The Janus Conspiracy

by

Michael Davies

The Janus Conspiracy

First Printing 2008
Second Edition Printing 2011

ISBN: 978-0-9818087-4-1

Published by The Mickie Dalton Foundation
Kempsey, NSW
Australia

www.mickiedaltonfoundation.com

In memory of Prue Mackay

A dear friend, a major influence on me and very badly missed

Other Works by Michael Davies

The Nightmares of God
The Janus Conspiracy
Accounts of a Killing
A Friendly Killing
Dreamkill
Ready, Steady, KILL!

For the Young Adults (12-18)
The Many Worlds of Mickie Dalton
The Many Galaxies of Mickie Dalton
The Many Universes of Mickie Dalton

For the 8-12 age group
The Quest for the Locket
The Secret of Yuri Kirilenko
The United Nations and the Extra-Terrestrial
The Secret of Charlotte's Cello
The Star of the Yshan Kings
The War of the Yshan Empire
The Red Fog of Time
The Mysterious Recorder and The Door to Elsewhere
Prisoners of the Picture

For the Little Ones (3-5)
Mary's World

And in non-fiction
The Business School Approach to Writing Your Novel

Janus, the two-faced god; one looked forward, the other back; one to the future and one to the past; one through new doors and one through old doors; and a god who might be one thing, or might be something else.

Prologue - Berlin, April 30th, 1945

It was the city's last day.

Not a building stood whole. Bodies lay in the streets like broken dolls after a demonic children's party. Some of the bodies wore the uniform of the Red Army, but most of them were in the dark field-grey of German troops. Many were corpses of children, women, old people who had watched the Soviet army units of General Zhukov drive through the last defenses of Berlin like a White Pointer shark attacking a wounded swimmer. The sharp stink of explosives mixed with the burning smell of charred flesh, pulverized stone and the stench of fear.

Dmitri Alexandrovitch was pale, his eyes black and haunted. No combat in the clean air, however filled with blind terror as aircraft flung themselves at each other like rabid hawks, nothing had prepared him for the death of a civilization.

"This is a vision of Hell, Yuri," Dmitri said into a small gap in the sounds of dying.

"This, Dmitri? Hell? It's just the antechamber. We have seen worse." Yuri's smile was cold. He would be twenty-three in four months, but his face was that of some ancient mystic in a painting by a Dutch master. A thousand years of pain burned in the blue eyes of his fine, aristocratic features.

The two brothers stood apart from the steady file of Russian soldiers walking along the rubble of what had been a broad, graceful street. The faces under the helmets of the infantrymen were no longer human. Too much death, too much killing, starvation and pitiless destruction had removed their souls. The men were now machines made of perishable and destructive material, quickened only by a lust to kill anything that was not one of their own. Ten minutes earlier, Dmitri had watched a trio of men bayonet a woman and her three children. There had been no joy in the savagery. It had been automatic, brutal killing on the way to the centre of the evil they had come to destroy. The *Fuehrerbunker*, the last refuge of Adolf Hitler lay only a few hundred meters ahead, and they wanted to be at the kill.

"Perhaps," Dmitri said. "We have both seen horrors. We have seen the best of our young men die. We have seen our Mother Russia battered to a pulp as that lunatic Georgian worked his insane fantasies on her, killing thousands if he felt that a man's eyes had looked at him wrongly. There is no hell like seeing one's own history and culture destroyed by a megalomaniac."

Yuri smiled without humor. "There was a time, dear elder brother, when you almost bowed when you heard the name of Joseph Stalin. The Great Father, we called him, the bearer of the mantle of Lenin himself, savior of all Russia."

"He killed our dreams, together with the millions of kulaks, the workers, the intelligentsia and the best officers of our army and navy." Dmitri watched another file of men pick their way through the rubble. "He betrayed the Revolution. We survived the Romanovs and the Mensheviks, and for what? To have another Tsar, ten times more bloodthirsty even than Ivan the Terrible or the hideous Catherine?"

"Why did you come here, big brother?" Yuri asked. "And in the uniform of a Colonel in General Katukov's First Guards? I tell you, it was a major shock to see you this morning, striding into the camp as if you had been an infantryman all your life."

For the first time, Dmitri smiled. "Instead of flying like an eagle above all this horror? Why, to save you, little one! I could no longer leave my baby brother to face the dangers of this war without the protection of his older and so much wiser sibling."

"A true brother," Yuri said, smiling back. "I am, of course, pathetically grateful for your protection, oh ancient one of such wisdom, but what is the real reason?"

A shell crashed into the walls of an already shattered building a few hundred yards away, and the remaining walls collapsed, the noise of the fall lost in the turmoil. Yuri pulled his brother inside the doorway of the church near which they had been standing.

"You still believe in the Revolution, little brother?" Dmitri asked, slapping dust and grime from his uniform.

"Dmitri! You want to discuss political philosophy at this place and time? We might be dead at any moment! And anyway, I want to be with my men as we catch that madman, Adolf Hitler. He is probably within two hundred meters of us right now!"

3

"I'm deadly serious, Yuri." Dmitri looked deeply into his brother's eyes. "Is your heart and soul still with the dreams of Lenin and Marx, that only through communism can we achieve world peace and fairness?"

Yuri stared at his brother. The deadly, intense seriousness of the other man's face and words rang through the death throes of the Third Reich proceeding with such slaughter and destruction around them. "Yes, Dmitri," he replied finally. "I am still a communist, heart and soul. Just because that Georgian lunatic betrayed that cause has not changed my views. I have fought these five years for Mother Russia, not the Soviet Union that Stalin has created. This Russia is no different from that of the Romanovs."

"Then will you help me make it so?" Dmitri took hold of his brother's shoulder urgently.

"Make it so? Dear elder brother, you babble as wildly as a drunken sailor on leave in our home town. How will you and I return Russia to Lenin's path when the Georgian madman rules with the blood-lust of the great whore, Catherine?"

Without answering, Dmitri reached inside his tunic and extracted a paper. He unfolded it and looked around him, sticking his head outside the doorway.

"What is that paper, Dmitri?"

"It's a map, little Yuri. And I got it from the same man from whom I got the uniform."

"He gave it to you?"

"After I'd killed him, yes," Dmitri replied, with a direct look at his brother.

"Good Christ, Dmitri, you killed a Colonel of the Red Army?"

"He was a Stalin supporter, Yuri. And he was very drunk one night last week. He was foolish enough to tell me his secret."

"That was enough to kill him? What is in that map?"

"It was. The map is our future, Yuri. Find us the corner of Hegelstrasse and Unter-den-Linden."

"And when we have found it?" Yuri moved out of the shelter and began to walk along the shattered ruins of the street. The soldiers had gone.

"There is a building. It was the home of a very senior officer of the Waffen SS. My late comrade who last owned this uniform told me that the honorable General had a taste for fine things. They had been friends many years ago. The fine things will be stored in a safe place in that house."

"And you think they will still be there? Dmitri, much as I love and respect you, this is madness! Our troops will have looted everything by now."

"I think not, little brother. The party officials move with the army. Their fanaticism is well known. Their only job is to find Adolf Hitler and finish off the Third Reich."

Yuri was walking briskly, carrying his city map. "We have three blocks to go," he said.

The three blocks took an hour. Several times, they had to wait while armored columns moved past them, heading for Hitler's Chancellery. At each corner they had to search the rubble to be certain it was a street junction, and to locate signs giving the road or street name. They were not always successful and dead reckoning was a large element of the navigation.

"This is the spot." Yuri spoke with confidence. Several buildings stood around them, only partially damaged.

Lying in the rubble was a street sign. It said *"Hegelstrasse."* In the distance, they could see the massive swastika standing proudly atop the huge walls of Hitler's headquarters. As they watched, several cannon opened fire, aiming directly at the symbol of the Third Reich. A shell finally landed on it, exploding with a massive roar and demolishing the hated sign. A bellow of triumph issued from the thousands of men who could see the final act of contempt for the enemy, and they began to rush forward for the killing stroke.

"Quickly, this way," Dmitri snapped, consulting his paper, and moving inside the doorway of the corner building. Inside, it was dark, but both brothers took out their flashlights and studied the room.

"The stairs should be over there." Dmitri pointed his light at the far wall. They strode in the path of the beam, and found a stairwell. Descending it, the blackness became absolute, but the beams remained strong.

"Under this board, here, if the paper is correct," Dmitri said. He stamped hard at one point, and a board reared up like a startled snake. Dmitri bent down and reached inside. With a grunt of triumph, he pulled out four packages, the size of large books. "The flashlight! Here, Yuri!" he called.

In the beams of the lights, Dmitri unwrapped the four parcels. Each was a box with a hinged lid. Dmitri opened the first and played his light on the contents.

"Dear God!" Yuri whispered. The light showed the exquisite beauty of a saint's face, the gold gleaming softly with its own internal voluptuousness. "Icons!"

"The very finest, if my dead friend is correct," Dmitri muttered. "And there are six of them in two boxes. They are worth millions of American dollars."

"And in the other two?"

"Let's see," Dmitri replied and opened another lid. Inside were several soft bags drawn at their openings with a string. Dmitri pulled one open, and the flash of precious stones under the torch beams filled the gloom with beauty.

"Quickly! Get these stored in our bags," Dmitri ordered and slid his backpack from his shoulders. Yuri did the same, and a few minutes later, they re-emerged into the destruction outside.

"And now what?" Yuri asked. "How will we use these treasures to restore the dreams?"

"We have to get to America." Dmitri looked carefully around him and selected a direction. "This way, do you think?"

"Dmitri, big brother, I know you are a fine pilot and a Hero of the Soviet Union," Yuri gasped, catching up with him. "And I agree, this direction is certainly west. But we have half of Europe and an ocean to cross to reach America. And how will we just arrive?"

"I will show you soon, little brother. We have a dangerous few miles to cross first."

"You are quite mad, Dmitri," Yuri replied. But he knew his brother's strength of will and the indomitable power that he applied to any decision. He stifled further objections and followed.

Two hours later, they had crossed two miles of the shattered capital of the dead Third Reich. The journey had been filled with fear and danger, and many times, the two brothers had hidden from Soviet troops on their final, triumphant lunge at Hitler's headquarters, or dived behind stone walls as random shells exploded around them.

Finally, Dmitri looked around him and nodded. "We are in the western sectors of the city," he said. "I recognize this part from my studies."

"And now that we are in the western sectors, what will we do?" Yuri was breathing hard in reaction from the perils of the last two hours.

"Let me show you," Dmitri replied with a slow smile. "See, over there?"

The shock hit Yuri like a physical slap. "Americans!" he gasped. "Dmitri, we must get out of here!"

"No! This is perfect. They are part of the US First Division. One of General Konev's divisions met units of this division near Torgau the other day. I knew we'd see them, eventually." Not looking backward, Dmitri walked firmly toward the small group of American soldiers walking through the ruined buildings with expressions of dismay.

"Hello there!" Dmitri called in English. "You must be lost!" Both brothers were fluent in the language, having kept up their studies since childhood, despite the war. Dmitri had insisted.

"Jesus Christ, feller! You speak English?" The soldier who replied was a corporal. Yuri could see the rest were privates. The corporal was in charge of his six-man troop.

"Of course," Dmitri said. "I am Colonel Dmitri Alexandrovitch. This is Major Yuri Kutasov."

The American corporal seemed to think for a moment, then slowly gave a reluctant salute, returned by both brothers.

"Then can you help us, sir?" the corporal asked. "We've become split off from the rest of our squad."

"Of course, Corporal," Dmitri replied. "I saw the lines of your First Division just a little way from here. Our two army groups are already working together. If you'll follow us, we'll take you there."

"You bet, sir," the corporal replied and fell into step beside the two Russians. The expressions of relief on the faces of the young Americans were vivid, thought Yuri, wondering what his brother was up to. They had seen no Americans other than this small, lost band. Yuri looked at the two men and saw that the corporal was of a similar height and build to his brother.

"What's been happening in your sectors, sir?" the American asked.

Dmitri smiled at him. "We have been entirely successful. The Red Army took the Seelow Heights a few days ago. Last week, General Zhukov finally broke into the city, and other units took the Berlin Town Hall just two days ago. Since our armies met in Torgau, we have crushed the last remnants of these German pigs. Within the hour, we should have the Reichstag."

"That's great, sir." The corporal and his men looked relieved. "We could be out of here in a few days."

"I'm sure of it," Dmitri replied. "Once we find the rat-hole where Hitler is hiding, it's all over and we can go home."

"Thank God!" The young American exchanged grins with his men.

"Where are you from, Corporal?" Dmitri asked as they worked their way along the street.

"Los Angeles, sir."

"You come from a pleasant part of the world," Dmitri said with a smile.

"You know it, sir?" The corporal looked pleased.

"Only through your movie industry," Dmitri replied. He pointed at one of the other Americans, a tall, slender-built man. "And how about you, young man? Where are you from?"

The private gave a shy smile. "Seattle, Washington, sir." The six Americans were looking cheerful, now that they were on the way back to rejoin their fellows and talking in English with a friendly allied officer who had given them such wonderful news.

"Splendid," Dmitri replied. He looked sharply at his brother. With a shock as severe as anything caused by the explosions of this historic day, Yuri comprehended what Dmitri intended. He pulled out his pistol as Dmitri did the same, and with three precise shots in the head, killed three of the Americans before they had time to see what was happening. All six men were dead within five seconds.

The brothers shook hands amid the rubble and ruins of Berlin.

"To the New Empire," Dmitri said.

"The New Empire," Yuri replied.

Chapter 1 - Martinsburg, West Virginia

Randy Crawford smiled through the glass at his producer sitting at her control panel. He knew he was in great form and the invective was flowing freely.

"Nothing that this sorry administration can do could ever match the economic mastery of the Reagan presidency or the sheer genius at international diplomacy that both Presidents George Bush brought to the White House," he said with powerful sincerity.

Crawford smiled again at Christiana. She was talking on the telephone and didn't see him. He leaned forward in his luxurious, leather executive seat and addressed the microphone with a loving, intimate tone.

"I tell you, my friends, as I sit here in West Virginia, in the heart of America's beginnings, looking out over the Appalachians, talking to you loyal Americans sitting at home or in your cars around the nation, this poor imitation of a president is destroying America. He's made an ass of himself on the international front, and don't be fooled by his arrogant claims that he's reduced the amount of terrorist violence around the world because he has started talks with those terrorist nations. The real reduction in violence has resulted from the previous heroic president beating the crap out of al-Q'aeda all over the world."

Crawford looked at his producer again. Christiana was still on the phone, but this time Crawford caught her eye. He smiled once more, but her face remained expressionless. She looked down at her desk and seemed to be listening carefully to the phone caller.

"And his claim that he's improved the economy already by placing tight controls over the banks and finance house, that's another librul lie," Crawford continued, an edge of irritation creeping into his tone. *That damned woman,* he thought. *Who the hell does she think she is? She comes to the studio dressed like a whore in her short skirts and then refuses any invitations for after-work activities. I'm Randy Crawford, dammit!*

He turned his attention back to the microphone. He let his annoyance show in his commentary to the outside world. "The collapse of the economy was directly the result of those commie policies that Clinton implemented. It took eight years of George Bush to replace those stupid policies, so it's no surprise that we had some troubles in his last year or so, what with those commie leftards in Congress blocking him at every turn."

He leaned back in his chair and took a sip of water from the glass on the table. "This guy is no better than the president who dodged the call to duty in Vietnam by sneaking off to England to pretend to study at some snotty-nosed British college. He talked his way into the White House with nothing but rhetoric, persuading millions of Americans that he was better able to run this country than a real, genuine war hero. This is the man in charge of our armed forces today. And you think we can believe his claims about improving the economy? You think the improvements result from his efforts? Hell no!

12

These falls in unemployment and the reduction in trade deficits, they were all the work of George Bush during the previous administration that's only now paying off. You think some liberal, pinko lawyer could have achieved this?"

Once more, he tried to catch Christiana's eye through the glass. He succeeded but she refused to respond to him. Her face was calm and without expression. She raised one hand with three fingers pointing up. Thirty seconds to a commercial break.

"No, my friends," Crawford continued. "This administration has been a disaster for America. We have some liberal whackos cutting the defense budgets. We have a vice-president who can't think about anything but saving trees ahead of saving American jobs, and both of them want to destroy the strength and vitality of the country by removing our guns and bringing in some crazy form of socialized medicine. Well, I have a message for both of them from all of us. And I know that when the time comes for the election next year, you and I will join together in ramming home this message. And it's a simple one, my friends. It goes like this. This ain't Russia, Mister President. It ain't communist China, or Cuba or North Korea. This is America, and we don't need you in the White House. And when America finally gets rid of this administration next election, you can go back to playing with your commie friends and leave a Republican president to bring this country back to greatness."

He took a sip of water and watched the second hand of the studio clock tick to precisely the right mark. He was, above all, a consummate professional. "And when we get back, folks, we'll take some phone calls from you true-blue Americans out there."

He watched Christiana carefully until she nodded to indicate that the commercial recordings were being transmitted then replaced the glass on the table. He pressed the communication switch on his panel to open up the connection to his producer. "So, how do you think it's going?" he asked with what he intended to be his most sincere smile. He was annoyed to see her face take on a look of distaste.

"About as usual," Christiana replied calmly. "We have three calls waiting for you when you get back."

"Well, I think it's going great!" he said loudly. "How's about we go for a drink after the show? You deserve it!"

"Thank you, no," she replied. "Ten seconds."

Annoyed, he looked at the small computer screen in front of him. Green letters on a black background showed three lines of data. Hal in Greensboro, North Carolina, said the top line of text.

Crawford watched Christiana's hand counting off the seconds. As she lowered the final finger and nodded at him, he pressed the switch on the telephone control system.

"And we go to Hal in Greensboro," he said, his voice gaining an extra notch of cheerfulness. "So how's it all hanging out down there in North Carolina, Hal?"

"Pretty good, Randy," a male voice replied through the loudspeaker. "Could be a damn sight better without all these liberals around the place."

"They do tend to mess up the country, that's a fact," Crawford replied. "So what's your particular comment, today, old buddy?"

"Well, I just want to tell yuh, Randy, God bless you, man. Keep up the fight."

14

"There ain't no doubt about me doin' that, Hal. It's my job to look after America's well-being, and that means doin' everything I can to get a Republican back in the White House."

Crawford disconnected the call. *Stupid jerk,* he thought. *I need something more interesting than morons calling in just so that they can tell their friends they talked to Randy Crawford.* He looked at the computer screen, and pressed the button again. "And so we go to Evanston in Illinois, to... Mark on a car phone. And what's happening in the Land of Lincoln, Mark?"

"What's happening," a clear, well-spoken, male voice said on the loudspeaker, "is that I'm listening to the longest, deepest and highest pile of garbage ever uttered by human voice."

Crawford sat back and felt a twinge of anger and worry. Educated callers were rare and unwelcome on this program. *What the hell was that bitch doing, letting this man get through to him?* He glared through the glass at Christiana and received a calm gaze back.

"Oh yeah? And how do you reckon that, Mark?"

"I reckon it by listening to you spout the most incredibly un-American nonsense and thinking just how like an old-style, hard-line communist you sound."

"You WHAT?" Crawford's well-trained good ol' boy mannerisms deserted him. "You're calling me a communist? How DARE you call me a communist! Who the hell do you think you are?"

"An American," the voice replied with a trace of amusement. "Unlike you, I suspect. And why should it be such an offense to call you a communist? It's what you call half the population of America every day."

Crawford fought for self-control. *I'll kill that bitch,* he swore to himself. *I've told her time and time again, weed out people like this. Listen for educated accents and make sure they don't get on. Just you wait, bitch. I'll teach you to cross Randy Crawford.* He took a deep breath. "Well," he sneered, "we've obviously got an *intellectual* on the program today. So tell me, Mister Intellectual, just how do you reckon I sound like a communist?"

"Easy." The voice was calm and composed. Crawford decided that, if he had ever before loathed educated people who spoke like this, he detested them even doubly now. "I listen to who it is that you hate," the distant voice continued, "and I find that they're the same groups that the old Soviet communists used to hate, and that the Chinese and Korean communists hate now."

"Yeah? And how come you know so much about the communists, Mister Intellectual? You lived with them for some years? You one of them, perhaps?"

"No, but I've studied them rather more than you have. I speak Russian and I read the Russian newspapers."

"You speak Russian? You're a commie sympathiser, then."

The laughter in the caller's voice was undisguised. "You mean anyone who actually studied the old Soviet Union and learned the Russian language is a communist?"

"Of course not!" Crawford snapped. "But it gives grounds for suspicion."

"Well, hell Randy, what are we going to do about all those card-carrying communists in the CIA, then? And what about those nasty, pinko commies who sat at Reagan and Bush's side when they talked to the Soviet and Russian leaders? And how about Condaleeza Rice?"

"What the hell are you talking about?" Crawford was feeling sweat running down his back. He looked through the glass at Christiana and tried to glare at her. She smiled back sweetly. *The bitch is enjoying this*, he swore.

"There are a lot of good, loyal people in the CIA, the armed forces and other branches of government who've studied the Soviets and speak fluent Russian," the caller replied. "And the interpreters for your little gods also spoke fluent Russian. By your standards, they were enemies of the USA."

Crawford realized his mistake. "They would be honest, real Americans who learned the language in the military with the intention of helping our country," he snapped, trying to recover the error. "Not like you."

"How extraordinary. You've no idea who I am, but by some miraculous means you know I was never in the military and I studied the USSR because I was a communist. Damn clever, Randy."

"Anti-American intellectuals like you wouldn't be allowed in the military," Crawford grated. He was desperately thinking of some way he could cut this bastard off without seeming like a coward and didn't see the opening he was giving the other man.

"Unfortunately, Randy, you're vocalizing through the wrong orifice, as usual. I learned about the Soviets while I was in the United States Navy doing my doctorate in Russian Studies. And you know what, Randy? The armed forces have a hell of a lot of people with Master's and Doctorate degrees. Intellectuals, all of them."

Crawford was silent. He understood exactly what the caller had meant by the reference to vocalizing through the wrong orifice. *Talking through my ass? I'll kill you, you bastard. And that whore in the control booth too, for letting that statement get through the five-second time-delay intended for just this kind of thing.* For the first time in his broadcasting career, he was stumped for a reply. But his caller saved him.

"But I was going to point out the amazing similarities between you and the communists."

Despite the dangers in the subject, Crawford took the opening. It was better than trying and failing to make a proper response to that astounding insult. "Yeah, let's hear this crap then, Mark," he said, emphasizing the sneer. He had practised for years to make his sneer a powerful weapon against the few callers who objected to his program. It seemed to have no effect on the present caller.

"Let's first look at the people you hate, Randy," the voice said from the loudspeaker. "Who hates environmentalists? The far right does. And who else? The Communists!"

"That's rubbish, caller," Crawford scoffed. "Those environmentalist loonies are all anti-capitalist, liberal activists, well to the far left."

"Really? So, in your fevered little imagination, if environmentalism is a feature of communists, then the communist countries would surely be the most pristinely perfect, manicured, forest-covered and pollution-free areas of the world, would they not?"

Crawford was silent. The trap into which he had fallen was all too obvious to him. The knife was turned another few degrees.

"But of course, they're not, are they Randy? The communist countries have avoided any sort of environmental controls over the years and their business operations are the foulest, dirtiest and least healthy in the world."

"That's because they don't have the technology we do," Crawford snapped.

"No, it's because they believe nothing should get in the way of industry. Just like the far right. And also because the country's leaders don't have to live in that filth, and they don't care about the common people. Just like you, Randy."

Mark's laugh echoed from the loudspeaker. Crawford decided he had never hated anyone as much as he hated this man in Illinois. He sensed the wide smile on Christiana's face and deliberately avoided looking in her direction.

"And who else does the far right hate?" the caller continued. "Well, how about liberal activists? And guess who hates them just as much? The Communists! You both hate anyone who believes in freedom of the individual over the state."

"Well now I know you're a lunatic," Crawford shouted. "This is America, the land of the free. It's the country where you can speak out freely and that's one thing we Republicans defend most of all."

"Oh yes? Remember when we went to war in the Gulf? Remember how anyone who spoke out against the war went in fear of their lives? Remember how people were hounded from their homes, even out of the country, because they disagreed with the war? Remember the people who called you up to support your suggestion that criticizing the president should be a punishable offense? Free speech only if it supports your party, eh Randy?"

"You're reaching far into left field here, caller. Once a country has gone to war, every citizen's patriotic duty is to support that war, not undermine the country's defense. That's what Socrates said, and that's a viewpoint I support entirely."

"Yes, I heard you declare that you felt like a blood-brother to Socrates when a caller first pointed out to you those words. When one looks at who else used those words to support the crushing of dissent, it puts you in a curious group of people."

"That's not crushing dissent, Mister Intellectual. That's enforcing security and moral support for the country's position." Crawford worked to keep his worry in check. He realized that it had been a long time since he had received a call that was not supportive of him, and he had lost his edge.

"An interesting justification," the disembodied voice said. "It makes you spiritually one with a raging homosexual, a Nazi leader and Joseph Stalin."

"What in God's name is this rubbish, caller?"

"Randy, Randy, I know you're a right-wing extremist and ignorant of all things, so let me point out that Greek society of the time of Socrates, your self-proclaimed blood-brother, saw heterosexual acts as merely for procreation. For real fun and games and true love among the intellectual and social leadership of the society, and that was of course, the adult male group, sexual love with young boys was the thing."

"You're talking nonsense!" Crawford was losing his temper and he felt his cheeks growing red. He refused to look through the glass at his producer. He almost sensed the shrug of disinterest in the caller.

20

"Suit yourself, Randy. But it is recorded that Joe Stalin quoted Socrates' words and used them for the same purposes you did. So did Joseph Goebbels."

"What?" Crawford was becoming overloaded and panicky.

"Joseph Goebbels. A European statesman I've no doubt you admire greatly. He was Hitler's propaganda minister. Nice company you keep, Randy."

"So now you're calling me a Nazi as well, are you? Make up your mind. Am I far right or far left?" The sneer was flung into the play again as Crawford fought to regain control of the conversation.

"What's the difference?"

"What's the difference? Some intellectual you are, caller, if you don't know the difference between political left and right."

"Okay, Randy, I confess my ignorance. I don't know the difference between the far left and the far right of the political spectrum. That's precisely my point. You and the Communist party have exactly the same philosophies."

"Well, all this is highly entertaining for my audience, caller, but I think it's time we cut you off. You've had more than your share of my time."

"Haven't got the courage to hear any more? You're a coward, Randy. You haven't the guts to debate somebody who actually disagrees with you."

Defeated, Crawford bowed to the point. He tried to laugh as if ridiculing the caller's words. "All right, caller, let's stick with this rubbish a little longer."

"Good. Some more similarities between you and the Communists. You both hate intellectuals, anti-war demonstrators, and homosexuals. In Russia, they used to shoot them. In America, you do the same whenever possible, and you'd like to do it more often."

"Garbage. Where the hell do you get that idea?"

"From you and most of your callers. How often have you said that those groups are enemies of the country and should be destroyed? And here's some more. Both you and the communists believe in one-party rule and also that the leaders of the party are above the law."

"What the hell are you talking about? We believe in democracy in this country. That's what America's about."

"Really? Then how come you say that anyone who opposes the Republican Party is a communist and therefore an enemy of the country? How often have you said that the Democrats are anti-American traitors and the root cause of the destruction of this country?"

"Most of them are," Crawford said coldly. "Though I suppose a few of them are merely misguided."

"So American values are only displayed by Republicans? You'd be happy, then, if the Democrats had the same philosophies as the Republicans?"

"Well, of course! Republican values are those of true Americans."

"That would mean two parties with identical philosophies. What's the difference between that and one-party rule? And you clearly see the Republican party as the only party fit to rule America, and it's obvious that you believe that the Chief of the Armed Forces should also have unlimited political and military powers. Just like any military dictatorship, and just like the Communist party."

"You're really off the wall now! It's clear to me that you don't understand any part of Republican philosophy at all."

"I think I understand all too well and I believe strongly in the genuine platform. My deep worry is that some people in the Republican Party don't seem to understand it any more. The last common feature between you lot and the Communists is that you clearly believe that senior party leaders are above the law. Amazing that, considering you whackos are always claiming to be a law and order party."

"And where do you get that silliness from, Mister Intellectual? Show me one example where I've claimed immunity from the law for Republicans."

"You mean since Richard Nixon? The man who single-handedly attacked the American Constitution and had to appoint someone to succeed him who would then pardon him? Let's not even talk about Spiro Agnew's brushes with legality. Let me just point out the high number of members of recent Administrations who had to receive presidential pardons for their crimes. Sixty-five of them, in fact. What does that do for the respect for the country's leaders?"

"All those men were trying to help in the fight against communism," Crawford blared. "They were hampered by all those un-American liberals in the House..."

"Who insisted on minor irritations like obeying the law of the land? As I said, you seem to believe that the law doesn't apply to the leaders, a sure sign of despotic leadership. And this is the party you want to rule America? It makes me wonder why, and I have only one answer."

"You have an answer, Mister Intellectual? So, let's hear this spark of genius."

"Okay, Randy, it's this. If I wanted to destroy American freedoms and democracy, I couldn't think of a better way than to cause a complete loss of faith in the country's leadership, and to generate so much hatred against a large segment of the population and the ruling administration, that an armed coup by the creators of that crisis would be welcomed by the rest of the country. I think that's what you're doing."

"I've given you all the time you deserve, Mister Intellectual. It's time to cut you off and let some real Americans speak." Crawford was almost trembling, and his voice shook.

"One *is* speaking, Crawford. So why do you espouse these policies, Randy? Could it be that you're not a loyal American after all, but someone dedicated to destroying this country?"

Crawford slammed the switch to disconnect the call.

"That lunatic has had all the time he gets, people," he said loudly. "We don't have to suffer through any more of that liberal nonsense. We'll take a break now and when we get back, we'll let some true Americans have their say."

He gestured to Christiana, a slicing movement that indicated she should cut him off. She was quick to respond, and almost immediately, a loud female voice with a strong Texan accent began to extol the wonders of a salsa sauce made in real cow-country.

Crawford opened up the line to the control booth. "What the hell were you playing at, letting that lunatic on my show?" he said furiously. "I've told you before, listen out for voices like that and keep them off the air!"

"I know you have." Christiana's face was expressionless. "Fortunately, my job description and also my professional ethics both tell me I have to let any caller through who isn't evidently drunk, abusive, or obscene. That guy was none of the above."

"He was a lunatic! That sort of call is bad for ratings."

"By lunatic, do you mean someone who likes to hear both sides of the question, Randy?"

"Jesus Christ, you sound just like that jerk! Is this some sort of plot between you two?"

"Plot, Randy? I thought belief in plots and conspiracies was the sole prerogative of liberals and communists. That's what you're always saying, anyway."

"You'd better watch it, young woman, if you want to keep your job."

"Threats, now? How interesting. You have twenty seconds."

"It's a goddam promise! You stick to the rules, or you'll be out of here by the evening."

"Exactly what rules are those, Randy? Fifteen seconds."

"My rules, dammit! You do as I say, or you're out! This is Randy Crawford speaking, not some limp-wristed, liberal station-manager."

"I'm sure Nick will be interested in that libellous comment, Randy. It's on tape. Five seconds."

Crawford leaned back in chair, the frustration threatening to blow his insides. *Little whore,* he thought furiously. *She's not going to get away with that sort of shit. Not with Randy Crawford.* He fought for self-control as he watched Christiana count down the last seconds and point at him. There were five names on the computer screen. Taking a deep breath, Crawford pressed the button.

"Well, hi there, Jack from St. Louis. I hope I'm going to hear a *real* American, this time."

Chapter 2 - Evanston, Illinois

Mark Ashton was having the usual sort of day. It had been frantic from the first moment into his office a few minutes before eight. The network had gone down at seven in the morning, and half the office was screaming blue murder. Mark's network specialist was hard at work on the job and he had reported he'd found the problem and things would be back to normal by nine. Until then, people would continue to scream.

He had meetings scheduled with a number of vendors and these would occupy most of the day. In between, he had performance-evaluations to prepare, requests for hardware and software upgrades from all over the country to examine and approve or disapprove, and a seemingly endless list of varied duties to complete.

By seven that evening, he was ready to call it a day. The company paid him well to manage the computer installation, but he gave back blood in return, he felt. A thousand people worked at the manufacturer of machine parts and the numerous branch offices around the country, and the demand for more and more sophisticated information technology never eased. The twenty people he

27

managed also had their problems and leaned heavily on him for support. Mark reported directly to the company president, but that youthful and energetic executive was in the office about one day in five and that one day was a feeding frenzy of meetings. Mark was basically on his own. At the age of thirty-six, the freedom and responsibility both excited and frightened him.

He walked out of the deserted office building that stood alongside the factory. Waving tiredly at the security guard who noted down the time, he found his Thunderbird standing alone in the staff parking lot and drove the short distance from the northern edge of the City of Chicago to his condominium in Evanston. He entered the underground parking area with an enormous sense of relief, the feeling of reaching a haven, a private, safe place where he could finally let down his guard. The feeling got stronger as he opened up the door to the apartment and closed it behind him. Throwing off his suit, shirt, tie, shoes and socks, leaving only his underpants in place, he padded into his kitchen and extracted a can of beer from the fridge. With a sigh of happiness, he folded onto the expanse of settee along one wall of the room.

It hadn't always been this warm a homecoming. He and Alison had moved into the apartment when they got married five years ago, and life rapidly deteriorated into some sort of hellish pain. Whatever warmth and femininity she had displayed during their short courtship quickly vanished under a constant tirade of disparagement, contempt and anger. Within weeks, the process of getting home had become a fearful exercise of wondering just what failure of his she had detected during her day at work as a market analyst. The only certainty was that she would find one. The tongue-lashing would start within minutes of his arrival home, continue through the miserable dinner and until the time he could retreat to the second bedroom which had become his within a short time of taking up residence. Mark felt as if he had taken a pet kitten into the house and it had turned into a ravening, bloodthirsty alien from a horror movie. In the years since Alison's furious walkout eight months after the wedding, Mark had often wondered just what it was he had done to fail her so catastrophically that she hated him so much.

No answer had ever come to him.

He threw the brief memory of the dark months out of his mind and switched on the television. He had the weekend alone, he reminded himself. Nobody would come to him whining about delays in system developments, demanding extra performance from an already maxed-out computer system, or requesting an upgrade in their personal computer while refusing to pay for it out of their departmental budgets.

Mark was in his cocoon for the weekend and that was where he was staying. But there was one thing on his mind that he couldn't seem to clear out.

Some weeks earlier, while looking for a classical station on the radio he kept in his office, he had accidentally tuned into the local station that carried the Randy Crawford program syndicated from somewhere in Virginia. He had listened, first in amusement at the simplistic raging against anyone with values different from those of the far right, then in increasing anger as he detected the hatred evidenced in both the host and the callers. The tone of the discussions reminded him uncomfortably of political attitudes he had encountered in some strange political regimes he had studied in his past.

"Are these really Americans?" he asked aloud. "Where's that good American tolerance for differences, the willingness to try change and variety? Where's the friendship?"

He took to arranging his schedules as much as possible so that he could tackle routine paperwork during much of the Crawford broadcasts, and listened to them with increasing worry. After a few days, he sketched out the standard philosophies and practices of the Soviet governments before the break-up of the old communist empire. His studies of these had been intensive during his years in Naval Intelligence. Alongside these elements of the cruel, restrictive and intensely reactionary administrations of Stalin, Bulganin, Khruschev, Brezhnev, Protopov and the others, he ticked those which Crawford and his listeners were propounding. To his appalled fascination, he had almost a perfect correlation.

"We don't execute homosexuals, and we don't refuse free travel to our citizens," he said to his friend, Andrew, one evening as they tackled a Chinese dinner at the local restaurant. "We actually have two political parties, and I used to believe the elections are carried out fairly, but the last two gave me some worries with those touch screen machines. We have a nominally free-enterprise system."

"Seems a fairly significant difference," Andrew said, culling the mixed vegetable dish for more mushrooms.

"It is," Mark agreed. "But I listen to these people on the radio, and believe me, most of those differences would be removed if they had their say."

"How so?"

"According to Crawford, well and loudly endorsed by his fans, anyone voting against the Republicans is a liberal. And liberal equals communist and communist equals enemy of America."

"Nasty," Andrew commented and added rice to his bowl.

"Very. And Crawford says anyone speaking out against war is a bleeding-heart liberal, which I assume is worse than any ordinary liberal, and dedicated to the destruction of America's manhood. The communists believe exactly the same thing. Crawford basically says there shouldn't be any opposition party to the Republicans."

"Still a long way to go." The last prawn followed the mushrooms.

"The communists hate liberals, environmentalists, free speech, criticism of the party leaders, anti-war activists, and any suggestion that they couldn't do anything they wanted, whether it was legal or not."

Andrew paused, his chopsticks an inch from his mouth. "Sounds like a couple of presidents I used to know."

"Exactly."

"Why do those differences exist then, if the two groups have identical values?" Andrew poured the last of the white wine into their glasses and studied the debris of the meal.

"Largely because our constitution is still too huge a hurdle for these loonies."

"Hard to imagine they could change that. It's a pretty powerful force."

"Thank God for it!" Mark spoke with force. "I've always believed it's the finest intellectual product known to man. But I really believe Crawford's crowd would like to suspend it. After all, the Soviets had a constitution which guaranteed individual human rights too, but look what happens when you get one party in power without an opposition."

"What about the whole free enterprise bit?" Andrew regretfully laid down his chopsticks. "Isn't that the primary difference between the two systems?"

"Supposed to be," Mark agreed. "But isn't it interesting that there's nothing the far right likes better than a war? And in a war, the government starts to control all the factors of production, communication channels, and every other economic and social feature. All in the name of democracy and the American way, of course. It means in practice, there's nothing more socialist than a war."

Andrew cackled and several diners turned startled faces toward them. "Now that's a statement that could get you into trouble!" he said semi-seriously.

"In America? The land of the First Amendment?"

"I see your point. "It seems to have bugged you badly."

"It has." Mark grimaced. "I'm not usually this concerned about such stuff. But the whole thing reminds me of some very ugly governments I used to deal with. Something in this situation frightens me."

"So, what can you do about it?"

"Dammit, I don't know! But there's one thing that bugs the hell out of me. Every day, Crawford starts with a wild rave against the president, or his wife, or both, alleging some sinful practice or act of moral depravity, or maybe the final break-up of the marriage. Where does he get it from?"

"Makes it up, I suppose."

"I don't think he's bright enough. But he gets away with it. There's one newsletter published in Chicago, *"The Lies of Randy Crawford"* that reveals the rubbish that Crawford spouts, and for which the publisher gets regular death-threats. But, apart from that, nobody ever accuses Crawford of lying, and the media often pick up on the so-called story and run it until it wears off. But look what happens when somebody raises the question of a previous First Lady's practice of running the White House with astrological charts. Couple of days of mild comment and it goes away. The last administration seemed to break numerous laws, they pardon the crooks and nobody bleats a sound. Could you imagine a talk-show host telling tales about these little details the way Crawford does about the president?"

"He'd have less than a week to live," Andrew answered.

"Exactly. So what the hell is going on?"

"Ashton, you're spoiling a very good Chinese meal and scaring the daylights out of me."

"Sorry!" Mark grinned and forgot the subject.

* * *

A couple of days later, he got an idea for following up on one of his concerns. He called up a number of people in branch offices around the country, and asked each of them the same thing. "Do you get Randy Crawford's broadcast in your area?"

With those who said they did, he thanked them, and ended the conversation. With the others, a second question followed. "Do you get any sort of right-wing talk-show program?"

Many of them did. Mark got the names of sixteen such hosts, and asked one more favor. "Would you listen in when you can, and note down just what the story is about the president or his wife that day? Send me a line by email."

He received agreement in all sixteen cases, but with varying degrees of amusement or hostility. A week later, he had an interesting fact. All sixteen radio personalities introduced the same stories on the same day.

Mark Ashton began to feel increasing anxiety. If there were sixteen of these people all following the party line, how many more could there be? He listened to Crawford's program for another three days, taking careful notes on the standard phrases and concepts that filled the man's pronouncements, taking special care to listen to how Crawford attacked any of the rare callers who were not fawning admirers.

Eventually, he planned his day to have an hour free, left the office and took his car out of the office parking lot. He drove to the waterfront at Evanston, parked and took a deep breath. Finally, he entered into his car phone the eight-hundred number which the radio station gave out at regular intervals, and pressed the "Send" button. Several attempts were needed before he got through, but at last, a melodious female voice answered him.

"This is the Randy Crawford program," the voice said. "Where are you calling from?"

"Evanston, Illinois," he replied, unexpectedly attracted by the voice.

"A mobile phone?"

"Yes, it is."

"Okay, that puts you at the front of the line," the woman said. "And what name should I give?"

"Mark," he answered. The feminine voice was causing a reaction in him that he found disconcerting. He heard a gentleness and a warmth, which touched a long-lost need in him. "Who am I talking to?" he ventured.

"Stand by," the woman said abruptly, and the phone's loudspeaker went dead. Mark stared out at the blue waters of the lake. A group of young people walked by the car, chattering loudly. Students at Northwestern, Mark assumed, then the speaker came back to life.

"I'm Christiana, Mister Crawford's producer. Sorry about that, I got another call."

"I imagine you get a lot of them. He seems to have a wide following."

"Indeed." The woman's voice was cool. "Is there a special topic you want to raise with Mister Crawford?"

Mark took a deep breath again, feeling the nervousness running through him. "I want to tell him he's talking a load of garbage," he said.

A second of silence echoed from the speaker. "That would certainly be a different call."

Mark thought he detected a warmer note in her voice but discounted the idea. Crawford's producer would undoubtedly be one of his strongest supporters, he assumed. "We'll see how long he lets me talk before he cuts me off," he said.

"Good luck," the distant voice replied. "Turn your car radio off. You're next."

With another deep breath, Mark tried to calm himself and looked out at the water. His radio was already

35

switched off, as he knew that live call-in shows like this had a few seconds of delay between actual speech and broadcast.

"And so we go to Evanston in Illinois, to... Mark on a car phone," the phone's loudspeaker said. "And what's happening in the Land of Lincoln, Mark?"

* * *

Twenty minutes later, Mark was still sitting in his car, deep in thought. The reaction to the discussion had not yet faded. Mark was feeling a mixture of exhilaration at the discomfort he knew he had caused Crawford and a sense of anger at the simplistic fury in the talk-show host's words after Mark had hung up. He had switched the radio back on as soon as the conversation had ended, and he heard the last few seconds of his own voice speaking, then Crawford's comments about "that lunatic" and his "liberal nonsense." He sat through a few minutes of advertisements then listened with interest to the next caller to Crawford. As he had imagined, the caller, a man with a strong Texan accent had joined in with Crawford for a hymn of unadulterated hatred aimed at Mark's words. Mark heard himself called "a sick commie," "a vicious hater of all things American," and "a traitor to the country." Crawford endorsed every one of the statements then the discussion focused back on the "liberal, pinko policies of that slippery coward in the White House."

Mark switched the radio to the Chicago classical music station, started the Thunderbird and drove back to the office. He hoped he had correctly set his recorder that morning. He wanted to review his conversation when he got home.

He parked the Thunderbird and returned to the frenetic zoo that was his regular working day. Occasionally, he thought of the voice of Christiana and wondered what she looked like.

* * *

"Listen Verity! I've told you before, the ratings depend on this being a show where loyal Americans can have a chance to speak their minds! I'm not going to have any more of that crap like we had this afternoon."

Crawford was sitting in the station manager's office in an armchair that was too small for his long, bony frame. Nick Verity sat behind his desk, lounging backward in complete relaxation. He was a thickset man in his mid-thirties. Red-brown hair lay thick on top of a broad face with a wide, generous mouth and intelligent eyes. He was dressed casually in jeans and a plain white tee shirt. In the other armchair, Christiana Girard sat upright, her legs crossed, and without expression on her face. Despite his attempts to avoid it, Crawford's glance kept returning to the long legs in the short denim skirt.

"I know that's what you've told me, *ad nauseam,*" Verity replied. "And I've told you each time, that we'll try and keep drunks, obscene callers and obvious crackpots off the air. And that's where Chris' responsibility ends." Verity's voice was calm.

"So what the hell do you call that bastard from Evanston?" Crawford snapped. "If that's not a crackpot, I dunno what is."

"You only know what your people tell you to know, Randy." Verity was unperturbed by the violence in the man across his desk. "That crackpot, as you call him, was an

37

educated man with a view contrary to yours and backed up by some solid ideas and valid questions. Made damn good radio, in my mind."

"Well not in mine," Crawford said coldly.

"He has a mind, Chris!" Verity raised an eyebrow at the woman in the other chair.

"The claim has been made before," Christiana replied. "Dan Quayle called him the intellectual giant of the right."

"Well that must surely prove it." A tiny smile hovered on Verity's lips. It infuriated Crawford who realized he was the target of a combined joke. He worked to take control of his anger.

"Now listen, you two," he said. His voice was tight with anger. "This program is heard all over the United States by over thirty million people. And I have some very powerful people behind me. You'll follow my orders or face the consequences."

"Back to threats, are we?" Christiana sat upright in her chair. "You implied something like this earlier, Randy. Do you care to tell us what will happen if we fail to buckle under?"

Crawford glared at her. "You could get hurt," he said.

"Hurt?" Verity leaned forward in his seat. "By people with guns, I assume?"

"People who believe in me," Crawford replied.

"People of very low intelligence, then," Christiana retorted. "Nick, I want off this man's program. He's scum."

"We don't have the staff," Verity answered. "And I know he's scum, but you'll have to stick with it until we can make other arrangements." He looked hard at the other man. "Crawford, don't make threats. To me, to Chris, to anyone. The first sign of intimidation, the recordings of your words to Chris this afternoon will go to the board."

"The board?" Crawford snapped. "The board's only interested in profits. Maybe I should have my people speak to the board. I could get you both fired."

"Possibly. But unlikely. Not only do I have a large share holding in this station, but we've tripled profits in the three years I've run the place. I could probably survive."

"Then we'll take my show off your station and give it to another one."

"Be my guest," Verity suggested. "I find your act personally offensive and I find the emails you get each morning from some group in Washington to border on straight-forward libel against the President and his wife. I have a copy of each of them, and I'd take great pleasure in sending them to the White House."

Crawford jolted forward in his chair. "You've got copies? How dare you keep copies?"

Nick laughed. "By following station rules, Crawford. The emails are stored on the disk, but we have to keep backups of everything, and that includes your nasty little emails."

Crawford struggled for self-control and to regain the power position in the meeting. The disdain with which Verity had received the threat dismayed him. "Those emails are accurate reports of failings by the President," he said. "We have a duty to inform the American people of just what sort of President they've got."

"No, you and your pals in Washington have a compulsion to make up dirt and spread it around the likes of you all over the country." Christiana's expression was of someone who has encountered a dog-turd on the carpet. "Every one of those little stories has been found to be false, but I don't notice that you retracted them."

Crawford ignored the statement. "Now, are you going to follow orders or do I have to take things further?"

"Take things wherever you like," Verity replied. "My orders to Chris remain what they have always been. Listen carefully for drunkards or obvious crazies high on any mind-altering substance, whether legal or illegal. But anyone with a genuine wish to be heard on the air will be let through. And that includes people who disagree with you. That's the American way, Randy, or had you forgotten?"

"Then I won't take their calls," Crawford snarled. "And that includes the loonie from today. He doesn't get heard again." He pulled himself to his full height and towered over the other two. It didn't seem to achieve his accustomed intimidatory effect. "Now, are you going to make sure whackos like that bastard from Illinois don't get on my program, or not?"

"Not." Nick smiled. "In fact, it was so much fun, if he doesn't call again, I'll persuade a few more people I can think of to make similar calls."

"I should have known all your friends would be anti-Americans," Crawford sneered. "Maybe we should do something about it."

"What, haul us up before the House Un-American Activities Committee?" Verity's face was alive with amusement and his eyes sparkled. "Sorry, Randy, but you may have heard, your old hero died some years ago."

Crawford's gaze was icy. "My what? Who the hell are you talking about?"

Verity shook his head in a mixture of disbelief and amusement. He looked across at Christiana who shrugged her shoulders. "McCarthy, Randy. Senator Joe McCarthy. Someone who seems to have been a role model for you."

Crawford pointed his finger at Verity. "Listen, you," he snarled. "One day, somebody's going to make you sorry you've behaved this way. There are a lot of people out there who may take objection to a commie faggot like you running a radio station."

"Do you actually have any words and phrases of your own, Randy, or have you always talked in fifties clichés?" Christiana was laughing outright, and Verity guffawed at her words.

"Fuck off, the pair of you," Crawford shouted and hauled the door open. He tried to slam it shut behind him, but the hydraulic mechanism refused to allow him the gesture and meekly slipped into its place.

*　　*　　*

At eight o'clock, Mark knew that he had successfully recorded his conversation with Randy Crawford. He got home and saw with relief that the tape had wound on, and the radio was still set to the correct station. He rewound the tape, set it running and walked in to his kitchen to prepare a meal while the earlier callers spouted their silliness to Crawford's warmly supporting commentary.

Mark poured himself a glass of beer and leaned against the door between the kitchen and the lounge while Crawford embarked on his raging attack on the president's policies. Fifteen minutes later, while sitting at his table attacking the steak, he heard his own voice on the radio and put down his knife and fork. The meal was forgotten for the next ten minutes.

"Ye gods, I really got right up that bastard's nose," Mark said to the unresponsive room. He punched the air with his right fist, walking restlessly up and down the room. He saw the part-eaten steak and grinned to himself.

"Well, I got food for the soul, instead," he said with a small laugh, and picked up the plate to return it to the oven for a few minutes. He left the tape running and listened to the remaining callers to Crawford without the irritation that he usually felt.

"Wait till tomorrow, Randy old friend," he said as he waited for the steak to heat up. "You'll get round two of our little battle. It's time some real Americans spoke up and revealed what you are."

Chapter 3 - Frederick, Maryland

"Jesus Christ, that guy was just too damn close!" Randy Crawford took a deep gulp of his bourbon and branch water. He had trouble looking at the man in the opposite armchair, but that had been a problem ever since meeting Vince Jerome.

Jerome had piercing blue eyes under a full head of pure white hair. He was every atom the aristocrat, and his presence disturbed and unbalanced Crawford in much the same way as the educated and confident voice of the afternoon's caller from Evanston had thrown him.

"I agree with you," Jerome replied calmly. "Of course, not too many people with education and analytical ability listen to you, Randy and this one appears not just to have listened, but listened with great care. He was astonishingly close in his evaluation of what is going on."

"Then you've got to put a stop to him!"

"Oh, I don't think we need to worry too much." Jerome took a sip of his malt scotch and looked deep into the fireplace where the flames leaped and danced like teenagers at a party. "The views he expressed are simply too far-fetched for any of your regular listeners to give him any credence. They'll just write him off as some intellectual left-wing lunatic and it will reinforce their views of their own righteousness."

"I don't want to talk to him again! The bastard straight-out called me a traitor! That sort of thing could cause people to think the wrong sort of thoughts." Crawford finished his glass of bourbon and sat fiddling with the empty container on his lap. Jerome smiled slightly and nodded at the bar by the wall. Crawford raised his long body from the armchair and went to refill his glass.

"I doubt it." Jerome was still watching the flames. "Nobody could doubt your loyalty to America, or the patriotism that we in the Council are showing. We're obviously saving America from the still-powerful communist threat. But, judging by the reactions of your radio staff, it sounds like you'll have to talk to that man again, or somebody like him." He smiled briefly at Crawford. "And I think it will help the cause rather than harm it," he added.

"I want those two bastards fired, then!" Crawford swore, returning to his seat. "They've disobeyed me all too often. They're out to get me, I can tell."

"I suspect some of your anger is because you failed to get the delectable Miss Girard," Jerome replied, looking sharply at Crawford. "You had better restrain yourself there. She is unlikely to find your peculiar brand of physical pleasures to her liking, and she could harm you. Leave her alone."

Crawford shrank inside himself. Jerome's knowledge of his private fancies shocked him. "What about Verity, then? Can we do anything about him?"

Jerome shook his head. "It's not worth it. Concentrate on doing your job and forget about your petty pride. Keep the objectives in view." His long, graceful fingers tapped the heavy, silver head of his walking stick that he kept by his side.

Crawford was silent in resentment for a few moments, but he knew better than to argue with Vince Jerome. Men had died for that crime. "So what should I do if that snooty bastard from Illinois calls back?"

"You'll listen to him. And you'll control your temper. You showed already that you can't match the man in verbal battle. Just let him ramble on and everybody will just write him off as a harmless eccentric."

"Jesus, I hope so." Crawford sank a large portion of his refilled glass. He felt a wave of anger at the man across from him. *Who the hell did he think he was, telling Randy Crawford he couldn't do his job right?* Then he subsided. Crawford was fully aware, as was almost everybody else, that Jerome was one of the most influential men in America. Jerome said what he wanted and people listened. He ordered, and people obeyed. Jerome was not a man to have as an enemy.

"Meanwhile," Jerome continued, ignoring Crawford's interjection as if it had never happened, "we might try and trace the man who called you. If, by any remote chance, he does start to have some effect, we can take care of the matter."

"How will you do that? He called on a cell phone. The number didn't register on the caller-identification system. There was no trace possible."

Jerome smiled briefly. "But there will be records in the computers of one of the cellular phone companies and the long-distance telephone companies. We can find him."

Impressed by this glimpse into the power that Jerome could use so casually, Crawford finished his drink. "It's probably time I was going," he said. "I've got another three hours on air tomorrow."

"Yes, of course, Randy." Jerome didn't bother getting up. "And don't worry. You'll handle it if he calls again. Just let him talk."

"Yeah, sure," Crawford replied and walked out of the room. A man was standing outside the door. He was well built and had the unremarkable face of a minor male model or a newsreader in a small television station. He wore a dark suit, white shirt and a striped military tie. He was the same man who had opened the front door to Crawford's knock some twenty minutes before and escorted him downstairs to the luxurious study. Now he reversed the earlier walk and led Crawford to the large, oak-panelled door to the outdoors.

"Good night, Mister Crawford," he said in an indeterminate middle-American accent. Crawford nodded and walked out into the night where his Cadillac was parked in the curving driveway. He opened the door and climbed inside the leather luxury, enjoying as always the subtle clunk as the door closed, the gentle interior lighting and the comfort of the seat. The rewards for success, he thought with satisfaction, forgetting the discomforts of his meeting with Vince Jerome. He drove out into the road and headed for his home, an hour away.

Alone in his study again, Jerome thought deeply for a few minutes, then picked up the phone. He dialed a coded two-digit number to access regular calls and waited for a few seconds.

"We've had an interesting development during today's program," he said when he heard the phone picked up at the other end.

"Yes?" The voice was deep and strong, the voice of a presence as powerful as that of Vince Jerome.

"You should listen to the tape," Jerome continued. "The caller displayed an astonishing grasp of common elements and analyzed them with some intelligence."

"And how did our man handle it?"

"Not well." Jerome gave a short laugh. "He got hot under the collar and made a fool of himself."

"Has he been to see you?"

"Just left."

"What did you tell him?" The other speaker seemed only partially interested in the conversation, but Jerome knew that the attitude was deliberate. Nothing the other man did was ever done with partial interest.

"That if the man calls again, to let him go on without too much editorial input. That sort of arrogant type will usually dig their own hole and bury themselves."

"How true." The remote voice held a ghost of amusement. "Keep me informed."

"Of course," Jerome replied. "Call me when you've had a chance to listen to the tape."

"I shall. Goodnight, young Jerome."

Jerome smiled at the thought of his many decades being called young. "And goodnight to you, you ancient old duffer," he replied. "I'll see you at the next general meeting."

Hearing nothing else, Jerome replaced the phone and returned to his thoughts.

* * *

At ten the following morning, Randy Crawford was in his office at the studios of WNDY in Martinsburg. He enjoyed being there, it reminded him of how far he had come. The pleasant, old-world architecture of the small town's streets made an attractive view out of the window, and inside, he sat in some considerable comfort at a huge desk. His morning had started as it usually did, with the short conference with his two staff members. They walked in behind him as he arrived and he reveled in the respectful air with which they waited for him to take his place behind the desk before taking their own seats across from him.

"So whatcha got?" he asked in his carefully developed folksy manner. He lifted the huge mug of coffee that Janice had brought in with her and placed on the electric warmer already switched on for him. The mug was decorated with three faces. Ronald Reagan looked to the middle from one side, George Bush the elder from the other, and in between, the apparent object of their friendly smiles was Randy Crawford. The mug was his pride and joy, presented to him by a group of elderly World War II veterans.

"Today's email is here," Janice replied. "Mister Verity gave it to me earlier."

The comment sent a small jolt through Crawford. *Christ, I'd forgotten about that little kicker,* he thought. *That bastard's got a copy of all these messages. I should have mentioned that to Jerome last night.*

"What's in it?" he asked, looking at his assistant. Once the view had excited him. Janice was a real looker, he thought. Blonde and blue-eyed, she had the large jaws and big teeth of the standard Texan beauty queen. Her superb breasts always seemed to be straining at her clothing as if struggling to be released, and long legs gave her a sweet sway to her walk that had entranced him. She had been delightfully submissive to his early approach when she joined his staff two years ago, starry-eyed at working for the great Randy Crawford, nationally renowned defender of America's conservatives against the encroachment of the liberals. It had been a deliciously easy conquest. She had joined him in a hotel room the first night and he had made use of that magnificent body with her full support and co-operation.

The second night had been a disaster. She had recoiled with distaste from the suggestions he had made to her.

"God, you're sick!" she said when he pushed the point a little further. "How could anyone possibly enjoy that?"

She had tried to get dressed but he had thrown her violently to the bed and beaten her face until blood flowed from her nose and bruises showed up on her cheeks. Weeping, she had finally been able to get away.

Crawford had assumed that she would leave his staff immediately. Instead, she had said firmly to him the next morning that she believed in his work and she needed the well-paid job. Whatever contempt she had for his sexual tastes would be ignored, she said. And that was the last time they ever spoke on any subject other than their work.

Crawford dragged his mind back from the delicious scenes in the hotel room and struggled to recall her words. "The.. er.. the email? Oh, great. What have we got for today?"

Janice studied the paper in her clipboard. "They've made up some rumors that the president's wife made an illicit fortune on gold trading. She was helped by a lawyer friend of hers who had connections in the gold business and slipped her insider information."

"Okay, we can use that," Crawford said. "It beefs up all that old stuff about her terrorist connections underlines her basic lack of any morality at all. What else?"

"Some changes in target. They reckon that stories about his infidelities haven't had any effect, so they've developed one about an affair she had with her daughter's baby-sitter back in Illinois."

"What, a lesbian affair?" Crawford sat up sharply. "Do they think that'll work?"

Janice shook her head. "No, they've made it a young man in his late teens. No name given, so no chance of trying to trace anyone who could dispute it."

"Oh yeah, I like that!" Crawford said with a pleased grin. "Maybe I can tart it up a bit with references to a staffer on the governor's team who wants to remain anonymous but confirms the story. This is great! Anything else?"

She shook her head. "Don't want to overload the listeners, they said. Just give them enough to get them excited."

"Okay, that sounds reasonable. Jimmie, anything from you?"

The young man broke his silence, having spent the entire discussion between Janice and Crawford with his eyes glued to the woman's breasts. He was in his mid-thirties and dressed smartly in a black blazer and grey flannel trousers. He had a military-style tie knotted in a

Double Windsor and his shoes gleamed in the lights of the office.

"Yes, sir," he said briskly. "We've got a guy who's going to call this afternoon. He'll tell you that he's got a friend in the White House who told him that he heard the two of them shouting insults at each other in their bedroom. He says the president was drunk and his wife was yelling about his affair with one of the secretaries during the last election campaign."

"How much are we paying him for this, Jimmie?"

"Five hundred, sir."

"And you're sure that nobody could trace him and refute the story in any way?"

"Quite sure, sir. I listened to him for a while, and he's pretty good."

"Okay, when is he going to call?"

"Around one, though when he gets through depends on the line-up. He'll give his name as Al from New Orleans."

"Good. Any more?"

"Yes, sir. One of my friends from the navy agreed to call early on. He'll say he's an ex-marine captain who saw combat in Panama and the Gulf, and he'll go on at some length about the president being an un-American, terrorism-supporting liberal and how he'd never follow him anywhere, and that's why he left the Marines. He'll be Jake from Sacramento. Actually, he's my old buddy from school in Pittsburgh."

"Fantastic! How much of that one is true?"

Jimmie laughed. "None of it! He was a maintenance mechanic. Never left the US in his whole hitch. I'm paying him five hundred as well, okay?"

"Well, that's all great, kids." Crawford grinned happily at his staff and lifted up his coffee mug again. Recognizing the signal, Jimmie and Janice got to their feet and quietly walked out of the office. Crawford settled down to reading the newspapers, searching for any other small items which could be used in the day's show.

At twelve-thirty, Crawford left his office and walked round to the studio. The familiar tension was building up in him, a mixture of excitement at the scent of the hunt, and the fear that this would be the day on which he finally met the bogeyman of his dreams, the caller who would rip him apart and leave him bleeding to death. Ever since he had got into this business, that nightmare had haunted him. Regardless of how many callers he demolished, the idea of meeting such a nemesis had scared him each day. The nightmares of his youth still haunted him. He could never forget the misery of being over six feet tall before he was fourteen, and his thin, bony body which never moved smoothly and which made him inept at any sport. Memories of the cruelty of his fellow students all through school, and his lonely, friendless childhood could still bring him awake at night in a cold sweat. Only when he discovered the effects of being able to attack new ideas, original thought or any concepts which could be labeled un-American, and demolish the proponents of such concepts, did he find some respect and admiration from others. With a small shiver, he remembered the shock when the caller of yesterday first tore into him. For a lengthy time, he thought his worst fear had come alive. Even when the call was over, he still trembled a little. He had come dangerously near the brink, he knew. He forced from his mind the perilous thought that the man might call again.

Christiana was sitting at her console checking out the system and the phone lines. She looked up as walked into the studio, looked coolly at him then returned to her systems check.

Damn you, you foreign bitch. He couldn't help staring at her crossed legs and the beautiful thighs displayed by the denim skirt riding up high. The exhilaration faded a little and the tension mounted. *You'd better behave yourself, you little tart.* He walked through the door into his own studio and settled down at the desk. The time was twelve thirty-five, ten minutes to air. He remembered that he had at least two prepared calls that would give him the atmosphere he wanted. He looked down at his notes. Al from New Orleans and Jake from Sacramento they said. *And if Mark from Evanston calls, well, fuck you, Mark. You'll get the silent treatment and you can talk yourself into a pit where I'll bury you.*

He reviewed the email sent that morning from Washington. Good stuff, he thought. Another row between the first couple, he drunk, she a jealous shrew. That was always good for juicy ratings. Nothing a puritanical America liked more than marital infidelity in its leaders. He frowned at the paper for a moment as a thought struck him. *Shit, hadn't they worked that one to the marrow by now?* He remembered the failed attempts to raise that bogeyman, and America had yawned the subject into oblivion. Oh well, the bright boys in the special section in Washington must have thought of that one. Maybe they reckoned it was time to dust it off again and bring it out. Okay, I'll raise it and play with it as I've been ordered to do, but I doubt I'll get much juice from it. Now, her affair with the baby-sitter, that had a lot more promise. And her illegal dealings on the gold market, that would be great. Nobody understood that shit, but the idea of her making a ton of money while the poor folk starved, that was always good for some dirt to stick when it was thrown.

He wondered who the group was that thought up this stuff each night and emailed it out to the others like himself. It sure as hell worked, he knew. Thirty or forty talk-show hosts, from the single-station, three thousand-watt transmitters to the national super-star network icons like himself, a concerted attack each day on selected topics, it wore away at the public like a Chinese water torture. *We should have achieved our aims and thrown the jerk out at the last elections*, he thought, but that damned asshole running as an independent screwed it up just like in '92. Ah well, the polls were really turning good now and the next elections looked a dead cert for the right party. The primaries would soon be off and running and the candidates were starting to show their form. There were a couple of strong guys in the lead right now, but they'd never let one of them win the nomination, Crawford thought. Much too bright. The Religious Right had a stranglehold on the thing, so one of their own would be Vice-President, for sure. The boys in Washington would make sure the presidential candidate was somebody they could control, just like the others had been. He felt pleased at the idea. Rampant democracy was a dangerous thing, he believed. How the hell could the great unwashed masses impose their views on America? Far better to make sure that men like Vince Jerome and his Council ran the nation, men who had proved their abilities and power to make decisions. He could hardly wait until the Council took over.

Three minutes to air. He settled back and watched Christiana. She ignored him until the last few moments, then raised her eyes to him as she indicated twenty seconds to go. His throat tightened up as it had done every day for twenty years as the last seconds dripped away. He took a sip of water, felt the throat ease and mentally counted down with Christiana.

"And a great good afternoon to all those true Americans out there listening. This is Randy Crawford, the voice of loyal Americans everywhere, here again to listen to your comments and show you even more of the damage this present administration is doing to this fine country of ours. Yessirree, people, listen up now, and Randy will tell you the crazy, liberal goings-on in the White House."

He took a deep breath, felt the power and energy flow into him. He was on the hunt, he was after blood and he knew that over thirty million Americans were out there listening to him. He had a job to do, and by God, he was going to do it. There were people depending on him as well as paying him.

"So here's the first thing all you Americans out there should know about your president and his wife. While you all out there were fighting to feed your families, keep your jobs and pay the rent or the mortgage, trusting in the president to try and do something about the economy, you should know that the First Lady was making a fortune trading on the gold futures market. To the tune of several hundred thousand bucks, it seems. Now I have to ask all you hard-working people out there, could you make that sort of money? Hell no, you aren't privileged with the sort of information you need to trade in that crazy world. And you think the president's wife isn't? Of course, she's got all her liberal lawyer friends to tell her what's going on, something we poor working stiffs don't have."

He grinned widely to himself. *Hell, man,* he thought, *nobody does it better than ol' Randy! This'll get up the noses of that awful pair in the White House.* He caught a glimpse of Christiana looking at him. Her face was cold with anger. Standing behind her was Nick Verity with a similar expression. *Fuck you both,* he thought. *It may all be stuff made up by the guys in Washington, but it works! And nobody can dispute this without getting themselves in a shit-load of trouble.* He pictured the frantic scrambling that would be going on already in the press lines of the newspapers around the country and the damage-control people in the White House.

"The word is," he continued, "that the president's wife made all this money because somebody helped her. And you have to wonder folks, did she pay tax on this little windfall? Well, there ain't no sign of it in her last couple of tax returns, so it seems unlikely, doesn't it? And isn't it illegal to use insider information to trade on the markets? Well, sure it is! So is our beloved first lady a criminal as well as a raving liberal?"

He grinned at the shocked faces through the glass. For a moment he worried at the thought that Verity would have seen the email he received this morning and would know there was no truth in either allegation. *Christ, if he sent it to the White House!* It occurred to him that the address of the email that sent the stuff would be on the computer and could be traced to a location. He relaxed again. His job was to stir up the mess, the others could clean it up if it went wrong.

Christiana showed ten seconds to commercial.

"And when we get back, folks, I'll have some even juicier stuff about the carryings-on in the White House. What was the president's wife doing with the young male baby-sitter some years ago? Don't go away, I'll be right back."

Crawford took a deep drink of water and leaned back in his seat, looking coldly at Verity and Christiana. "So, how does that grab you?" he said loudly.

The other two looked at each other briefly.

"Who makes up that shit?" Verity asked.

"It's no shit. Very reliable sources get that sort of information for us because the liberal press wouldn't report it, you can bet." *Hey, that's a good line*, he thought. *Must remember to use it.*

"Tell me, Randy, do you actually believe any of the stuff you say, or is it just like verbal diarrhea?"

"It's true and I just report it." Crawford tried to stifle the anger he felt. Christiana was grinning at Verity's comment and it annoyed him even more.

"Ten seconds," she said. "We've got every line already waiting."

So there, bitch! The whole country wants to talk to Randy Crawford. And you can bet your sweet little fanny they'll all believe it, whatever you think.

He scanned the screen on his desk and saw the name he wanted. Jake from Sacramento was already on the line. Good man, thought Crawford, he must have called real early and just kept plugging until he got through.

He watched the fingers in the other booth and came in on cue. "Okay, America, we're back! This is Randy Crawford telling you all the real stuff about the present and very temporary occupants of the White House that the liberal pinko press wouldn't dare tell you. So we've already told you about the highly questionable trading on the gold futures market which your first lady indulged in. I was going to tell you about some other stuff about that lady, but we've got calls on the line and I don't want to stop honest, loyal Americans from having their say. So we go to Jake in Sacramento. Hey there, Jake, how's it all going in California?"

"Not that good, Randy," the voice said in the loudspeaker. "Ever since that lunatic moved in to the White House, there's been such a crazy slicing away at our defense forces that the economy's gone to hell."

"We're sure at risk," Crawford agreed. "Just about any half-assed bunch of commies could invade America right now and there's nothing we could do about it. All Reagan's good work undone by a socialist."

"Damn right, Randy. I'm a veteran, I saw combat in Iraq when President Bush sent us in to protect democracy, and before that, I saw action in the Gulf."

"A real, certified American hero, Jake. What branch of the armed forces were you in?"

"I was a marine captain, Randy."

"An officer? Hell, Jake, it takes a real man to be a marine officer. And what's your comment on the day's news, my friend?"

"Well, what I just heard about the president's wife doesn't surprise me one damn bit, Randy. I left the Marine Corps when she took over the White House because there's no way in hell I could serve in the armed forces with that yellow rat as my Commander-in-Chief."

"So the services lose a good man, Jake. It's the sort of thing that happens when you put a liberal in charge of the country's defense."

"And there's more leaving, I can tell you," the voice said. Now that he was listening for it, Crawford could hear the slightly false note in the California accent. *Stupid jerk,* he mused. *You were a mechanic who never saw action anywhere except in the bars around your base in San Diego. But it's good copy.*

"And that's the tragedy of all this, Jake old pal." Crawford knew that people loved to hear their names and he had developed the habit of using them as often as possible, even when he knew that Jake was no more the man's name than his claimed service record was accurate. "These losses take years to make up. Our president has done more damage to this country's defense capability than if he was an Arab jihadist."

He cut off the caller, his superb instincts telling him the man didn't ring true. He had served his purpose. The next caller was shown as Margaret from Boston. Crawford pressed the button and spoke warmly.

"Hi there, Margaret in beautiful Boston on the harbor. What can we do for you, today?"

There was only a click and Crawford grimaced. Callers who lost their nerve at the ultimate moment were common. *Stupid bitch. I know exactly the sort of crap you would have spouted, too. Girlish squeals and worship. God, I hate that! But it's useful padding.*

"We'll take a break for station identification," he said. "And when we get back, more of your calls."

He watched the signal for the cut-off, and took another drink. That first call had gone well. It would trigger a lot of hostility from war vets and some of them might call in.

"So that was Jake from Sacramento, was it?" Christiana's cool tones echoed through the speaker.

"That's what it said," Crawford replied.

"Except that the call came from Pittsburgh if my caller-identification system is working right. So what else was he lying about, Randy?"

"Hey, maybe he was just passing through Pittsburgh. What the hell does it matter?" *Christ,* he thought. *She's getting a bit close with this.*

"That was no more a Californian accent than mine," she persisted. "Are we so short of callers that we have to set them up, these days?"

"Shut up and do your job," he snapped and was relieved to see the clock running down to air time again.

"And we'll get to the nasty question of the first lady and the baby-sitter at a later time, folks," Crawford declaimed in the warm, friendly tones he was usually able to summon up with ease. "But right now, we go to... Mark on a car-phone in Chicago. What's up, Mark?"

At eleven-thirty, Mark had the Thunderbird sitting in the same spot as the day before, facing the waters of Lake Michigan in Evanston. A canceled appointment with a sales representative from a chain of computer stores had given him an unexpectedly free hour, and the summer vacation period at the office had reduced some of the crises to merely inconveniences. Mark wanted to hear the whole program today and make sure he got in his own call. A tiny thought flickered through his mind that he also wanted to talk to Christiana again, but that idea was submerged under the nervousness he was feeling at tackling Crawford for the second time.

He watched the clock on the dashboard. Crawford's show started at twelve-forty-five Eastern Time. Chicago was an hour earlier. He decided to tell the producer he was in Chicago, rather than give her a chance to recognize the combination of his name and Evanston that he had given her yesterday, and possibly cut him off. Despite the slightly warmer note he had detected in her voice when he announced that he was hostile to Crawford, he still felt convinced that she would have to be a Crawford believer to be his producer.

A few minutes before the quarter hour, he switched from the classical station to the local station that carried Crawford's program. The local talk-show host was still engaged in his own program and was arguing with a woman about some topic related to the Chicago School system. Mark called the eight hundred number and to his surprise, it took only three attempts before he got through.

"This is the Randy Crawford program," the delightful tones of Christiana said. "Where are you calling from?"

"Chicago," he replied, feeling a small tremble of pleasure at hearing her voice. "On a cell-phone."

"It's Mark again, right?"

"That's clever," he said, sensing a mixture of delight that she would remember and worry that it might result in his being cut off again without getting to talk to Crawford.

"I'm very glad you called," she said. This time, Mark had no doubts. There was warmth to her voice.

"A corporate or personal pleasure?" he asked, taking a risk. *I haven't flirted with a woman in two years,* he

61

thought to himself, and heard with delight her slight chuckle.

"I'll take the fifth on that."

The accent's interesting, he thought. *Slightly European...? No, I've heard that tone signature before... Montreal! I'll bet on it. She's French-Canadian.*

"Okay," he replied, feeling more confident at her evident response to him. "And how is *la belle Province* these days?"

"Good lord! How did you pick that? It's years since I left Montreal."

"It's what I do best," he replied. "Languages, accents, all that stuff. I'm good at it."

"That's right, you were a Russian speaker in the navy."

"Yes I was. Also German, French and Spanish."

"Wow!"

He laughed at the girlish expression. "Wow, indeed." A couple walking a dog in the park outside looked at him strangely. With the hands-free system on his phone, he supposed that it would look strange, a man sitting alone in his car talking to nobody.

"Okay, Mark, he has two callers ahead of you, then I'll put you on."

"You're letting me talk to him?" Mark was surprised, despite the apparent friendliness she was displaying.

"Good lord, why not?"

"After yesterday, I wondered."

"It was the best moment of the year, Mark," she replied, and this time the laughter was evident in her voice. "At least for us, if not for Mister Crawford."

Astonished, Mark said nothing, and the sounds of the radio program came through the small speaker of the car phone. Mark knew that if he turned on his radio, he would hear the same program about five or six seconds later than what he was hearing now. The introductory music came on then Crawford's bombastic tone came through the speaker.

Mark listened, working at keeping calm, knowing that two callers were ahead of him. He shook his head in disbelief as Crawford launched into his tirade about the supposed gold market trading by the president's wife and the implications of her sexual impropriety that Crawford promised to reveal later in the program.

When the first caller came through, Mark's attention was on a group of young women settling down on a blanket spread out on the grass of the small park next to the parking lot. They were removing their clothes to reveal bathing suits, when his attention was dragged back to the radio program.

The caller's voice was familiar. Mark concentrated on the tones. Jake from California, the man called himself, but Mark could tell immediately that the accent was not from the west coast. And the voice... despite the forced overtones, Mark knew that the voice was somewhere in his memory banks. He stared at his telephone as if to concentrate his thoughts on the tones. Somewhere in the last few years, he knew, he had met this man. His attention became deeper and deeper as he focused on vowel sounds, intonations... this is what he was good at, the skill that had let him become a fluent speaker of several languages.... Simpson! Dammit, it was Seaman George Simpson!

Mark recalled the man clearly. A large, muscular man in the mechanics section at the station in San Diego where Mark had done his basic training. An unpleasant bully of a man, Mark recalled. In trouble a couple of times for drunken behavior. And now he was claiming to be a Marine captain with combat experience? Mark wondered if Crawford knew that the caller was playing a role. *Good grief,* he thought. *Do they go so far as to set up dummy calls?* The idea made him laugh at first then he shivered slightly at the implications of the idea. Was the whole thing a well-planned, co-ordinated set-up? The network of talk-show hosts with a common agenda, dummy callers arranging to spew forth hatred, and created stories about the president, were these all part of some lunatic scheme to discredit anyone who opposed the right-wing viewpoint?

His attention was snapped back to the radio program.

"And we'll get to the nasty question of the first lady and the baby-sitter at a later time, folks," the warm, friendly tones of Crawford radiated from the telephone. "But right now, we go to... Mark on a car-phone in Chicago. What's up, Mark?"

Mark smiled to himself and went to war.

Even as he asked, Crawford felt the warning shiver. Something about the name...

"Much the same as yesterday," that hated voice said from the speaker. The amusement was stronger than Crawford remembered. *Jesus, it's that bastard again!* The name had not registered because the caller location said Chicago, not Evanston.

"Oh, it's the left-wing intellectual from yesterday." Desperately, Crawford called up The Sneer in full force. "Didn't you make a big enough fool of yourself in your last call?"

"Is that how you saw it? Most people seem to think you have it the wrong way round."

"Impossible. So what crazy liberal stuff do you want to force on us today, Mister Intellectual Mark?"

"It's interesting, Randy, how brilliantly you and your regular callers emphasize the truth of what that great English political commentator, John Stuart Mill said, many years ago."

Crawford was confused. The sudden tack had been unexpected and he had never heard of John Stuart Mill. "What the hell has some stupid British politician got to do with this?" he demanded.

"He wasn't a politician, Randy. Don't you listen? It proves his point even more. Mill said that while not all conservatives were stupid, it was a certain fact that all stupid people were conservatives."

"Then he was obviously one of your people, caller, an idiotic, liberal, trouble-maker, which is what I expect of any Britisher. Now, do you have something useful you want to say?"

"You're talking a great deal of bilgewater, Randy, even more than usual, and I wonder where you get it from."

"Damn good sources, I assure you," Crawford said sharply. "More reliable than the liberal press who try and protect their little friend as much as possible."

"Well, I'd say if they're as reliable as that last character who called, you might as well use your information as toilet paper, Randy ol' pal."

"Just what the hell does that mean, Mister Intellectual?"

"You might recall from yesterday, Randy, that I was in Naval Intelligence, and I learned Russian in that time. The reason I did that was that I've got a good ear for languages, and therefore accents too. And I tell you, Randy, that last caller sure as hell was not from California. I'd say he was from Pittsburgh."

The shock ran through Crawford like storm water. *Pittsburgh? Jesus Christ, he really could tell accents.* "People move, caller. He may have grown up in Pittsburgh and moved to California."

"Sure he could, Randy. But there's another problem. He was in the regular navy, not the marines, and he was no captain, nor any other commissioned rank."

"How the hell could you tell that, Mister Russian Speaker? Your ear for accents can identify military ranks, too?" The Sneer was in full force and Crawford was starting to enjoy himself after the initial shock.

"Don't be silly, Randy. I knew that man twelve years ago. He was a seaman in the engineering section at the base in San Diego."

Oh God, the one-in-a-million chance, and it had to be this bastard! Crawford groaned internally. "You're being stupid, caller, even for a liberal. There's no way you could recognize a voice that way, not after twelve years."

"Voices are my specialty, Randy. I knew that man."

Calling on his training and experience, Crawford pulled sharply away from the topic. "Presumably you had something useful to share with us, not this stupid attempt to disparage a genuine combat veteran?"

"Well, of course, Randy," the voice replied. It irritated Crawford that the caller used the same technique of quoting his name as often as possible. "We were discussing yesterday how like the communists you right-wing types are, with the same policies and philosophies.

And I think I raised the question of whether you really are a loyal American like you claim so loudly."

Despite a sudden wave of fury, Crawford remembered the instructions he had been give the previous night. Let the man talk, give him rope. "Go on," he said shortly.

"Let's recap, shall we?" the hated voice said. "We've already determined that you and the communists share the same stance on the environment, the preference for a military dictatorship to run the country, the hatred for liberal activists, intellectuals, environmentalists, anti-war philosophies and freedom of speech, and we've also agreed that you both believe the law doesn't apply to the party leaders. Right so far, Randy?"

Remembering his instructions, Crawford kept silent.

"I'll take your silence as agreement. So let's look at another topic, the question of gun control. I listen to you whackos screaming that guns are an essential part of liberty and that controls would not affect their availability to the criminals. But other countries manage to keep guns away from criminals fairly well, if not entirely. So when I see over thirty thousand Americans killed every year by gunshot, it's obvious that the people who benefit most from this situation are the gun manufacturers and big crime. So is it possible, Randy, that those two groups are funding the efforts to oppose any sort of gun control?"

Christ on a crutch! Crawford physically sat back from the microphone as if he had been slapped. He struggled for self-control and said nothing. He saw that both Christiana and Verity were listening with intense interest in the other booth.

"Your silence is interesting, Randy." The laughter in the voice was obvious. "When interrogating prisoners-of-war, we were taught to let them talk if they would. Give them room to talk themselves into a pit. Is this what you are doing? Because if so, it's most unlike you. Which probably means you're following somebody's instructions. And that somebody knows about interrogations. Who's your controller, Randy? Somebody with a military background?"

Crawford was desperately seeking an end to this. He decided that the best way was to encourage the caller to make his point then he could turn him off. "Do you have a point in all this lunatic rambling?" he asked.

"I sure do, Randy. My point is this. You're obviously aiming at some sort of destruction of American freedoms and democratic heritage, to be replaced by a military dictatorship. You're not bright enough to do this yourself, and it's interesting to hear any number of talk-show hosts like yourself all leading off with the same topics each day. I suggest that you're part of a group aiming to break down the American way of life. Somebody's coordinating the efforts. So, far from being the patriotic American you claim so loudly, I believe you are the real enemy of this country, not the liberals you so furiously attack. Who's behind you, Randy?"

Slamming his fist at the switch, Crawford disconnected the call. He was sweating heavily and his hands were trembling. He risked a look at Christiana and she was staring at him in a way he had never seen before. Verity's face was expressionless.

Crawford forced some sort of control on himself. "Well, after that lunatic's ramblings, we all need a break, folks," he said. "You can all go outside and be sick, and we'll be right back after these messages."

He gestured the cut-off sign at Christiana, and the room went silent. Crawford let out a long, trembling breath.

For the whole of the commercial break, there was silence in the studio. Crawford took the time to force calm on himself and ignored the presence of Christiana in the control booth. *I'll have to talk to Jerome again, tonight. That guy was scary. How the hell did he work it out, anyway? Jerome's going to have to do something about him. He could destroy the whole set-up.*

"Twenty seconds." Christiana's voice in the speaker.

Crawford looked at the list of waiting calls on his computer screen. The second plant was there, he could see. Al from New Orleans. Good, that would be the first call he'd take. That would send the discussion along the lines he wanted and give him the chance to introduce the second topic on the email from Washington. The show could be a success yet, he decided, feeling a rush of wild hatred for the occupant of the Oval Office. *Just wait, you bastard. You'll be finished soon and the whole world will know that it was Randy Crawford who destroyed you. You and your bitch-goddess of a wife. Your time is done, jerk, and I'm the one that did it to you.*

"Ten seconds."

He ran through the words he would use to introduce the tale of the first lady's dalliance with the male baby-sitter. He'd introduce it as a story he'd heard going the rounds in Washington. He'd deny any thought that it was another fabrication aimed at the president, and claim that these stories had to be told so that American voters could make up their own minds about the morality of the couple in the White House. It would be added to the next caller's story about the screaming match in their bedroom. *Yes, this could set the fur flying. Just think what a lovely scene it will be in the White House today as the spin-doctors start working out a defense against this bombshell from out of nowhere.*

Crawford smiled to himself.

"And we're back, America. You've all had a chance now to puke up the garbage that the last caller tried to feed you, and of course you've already worked out that he was a real lunatic who made up all that drivel. Just like all these crazy liberals, he's going nuts at the knowledge that his little tin god in the White House will be just another has-been by next year and we'll have a true American back in the Oval Office. So let's get back to the real world and our next caller. Al from New Orleans. What's happening in Creole Country, Al?"

Through the glass he saw Christiana shaking her head with a cynical smile. *Damn, she's seeing on her call-identification that the call's not from anywhere near New Orleans. She'll know it's another plant. To hell with it. This call will wipe the smile off that damn face.*

"It's a great show, Randy," the new voice said. "Ain't nothing you can tell me about that woman that would surprise me no more. And I got some more stuff for you."

"Let's hear it, Al." Crawford sat back in his seat with a wide grin at the woman in the control booth. This was going to be good.

Later that evening, Mark reviewed the discussion with Crawford on his tape. As before, he prepared a meal, listening to the callers to the show. The same stuff he had heard before was repeated, the allegations of illicit trading in gold by the president's wife, and he heard the promise of revelations about her sexual misdoings.

"We'll find out tomorrow if the other puppets have the same message," he said, took a gulp of beer and returned to the kitchen to check on the progress of his fish fillets.

Within a few moments, his own conversation was repeated for his edification, and Mark grinned as he heard the raw tension in Crawford's voice.

"Got you again, you bastard," he muttered. "You're running scared." He wondered what Crawford would do after that second call, to whom he would report, and what the unknown forces behind him were. A slight chill ran through him at the possibility that Crawford's masters were powerful enough to do something about the attack on them, then he calmed down. "There's no way they can trace me, anyway," he said, taking a second can of beer from the fridge. "That's why I used the car phone with ID suppression. You can't trace those."

He waited for Crawford to bring up the question of some sexual misadventures by the first lady as he had promised, but the tape ran out before the topic was raised.

The next morning, however, he found the messages on his computer system. His reporters around the USA all reported that the local talk-show hosts had initially discussed the first lady's dealings on the gold markets. Then all but Crawford had told their listeners how "highly credible resources" had told them about sexual dalliance between a male baby-sitter and the president's wife some years ago when the president was still a state governor.

The information dampened Mark's delight in the punishment he had dealt Crawford the day before, and firmed his resolve to carry on his personal war. Just what else he could do, he had no idea.

*   *   *

"The mysterious caller from Chicago called Crawford again today."

"How interesting. I reviewed yesterday's conversation. Was today's discussion equally as revealing?"

"Indeed it was. Essentially, the man described the exact situation."

"And how did Crawford handle it?"

"Better than yesterday. He followed my suggestion to let the caller speak at length and then ridiculed the performance later. He used the emailed material rather well, weaving it into one of the planted calls."

"Good. I'm relieved. The man's a buffoon, but we need him. He's the biggest name among the radio hosts and carries a lot of weight."

"I agree, which proves that we're achieving one of our goals in downgrading American educational levels. Another small problem revealed itself. The producer detected that there was something unrealistic about the two calls. She saw that neither of them came from their claimed origins and literally accused Crawford of planting them."

"Another bright woman. Shouldn't be a problem. Nobody would believe her and she couldn't prove her claims."

"I suppose not. But the station manager has also told Crawford that he has copies of all the emails and has threatened to send them to the White House."

A small silence echoed in Jerome's ear.

"That could present an embarrassment," the remote speaker said. "Let us do nothing about that for the moment until events develop."

"Agreed. But I suggest we raise the issue of this man in Chicago at the next board."

"A good suggestion, my young friend. We'll do that."

Jerome grinned. "Good-bye, old man. See you next week."

Chapter 4 - Frederick, Maryland

Charles Dansbury was the first to arrive. His stretched Cadillac limousine gently rolled up to the gates of the Maryland estate and stopped, the massive hood of the car barely an inch from the wrought iron. Dansbury did not look up from his papers as his driver went through the clearance checks through the intercom system by the gate. The gate swung open under the electronic instruction of some unseen controller and the Cadillac rolled its supremely elegant way along the curved driveway up to the house. Only when the car stopped for the second time, did the man in the rear seat fold away his papers and pack them in his briefcase. He took the crystal glass from its holder by the seat, drained the remnants of the fine malt scotch and placed the glass inside the cabinet in the back of the forward seat.

Dansbury waited for the driver to come round and open his car door, then climbed out into the warm morning sunshine. His gaze passed through the uniformed chauffeur as if he were invisible, and looked around him. The view was worth the effort. Gentle hills sloped away into the distance. The house was surrounded by trees so that there was no sign of a roadway or even of the gate through which the Cadillac had just passed. Dansbury looked up and smiled with pleasure as he saw a hawk floating motionless above the trees. He could just make out the tiny flickers of movement in the bird's wingtips as it corrected for air currents. At eighty-four years of age, Charles Dansbury still could still boast the long-range vision that had once served him well in the Second World War.

The huge front door of the mansion house opened smoothly and Vincent Jerome walked out to greet his first guest. His walking stick made no sound as the rubber base touched the floor, and Jerome seemed not to put any weight on the silver handle. "Hello, ancient one," he said with a tiny smile. "Your visits almost make these events bearable."

"Ah, young Jerome." Dansbury extended his hand. "It remains a source of astonishment to me how you have acquired such wealth while still in your tender years."

The two men laughed and shook hands. They were quite unalike. While Jerome was built along the tall, elegant lines of the old-fashioned patrician, Charles Dansbury was broad and stocky, his face more like that of a farmer than of a man who controlled much of the wealth and political power of the United States. Dansbury was the elder of the two by a little over two years.

Jerome turned back toward the house. "I have a new *Fumé Blanc* you must try," he said as they climbed the steps and entered the cool, airy hallway of the house. A massive, antique grandfather clock stood impassively against one wall. The heavy, complex-patterned hands pointed to fifteen minutes before eleven o'clock. As

Jerome and Dansbury walked to the middle of the black and white marble-tiled floor, a silent young man swung the door closed behind them. Dansbury's gaze flickered rapidly to the attendant as he walked past and studied the well-tailored coat which, to his educated eyes, showed the small swelling of a shoulder holster and the automatic pistol held inside it.

"*Fumé Blanc?*" Dansbury curled his lip. "A drink for young, uneducated palates, I suppose, but what can one expect of one so unlearned as yourself? Would this kindergarten happen to have a drink fit for a mature man like myself? A Laphroaig, perhaps?"

Jerome smiled and gave an almost imperceptible nod at the hovering attendant. "I'm sure we can find something among the bottles of kiddy stuff that might please you. Let's go to the conference room and wait for the others."

He walked ahead of Dansbury and opened the library door. The heavy oak swooshed over thick carpet and Dansbury lead the way in. The room was capacious, well over forty feet long and twenty wide. Down the middle, stretched a conference table that glowed with a gentle, self-contained gleam. There were no windows to the room. Although twenty seats were placed at the table, nine down each side and one at each end, only eight places had notepads before them. These places also had a drinks coaster next to each pad. Three water jugs on small trays were lined up down the middle of the table, each with four upturned glasses by them.

"Your knee pains you, young man?" Dansbury asked as they entered the room.

Jerome smiled. "Hardly at all. I only carry this stick to give some gravitas to my image of extreme youth."

"Hah!" Dansbury snorted mildly.

Another young man was in the room, and he turned as the two older men entered. Jerome nodded at him, and the man continued walking slowly round the conference room, carefully moving a metallic rod up and down the walls and along the table. A pair of light earphones on his head, and a glazed concentrated expression in his eyes placed a barrier between him and the other two. Jerome took the chair at the head of the table, and Dansbury sat in the chair at his immediate left. They said nothing as the third man continued his sweep of the room. Finally, the young man removed his earphones. "Clear, sir," he said and moved to the door. It opened as he reached it, and a woman of considerable beauty walked in, carrying a tray. She wore a short, black, sleeveless dress with a low, scooped neckline. The tops of her breasts stood out above the line of the dress. The man walked out with a brief glance at her, and she advanced to the table.

"Good morning, Mister Dansbury," she said with a glowing smile. "How lovely to have you back."

Dansbury grinned cheerfully at her as she bent over him, deliberately revealing her breasts, and placed the crystal glass of scotch on his coaster.

"You know you're the only reason I come here, Angela," he said, staring unabashed down her dress.

"Then when are you going to make an honest woman of me, Mister Dansbury?" she asked with a little chuckle. She turned and placed a gracefully-shaped wine glass on Jerome's coaster.

"Angela, you'll give the old man a heart-attack if you behave like this," Jerome said. "He still has dreams of his lost virility. Now run away before he starts drooling."

"Yes, sir," she said primly, and stood upright. Both men watched as she swayed out of the room with an exaggerated hip movement.

"Precocious child," Dansbury said as the oak door closed behind her. He sniffed carefully at his glass. "Laphroaig," he said. "At least twenty years old."

"We try and look after our older guests."

Both men laughed out loud, and each drank from their respective glasses. For a few moments, they lost themselves as they savored the drinks, then placed them back on the table.

"Anything unusual on the agenda?" Dansbury asked.

Jerome shook his head. "Just the usual bean-counting reports. The treasury will be taking a beating over the next few years and I want to ensure everything's kosher."

"What about the recent events with the broadcaster?"

"We can raise it if you like. I'm not concerned about it as yet."

"I think it should be raised," Dansbury murmured, taking a delicate sip of his scotch. "The reaction might be interesting."

"By all means." Jerome gave with a small shrug. "There's nothing lost by it, and we shouldn't have a heavy session today." He lifted his own wineglass and took a mouthful. As he replaced the glass, the door opened again and Angela reappeared.

"Mister Armstrong is here, sir," she said. Her voice held a note of disapproval.

"Send him in, Angela." Jerome rose to his feet, taking hold of his stick with his left hand. He looked down at the raised eyebrow of Dansbury. "Common courtesy," he said softly.

"Very common," Dansbury agreed and remained seated.

The man who entered was about six feet tall and lightly built. His hair was sparse and light-colored, his face so thin as to be almost skeleton-like. The mouth was merely a narrow line under a razor-sharp nose. His dark suit hung loosely on him. Cold blue eyes stared at the two men in the room and he paused for a moment before advancing to the table.

"Good morning, Vince," he said. He nodded to the seated man. "And to you, Charles."

Dansbury nodded, but said nothing. The dislike of the new arrival was obvious, and it seemed to be mutual.

Jerome smiled pleasantly and extended his hand. "Welcome to our meeting, Grant," he said. "Please take a seat. Can I offer you a drink?"

Armstrong shook his head. He studied the table for a moment, then moved to the line of seats down from Dansbury. He slid one of the note pads along the table to a seat leaving two empty chairs between himself and Dansbury and sat down. He took a black fountain pen from his jacket pocket and laid it on the note pad, laced his fingers together under his chin and stared at the table without further movement.

For a few uncomfortable seconds, silence hung over the boardroom, while a barely perceptible smile hovered over Dansbury's lips. The sound of voices from the hallway broke the discomfort and Jerome turned to the doorway expectantly.

"Senator Eckhard and General Rollings," Angela announced. She squeaked as two men swept by her, the leader of them obviously relishing the gentle pat he had given Angela's buttocks. She didn't seem upset by the contact.

"Morgan, always a pleasure." Jerome shook hands with the first of the newcomers. Eckhard was a heavy-set man in his fifties. A full head of black hair topped a face made of masculine craggy lines, with grey eyes that looked calmly at the world. The dark blue suit he wore was tailored with class and fitted him perfectly. Gold cufflinks gleamed from pure white shirt-cuffs and his tie was a deep burgundy with blue stripes. One stripe exactly bisected the knot.

"Hi there, Vince," Eckhard replied and shook hands enthusiastically. His voice was firm and the accent Ivy-League. "Good to see you, too. And you, Charles. Keeping fit?"

Dansbury had risen to his feet and also shook hands with a friendly smile. "Pressures of keeping the world safe make me tired sometimes, Senator," he answered. "But at my age, that's no surprise."

"Hah!" Eckhard laughed. "You're a walking advertisement for a fitness club, Charles. What's that you're drinking?"

"Nectar of the gods, my friend," Dansbury said softly. "We'll organize some for you."

Jerome had meanwhile turned to the second man who had entered. "General, delighted you could make it," he said with a warm smile.

General Corley Rollings was dressed almost as a twin of the senator. His suit was a shade darker, and the cufflinks were a gunmetal grey, but his tie was a similar military pattern and as immaculately tied as the senator's. Rollings' hair was receding from the forehead and cut short. His eyes were a bright blue, and they flashed with intense energy.

"Wouldn't miss these meetings, Vince, you know that," he said firmly. He shook hands, then repeated the exercise with Charles Dansbury who smiled at him and resumed his seat.

Eckhard took a seat at Jerome's right, but one chair down, leaving an empty chair directly across from Dansbury. Rollings left another chair empty and took the next seat on the senator's right. The spacing seemed to indicate an acknowledgement of the need for a private area without a requirement to be any further distant from each other.

The two new arrivals looked across the table at Armstrong. No friendliness was evident in their expressions.

"Grant, how are you?" Eckhard enquired politely.

"Fine, thank you, Senator." Armstrong's mouth seemed barely to move and he looked at Eckhard only briefly before his eyes turned back to the table.

"The CIA keeping you busy?" Rollings asked. His distaste was not concealed.

Armstrong's eyes lifted to stare at the General. The difference in the color was sharply evident. Whereas Rollings' eyes flashed and sparkled, Armstrong's were pale and washed-out, hiding any personality behind them. "As always, General," he replied, then looked down again.

The door opened and Angela returned, breaking the tiny air of tension in the room.

"Perfect timing," Jerome said and smiled at her. "I think these gentlemen need refreshment."

The woman surveyed the room, standing at Jerome's left shoulder. Dansbury was admiring the line of her waist and bosom. Both Rollings and Eckhard were looking at her in frank admiration, while Armstrong did not raise his eyes.

"The same as Charles is having," the senator said.

"Bit early for me," Rollings said. "Make it a mineral water."

The woman nodded pleasantly and looked at Armstrong.

"Nothing," he muttered.

"And the same again for us, please," Jerome said. "And no flashing your boobs at these gentlemen, Angela. They're a lot younger than Mister Dansbury and I can't vouch for their reactions."

Amid a chuckle round the table, Angela left the room.

"The others are coming, Vince?" the General asked. He sat firmly upright in his chair, his hands resting on the table, fingers interlaced.

"It's a full meeting," Jerome replied with a friendly nod, then looked sideways at the door as the sound of voices reached him. A few seconds later, the door opened.

The first man to enter was short, stocky, with a chest like a bull. His face was square, firm and authoritative. His presence projected ahead of him.

"Good morning, gentlemen," he said, walking briskly up to the head of the table. He shook hands with Jerome, who had risen to his feet.

"Geoffrey, always a pleasure," Jerome said. The other man grinned at him, then looked down at Dansbury.

"Don't get up, Charles," he said and took Dansbury's hand in a firm grip. "Good to see you, old friend," he said.

"Mister Payne, why are you so damned noisy?" Dansbury asked with a smile. "You hurt an old man's ears!"

Payne let out a laugh. He walked round the table and shook hands in a friendly manner with Eckhard and Rollings, then carried on to take a seat leaving one empty space between himself and the General. The three men obviously liked and respected each other. Payne merely gave a nod to the CIA man across the table. Armstrong responded in the same way.

Two other men had followed Geoffrey Payne into the room. The first, like Payne, carried himself with a sureness and confidence that surrounded him like an aura. But whereas Payne's ego projected an air of expectation and excitement, Anthony Redman emitted tension and fear. He was a handsome man, his face well shaped under a head of gleaming black hair. His eyes were large, dark, and almost hid the person behind them the way reflecting sunglasses did. Like the others, Redman was dressed in an immaculate, expensive suit, though his tie was more ornate and decorative than the others, an explosive riot of color. Despite that, there was a darkness surrounding Redman and it reflected in Jerome's greeting.

"Good morning, Anthony," he said briefly. His expression was subdued and no smile alleviated it. Redman nodded, briefly shook hands then walked firmly to the far end of the table. He made no sign of recognition to any of the other men in the room. He took his seat and sat motionless, impatience showing in his face.

he last man seemed to slide in to the room.

His walk was smooth and silent, like a predator. But the man's appearance was oddly contradictory to the movement. Of medium height, he was overweight, a round belly pushing out the single button of his light grey suit. His face was circular, fleshy lips under a snub nose and pink cheeks. His eyes were round, colored the same cold, light blue as Grant Armstrong's.

The Reverend Jackson T. Vanderbilt walked up to Jerome and offered his hand.

"Welcome, Reverend," Jerome said. "I'm glad we're all here at last. Angela is getting drinks for all of you, I believe?"

"I believe she is, yes." Vanderbilt's voice was a powerful, orator's broadcast. It reflected intensive training, echoing upward from the oversized belly.

Vanderbilt smiled at all the others in turn as he studied the layout of the table and the distribution of occupied seats. He walked down the left-hand side to take a seat between Redman at the foot of the table, and Grant Armstrong, leaving two empty chairs between each of them and himself. He received a courteous wave from Eckhard, Rollings and Payne, and a cold nod from Redman as he sat down. Armstrong shifted his seat slightly, as if to ensure he maintained the maximum distance between himself and Vanderbilt on one side and Dansbury on the other.

Angela returned, carrying a tray of drinks. She replaced the two glasses of Dansbury and Jerome then carried on round the table, depositing a scotch glass in front of Eckhard, a glass of bubbling mineral water by the General and another scotch glass by Geoffrey Payne. She seemed to hesitate before moving to the foot of the table where she carefully placed a large glass of red wine in front of Redman. The last glass was another scotch, and when she had placed that by the Reverend Vanderbilt, she walked back to the door, acknowledging with a small smile, Jerome's silently mouthed words of thanks.

None of the men had made any playful comments to Angela as she passed. Tension in the room had built rapidly as the last three men had entered, and went up yet another notch as Vanderbilt, the last of the group sat down. Dansbury was watching Redman at the foot of the table as Angela moved down the room, but Redman seemed not to notice the gaze. General Rollings sat stiffly as his drink was placed down, while Payne acknowledged his with a murmured word of thanks. Reverend Jackson T. Vanderbilt stared at the ceiling until Angela had passed. When the woman closed the door behind her, a small stir went round the table.

Jerome broke the silence. He raised his glass and looked round the table. "Gentlemen," he said, "I give you the New America."

"The New America," the others replied. All of them took a drink from their glasses and set them back on their coasters.

"By God!" Senator Eckhard grinned widely. "You're right, Charles. This is the nectar of the Gods!"

"Tell that to my young friend here," Dansbury replied with a smile at Jerome. "He insists on drinking that French soda pop."

"You may all want a notepad, gentlemen." Jerome deliberately ignored the jibe and waited a moment as pads were slid down the table to those who had not taken one before. "Good," he continued when the table had settled again. "Our quarterly meeting of the Council is now opened. We have little new business to discuss, but we must review the status of current projects. Grant, perhaps you will start?"

Armstrong stirred in his seat. He referred to no papers and spoke from memory, looking down at the table as he did. The others picked up their pens and looked expectant.

"Imports of all narcotics controlled by my group are now averaging just over a billion dollars per month at street value," he said. "In the last three months, CIA and DEA agents have destroyed six more major importers and we have taken over their delivery systems effectively. That increased our income by fifteen percent."

"Excellent," General Rollings said, writing figures on his pad.

"Indeed," Payne agreed. "Well done, Grant."

Grant ignored both comments. "Cash reserves now total fifty-four point two billion," he continued. "This money is distributed between nine different accounts in Switzerland, the Caymans and Luxembourg. However, we've had a fairly heavy cash outlay to replace the aircraft, vehicles and men that were destroyed by the US narcotics agents in the process of removing the competition. I had to buy two new twin-engine aircraft and a variety of vehicles. That cost over thirty-two million, allowing for black-market costs and fees to cover up the deals. We recruited all the men we need in Bogata and Medellin, and a few in Mexico. The usual checks were made on them, and of course, my resources have the best facilities for that process."

"I bet they have," Senator Eckhard chuckled. "You'd be the first to know if any of the recruits were DEA or CIA infiltrators."

Grant looked impassively at the senator. "Of course we would," he said without expression. "I'm in charge of the CIA anti-narcotics forces."

"I know that," Eckhard snapped in irritation. "It was a joke, Grant, for Christ's sake."

Armstrong blinked, and resumed his head down pose.

"Grant, that's an excellent performance," Jerome broke in to ease the irritation from Eckhard. "Are you absolutely certain that Hennings doesn't have any wind of what's going on?"

"John Hennings is a fool," Armstrong said, the first time any emotion had appeared in his voice. "He may be the Director of the CIA, but he trusts me with the anti-drug forces. He has no idea at all of the real objectives."

"How do you keep it covered?" Rollings asked curiously.

"Easy," Armstrong replied. "Every time we make a major bust, we do a big song-and-dance act about the recovered drug pile and make certain the press sees us destroy it. And of course, we really do burn it up. It helps increase the shortage for a few weeks and pushes up the price. So once we bring in the next batch under our own control, we make up for the lost product immediately. After all, I'm doing my job. I'm destroying drug importers."

"And I suppose you can then hide the imports more easily by being in control of the mechanisms." Geoffrey Payne seemed amused.

"Of course," Armstrong agreed. "I have my people at the key entry points and we ensure it gets through without fuss."

"Nothing like having the crooks in charge of the police," Payne said with a laugh. It was echoed by Jerome, the senator and the General. Dansbury merely smiled politely, Redman ignored the comment, and the Reverend Vanderbilt looked offended. Armstrong said nothing.

"I hardly think in this case we could be classed as crooks," Vanderbilt said. "We're on the side of goodness here. These methods merely help us achieve godly aims."

"It was a joke, Reverend," Payne said, echoing the irritation that Eckhard had displayed earlier.

"Thank you, gentlemen," Jerome said firmly. "Geoffrey, how about you?"

"Much as before," Payne said. "United Armaments continues to build up sizeable stocks of automatic weapons and ammunition for distribution as required. And we continue to build up control of retail outlets so that we can get as much of the stuff out and into peoples' hands as possible."

"How do you hide the reserves from the auditors?" Dansbury asked.

Payne turned to him with a smile of pride. "I established a secret testing plant in Arizona," he replied. "I had it placed directly under my control and got it classified top-secret, so not even the auditors can inspect it. We do test weapons there, of course, but mainly it's an assembly line big enough to build what we'll need."

"And normal retail movements are healthy?" Eckhard inquired.

Payne looked up the table to his left and nodded. "With the help of your good self and your party," he said.

"I don't think so," a soft voice said from the end of the table, and all faces turned in that direction. Redman had not spoken loudly, but he had established his authority immediately. "You've had too many failures these last few years," Redman continued. "My colleagues and I have put millions into the National Rifle Association and your party for you to make sure there's no restriction on gun sales. And look what happens."

"Anthony, I hardly think the recent legislation hurts us," the senator replied. "We managed to stall it and cut it until it only banned the import of automatic weapons. In fact, that helped Geoffrey, because his sales went up immediately."

"I don't give a damn." Redman's eyes had lost their secretive dullness and were flashing with anger. "Any restriction at all is just the start. The more guns get sold to legitimate buyers, the more my people can relieve them of the weapons and use them for my purposes. I can't afford any slow-down in that process."

"And that's our objective," Jerome interjected smoothly. "The more we break down the established structure of law enforcement and get people panicking, the quicker we achieve our own aims. I agree with Morgan. The new laws didn't hurt as at all, any more than the seven-day waiting legislation did."

"They may not have hurt any of you lot," Redman whispered. "Payne's only concerned with selling guns, so he doesn't care. But my people need guns, and we can't always get them through legitimate channels. And if we can't get them, we can't sell them to the single operators. I lose money both ways. It's essential that people remain free to buy guns with no limit, so that we can grab them."

"I agree with you," Eckhard said soothingly. "But the legislation was purely symbolic."

"Well just make certain no more of it goes through." Redman's voice held a dangerous edge. "I'm not wasting any more money on your bunch if it does."

"Logistics, Geoffrey," Jerome said, working to keep the atmosphere calm. "Some figures, please?"

Payne looked briefly at Redman, then, like Armstrong, spoke without notes. "I have a hundred and twenty thousand handguns in the stockpile. Twenty thousand are twenty-two caliber, the rest are all nine-millimeter automatics. I have forty thousand AK-47 equivalents, made in the same style as the Kalashnikov. There's enough ammunition for twice the duration of the action we've estimated in the worst-case scenario. Of course, the plan indicates no need for any such action."

"And retail sales?" Jerome asked.

"They continue as healthy or healthier as before. Our program of recruiting crazies and sending them out with an assault weapon to schools and malls and letting loose has been most successful. We have a stable of such loonies and when sales sag a little, we bring one of them in, get them hopped up and send them out. The Virginia Tech shooting was one of ours and it sent sales soaring that weekend at guns shows over the country. Same with those episodes in Tucson and Connecticut."

"And the lists of retail outlets and their purchases have been sent to me?" Redman demanded.

"As always, Anthony," Payne replied without looking at the man at the end of the table on his right. "You can follow up and apply whatever muscle you want to the store holders. I'm sure they'll give you the details of who bought them. It's up to you to get your hands on those guns any way you want."

"Of course," Redman replied. The satisfaction was evident in his voice. "I'll get my share."

"I'm sure you will," Payne concurred, ignoring the glare he received from Redman.

"Good," Jerome said. "Morgan, your turn. What's happening on the political front?"

"Continuing the good work on both fronts," Eckhard said with a smile. "We're forming public opinion with the broadcasting network just the way we want it, and the polls are looking excellent."

"Ah, yes," Dansbury broke in. "Vince and I have a question for you on this topic when you're done."

"Really?" Eckhard raised an eyebrow. "Anything serious?"

"I doubt it," Dansbury said with a friendly smile. "But it needs raising. Finish the report, Morgan, and we'll get to it."

Eckhard looked briefly at Dansbury and Jerome, and continued. "The network is now forty-one talk-show hosts. All of them receive their daily emails of topics to be used to attack the current administration, and the group that develops these topics each day continues to be creative and aggressive. Crawford remains the highest profile of all of them, of course. He's carried to an audience of over thirty million listeners around the US, and the others between them talk to more than twenty million. As I said, the polls are showing a continuing and steady climb for the Party."

"What about the other side?" Payne asked. "There must be a number of radio hosts pushing the liberal side, surely?"

"Almost none," Eckhard answered. "We keep a careful ear open for these types all over the country, including any possible enemy types in Canada who might be heard on this side of the border. Any time we find one, we can exert considerable pressure on the station to cut them."

"What sort of pressure?" Payne was curious. This aspect of the system had not been raised before.

Eckhard shrugged. "Mainly economic," he said. "We contact the advertisers. We've got enough heavy financial organizations under control so that threats of financial restrictions can be applied. Then they threaten to withdraw their advertising. If that doesn't work, we get some grassroots organizers to set up boycotts of the advertisers' goods. It's amazingly easy to do that. People are very quick to believe that anyone who supports this administration is a raving communist and anti-American."

"And it's worked every time?" Payne asked.

"Almost," Eckhard replied. "We had one hard nut in Chicago. Eventually we had him removed."

"I think I understand," Payne said. "It was an accident, of course."

"A drive-by shooting," Redman added. "Happens every day in Chicago."

"Ah." Payne smiled coldly. "Your people?"

Redman simply nodded.

"On the second front," Eckhard continued, "there's nothing new to report. The selection of the presidential candidate for the next election is still in progress. The primaries begin in earnest in a few months, and we're setting it up for the favored man to get the nomination."

"The same bunch of bird-brains, I trust?" Rollings asked.

Eckhard looked irritated for a second, then seemed to take control of himself. "Of course," he replied. "Somebody we can control. The main program right now is to dissuade the bright guys from running, not that there are many of them, and to get the dummies into gear."

"That's where a lot of the funds in our accounts will be used," Jerome said with a nod. "We'll be sharing out the cash very liberally to each of the selected few. They need bright staff and spin-doctors and a hell of a lot of training to sound like intelligent human beings."

"And of course, the more we give them, the more certain we are to control them once they're in the Oval Office," Eckhard agreed. "That's about it, Vince, the situation as before. You said you had a question, Charles?"

"I did," Dansbury said. "It's about your leading star, Randy Crawford."

"A problem?" Eckhard seemed concerned, and all the men at the table looked at him, then at Dansbury.

"Unlikely." Dansbury gave a small shrug. "A few days ago, he received two successive calls from a man in the Chicago region who ripped him apart. We have the tapes if you want to review them later. Not only did he make Crawford look stupid, but he came dangerously close to specifying exactly what was going on."

"How close?" Payne asked, leaning forward on the table.

"Remarkably close," Jerome answered. "Some of his conclusions were wrongly drawn, but he saw the factors in play. For example, he stated that he thought the existing gun laws only benefited the criminals and the gun manufacturers, and deduced that representatives of those bodies were funding the NRA and Morgan's party to maintain pressure on Congress and the Senate never to tighten gun control."

"Jesus! He was right on target there, all right!" Payne sat back in his seat in astonishment and finished his scotch in one gulp.

"That's a dangerous man," Redman said softly. "I don't like this. What else did he say?"

"His remaining conclusions were quite wrong, based on silly philosophy," Jerome said. "But his deductions were based on correct observations. He said that there was a conspiracy to destroy personal freedoms in the country and replace the political system with one-party military rule."

"So how was he wrong?" General Rollings asked. "That's sure as hell what we're going to do. This country won't keep going without some strong leadership and real discipline."

"Well, this caller said that it was obviously a communist conspiracy, because there was no difference between hard-line communism and right-wing fascism."

"Then the man's a fool!" The Reverend Vanderbilt's face flushed. "The communists don't believe in God! When we're in power, God's words will rule this country and anyone who objects to that can kiss their ass goodbye."

"Of course," Dansbury said with a smile. "The man's conclusions were stupid. But he did see what was in process, and he accused Crawford of representing what he called anti-American interests. The diminution of free speech, immunity from prosecution for senior party members, and so forth."

"I don't care about his stupid political thoughts," Redman broke in from the foot of the table. Again, all attention swung toward him. "But I do care that someone is catching onto the fact that my people depend on the current gun laws to obtain our weapons. Find out who this man is and have him removed, Jerome."

Jerome looked round the table. "Do I hear a second for that motion?" he asked.

Payne raised his hand firmly. "Damn right, you do," he intoned. "I sure as hell don't want anyone thinking I might be subsidizing Morgan's party, or seeing a link between United Armaments, Redman's people and the NRA. Get rid of him."

Jerome leaned back in his chair, holding the head of his walking stick. For a few seconds at a time, he looked at each of the men round the table, starting with Morgan Eckhard on his right. He received a nod of assent from each one. Finally he looked at Charles Dansbury.

Dansbury looked back with a small smile. "See," he said. "I told you it needed raising."

"You did," Jerome agreed. "So how say you, old man?"

"Remove the bastard," Dansbury said.

Jerome nodded. "The chair agrees. I'll organize it. The next report comes from you, Jackson."

The Reverend Vanderbilt cleared his throat. "Situation as before," he said loudly. "My people have been winning office in all states, at all levels, concentrating on school boards. As soon as we feel able to swing the votes, we start pushing for firm, religious-based educational standards. We've managed to cut down scientific education in a lot of areas already, we get maths, physics and chemistry sharply downplayed, and of course, insist that all evolution teachings are matched by Creation Theory. Reading and writing skills have been declining sharply over recent years."

"What about libraries?" the General asked.

Vanderbilt smiled. "I've got people organizing book removals all over the country. We're moving in on any old American histories, literature and of course the scientific stuff, and downgrading the entire stocks. Give me another few years, I'll have not an American in the country capable of any critical thinking. They'll do what my church tells them to do. And of course, with the help of Morgan's people at state and federal level, most university curricula are going the same way. The quality of education is being depressed everywhere. I think that the way we have created the social pressure to ensure everybody gets a passing grade, and pass it off as a liberal agenda is brilliant. It's helping that decline of education standards enormously. The level of literacy in the country is dropping sharply, together with knowledge of history."

"Good, keep it up," Jerome murmured. "Anthony, anything you wish to add?"

"No," Redman said. "I came to see what you people were doing. I'm on top of all my plans."

"General, what about you?" Jerome asked. "Any changes to your plans?"

"None," Rollings said firmly. "All plans to take control of radio and television stations have been in place for three years. We have the expected control already of most

National Guard units in case of civil unrest. A number of crucial military bases are personally committed to me, and I control the postings to ensure my men stay in control. But as we have always known, this whole action will result from a legitimate win at the voting booths when our man will take the White House. I expect no problem with any military units because the legal Commander-in-Chief will be in place."

"Good," Jerome said with finality. "Any questions from anyone?" He looked round the table again, and received a series of shaken heads. "Then as usual, let's give ourselves ten minutes to review and absorb our notes, then you'll each please give me the complete note pad for shredding."

"Perhaps some discussion is called for, Vince." The General leaned forward on the table and looked round the room.

"On what, Corley?" Jerome seemed surprised by the interruption.

"Progress generally," Rollings replied. "We have these meetings and all seems very fine. The money is building up nicely, and we all have our plans in place. The public polls show the mood is swinging the way we want it. But is this enough? Are we really on track for our New America?"

Jerome sat back and exchanged a brief glance with Dansbury.

"This group has achieved many significant objectives, Corley. Your predecessor laid down much of the groundwork, as did the predecessors of all of you since Charles and I formed the group nearly sixty years ago. But such a massive change in national culture so that power can be restored to the rightful holders without risk of damaging the country beyond repair is a monumental task. So let's review our progress, shall we?"

The room stirred slightly as all the men sat back in their seats. Several took sips of their drinks and watched Jerome carefully.

"We arranged the deaths of both the Kennedy brothers in the early years of our plan," said Jerome. "The key result of the killing of the president was to ensure that a huge official enquiry took place and came up with results that few Americans believed. That took enormous pressure, but we were totally successful. Public confidence in the leadership took a severe beating. The studies show that, even today, over eighty percent of Americans consider the Warren Commission report to be a cover-up, as, of course, it was."

He looked round the room as several nods of agreement followed his words. Only Redman remained motionless and expressionless behind his secretive eyes.

"Nixon was entirely serendipitous," Jerome continued. "He needed almost no prodding from his associates to walk into the Watergate fiasco, and we needed no influence on those associates to do the prodding. Call it merely fortuitous. We had no trouble catching Agnew in a sting to get him to accept bribes over several years, and that increased the damage to leadership credibility. And Nixon's propensity for abuse of power opened up the door we had been seeking with Johnson. Nixon confirmed and expanded the laws first enacted by Johnson, for the use of emergency powers. Sections of the law exist, as you all know, for the creation and use of internment camps. It only requires a State of Emergency to be declared on a national basis for these camps to be set in construction.

"During the Carter Administration, our main efforts were financial. We manipulated the markets and the institutions to force a massive rise in interest rates, causing many hundreds of thousands of Americans to lose their homes and jobs as companies were forced out of business. So, as we dealt with the Ayatollah Khomeini in Iran, we set up the capture of the hostages, which further damaged the public's respect for authority, but also set up enormous expectations for the Reagan Administration. Apart from that, the Carter years were fairly uneventful for us as we gathered our forces and arranged some financing to ensure Reagan took office in 1980. The first Bush administration was just a cooling off period for us, Clinton couldn't be helped, but we had to ensure nobody shot him, because that would have caused strong pro-democratic reactions. And I know that we had planned for the take-over during the second Bush administration, even though he wasn't our puppy, but the fool got carried away by being a war president and ignored our instructions. He screwed up everything, so this last bastard in the White House was an unexpected hurdle. But we're doing everything necessary to bring on the climax after the next election and we've got a tame chimp in the Oval Office."

Eckhard looked embarrassed. "It put my personal plans well behind. My wife still gives me hell for that."

"Then you must remember that your personal comfort takes second place to our cause," Jerome said with acid. The senator looked down at his pad.

"After all," Jerome continued in softer tones, "look at what we achieved. We applied pressures in financial or other forms to the opposition party and to the Republican staffs and their people so that the country followed economic policies designed to damage the economy and largely succeeded. The size of government expanded hugely, the deficit rocketed upward, America became a debtor nation after being the greatest creditor in the world, and a nice little artificial boom was put in place with everything set up to collapse soon after. Which, of course, is what happened. Clinton was actually quite fortuitous because the economy did very well for eight years. The next eight of course, helped the nation's mood to decline even further, so despite the fool's failure to follow orders, those eight years, gentlemen, were the most effective years ever. The downward path of the public respect for authority was set at an irretrievably steep incline."

"I suppose so," Eckhard muttered.

"You know so, Morgan," Dansbury interjected with a smile that removed the admonition from the words.

"And it keeps going," Jerome continued. "Crawford and the rest of the network are performing sterling service in raising the levels of hysteria and irrational hatred against this Administration. The improving economy has worked against that, of course, but when we manipulate the crash, that will do the utmost damage to public confidence. Of course, the Reverend Vanderbilt and his team of televangelists back up the efforts splendidly. The levels of crime and especially violent crime are rising most satisfactorily under Tony's prodding and leadership, and the acceptance of murder as a solution to any dispute is almost complete. The public mood is nearly ready for violent overthrow. Another couple of years will do it. We'll have the whole of America ready for blood.

Obviously, the next administration will be ours, coming in with huge public hunger for change. Naturally, they won't get it, and the people will be ready to follow anyone who promises real results and strong leadership, regardless of the method."

"Exactly the way Hitler achieved power in the thirties," Vanderbilt said with a nod.

"And how the Communists swept out the Tsarists," Jerome concurred, receiving an amused glance from Dansbury.

"Hardly the same thing," Vanderbilt retorted with an irritated glare. "This group could never be called supportive of Communist philosophies!"

Jerome shrugged. "The man who called Crawford might disagree with you," he murmured.

"Then he's a fool," Vanderbilt snapped. "Equating us with Communists? What rubbish!"

"Of course," Jerome said gently. "Nobody could make that mistake."

"So, I believe we are well on track, gentlemen," Dansbury said. "In the first year of the next administration, which we will own, we will pull a trigger to set massive public upheavals into motion. Our tame president will declare a state of emergency, the camps will be used for political dissenters, military force will take command and remain in power when things settle down again, leaving our compliant president happy to play golf and enjoy the fruits of office. Things will then be as we want them for maximum control."

A few minutes of silence hung over the room, then all the notepads were passed up to Jerome, who collected them in a neat pile. He stood up, took his walking stick and moved to the side of the room by a walnut cabinet where another chair stood. He opened the doors and pulled out a shredding machine on a sliding rack. He sat down, pressed a button, and calmly fed every sheet of each pad through the machine. Twice, he had to stop feeding paper in order to clear the pile of shredded material at the rear of the machine, but after twenty minutes, all the pads were consumed. He was watched intently by every man in the room.

When he was finished, Jerome stood up and turned to the room. "I think that does it," he said with a smile. "Lunch as usual will be in the dining room. If you gentlemen would like to move over there, Angela will naturally see to your drinks. Charles and I will join you in a few minutes when I have wrapped up the room here."

The room erupted as the other men stood up and moved to the door. In a few moments, Dansbury and Jerome had the room to themselves again. Leaving his stick by the shredder, Jerome walked round to another small cabinet, opened it and extracted a bottle and two crystal glasses. He walked back to his seat, and placed the bottle in front of Dansbury who studied the label with interest.

"Bowmore?" Dansbury gave a pleased smile. "Twenty years old, as well?" He opened the bottle and poured two healthy portions of the ancient single-malt scotch. Jerome took a glass and gestured to the older man.

"Well, old man," he said. "How do you think that went?"

"Well enough," Dansbury said. "Our little group is doing everything we asked to make sure the right people take power in America."

"Good, American patriots, every one of them," Jerome agreed.

"Bless their all-American cotton socks." Dansbury swallowed his scotch. "Shall we join our friends for lunch?"

"Of course," Jerome agreed, and both men stood up.

Chapter 5 - Illinois

"Hi, Sally! It's Sam!"

Sally Andrews froze for a second at her desk. The call had come only a few minutes after she had arrived at the office that morning, and she hadn't settled into the day's routine. She quickly looked around the open-plan office, but nobody was within earshot. Nearly everybody else was clustered round the coffee machine in the far corner before moving to their desks and computer screens.

"Hello, Sam," she replied cautiously. "How are you?"

"Alive and kicking!" the male voice said. It was the second of three identification codes she had been told to expect if her services were ever to be called for. The third came immediately. "I'm getting the six-fourteen flight to Monterey this evening, but I hope you can find time for a coffee with me at the airport?"

She took a deep breath. Her country was calling her. "Of course I can," she replied. "Where will I meet you?"

"The American Airlines terminal. At gate H14."

"I'll get there about five-fifteen," she said, trying not to let the tremor show in her voice.

"Great! I'll see you then." The caller hung up.

Sally Andrews returned to her computer screen and tried to still the trembling in her hands. She prayed nobody would come near her desk for a while, and her prayers were answered.

She had tuned in to Randy Crawford's show one morning two years before, during a short and unusual bout of 'flu.   She had been instantly thrilled to hear the courageous attacks on the president and delighted, though horrified to discover the depth of depravity to which the White House had sunk during the first term of the terrorist-supporting, liberal-communist president she hated so much.   No hint of the horrible, disgusting behavior that Crawford reported so openly and bravely had ever been reported in the press, a fact that she attributed to the well-known communist bent of all journalists. At least, that's what Crawford said the journalists were like. Sometimes, she tried to read the political reporting in the Chicago Tribune, and she looked hard for pro-liberal biases, but had to admit to herself that she couldn't detect it.   But Crawford, like her father, said all the press was liberal-dominated, so it had to be.

Sally Andrews hated the current president with all her heart, almost as much as she hated the first lady.   Things just weren't as simple and obvious any more, not like they had been under Reagan and Bush.   Then she understood what the world was about.   It was about fighting communism, and nobody did that like the Republicans. And first ladies were proper ladies, she knew.   They supported their husbands, ran White House parties and kept out of politics because they couldn't be expected to understand a man's world.   Then this new first lady had come along and messed things up by becoming involved in the running of the country.   Women shouldn't be that

105

clever, she had heard her father say, and she agreed with him, as she always did. Women were supposed to work until they got married, and then have kids and stay at home. This witch of a first lady was giving other women of America the wrong idea, trying to show that women were as good as men. *God knows where that was leading the country,* she thought to herself, echoing her father's words.

When the 'flu had died enough for her to feel fit enough to talk, she worked up the courage to call the Randy Crawford show on the number that was given out every few minutes. Crawford had been running a blistering attack on the president's wife that morning. He had been accusing her of looking after special interests in her health-care proposals, and implying that a personal financial interest was involved. Sally felt her anger rising as Crawford's vitriol increased, and eventually felt she would burst if she didn't call Crawford and express her support for him. It took a while to get through, and she blessed the redial button on her phone. She simply kept trying. As soon as she heard the busy signal, she pressed the disconnect button and the redial button. After five minutes, she was thrown off balance by a woman's voice answering.

"The Randy Crawford show," the woman said. She seemed to have some sort of accent, Sally thought and she felt irritated at that. Foreigners had no place on this patriotic hero's program.

"I'm Sally Andrews," she said. "I'd love to talk to Mister Crawford."

"Where are you calling from, Sally?" the woman asked.

"Streamwood, Illinois," Sally replied, her nerves threatening to overwhelm her.

"Okay, Sally, it will be just your first name we use. The board's full at the moment, so it could take a while. Just hang on, and Mister Crawford will finally say he's going to Sally from Streamwood. Turn your radio off and listen only to the phone, because the broadcast is delayed by a few seconds."

Sally hadn't known that, and she was disappointed. She was hoping to listen to her own voice coming from the radio as she talked to Crawford.

"Okay," she said, breathing deeply to control her nerves. She kept the phone close to her ear, listening to the conversation going on between Randy and a man from Sacramento describing how he had heard that the president gambled secretly on the horses and had lost thousands, all taken from government funds. She felt outraged. She reached over and turned the radio on, keeping the volume low, and heard the words over the air that she had heard a few seconds before on her telephone. She turned the radio off again.

Finally, she heard the words she had been waiting for.

"And we go to Sally in Streamwood, Illinois. Lincoln country! Hi there, Sally, how are things in the mid-west?"

She grabbed her courage. "Hello there, Randy, it's wonderful to talk to you! I've been listening to you only a few days, and I have to tell you, I think you're a real American hero!"

"Well, dang me, that's nice to hear," the good-ol' boy accents echoed in her ear. "It's good to have my poor efforts appreciated by a true American woman."

"I just want to say, Randy," she continued, emboldened by the wave of support she had just heard. "Anything I can do to help you get rid of this communist terrorist in the White House, please just ask. Anything at all."

"There's always work for good Americans to do to help save the country, Sally," Crawford replied. There was an extra warmth in his voice, and Sally felt a wave of corresponding electricity run through her body. *God, he sounds sexy,* she thought to herself.

"So I tell you what, Sally," Crawford continued. "Don't hang up, now. I'll let Christiana get your details, and I know we'll be able to use your valuable help one day soon."

She heard a tiny click, then Crawford said something about going to Jeremy from New York, but she hardly heard it, so excited was she. The woman with the foreign accent came back on.

"Let me have your full name and your home telephone number, Sally," she said. She sounded cool, and Sally found it hard to control her jealousy. *Christiana? What sort of foreign name was that, then?* She gave her home phone number.

"And is there a work number we can get you at during the day, Sally?"

"Er.. yes." Sally gave the number of the cellular telephone company where she worked.

"Thank you, Sally," the odd accent said, and the line was disconnected. For a few moments, Sally felt furious with the foreign bitch, then the excitement of actually having talked to Randy Crawford overwhelmed her. She had offered her help, and he had accepted it! She hugged herself with delight. Two days later, she returned to work, the memory of the conversation acting as an amazing medical boost to her. From then on, she had set an electric timer and her tape recorder to record the Randy Crawford show every day, and played it in the evening when she got home.

Two months later, on a warm early Fall day, she was sitting on a bench in the nearby park, her regular stopping point in the two mile walk she took every Saturday and Sunday at the same time. A shadow crossed her face, and she opened her eyes to see a young man sit down on the other half of the bench. He looked rather smart, she thought, quite tall, and nicely dressed. When he spoke to her, she was astonished.

"Sally, my name's Jimmie Wanlyn. I'm from the Randy Crawford show."

"Good God!" she exclaimed in shock.

He smiled pleasantly at her. "Sorry about the unusual way of making contact. We have to very careful. We get a lot of attacks from liberals and communists, and I don't want to risk your safety."

She calmed down. His words made sense to her. Any American hero could expect to be savaged by the liberals in this country. Excitement ran through her. Randy Crawford had made contact with her! It hadn't just been a way of keeping her off his back. He really needed her! All sorts of pleasurable fantasies ran through her mind.

"Is there something you want me to do?" she asked the charming young man. She was horribly disappointed when he smiled and shook his head.

"Not immediately, Sally, no," he said. "But I wanted to talk to you and assure you Randy really appreciates the offer of help. One day, I know he'll need your assistance, and we'll make contact with you again."

Stifling her disappointment, she smiled back at him. "Of course," she said. "You know I'll do anything I can."

"We know that," he replied. "The main problem is this, Sally. The liberals have ears everywhere. They control the media as you know, and they've got spies in the US Mail, the telephone companies, all over the place, all looking to bring down a true patriot like Randy."

She nodded enthusiastically. It was exactly what her father had said only a few weeks ago.

"So, here's how it will work," Jimmie continued. "When we need to ask for your help, somebody will call you on the phone. He'll call himself Sam. You don't know anybody called Sam, do you?"

She shook her head. This was all so thrilling, just like a spy movie. But it was to protect America against the liberals, so it was especially wonderful. Her blood raced through her body like the Mississippi in flood.

"Good," Jimmie said with a smile. "When you hear that, you'll ask him how he is. Nothing unusual, nothing that could cause anyone to get curious if they hear you. He'll reply that he's alive and kicking. If he doesn't say that, then you've had a weird coincidence, and you just hang up. Okay?"

She nodded, unable to speak, so excited was she.

"Good. Then he'll say he's catching the six-fourteen flight to Monterey. Not six-fifteen, six-*fourteen*. That's just another safety feature. Once that's all established, he'll arrange to meet you. Whatever you're doing, you must meet him. Got that?"

"Yes, but what if I'm at work?" she asked, the excitement tempered by the cold reality. She couldn't just walk away from her desk.

Jimmie shook his head. "We understand. We'll try as hard as possible to make it a reasonable time for you. And he'll know you, so you don't have to worry about asking anything that could make a listener curious. It will just be a pleasant call from a friend to have coffee somewhere."

"Okay," she replied. *After all, a girl had to make sacrifices to save her country.*

"We'll be in touch," he said, and stood up. She watched him walk away with a little regret. He had a nice walk, she thought. *But maybe I'll get to meet Randy,* she said to herself, and lost herself in a flood of pleasant images.

At fifteen minutes before five that afternoon, her regular quitting time, she stood up from her computer screen and prepared to leave. It had been a hard day, with a number of program bugs to be fixed in the new accounting control system, and she hadn't been able to think much about what the afternoon meeting would bring.

She made her way down to the car park, saying little to anyone around her, for she had few friends at the cellular phone company. She found her little Chevy and joined the line of cars to the exit gates. Twenty minutes later, she had stopped the Chevy in the covered parking building at O'Hare Field and was walking into the American Airlines terminal, her heart pounding at the thought of this coming meeting.

She walked through the security checks and along the corridor till she saw gate H14. She had no idea of what the man meeting her looked like, but she remembered Jimmie saying that Sam would know her. For the first time, she wondered how that could be, or how Jimmie had found her in the park that day. She took a seat at the gate, and looked at the crowds around her. There was a huge 767 parked at the gate outside, and she envied the people who were going to board the monster and fly somewhere remote. Sally had never been further than St. Louis or Detroit. She had dreamed about going to exotic places like Hawaii, or even Europe, but she had never done so, despite her reasonable income as a computer programmer. She might make Hawaii one day, she thought, but Europe frightened her. Her father said it was full of communists, liberals and foreigners.

"Sally! It's good to see you!" a firm male voice said next to her. With a slight shock, she looked up to see a young man standing there. It was Jimmie Wanlyn, the same man who had spoken to her in the park. She stood up and extended her hand.

"Hello, Sam," she said nervously. She hoped she was doing the right thing, playing along like this.

"That's a hell of a welcome for an old friend," Jimmie said and utterly shattered her composure by wrapping his arms around her and hugging her. Just as suddenly, he let her go. "There's a coffee bar down the way," he said cheerfully, and placed a hand in the small of her back, leading her firmly away from the crowd at the gate.

A few minutes later, they were seated in a coffee lounge and a waitress had taken their order. Sally's head was still spinning from the force and speed of the meeting.

"Okay, here's the deal, Sally," Jimmie said. "We need your help, and it's rather urgent. The boss has had a very threatening call from a man in this location, and we need to find out who it is so we can protect ourselves.

112

"What sort of threatening...?" she began, but Jimmie waved a hand firmly in front of her face.

"You don't need to know that, Sally. Just be assured that whoever made the call is a communist and a threat to security."

"So how do I..." she began again.

Wanlyn looked irritated. "Sally, we don't have much time," he snapped. For a second, she felt frightened. The waitress appeared with a tray, and Jimmie sat back in his chair until the coffee had been placed on the table.

"The call was made to the studios from a cellular phone," Jimmie said when the waitress had gone. "It was at twelve-forty on Thursday, June eleventh. A second call was made the next day, five minutes earlier. I want you to find those calls and who made them."

Sally felt cold inside. "But that's illegal," she whispered.

Jimmie grinned without humor. "Randy's in danger. We need you to protect him. Destroying America's illegal too, but the liberals are doing it. We need you, Sally."

She took a deep breath. What Jimmie said made sense. Saving America was the only important thing, she realized.

"Can you do it?" Jimmie persisted. "We know you work in the computer systems department. Can you get into those files?"

"Yes," she said. "That's no problem. I work in the active systems maintenance group, so I have access to current files. But what if he's not a customer of ours? There are other cellular companies."

"We know that," Jimmie said impatiently. "And if you don't find him, we'll look at the others. But you have to try."

"Of course," she agreed. "Give me the details again so I can write them down."

He shook his head. "No way, no paper trails. The first call was at twelve-forty on June eleven. The second was at twelve thirty-five on the twelfth. That's all you need, so remember it. His name may be Mark, but it could be a fake."

"What do I do if I find him?" she asked.

"Then you send the man's name and address to a box number in Roanoke, Virginia. I'm going to say that number to you, and the zip code. You repeat it back and memorize it. Do *not* write it down, okay?"

"Okay."

Jimmie recited a box number and a zip code. She repeated it.

"Again," he ordered, and she repeated the numbers.

"Once more."

She obeyed.

"Good," he said. "Don't write it down." Without another word, he walked away from her.

She realized the coffee bill was on her, and she felt irritated. *She was saving her country,* she thought. *Surely Jimmie could have bought her a coffee.* She watched his back vanish into the crowd, then despite his order, she extracted her notebook from her handbag and wrote the Virginia box number down, together with the dates and times of the phone calls she would seek.

The assignment was easy. She had regular access to current master files, and an inquiry routine had no security restrictions on it for her, because no change to the master file was involved. If it had been, the task would have been a lot more complicated, requiring access codes that she did not have. She came into work the next morning with a surge of excitement at the importance of the patriotic duty she was about to perform.

She rapidly formulated the inquiry routine she would need. The little program would scan the call file, looking for calls on the eleventh and twelfth of June from the 312, 847 and 708 area codes, the codes for Chicago and the collar suburbs around the city, to the studio number of the Randy Crawford show, a number that was firmly stored in her memory. When and if she found such a call, she would extract the caller's identification number, and from that, locate his name and billing address in the customer master file. The computer logic was simple. She set the search parameters for calls originating between ten in the morning and one in the afternoon, knowing how long she had waited herself to get through. She added an instruction to issue a warning beep at her terminal when the job was complete, and returned to her legitimate assignment of seeking and correcting a bug in an accounting routine.

The search took twenty minutes. She had deliberately given her program a very low priority in the computer's job queue, so as not to call attention to it. As she was setting up a trace routine in the file update program, her terminal emitted a subdued beep, and her heart jumped. She quickly stored her trace routine, and switched back to the search program. The details on the screen were starkly uncompromising. "Mark Ashton," the first line said. "237, College Park Road, Apartment 505, Evanston, Illinois."

She wrote the details down in her notebook, on the same page she had scrawled the Roanoke address to which

115

the data should be sent. With a sense of immense relief, she cancelled her inquiry program. There would be a record of it on the security journal records, she knew, but nobody ever looked at that, and it was too small a routine to have caused any delay to anyone else's more important programs.

A few miles away, Terry Seymour performed a similar routine with the computers of the major cellular competitors of Sally's employees, but his search came up blank. Terry worried for several days that his failure would be seen as his fault, but after a week of silence from the date he sent a note to a post office box in Roanoke, Virginia, he put the odd incident behind him. He hadn't liked Jimmie Wanlyn at all when he had met him first while walking in the park in Barrington Lakes, and even less the second time, when he had been summoned for a cup of coffee at O'Hare Field at gate C14 of United's Terminal One. The tense, difficult conversation with the condescending Jimmie almost made Terry regret the time he had called Randy Crawford and offered his help in the fight against liberalism and communism in America.

Chapter 6 - Martinsburg, West Virginia

"Ooooh, Randy," the woman breathed. "That was marvellous!"

She lay on her back, her arms stretched above her head to the brass rails of the massive bed. Velvet-lined handcuffs held her wrists to the rails, and her legs were folded over the now-quiescent buttocks of Randy Crawford. The thrashing had gone on for several minutes and the woman's well-practised, high-pitched squeals had played a perfect counter-point to the bellows and grunts of the frenetic Crawford. These had faded now, to be replaced by heavy breathing as Crawford buried his face in the woman's neck

"And you can stay right there, you lovely man," the woman said gently into Crawford's ear as she gave a gentle thrust of her thighs against his groin, receiving a small gasp in her own ear in return. Monique Lamoureux, née Irene Wilson of Des Moines, Iowa, knew her trade well, and believed she was worth far more than the three hundred dollars-an-hour that her clients paid her. She had been called by Crawford once before, after one of her regular johns had given Randy her number as a gesture of appreciation for his relentless and gallant fight against the evils of liberalism and moral collapse in America. She had endured the session three months ago without difficulty. It had been a perfectly conventional trick, though Crawford had shown unexpected stamina and had held her back longer than planned, so that she had to call her next assignment and reschedule her visit to a businessman staying at the Holiday Inn. Today's request for the use of handcuffs was nothing out of the ordinary, and she had extracted her custom-made pair from her bag of props with a smile that had sent a look of eager delight over Crawford's face.

She looked sideways at the clock radio on the bedside table of Crawford's bedroom. She had plenty of time left, she thought. Anticipating another of Crawford's extended performances, she had allowed two hours before her next appointment at a hotel a few miles away. But Crawford had exploded within her remarkably soon, the jolt of his orgasm easily felt through the latex protection. *Maybe I can call in at the donut store on the way,* she thought with a smile of anticipation. Such a treat was a rare event, what with the need to take care of her splendid body and the busy, profitable schedule which that splendor gave her, but she did love a Boston Cream with a rich coffee now and again. She'd do an extra thirty minutes on the Nordic Track that evening, she promised herself.

She felt a stir of previously flaccid tissues against her inner thigh.

"Oh my, Randy," she said, pushing a practised note of delight into her tones. "Are we ready for another one, so soon?"

"Damn right," Crawford grunted, moving one hand from behind her back to lay it on her left breast.

"Well, just roll off for a moment, darling," she said huskily, "while Monique gets you set up. You'll have to let me out of these cuffs, though."

"I'll do it," Crawford muttered, easing his weight off her. He reached under the pillow and extracted another condom as she took the opportunity to stretch her slightly cramped legs. A few moments later, he rolled himself back on top of her and drove himself straight into her body. She gasped, hiding the pain. She was a highly paid professional, after all.

"Oh, Randy! You are ready, aren't you?" She gave up the ideas of the donut break. Crawford was thrusting into her wildly, like a teenager on his first sexual encounter. After a few moments, however, he stopped. She hadn't felt any signs of an orgasm, and wondered if perhaps he was just too tired for any more. He was still solidly erect within her. She hadn't had time to prepare her own faked climax, so sudden was his stoppage of action, and felt angry with herself. *Think about the job, Irene,* she told herself in irritation. *Can't have the customer feeling he's not had his money's worth.*

She emitted a long sigh of artificial satisfaction. "That was so nice, Randy," she whispered into the large ear which had returned to her neck.

"Shut up," Crawford snapped. Astonished, she obeyed. This was a new aspect of the man.

Crawford pushed himself up on his arms, and back into a kneeling position, placing one hand behind her back and pulling her so that he remained within her, her legs across his thighs. The cuffs pulled at her arms and she

119

squeaked a little with the pain. A look of pleasure crossed his face and he placed both hands on her magnificent breasts, squeezing hard so that she gasped again.

So that's what turns him on, she thought in sudden understanding. *He's a pain freak. Oh shit, I wasn't ready for this. Irene, you idiot, you let him handcuff you, as well. Better play the bastard along and stop him getting too extreme.*

"Randy, that does feel lovely," she gasped in faked excitement. "Fuck me some more, darling, please."

His right hand left her breast and slapped her hard across her face. She screamed with the shock of it. He reached under the pillow again and this time, his hand came out, not with another condom packet, but a stiletto knife. The sight froze her, and she could only watch as he released the blade.

He placed the point against her chest under her breast where his hand had been before. She felt the point dig into her skin. Terrified, she could only stare at the face above her and pray that he was merely playing games.

His hand swung again, and the jolt shook her whole body, jerking her upward a little so that the knifepoint dug hideously into her skin. She knew blood was rolling down her side. Another vicious slap sent her face hard against the pillow and the pain of the blow was matched by the agony of the knife.

"Randy!" she screamed, "please don't! Please darling, no more!"

Crawford was gasping, slamming his left hand against her face and thrusting his penis into her with every slap. As one more blow made her shudder and the blood flow more freely, she felt the massive trembles within his body, and the huge organ within her suddenly went slack.

Crawford removed the knife from her skin, dropped it on the floor and collapsed back on top of her, breathing in huge gasps from his release.

Irene felt her fear subside, and exercised her well-honed professional skills.

"Randy! Oh Randy, that was fabulous!" she squealed. "I've never come so hard before in my life! You really are fan*tastic.*"

A grunt echoed in her ear. "You really did come, eh?"

"Oh yes, sweetheart," she replied, looking across at the clock again. "The best ever. We'll really have to do that again, some time." *That's the last time you ever see me, you pig,* she thought. *Give me a Band-Aid and undo those fucking cuffs and I can still get that Boston Cream before the next trick.*

* * *

"Heavy date, tonight, Chris?" Verity grinned cheerfully at his producer. "I heard the guy who was in yesterday was quite a hunk!"

Christiana pulled a face. "God, is it all over the station? A man comes in to arrange a new affiliate, asks me to dinner, and you've all got me married off already, I suppose."

"That's the problem with small offices," Verity agreed. "Ain't no such thing as a private life."

"You seem to manage." She switched off her computer terminal and folded some papers into her desk drawer.

"I'm just a boring old married man," he replied. "A father, yet. Not worth making a fuss about."

She smiled at him as she stood up. "The entire Crawford program revolves around destroying a married man and a father. Why not you?"

Verity grimaced. "Yeah, but that married man's the President of the United States. A lot of people have a vested interest in pulling him down."

"It seems. I never planned to be part of such a criminal assassination exercise. I'm serious, Verity. I don't feel capable of putting up with Crawford's lies much longer."

Verity sat down across from her desk. His expression was intense and worried. "How much longer do you think you can carry it? I need to know if you're thinking of quitting on me."

Christiana resumed her seat and looked clearly at him. "Verity, I've never been so happy as since I came here two years ago. Until we took on Crawford, that is. I really don't know how long I can stand it. He makes my skin crawl."

"Is that because of his political crap, or because he made a play for you?"

She blushed. "You know about that?"

"Chris, the whole station knows about it. It's a microscopic world, remember. He did the same with Janice when she arrived."

"But she went out with him."

"She sure did," Verity agreed. "She was so besotted with the great Randy Crawford that she was prepared for anything."

"It didn't seem to last very long. I don't think she still dates him."

"Just the one evening." Verity grinned. "I suspect that Crawford's idea of fun frightened even the gorgeous Janice."

"What sort of ideas were they?" Christiana was curious, and Verity shrugged.

"I didn't ask," he said. "The less I know about our fearless, all-American hero, Randy Crawford, the better I like it. But it was obvious that Janice was very cold to him for a few days after that evening."

"But she stayed on. Can't have been too bad."

"Maybe not. I think that Janice's ideology is still too strong to abandon the fight for Randy's philosophies, however. So is her need of a job. Anyway, what about this date for tonight?"

She stood up and looked at her watch. "He's a director of a station in Phoenix. Seemed okay as men go, these days."

"And what does okay mean in today's vocabulary?" he asked, his smile broadening into his customary grin.

"He washes, he has his teeth and most of his hair, and he has a pulse. He was polite enough not to grab my boobs and he didn't drool too obviously. This puts him in the probationary gentleman class."

"Christ, that bad, eh?"

"That bad. How you and Carolyn have managed to get together and stay that way long enough to have a kid escapes me. You still talk to each other, as well. You're a vanishing breed, Verity."

"I think you're just cranky about Crawford. A girl like you shouldn't have troubles finding suitable men, Chris."

"There's no shortage of men, Nick. But men with intelligence and horizons extending beyond their bedroom walls, now that's another thing."

"What about that guy who kicked the stuffing out of Crawford the other day? He seemed quite a character."

She stopped her movement toward the door and turned back to him with a thoughtful expression. "You're probably right," she said. "If he calls again, I'll propose marriage to him."

"Hah! Why don't I make it easier for you? If he calls again, invite him to the station. I'd like to meet him myself, and there may be an interesting program in his ideas."

"I'll do that. Then can I propose to him?"

Verity chuckled. "You really are in a lousy mood! Go off and be wined and dined. You never know, this Phoenix guy might be all the things you're looking for."

"Yeah, yeah," she muttered and waved a hand at him as she walked out.

By seven, she was ready. She had dressed in a simple black dress that gave just a hint of cleavage and was not as short as the denim skirts she favored for the office. She was unsure about this date. Jack Rylett was good-looking enough, and certainly had been charming to her. But there had been no sense of chemistry with him. However, her social life had been arid for some months now, and felt the time lost as something never to be recovered.

"Hell, it's an evening out and a decent meal again," she muttered to her reflection as she put the final touches to her make-up. "Can't imagine wanting anything else to happen, though." She thought about the man who had called with such a devastating effect on Randy Crawford and smiled. Mark from Evanston, she remembered. He had a gentle, baritone voice and he had identified her Montreal accent immediately.

"A listener, would you believe," she said aloud as she laid down the mascara brush. "Not many of those around. And sure as hell educated. What did he say? Russian, Spanish, German and French? Don't think I've ever met anyone with that sort of linguistic skill."

She checked her watch. Jack had said around seven o'clock. It was five minutes after. She probably had a few minutes left. "Wonder what Mark's second name is," she said as she stood up from her dressing table, then chuckled at herself. "Come on, Chris, he's bound to be married, probably fat and balding and sixty, and he's not going to call again."

She mused for a few moments about what she would say should Mark tackle Crawford once more. Could she ask him about himself? Not professional, she decided, then the door buzzer sounded and she returned to the here and now.

"So where are you from, Christine?" Jack Rylett asked. He had downed his first martini in a few seconds and had just received his second from the waiter. He was a large, well-muscled man with strong, regular features. He looked about thirty, Christiana estimated.

"Christiana," she said. She was already feeling uncertain about the man.

"Christiana?" Rylett looked puzzled. "That's a first for me."

"It's Italian," she said, "but I was born in Montreal."

"Montreal? I'm not sure where that is."

"Canada," she replied shortly, a small irritation growing. "That's a country generally to the north of here." She sipped at her red wine.

"So that's the accent," he said, not appearing to notice her sarcasm. "I couldn't make it out."

"French is my first language. We tend not to lose the accent."

"French? Why French?"

She looked curiously at him. "French is the language of Quebec," she said. "I'm from there, of course I speak French."

"Quebec's the state? And they speak French there?" The information seemed to astonish him.

"Province. We call them provinces. And yes, Montreal is in Quebec Province, and the capital is Quebec City and yes, we're weird enough to speak another language."

"Gets pretty cold there, I believe," he said, again failing to sense her growing irritation and caustic comment.

"All the year round," she replied, deciding to have some fun at his expense and wondering when he would detect it. "It *can* get above freezing in mid-summer, but things get dangerous in the winter with all the polar bears wandering around. But a lot of the city is underground, so we manage."

"Gee." Rylett gulped at his martini. "How do you get around in that sort of weather?"

Oh God, he's taking it all in, she thought in derision. "We use the heavy-duty, Arctic snowmobiles," she said. "And if it's really snowy, we use dog-sleds."

"Yeah?" His eyebrows raised. "Borrow them from the Eskimos, do you?"

126

"Sometimes," she replied. "But if anyone doesn't have their own sled and dog-team, they rent them from Avis."

She was losing him, she could see. The puzzlement in his eyes was growing, with the first sense that she might be laughing at him. She felt a little ashamed of herself, and eased off the torture.

"How about you, Jack? Where are you from?"

Twenty minutes later, she had more than she wanted to know about Jack Rylett. Into his fifth martini, his face showing a strong ruddy flush, she interrupted him and suggested they order dinner.

His monologue continued through his steak and her sole almandine. She refused a desert, hoping to end this evening as soon as possible, and mercifully, he followed her lead. She was totally bored by the tales of adventure on the football field at Arizona State University, his draft into the National Football League and the knee injury that prematurely ended a brilliant career with the New Orleans Saints. His ignorance of anything outside the USA irritated her beyond measure.

"Say, do you think we'll get the pickup of Randy's show?" he asked as coffee was served.

She shrugged. "No idea," she said. "That's between you and the station management. I just produce the show."

"You must be proud as hell, working with Randy Crawford." Rylett's speech was becoming slurred and Chris began to worry about the drive home.

She almost said exactly what she thought about Crawford, but held her tongue. "He has a big audience," she replied noncommittally.

"And goddamn well deserves it," Rylett burped. "That guy's a genuine American hero. Anything it takes to get that pot-smoking bastard out of the White House is okay by me."

"Even an armed attack?" she replied sweetly, but it was lost on Rylett. He was staring at her breasts.

"Why don't we just go back to my hotel?" he slurred. "I tell you, Christine, you're driving me crazy."

"Then you'll have to live with your insanity," she snapped and got up. He tried to get to his feet but stumbled on his chair legs and nearly fell. Faces turned toward them and Christiana thankfully walked out of the restaurant. At the door, she asked the doorman to call a cab, and she was home twenty minutes later.

"Mark from Evanston, I hope you call again," she said angrily as she hung away her dress. "Just to talk to an intelligent man who knows where the world is would be a treat."

She took a long shower to try and wash away the memory of Jack Rylett's courtship and only partially succeeded. Midnight came before she was able to sleep, and her last thought was to wonder what it would be like to have dinner with a man who spoke five languages and had seen the world.

* * *

In Evanston, Mark Ashton reached home at just before seven-fifteen. Though tired, he felt good about the day. The finance department had finally agreed to the specifications drawn up for them by the systems analyst. A nagging problem with the network controller had at last succumbed to intensive investigation by the external wizard that Mark brought in for these situations, and he had interviewed a young man for the position of communications specialist who had fitted the bill neatly. All in all, Mark decided, a better than average day at the coal face.

In such a positive mood as this, the television had no attractions. He scanned the movie programs to see if there was anything other than the standard, mindless epics of death and destruction, and found nothing in any of the four premium channels for which he paid.

"I wonder why I buy this crap," he muttered as he threw off his suit, hung it away and wrapped his dressing gown around himself. He switched on his CD player instead, and began to look for a disk in the tall and ever-growing stack. Jazz, he decided, and found one of his old Dave Brubeck collections. He opened the case and placed the disk in its slot, pressed the "play" button and walked into the kitchen.

He felt no desire to cook so he extracted a packet of sliced roast beef from the refrigerator and pulled a pair of fresh bread rolls from a sealed bag. A jar of the finest English mustard followed the beef to a tray, as did a small container of margarine and a can of beer, and he was about ready. As the complex variations of the Brubeck sound emanated from the speakers in his lounge, he reached for the knife from the stack of utility knives on the counter-top and stopped, puzzled. The knife was missing.

He looked round the kitchen and couldn't see it. Slightly irritated, he opened up the dishwasher to see if he had placed it there, but the machine was empty.

"What the hell?...." he murmured and thought back to the last time he had used the knife. It was two days ago, he remembered, and he had sliced a wonderfully fresh loaf of bread to make toast in the morning. He clearly recalled replacing the knife back in its slot in the block of wood in front of him, taking care with the lethally sharp blade.

He shuffled slowly round the large kitchen, looking at every point on the counter top, in every drawer and in the sink, but the knife was stubbornly absent.

"All right, Mark," he said aloud. "It's probably in front of your face, but you've got a blind spot tonight. You just can't see the damn thing."

Stifling the annoyance, he picked out an alternative knife to cut open the bread rolls and carried the tray into his lounge room. Within a few moments, the smooth perfection of Paul Desmond's saxophone had soothed his nerves and he settled down to enjoy the fresh bread, beef and mustard washed down with the Heileman 'Old Style' beer.

It had been a good day. He wasn't going to allow anything trivial to spoil it. He mused over the invitation he had received last week. His friend Andrew had been given the keys to a chalet in Wisconsin while the owner was in Europe.

"It's a goddamn country mansion!" Andrew had enthused. "Four bedrooms, two bathrooms, log fire, fridge, and it's right on the lake's edge. There's a canoe, fishing gear, everything."

"Some people sure know how to live," Mark said with a laugh.

"Damn right! How about we go and pretend to be bloated industrial giants for a weekend?"

"Sounds wonderful," Mark sighed. "Let me find a weekend when I can get away earlier on the Friday and we'll do it."

"How about next week?"

"Let me check."

"Check hard, young Ashton. You need time off from your war with the lunatic right wing of America."

"That's for sure."

Mark felt at peace, despite the puzzle of the carving knife. The workload was down a bit. The car was booked in for a major service this Friday, so going to Wisconsin could be delayed if anything extra needed doing to the machine. Maybe the weekend after could be the one. A couple of days on the lake, no phone, no television, no people, it was all just what he needed.

"I'll do it," he said with a wave of enthusiasm, and reached for the phone to call Andrew.

* * *

Bob Merton was a loser. When he bothered to think about it, which was hardly ever in recent years, he had always been a loser. School days were a misty memory of indeterminate aeons ago. He had struggled every day to survive the tortures, unable to understand what the teachers wanted, or what he was supposed to do, and whenever he could, skipped out of that hideous place. His mother never cared. On the first few occasions of playing hooky, the principal had called on the tired, washed-out shadow of a woman, but could extract no commitment from her to ensure her son's attendance. After a while, the authorities gave up caring. In Chicago, Bob was simply one of thousands failed by the system every day.

He stayed away from school most days. He scrounged food from the garbage bins behind restaurants, earned a few nickels here and there by running small errands for people and somehow survived. When he came home one night and found the apartment locked and bolted and his mother gone, it made little difference. He began to haunt the shelters, begged the odd meal from the Salvation Army or other soup kitchens and slowly lost any recollection of being an individual with an identity. At fifteen years of age, Bob was a lost soul in the garbage stream of Chicago.

One night, his scrabbling in the refuse bins resulted in a half-bottle of rum. He downed the lot and had no memories of anything else until he came to, lying in a pool of his own urine and vomit in the lower levels of Michigan Avenue, just north of the Wacker Drive bridge. When he found a few bucks in a purse in the gutter five days later, he bought a bottle of muscatel from a liquor store where the man behind the counter preferred to ignore the law in favor of a small profit. Bob repeated the alcohol experience, this time waking up in the cells of the local police station. He was eighteen.

Three years later, he had no idea where he was. He couldn't remember his name, because nobody had asked it of him in that time. Life was merely the confusing fog that filled the times between the acquisition of another bottle. He had no idea that he had somehow drifted up to Evanston, and that this mild summer night would bring to an end his short, catastrophic existence.

He had found a bottle. What was inside it, he neither knew nor cared, but it was alcoholic. The treasure had come to him a few minutes ago, just after midnight. He was shambling along Ridge Road and steered his mindless way into a small park at the corner of Main Street. He had heard the muffled grunts and thumps and stopped as the noise permeated the foggy recesses of his mind. Two men were fighting on the grass. They were like himself, flotsam of his society. The smell of their bodies drifted to him together with the soggy sounds of ineffectual combat.

Bob shuffled along to the shadowy scene. As he appeared, silhouetted in the glow of a street lamp, the two combatants gasped, took a brief glance and ran without verifying the helplessness of who was watching them. He watched them go without thought. The incident had not made any impact at all on his mental processes, such as they were. He began to move on, when he stumbled over the bottle that had been the cause of the fracas. With a warm glow of pleasure, he picked it up, unscrewed the cap and took a swig, not bothering to smell the contents. It was a bottle of sherry, the first time he had encountered such a flavor. Moaning softly to himself, he slid into the bushes at the rear of the little park and settled on the ground. At no time had he seen the shape that had followed him ever since the bright lights of Howard Street.

The man in the shadows watched Bob settle down and smiled to himself. It could not have been made easier. His target had voluntarily sought out the darkness and had reduced himself to a drunken stupor without any investment or assistance on the hunter's part.

The man extracted a pair of fine, chamois-leather gloves from the pocket of his light jacket, and slid them onto his hands, taking care that the fingers were fully in place and had free movement. Then he took out the carving knife from inside the sleeve of his jacket, unwrapped the covering of plastic from the handle and took it firmly, the blade pointing forward. Softly he slid forward until he was standing over the man on the ground. Bob was chuckling softly to himself, taking regular gulps of the sherry and almost crying with joy at the sensations as the fortified wine slid down his throat.

When the man above him bent down, seized Bob's hair and hauled his head back, Bob was only a little surprised. The keen blade sliced sweetly through Bob's windpipe, round to his ears and opened up the jugular. Blood gushed out with a light bubbling noise, almost the same sound as the sherry had made leaving the bottle. Bob just had time to feel regret that he hadn't finished the serendipitous treasure, when he died.

The killer plunged the knife through the other's chest, released the handle and walked quietly away, peeling off the gloves as he walked. The handle twitched a little then moved no more.

Bob Merton's utterly valueless life ended after twenty-two years.

Taking notice of established wisdom had never been a failing for Miranda Foulkes. She refused to listen to the warnings that going jogging in Evanston after dark was the act of a lunatic with a highly developed death wish. Miranda was fifty-three and she had gone jogging almost every night for the last twenty-four years without incident. The fact that she invariably ran with Sackville might have helped that fact. There had been four Sackvilles in that time, each different in shape and temperament, but all sharing the characteristics of being large, energetic, and highly protective. The current incarnation was no exception. A mixed Doberman and Border Collie, this Sackville was, in Miranda's expert opinion, the most rambunctious and protective of the lot.

Miranda's normal time for exercise was ten o'clock. She was late this evening because she'd had friends round for dinner and she was incapable of leaving the house until everything was stashed away in the dishwasher and the kitchen clean. Despite the increasingly agitated protests of Sackville, Miranda only got round to donning her warm-up suit and sneakers at twenty minutes after midnight. Sackville almost tore down the door as they left the apartment on Church Street and she made a beeline for the bushes before racing after Miranda. She turned south along Ridge aiming for her usual circuit down to Main Street, along Main to Chicago and back up to Church, a route that provided a number of large gardens for Sackville to explore and hunt squirrels. She reached the small park at the corner of Main, and Sackville leaped forward with a bark of delight as she normally did, eager to expend huge amounts of energy chasing round the grass. Miranda grinned through her deep, controlled breathing.

The grin changed to a frown as Sackville let out a hunting dog's hysterical baying.

"What the hell's the problem, you scrofulous excuse for a dog?" she muttered and came to a halt in the middle of the park. Sackville was not to be seen, but the hunter's bay was coming from a deep cluster of bushes against the rear edge. "Sackville, for Christ's sake, what's got into you?" Miranda called and strode across the grass, just as the dog leaped out at her, ran two quick circles round her and shot back into the bush. Clearly, something had to be investigated. Miranda followed.

Thirty seconds later, she pulled out her cell phone that she kept on her belt.

The little park had become an oasis of light. The line of spectators was kept distant from the fearsomely well-lit scene at the rear of the park. The flashes of the police cars and the ambulance parked on the roadside streaked out in all directions, diving into oblivion as they hit the glare at the focal point of the action.

"Fairly straight-forward, I believe," the Evanston Medical Examiner said. "His throat was cut first, then the knife was pushed into his chest."

"Why the hell would the perp leave the knife there?" the Homicide Division cop asked, looking with distaste at the grisly scene.

"God knows," the ME replied, wiping his hands on a rag he took from his briefcase. "The poor bastard was already dead when he stabbed him. You can see, there's not a lot of blood around the chest wound. So the killer waited until the victim was dead from the cut throat before stabbing him again. I'll be more certain after the autopsy."

"Damned stupid," the cop said.

"Almost as if he wanted the knife found." The ME replaced the rag in a plastic bag and closed his briefcase.

"Yeah, right!" the cop snorted and waved the photographer in to complete the process of recording the scene. "We'll look at the knife, but any prints would be too much to hope for."

"Poor bastard," the ME said, walking away. "Couldn't have been more than fifty. What a way to go."

* * *

"Look at that!" the lab technician said. "That's a complete set of prints, all five fingers."

"Never seen anything like it." The homicide cop emitted an appreciative whistle. "Who the hell would be so stupid as to leave their prints all over the thing? Now it's just a matter of seeing if these are on file anywhere."

"You never know," the detective-sergeant said. "We could be lucky here. You'll probably find they're some young punk's we've had for breaking and entering, or assault, or such like, and we'll have 'em in our own files. But just in case they're not, put 'em on the computer to the FBI. We could wrap this thing up in a couple of weeks with a bit of luck."

"Sure thing, Frank," the cop said.

Chapter 7

The day had been another one of those that Mark thought of as "shit-eating days." Little had gone right. The computer network had erupted with yet another of those silly, infuriating, inconsistent faults that not even the brought-in wizard had as yet been able to identify. Mark had taken calls from all over the country, some furious, some irritated, some sympathetic, but all expressing the same basic idea - when would the network be up again? Mark had been unable to offer anything more constructive than "we're working on it," and nobody had been satisfied with the answer. Even the president of the company had chosen the day for one of his rare appearances in the office, and had expressed his annoyance to Mark that he couldn't get to his electronic mail-box.

One of his systems analysts from the New York installation had quit, leaving a project in a precarious state of incompletion, and the project leader had called to confess that documentation of the analyst's work had not been checked for some time, and had now been found to be inadequate. Several days would be lost in the project schedule, as somebody had to be diverted to bringing the documentation up to date.

Mark left the office at seven-thirty, exhausted and cranky, leaving the wizard staring gloomily at the innards of the file-server, muttering about mother-board replacements being the only solution. He walked into his apartment in a high state of ediginess and poured a stiff glass of scotch as soon as he laid his briefcase down.

"God, I need that weekend in Wisconsin," he grumbled, wondering if he could last the ten days to the Friday of the following week when he planned to meet up with Andrew soon after lunch and drive north. He threw off his jacket, loosened his tie and carried the glass of scotch through to his lounge room.

Sitting moodily in his armchair, staring sightlessly at the blank television screen, his eyes caught the red "power-on" indicator of his tape-recorder. For the last few evenings he had felt too irritable to play his recording of Randy Crawford's two-hour radio show, though he had set the timer each day.

"Maybe it's time to kick the shit out of Crawford again," he said aloud. The idea appealed to him. Crawford had shown a delightfully strong propensity to react badly to Mark's goading. "A little bit of blood-sport at that bastard's expense is perhaps just what I need," he said, feeling immediately better at the prospect. "Let's see what garbage the idiot was spouting today." With another small jolt of excitement, he also thought that it would give him the excuse to talk to the delightfully accented Christiana, Crawford's producer.

"She's probably over two hundred pounds, ugly as sin, and married six times with ten children," he said, and took a gulp of his scotch. The liquor burned a comfortable river of warmth down his guts and he began to feel better. He got up from his chair, carefully carrying his glass, and pressed the rewind button of his tape-recorder. He waited until the tape had stopped, pressed the play button then carried his glass back to the kitchen to prepare a meal while listening to Crawford's rabid pronouncements.

"Okay, listen up, America," Crawford said in the carefully cultivated good ol' boy accent which he had lost so quickly in his anger at Mark's attack. "Just sit back and don't bother to think, 'cos old Randy here will tell you what to think."

"Yeah, I'm sure that's what you'd like," Mark muttered. "Same as any despotic government the world over, a thinking population is the most dangerous thing in the world. You'd love a system in America where the authorities told the citizens what to believe and they'd do it. Our education system certainly seems to be modeled with that idea in mind."

"And we all know that we agree with each other," Crawford continued, "that the dope-smoking, yellow-bellied little terrorist-supporter in the White House has no right to be there."

"Except by the democratic process of a national election," Mark said as he sprinkled meat tenderizer and spices on his steak. "Interesting that, Randy old pal. You're starting to say it out loud and directly, anyone from your opponents shouldn't be allowed to be in office, regardless of what the citizens vote for. And I notice that you never criticize any of your bunch who avoided the Vietnam draft. Maybe that's what I'll call you on tomorrow."

He listened for another hour of Crawford's ranting and the groveling adoration of his callers, and decided that any more would put him to sleep. It had become monotonously repetitive. He checked the television guide and found he had picked a rare night when one of his four movie channels had something he wanted to see. A replay of the old Beatles' movie, *"A Hard Day's Night"* was exactly what his prickly soul needed to smooth itself out. He packed the plates and frying pan into the dish washer and settled down for a couple of hours of sixties' nostalgia.

The next morning, things fell into place quite rapidly. The wizard of the network, looking unshaven after a night of hardware testing, announced that he had finally identified a hairline crack in a chip on the mother-board at five o'clock that morning, replaced it, and all was well, and could he now go home and get some sleep? Expressing his appreciation, Mark signed the man's timesheet and waved him to the door.

At nine, he got a call from the plant manager at the Hagerstown metal extrusion plant. A modification to the control system was needed. Would Mark send a systems analyst to have a look at the requirements?

"No problem," Mark replied. "When's a good time?"

"Tuesday of next week, if possible," the plant manager answered. "We've got some consultants finishing up some work this week, and I'd like to get them out of my hair first."

"Let me work on it," Mark said. "I'll see who's free and confirm it with you by Friday morning." He wrote the details of the requirements in his day-timer.

"Sounds good," the other man said. "Thank God you've got the network going again."

"Not God," Mark chuckled. "Some poor, overworked and sleepless contract engineer. He's been working all night."

"Give him a kiss from me."

"Not likely!"

"All right, a bonus then."

"I'll talk to you Friday," Mark said and hung up. He was getting nervous about the impending call to the Randy Crawford show later that morning.

*   *   *

Soon after mid-day, after thirty-two re-dial attempts on his phone, he got through.

"The Randy Crawford show, good afternoon," the well-remembered French accent said into Mark's ear.

"This is Mark on a car-phone in Evanston," he said. *Would she remember him?*

"Well, hello!" she replied, the pleasure evident in her voice. "I hope you're calling with another bombshell for Randy."

"You do remember me, then?" he asked, feeling a rush of excitement in his stomach. *Her voice is really lovely,* he thought.

"But of course," she said. "We hardly ever get anyone calling in who disagrees with Randy, and certainly nobody who has given him such a difficult time."

"You approve of that?" he asked curiously. "I thought you'd be of a similar view to his, being his producer."

"Not only do we approve, but the station manager said he'd like to meet you. He thought he could do an interview with you about your rather interesting viewpoint."

"I'm astonished, and a little honored. He really said that?"

"He sure did. What chance of you getting to West Virginia some time soon?

"Not sure. Can I call you if I work something out?"

"Let me give you a different number for the station. The manager's name is Verity."

"Verity? First or last name?"

"Last, but that's all he uses. Here's the number."

She read out seven digits and Mark scrawled them on his notepad. "Area code 304," she added. "We're in Martinsburg, West Virginia."

"Thank you," he replied uncertainly. This was a wholly unexpected development, but the idea of having an open discussion on his views was intriguing.

"You're on next," she said, a laugh evident in her voice.

"You certainly know how to un-prepare a man for combat."

"I'm sure you'll cope," she responded, and Mark was certain. There was a distinct warmth in her tones. Trying to stifle his excitement, he tuned in to the conversation Crawford was having with a woman from Minneapolis who was expressing the view that while she didn't hold with what the Nazis had done, she felt that what America needed was a strong leader like Hitler who would show the world that America was the only real super-power left. Crawford diplomatically declined comment on her obvious sympathy for the methods of the Third Reich, and cut her off gently.

"And so we go to Mark on a car-phone in Evanston...." Mark heard the sudden uncertainty in Crawford's voice as the radio host obviously recognized the caller's identity. "So it's the liberal intellectual from Evanston, again, is it?" Crawford said. "What rubbish have you got to insult America's intelligence this time, Mister Intellectual?"

"I do so admire the courtesy with which you greet your callers, Randy old pal," Mark said. "It's so nice to see somebody who doesn't let their bias interfere with the social niceties."

"Have you got something you want to say?"

Mark decided that the three weeks since his last onslaught had left Crawford unprepared for another attack. *Lulled him, did I?* thought Mark. *Great tactics. Must remember them.*

"I've been wondering, Randy, why you're so hostile to the fact that the president has never served in the military. You never shut up about it."

"Because military service is an honorable act, that's why."

"Well, I do agree with you for once. But does that mean everybody should do it? How about you, say? Tell me, Randy, in what way did you serve your country? Were you in the military?"

"Damn right, I was!"

Mark could hear the fury and the tension in the host's voice. Something was brewing nicely here, he decided.

"Yes? So tell us, Randy, me and all your loyal American listeners, exactly what branch of the military service did you serve in?"

The silence rang out of the earpiece like a gong.

Gotcha, you bastard, Mark exulted. *You've never been in uniform either.*

"I served," Crawford said shortly.

"Let me remind you, Randy, that I served in the US Navy in the Intelligence Branch..."

"So you claim," Crawford interjected, desperate to regain control of the conversation.

144

"Yes," Mark agreed. "So I claim. A claim very easily verified. I'm perfectly prepared to email you a copy of my service record, right now. Could you do the same for me?"

"Not immediately," Crawford replied. "I don't carry it around with me."

"I bet you don't," Mark concurred. *Because it doesn't exist.* "But as I said, I was in Intelligence. It would take me two days, max, to verify your claim myself. I still have friends in the service. I'm prepared to bet a thousand dollars you were never in the military."

"I don't make stupid bets over the air," Crawford snapped. "Let's move on. Is there something intelligent you want to discuss?"

"I started that way," Mark replied. "It's interesting, Randy, how you remind me of a famous book. I know you'll never have read George Orwell's *Animal Farm* because I'm sure it's not on your party's approved list. You haven't read it, have you Randy?"

"Yes, I have read it, you supercilious jerk," Crawford rapped. "Exactly how do I remind you of it?"

"I'm impressed, Randy. I see why you're considered to be an intellectual giant among your people. Then you'll recall how the horses developed the chant of *"Four Legs Good, Two Legs Bad,"* to represent their simplistic view of the world after the animals had taken over the farm from the humans."

"Yes. What of it?"

"It's what you've done. You've reduced the level of political debate to the same chant. *"Republicans Good, Democrats Bad."* Funny, isn't it, Randy? Orwell was warning against the evils of a communist take-over in Europe, and here you are, displaying exactly the sort of behavior to be expected of communist apologists. Odd behavior for a loyal American, don't you think?"

"You're a liar, a liberal and a traitor," Crawford said loudly. "It's time we shut up this crude attempt to smear patriotic Americans."

"You can't handle opposition, can you, Randy? Is that why you tell your listeners that you'll do all their thinking for them?"

"No, it's because they'll otherwise be corrupted by the left-leaning, liberal press that infects this country."

"No, it's because all dictatorships hate a thinking populace. Is that's what's going on, Randy? Are you and the people behind you working to that end? Is the deplorable standard of education in this country a deliberate move to keep the citizens ignorant and incapable of dissent?"

The shock in the other man nearly blew Mark's ear off. He heard an audible gasp then he sensed the silence as his call was cut off.

My God, we really hit a sensitive chord there, thought Mark as he slowly replaced the telephone. He opened his pocket diary and looked up a number in Washington.

"Commander Featherstone, please," he said when the phone was picked up at the other end and a cool, female voice answered.

After a few seconds, the deep voice of his best friend in the Navy spoke into his ear.

"Commander Featherstone."

Mark grinned with affection at the memory of some of the wild evenings he had spent with this naval officer. One of the finest wide receivers that had ever graced the Annapolis football team, Featherstone had an exceptional intelligence. He spoke all the languages Mark could claim and Portuguese as well.

"Hey there, Feathers! Still slacking off all day?"

The laugh in Mark's ear nearly deafened him. "I've been expecting you, little guy! How are you keeping in that hell-hole of civilian life?"

"At least I work for a living! Good to hear your delicate soprano voice again, old buddy."

"Well, is that so? I've been hearing yours a lot, recently."

"You listen to that jerk, Crawford? Hell, Feathers, I thought you were brighter than that."

"Obviously as bright as you are, little feller," the officer replied. "How come you're giving that all-American hero such a hard time? What's he ever done to hurt you?"

"Actually, I think he's planning more than just hurting me," Mark said, becoming serious. "The crap he spouts sounds dangerously like the stuff we used to monitor from some very peculiar people of extreme political persuasions."

"Yes, it does. And you're right on one claim. The bastard has never served a day in the armed forces in his life. I checked the computer as soon as you raised the question a few minutes ago."

"Of course."

"Yes. Now, to serious matters, young Ashton. When are you coming over to this part of the country? It's not far, and you owe me several drinks. And I think we need to talk about this sudden crusade of yours."

An idea struck Mark. He thought quickly, and a number of possibilities opened up in his mind like flowers in a spring shower. "Are you in Washington next week?" he asked.

"Of course. A loyal serving officer like me, a devoted servant of his country just like Randy Crawford, when would I not be at my post?"

Mark struggled to control his laughter. "I'll get back to you, but I think I might be able to swing a break in that region."

"That would be good. But of course, whether I can be seen with a left-wing, commie, pinko traitor to America like you remains to be seen."

"Risk it! Call you later when I know the schedule."

"Great!"

Mark hung up, grinning widely at the idea that had come to him. He drove back to his office, checked the corporate telephone directory and called the plant manager in Hagerstown.

"I'll come and do the review myself," he said when the manager came on the phone.

"You will? That's slumming with the peasants, isn't it, for a man from head office?"

"We have to get out there and see the real world once in a while," Mark agreed.

"Glad to hear it. I'll reserve a room at the usual hotel?"

"Please. Just for the Monday and Tuesday nights. I'll take a few days off and spend some time in Washington, sight-seeing."

"They let you take time off?" The manager laughed. "What sort of loose operation are we running over there?"

"See you Tuesday morning," Mark said, and hung up.

That evening, feeling much better than he had the previous night, Mark got home by six, an exceptionally early hour. He switched on the television, thinking how rarely he was able to hear the six o'clock news. He tuned to the local Chicago channel and sat on his couch as he undid his tie and shirt.

With half an ear, he listened to the seemingly endless parade of news items of violence, thuggery and murder of the Chicago region. One item attracted his attention because of the location.

"Police are confident of an early arrest in the murder of an unidentified man in Evanston two nights ago." The blonde newsreader maintained the same plastic smile she had worn during a story of a lost child's recovery in Wisconsin. "The victim is believed to be a homeless person, aged between twenty-five and forty. The body, which was discovered by a late-night jogger in a park at the corner of Main and Ridge in Evanston, was stabbed to death. The murder weapon was recovered at the scene. A police spokesman said the weapon was an ordinary kitchen-knife, and a good set of fingerprints had been taken from it. Police expect to identify the killer very soon."

That reminded Mark. Despite the disturbance he felt about a brutal slaying so close to his apartment, he remembered the mystery of his missing knife. He stood up and walked into his kitchen. The knife was still nowhere to be seen. It puzzled him. Where the hell could it have gone?

Then he forgot the oddity in the excitement of visiting the radio station, confronting the issues, and maybe seeing if Christiana was as attractive as her voice indicated.

* * *

"Our young critic called Crawford again, today."

"I thought we had agreed to remove this little thorn from under Crawford's saddle?"

"Don't panic, old man, it's bad for your heart. Yes, we did so agree, and the matter is being taken care of. However, a straight-forward killing of the man would only arouse attention, and perhaps focus public interest on Crawford."

"The subtlety of extreme youth, I see. I suppose you have implemented a plan of enormous sophistication to satisfy your creative mind, young Jerome?"

Jerome smiled. The verbal fencing over the decades had always been a source of great pleasure and satisfaction to him. "Indeed I have, my geriatric colleague," he replied. "A better approach was to cover the man with problems and remove him from further interference. I have given him such difficulties as might silence him for ever, though he hasn't yet discovered that fact."

The silent laugh echoed down the line. "Exactly what has your undisciplined, if imaginative mind come up with, Jerome?"

"I arranged a discrete entry of Ashton's home. A knife was removed, with excellent fingerprints on it. That weapon was later used to murder an itinerant wanderer not far from Ashton's home. In time, even the local plod will locate the prints' owner."

"The local what?" This time, Dansbury's chuckle was loud and relaxed.

"Plod. A British term. It comes from an old series of children's books where the policeman was called Constable

Plod. The British police use it themselves to refer to each other."

"My dear young friend, you always were such an Anglophile. However, I do admit to being somewhat attracted and entertained by your plan. And what weapon did Ashton use to attack Crawford's delicate ego, this time?"

"Yet again, he showed remarkable perception." Jerome's voice held a dry note. "He accused Crawford's backers of deliberately suppressing the standard of education in America so that the capacity for critical thought would be eliminated, thus allowing a dictatorship to flourish."

"I believe we made the correct decision to eliminate this young gadfly. If Crawford had much more of such discussion on his show, even the people who follow him so avidly might start to think about the topic and question the validity of the philosophies being propounded."

"Yes," Jerome agreed. "Though I must express my regrets at losing the entertainment. I did so enjoy hearing Crawford being mangled so effectively."

"We all have to pay the price for the cause," Dansbury said dryly. "And now that we have located and taken care of Ashton, need I remind you to wipe the trail clean?"

"That is also in progress. Charles, my respected elderly friend, you may return to your milk and cookies and ancient dreams of past glories in forgotten wars. We energetic youngsters will continue to guard the ramparts against the Mongol Horde invaders."

"I shall sleep easily, knowing that," Dansbury replied with the ghost of his laugh whispering down the secure phone line.

* * *

The day was almost peaceful. Mark leaned back in his chair and realized that he had two hours before his next meeting, there was no immediate crisis with any system or hardware component and he had nothing specific to do. What the management textbooks described as thinking time to anticipate the next problem and prepare for it.

Instead, he reached for his notebook, located the telephone number of the radio station in Martinsburg and punched the numbers. A youthful, female voice responded.

"Let me speak to Verity, please," he said.

"Sure," the voice replied with a cheerful energy. "Who can I say is calling?"

"Mark Ashton."

"Stand by."

For a few moments, he was treated to the broadcast of Crawford's program, then a man's voice broke in.

"This is Verity. How can I help you, Mr. Ashton?"

"Christiana asked me to call. She said you were interested in my anti-Crawford performance."

Verity's laugh exploded in Mark's ears. "Oh, *that* Ashton! Mark, I owe you a vote of thanks! You've given us some of the best radio in years."

"Happy to oblige. But I'm surprised. I thought you'd all be Crawford fans there."

"It's good business to host his show, but we don't have to like him. Chris has already asked to be taken off the program. So how about visiting here? I think we could do an interesting counterpoint to the Crawford crap."

"Wednesday, next week, if that's not too soon. I have to visit our plant in Hagerstown, and that's near enough."

"Great! I'll set up an interviewer for when you arrive. When is that likely to be?

"Some time around four okay?"

"Perfect. We'll look forward to seeing you. Chris is absolutely breathless at the idea."

"I'm overwhelmed. She seems nice." Mark threw in the bait but didn't get the catch he wanted.

"She's very bright," Verity said, and the laugh in his voice was obvious.

"See you next week, then," Mark said, and hung up. He wasn't sure which part made him more nervous, a live radio interview, or meeting Christiana.

Sally Andrews drove her small Toyota down the ramp into the garage of her apartment block in Streamwood. She was feeling irritable. It had been a week since she had sent the results of her computer search to the post office box in Virginia and she had heard nothing back.

"At least a thank you would have been nice," she muttered as she negotiated the narrow lanes to her parking spot. The wheels squealed noisily on the surface of the basement level. "I risked my job doing that search, and what do I get? Sweet nothing."

She slid the Toyota into its spot and switched off the engine, gathering her bag from the passenger seat. She had been to a local bar with several friends to celebrate the engagement of one of them, and the occasion had left her mood a little darker. She had held high hopes of meeting the sexy Randy Crawford and nothing had come to pass. Even that Jimmie Wanlyn would be better than nothing, she thought. It had been months since breaking off with her previous boyfriend. Roy had been nice, she thought, a business school graduate from Chicago, working as a systems analyst at her company. But after a few weeks, she had become increasingly irritable about her inability to understand some of his jokes, and she had never heard of most of the books he had read and referred to in some of the conversations. When she had told him about calling the Randy Crawford show, a look of distaste had crossed his face.

"You called that idiot?" he asked. "I hope it was to tell him what a lying jerk he is?"

"What?" she said, realizing her voice had leaped a few tones. "He's a hero! He's a real patriot, trying to protect Americans from the communists."

"He's a liar, a pig, and his whole performance is to be a loudspeaker for the far right. I'm astonished that someone as bright as you are would swallow that lunatic's garbage."

The relationship had ended at that moment.

Sally opened the door and climbed out of the car. She closed the door behind her and began to walk to the stairway up to the lobby. It was after ten, and she was tired and cranky.

"Hello, Sally!" The voice came from behind a Jeep parked a few spaces down from her own car. Sally gasped, then relaxed.

"Jimmie! What on earth are you doing here?"

"We have to be careful for your sake, Sally," Wanlyn replied. "We don't want anyone to see you associated with Randy or his staff, not if they're the enemy. They might hurt you." He stayed in the shadows behind the large Jeep.

"I see." Sally felt better. It made sense to her. "What did you want to see me about?" she asked, walking towards him.

"Just to say thank you," Wanlyn replied. "And I have a gift to you from Randy as a gesture of his gratitude."

"Oh!" Sally squealed. Her crankiness vanished. Randy had thought of her, after all. She walked up to Wanlyn and stood close to him. She decided he was rather nice, really. She thought about inviting him to her apartment for a drink. It had been a while since a man had been in her apartment. She began to feel pleasantly warm inside.

Wanlyn reached into his pocket and she followed the move expectantly. She couldn't see what it was in his hand when he brought it out again. It looked metallic. She looked up to Jimmie's face. Nice bright eyes, she decided.

"Would you like to come up for a drink?" she asked.

Wanlyn smiled. "I'm sorry, Sally. I have to get going again."

She heard a small click then the pain hit her. It was the most horrible agony ripping into her stomach. Nothing could be this dreadful, she thought in confusion. She bent over to shield the pain but nothing stopped it. The sight of the blood pouring all over her dress bewildered and terrified her. She tried to scream, to beg Jimmie for help, but he seemed to be standing quite still, very close to her.

The pain declined, and her vision began to grow dim. Her last thought was that she wished she had asked Jimmie up to her apartment earlier. It had been a long time....

Chapter 8 - Martinsburg, West Virginia

Mark had no trouble spotting Feathers in the bar. The man stood out in any social gathering. It was not just the six-feet-five inches of him, nor the ebony features with the classically North African beak of a nose, nor even the width of the athlete's sloping shoulders hunched over the corner table. Commander Featherstone simply had a presence that demanded attention and respect. Mark had spent the whole of the first year of his friendship with Featherstone battling to discover the name hidden behind the uninformative "Lieutenant (JG) B. Featherstone" labels on all the man's possessions.

"C'mon, man," Mark begged time and time again. "B. Featherstone? Everybody has a name!"

"Call me Feathers."

"Feathers? A man of six-five and two-fifty pounds? *Feathers?* That's dumb."

"That's my name." Feathers gave a smile that dimmed the lights of their junior officers' barracks room. "It's done me well for twenty years."

He refused to give any details. It was only during classes in military studies when Mark learned the truth. The group of fifteen junior officers was studying the campaigns of the American War of Independence.

"A small, but pivotal battle took place early in the new year, soon after the American victory at Saratoga," the lecturer said. He was a Scottish civilian academic on assignment from the Royal Military College at Sandhurst, the British Army's opposite number to West Point. His accent had caused occasional difficulties for the young men and women in the class. "Morgan's Continentals had settled on the high ground near the Broad River," continued the Scot, "a well-chosen base from which to observe the approach of the British, and easily defended. The weather had been exceptionally wet and cold for several days and the British troops had a long way to come to attack Morgan. But come they did. In an eight-hour, overnight forced march, the combined British and Loyalist troops under the command of Lieutenant-Colonel Banastre Tarleton...."

Mark sensed the tiny reaction in the huge man sitting next to him, and looked sideways at Feathers. The wry grin and shake of the head told him everything. Feathers, that massive African-American, had been named after an obscure British commander in the War of Independence. Mark smiled and returned his attention to the lecture. The secret would remain with him.

He walked through the gloomy surrounds of the bar, past the little oases of candlelights at each table and advanced on the table in the corner. Feathers unfolded himself like a crane raising its boom and laughed.

"Hey there, little commie, pinko, liberal intellectual! Come and whisper traitorous thoughts into my delicate shell-like ear!"

They shook hands with the delight of old friends meeting again. Drinks were brought by a tall, elegant waitress in an astonishingly short skirt that caused a halt in the conversation for a few seconds while she placed the glasses on the table. Then the two men carried on a conversation that almost seemed uninterrupted since they had last met over three years ago.

"Since when have you been attacking the heroes of America?" Feathers grinned over his beer.

"I needed to exercise my debating talents."

"You always were good at the bullshit, that I agree," Feathers agreed with a chuckle. "You saved both our skins a few times."

"Me? I just think you scared everybody shitless, including the military police."

"Maybe," Feathers agreed. "Hey, man, I was sorry to hear about you and Alison. What the hell happened?"

"I'll never know. She just became someone else once we were married. Enough of that. What are you up to these days?"

Feathers was silent for a few moments, studying the tiny stream of bubbles in his beer glass. "You're still in the Reserves?" he asked quietly.

"Naturally." Mark sensed the seriousness in his old friend.

"Still got all your clearances?"

"Yes, I do. Feathers, old buddy, if this is something you'd rather not tell me, that's okay. I know the system, remember?"

"You can have some of it, Mark." Feathers blew out the candle on the table. "I joined a special group a few months ago," he murmured. "We're known as Task Force

Five. I have no idea what Task Forces One through Four are, or even if they exist, and I've even less idea if there's any Task Force Six or above. I don't even know my boss's name, but I do know that he's a civilian and he reports to a group of joint military and civilian heavies. I don't know who they are, either, and I don't want to."

"I get a distinct impression that you're a little uncertain of this whole thing." Mark had heard the tones of doubt in Feathers' voice and he knew his friend well.

"I'm not sure what's worrying me," Feathers admitted. "Maybe it's the question of whether there are any absolute rights and truths in the world."

"And what do you do, this mysterious Task Force?" Mark was fascinated. There was a tone of such gravity in his friend's voice as he had never heard before.

"I can't tell you all the details. But let's say that the things you said to Randy Crawford would generate interesting vibrations."

"You mean you'd want to shoot me, or you'd want to examine the activities of Crawford?"

"I'd say that Mister Crawford might just merit some interest from Task Force Five."

Mark went silent for a few seconds. "I see your problem," he said eventually. "Crawford has a significant and rabid following in this country. A lot of Americans, possibly even the majority of Americans see him as a savior of the nation."

"Eighty-five percent of Germans voted for Adolf Hitler." Feathers swallowed the remains of his glass and waved at the waitress for a refill.

"It does raise interestingly philosophical questions, doesn't it?" Mark watched the beautiful waitress approaching. He finished his own beer and waited until the minimalist skirt and endless legs had departed again. "In a free, democratic society, we must allow free speech, regardless of our views of it. 'I hate the words you are saying, but I will defend to the death your right to say them' and all that stuff. And we are free to elect any government we choose if the process is by democratic means. Even if we choose to elect a despotic, tyrannical government by such means."

"Exactly." Feathers nodded. "That's why I can never support the sort of thing we did in Chile when they elected an openly communist president. We had no right at all to bring down Allende by covert means. Least of all when you look at the alternative we got."

"That's why you're a little ambivalent about the role of Task Force Five?"

"Yes. And yet, who is there to protect those classic, yet sometimes derided concepts of Truth and Justice and the American Way? If some faceless group is truly behind Crawford, and they are using legitimate, democratic means to bring about a despotic government that can then dismantle all the things we value in this country, what can we do about it? Are we even *supposed* to do anything about it, or must we wait until the deed is done?"

"What if those ostensibly legitimate means are mis-representations, though?"

Feathers raised an eyebrow. "Explain," he said.

"Remember George Simpson?"

"Simpson? Loud-mouthed bastard in the motor pool at San Diego who kept getting into disagreements with people. Especially people not born into the God-blessed ranks of the white-skinned?"

"That Simpson. I last heard his dulcet tones talking to Crawford, claiming to have been a Marine Captain in the Gulf War, and pouring out crap about the president."

"So that's who that jerk was! I thought I found his voice familiar. Now, do you think that Randy-baby knew about the deceit?"

"Can't say. I have no way of knowing. But supposing he did, and supposing Simpson was just one of any number of set-ups like that?"

"Then it's mis-representation, and may contravene FCC regulations." Featherstone's smile reflected none of the man's warmth.

"That's what somebody else said to me a few days ago." Mark felt a sudden glow of delight as he thought about meeting Christiana in a couple of days. "But I can't help wondering if perhaps even the control of the FCC is already in the hands of people who believe Crawford is a demi-God."

"It's a thought," Feathers agreed. "Here's another thought. Just supposing all this *is* a deep, dark plot to put into place a legitimate government that then destroys the American democratic institutions in the same way Adolf did in Germany. What is the position of the military? We've taken an oath to protect the US and the Constitution against all enemies, domestic and foreign, but we also commit to obey orders from superior officers, especially to the Commander-in-Chief. So what if that Commander-in-Chief is the head of state of a government which has legally and legitimately changed the constitution to one which abuses human rights? Must we still defend that constitution, despite our consciences? If we try to bring down the legally-elected government of the United States, if, for instance, we took military action against other units of the armed forces who remained loyal to the new Whacko-in-Chief, are we guilty of treason? Who are the traitors here?"

"The Nuremberg trials after World War Two indicated that human rights take priority over the niceties of national legalisms." Mark was disturbed by the conversation.

"Yeah, sure. But whose judgment is the right one? There are a hell of a lot of Americans right now who would still say 'My country, right or wrong.' Who judges whether it's a case of human rights abused or national security defended? Who watches the watchers?"

"I don't know." Mark's beer was forgotten. "Does Task Force Five know?"

"I think that's what we wrestle with every day. I don't think we've conducted any sort of action since I joined and I don't know anything about any activities before that. You see the danger, don't you?"

"Of course," Mark replied. "There's a fine dividing line between patriotism and defense of true liberties, and repression of dissent. Could you become somebody like the late, unlamented J. Edgar Hoover, that famous cross-dresser, and attack people with genuine grievances against the government, people like Martin Luther King? Or could you become like the celebrated military dummies who court-martialed General Billy Mitchell because he told them that the army establishment had its head up its own ass on the subject of air power?"

"Precisely," Feathers agreed. "Both of those guys had genuine concerns about the values of their country and yet were right royal pains in the asses of the authorities. Both of them could be classified as "liberal activists" in today's right-wing version of political correctness. You could probably argue that Adolf Hitler also had quite genuine complaints about the leadership in Germany." The big man looked thoughtfully into his beer. "Heaven knows, the Treaty of Versailles was a grotesque arrangement by the winners of World War I. It was vengeance, vengeance all the way, no room for recuperation and healing. It's only when you see some of the nasty things old Adolf did to get to the Chancellorship that you can see why things happened the way they did afterward. There are several quality thinkers who have raised concerns about the similarities between today's America and Germany in the 1930s, and Crawford's blistering invective against anyone who fails to conform to right-wing dogma is one of those similarities."

"So you're really dependent on your group being led by a man or woman of absolute integrity and honor?" Mark said. "I wonder how many of those there are still in the USA?"

"More than either of us could pray for, I hope," Feathers responded grimly. "I believe my boss is one of them."

"You make me feel ashamed, Feathers. I joined the navy because it gave me an educational opportunity that paid off in civilian life. I was happy to serve my country for eight years to get a great education, but you know me, I was never the deeply patriotic type. I think you are, in a truly intense way."

"We all do our bit," Feathers replied with a deprecating shrug. "I don't think I love my country any more than you do, old pal, but I just got the opportunity to join a group that can do something special."

"It means a hell of a compliment to you that you were asked to join." Mark was deeply aware of just how fine a man was his friend of the last fifteen years.

"It just reflects my boss's superlative judgment," Feathers retorted, and this time, the grin lit up the gloomy air of the bar. "Okay, buddy, just why are you on this crusade?"

Mark frowned. "Another friend of mine asked me that a few days ago. I still don't know, but something is disturbing me about the whole thing."

"What whole thing?"

"The fury, the hatred, the obvious preference for an autocratic rule, for a moral structure thrust down people's throats. It's too much like the shit we used to hear from the old Soviet Union, from Chile, Argentina, Romania and Albania and similar places. Hearing it in America is frightening me. It's concerted, it's orchestrated, and it's powerful."

"Yes." Feathers' answer was short but implied a lot. Mark looked up at him.

"And Task Force Five thinks the same?"

"No. Feathers does. I'll run it by the boss. I think he'll listen."

"So I'm not totally bat-shit crazy?"

Feathers laughed. "Only a bit. Enough of this cataclysmic topic, old buddy, we have some beer and three years to catch up on. And tell me why else you've come to Washington, apart from worshipping at my feet."

"Now this you're going to find funny," Mark said as the waitress approached them once more. "Let me tell you about the gorgeous voice, and, I suspect, equally gorgeous appearance of Christiana."

"Christiana?" Feathers was amused. "Sexy name."

"Sexy voice. She's Crawford's producer. I'm seeing her for dinner on Wednesday."

"Oh my, oh my, oh my," Feathers intoned in his finest, most musical bass-baritone. "My little buddy, what in hell have you got yourself tangled up in?"

* * *

Mark drove through the outskirts of Martinsburg with excitement building up within himself, and also nervousness.

"Just take it as it comes, kid," he muttered to himself as he followed the directions to the radio station he had been given by the young man in the gas station at the edge of town. A line of attractive old buildings had replaced the visual squalor of the outskirts. An open-air café seemed to have a clientele of young people. He decided he liked Martinsburg, and checked his watch again. Just a few minutes before four o'clock, about when he had said he would arrive.

He saw the red brick building on his right, a hundred yards or so ahead, and felt another surge of nervousness. The station's call sign was emblazoned on the roof, and on the wall was a large advertisement. Above the head of a long-faced man wearing a cynical smile were the words "Randy Crawford - the Right Voice of America!"

"Yeah, yeah," Mark grumbled and slowed the rented Ford to turn into the parking lot at the rear of the building. He climbed out, locked the door, walked back to the street and walked inside. He found a small lobby with a single desk, and three armchairs round a coffee table covered with magazines. Behind the desk was a girl apparently in her teens, dressed in a white blouse and stylish black jeans. Her make-up was immaculate, thought Mark, enjoying the smile of welcome she gave him.

"Hi!" she said. "Welcome to Station WNDY! Can I help you?"

"You can," he said, returning the smile. "I'm here to see Verity. My name's Mark Ashton."

The girl studied her control panel. "Mark's on the phone. I'll call Chris. Take a seat."

Mark nodded and sat at the coffee table, too nervous to read. He listened as the girl dialed a number, waited a few seconds and then spoke. "Hi, Chris!" she said brightly. "There's a Mark Ashton to see Verity."

Mark felt so nervous he was sure he was trembling. He wished he had a drink to wet his dry throat. He swallowed.

"She'll be right out," the pert young lady at the desk said. Mark waved his hand in thanks, uncertain of his ability to speak clearly. He waited, the nerves building. He tried to laugh at himself for being as silly as a teenager asking a girl to the school prom, and it helped a bit. *Dammit, Ashton,* he snarled at himself. *You're a senior corporate executive, you've been an officer in the United States Navy, and you're scared shitless about meeting some girl? Get hold of yourself, man!*

The door into the lobby opened and Mark rose to his feet. Christiana walked in and for a moment they stared at each other. She was dressed in a denim miniskirt and a light, white sweater. Her hair was tied behind her neck with a simple blue ribbon. Her face held delicately sculpted planes and her eyes seem to smile at him.

"I'm glad you made it," she said.

Mark swallowed again and took a deep breath. "So am I," he responded.

"Come on through," she said, looking firmly into his eyes.

Mark walked up to her where she was holding the door open. As he reached her, he looked into her face from only a foot or so away. Her complexion was perfect, he thought, and found he was holding his breath.

When she smiled right into his eyes, he felt a thump in his chest. She touched him on the elbow to move him into the corridor, and at last he relaxed.

"I wish I could think of some original way to tell you how delighted I am to see you," he said.

She let the door close behind her. "I'm sure you will," she said. "But let's get the social amenities done first."

He chuckled. "Lead on," he said.

A tall young man walked out of the washroom as they passed. He wore a black blazer with a military crest on the pocket. Mark couldn't identify it. The man beamed at them.

"Well, hello there, Chris," he glowed.

Christiana merely looked at him coldly. "Jimmie," she said shortly, and the young man looked peeved. He gave a short glance at Mark then stood still, obviously watching Christiana as she walked along the corridor. Mark felt a sense of hostility at the man, echoing Christiana's obvious dislike of him.

She looked back at him again, and her cool gaze softened. "One of Randy's assistants," she murmured. "A true slimeball."

"Like master, like servant?" Mark suggested, and was rewarded with a glow in her smile. She turned back to look ahead, and Mark followed her.

"Verity's waiting," she said, looking back at him as they walked along. He felt a little embarrassed for a second, realising she had seen the admiring way he was looking at her, but she didn't seem annoyed by it.

"Any other name but Verity?"

"Nick, but it's rarely used. He prefers just Verity."

She stopped by an open office door, and waved him inside. "The Crawford-Killer has arrived," she announced with a small laugh.

Mark smiled at her and went into the office. Behind the desk, a stocky man of about Mark's age rose to his feet with a wide, welcoming smile.

"I'm Verity," he announced. "Man, I'm delighted to meet you, Mark! You've given me more fun than I've had in years."

Mark responded to the warmth of the welcome and shook Verity's hand. "I'm glad I've helped. I rather enjoyed the process myself."

He took a seat across from the desk as Verity sat down again, and Christiana took the other seat. Mark looked at her again and sensed a moment of humor as he recalled his concerns that her appearance might not match her voice.

"You're obviously a natural killer," Verity said. "Crawford is still sulking after your two sessions with him."

"I just detest lies aimed at fomenting inter-group hatreds." Mark felt relaxed. The immediate friendship he sensed from Verity had touched him

"That's Crawford's thing, all right," Verity agreed. "Can I get you a beer, soft drink, anything?"

He opened a small fridge behind his desk and moved his seat to allow an inspection of the contents. Mark asked for an apple juice, Christiana followed suit and Verity settled for a beer.

As the cans were opened with a hiss, the door opened without ceremony. A tall, rangy man walked in.

"Verity, I need to talk to you about..." He stopped and looked at Mark. "Didn't realize you had company," he continued. His face adopted a wide, folksy grin, and he advanced on Mark, extending his hand.

"Hi, there," he said. "I'm Randy Crawford."

Mark stood up, aware that the other two were watching carefully. "Of course you are," he said coolly. "I'm Mark Ashton." He shook Crawford's hand, but pulled away from the extended, enthusiastic pumping which Crawford began.

"Well, just great to meet you, Mark! I hope you listen to my program."

"Indeed I do." Mark sensed the repressed giggle in Christiana.

"So where are you from, Mark?" Crawford asked.

"Evanston, Illinois."

"Well now, that's Lincoln country...." Crawford stopped short and stared hard. "Mark? From Evanston?"

"That's me. We've talked, you might recall."

"Jesus Christ!" Crawford grated, and turned his furious face to the station manager. "Verity, who the hell let this jerk into the station? Get rid of the bastard at once!"

"He's my guest, Randy, and he stays because I say so," Verity replied with a cold smile. "If you don't like the scenery, move. This was a pleasant conversation with an intelligent man until you came in. And next time, have the courtesy to knock."

Crawford turned the full force of his stare at Mark and pointed a finger at his face. "You're in danger, jerk. There are a hell of a lot of people might want you hurt after that crap you spouted on my show. Make sure you're gone before I get back."

Mark smiled. "And very nice meeting you, too, Randy. I'm sure we'll talk again."

"Like shit we will," Crawford snapped and stormed out. The door closed softly behind him.

Mark returned to his seat, feeling his heart pounding from the fury of the short encounter. He saw Christiana's sympathetic smile and returned it with warmth. "I envy you," he said. "Working for a charming, gentle person like that."

She laughed softly. "You can see why we enjoyed your calls so much. They were the complete opposite of the usual fawning garbage he gets, and the only time anyone has actually spoken with intelligence to him."

"I agree," Verity said. "Watching him sweat was our finest hour at this job."

"It was fun for me, too," Mark said. "I'm not one for blood-sports, but cutting him up was highly satisfying. The only problem is, while I was initially exaggerating my accusations a bit, just to stir him up, I think there may actually be something coordinated going on."

"Damn right there is," Verity replied. "He gets an email every morning from Washington with the topics for the day."

"The same email a whole lot of other similar people get, I bet," Mark said. "I've been doing some checking around, and I found out that at least sixteen other lunatics around the country have exactly the same scandals and lies every day. These emails must be the mechanism."

"Sixteen? I think it's over forty," Christiana said. "We've been doing the same checking around, and we know the people in the industry."

"Over forty?" Mark felt a twisting sensation. "That's a national campaign! Could I see some of those emails."

"Be my guest." Verity opened a drawer. "I printed a sample off the computer." He extracted a pile of papers and slid them across to Mark who leafed through a few of them.

"They all come from the same place?" Mark asked.

"Possibly," Verity said. "The address is the same, but they could be coming from any group using a corporate web address."

Mark studied the address but it told him little, just a common public email system. He memorized it and slid the papers back.

"It's nasty," he said.

"It's worse," Christiana interjected. "A lot of people call in and offer any help they can in Randy's so-called "fight for freedom." I'm supposed to get their names and addresses and give them to Jimmie after the show."

"And what do they do for him?" Mark asked curiously.

"I don't know," she replied. "I never hear any more about it after that."

"This is not a pretty picture," Mark said.

"Ugly," Verity concurred. "However, I'm sure that you've got better things to do than worry about the delightful Randy Crawford. I think Chris wants to show you round the station, so please enjoy the trip. And then we'll do the interview. And I assume you're staying for the evening?"

"Er.. yes." Mark felt anxious. Much as he liked Verity, he was hoping that the evening could be with Christiana and nobody else. But Verity seemed to understand.

"I know you'll be grief-stricken," he said with a small grin, "but I have a wife and young John Power Verity to attend to, so I'll have to let you be alone with Christiana. I'm sure you'll understand."

"We'll try to cope," Christiana said. "I know we'll be bored out of our skulls without your stimulating company, but Mark will be polite enough not to mention it."

"Careful, woman," Verity replied. "Salary review time is approaching." He laughed, stood up, and extended his hand again. "Great meeting you, Mark. I hope we see you again."

"That depends on this evening, I suppose," Mark admitted, with a quick glance at Christiana. She smiled.

"I think you'll see each other again," she said, and stood up. "Come, Mark, the station calls us."

* * *

"We're just two tables away from where I sat with the wonderfully subtle Jack Rylett a few nights ago," Christiana said with a laugh.

"I'll try and be equally charming and sophisticated." Mark was entranced by her appearance. He had picked her up at her apartment just half an hour ago, after going back to his hotel to change. The attractive woman in the casual office clothes had become a beautiful woman in a blue, figure-hugging dress, her hair swept up, and her face delicately made up to enhance wide, almond eyes. She had attracted attention as they walked to their table.

"Oh God, please don't," Christiana responded. "Rylett displayed more of his brand of sophisticated courtship than I ever want to see again."

He decided he had to throw the dice and see where they fell. "Christiana, I must tell you, part of the reason for coming here was to see you. Your voice is very attractive."

She was still for a moment, then smiled. "Confession time? Then I have to tell you, I think I probably gave Verity the idea of inviting you. I was intrigued by the giant-killing talents you had shown."

"That's nice. So we have each seen enough to think we want to keep this going? I know I have."

"I think we should certainly explore possibilities. You're a nice, gutsy man, Mark Ashton. I'd like to find out more about you."

"Good. Then it's mutual. I'm a lot out of practice, Christiana. I had a really nasty marriage experience a couple of years ago. I'm divorced, but I've been gun-shy with women since then."

She looked down at the tablecloth. "When I got home from the awful Jack, I wondered what it would be like to have dinner with you, somebody's who's been around the world, speaks several languages, listens to me with real interest enough to spot my accent and is clever enough to handle the likes of Randy Crawford. I thought it was something unlikely to happen after all these years of dating the Jack Ryletts of this world. And now it's happened. And I like it, certainly enough to want to give it time to see."

Mark felt the other diners were a million miles away and the universe belonged only to them. "Thank God for Randy Crawford," he breathed. "How would I ever have met you without him?"

"Even Crawford has his uses," she agreed.

They were interrupted by the waiter with menus, and for the next two hours, Mark felt he was in a private world with Christiana, where nobody could break in. Conversation flowed easily, and the mutual attraction provided a spice to the night that not even the excellent food could match.

At eleven, Mark suddenly looked at his watch and was startled to see the time.

"We should probably be going," he said, looking back into her eyes. "You have a working day, and I have to get back to Chicago tomorrow."

She nodded. "I know. When will you come back?"

"About a week," he replied. "I have a promise to spend this weekend in a friend's cottage in Wisconsin, which I really wish I hadn't made now. But I'll fly back to Washington the following Friday."

She smiled. "Our phone bills and travel bills are going to get a bit steep, aren't they, if this works out the way it seems to be?"

"We'll have to discuss that," he agreed. "Let's just be careful and see how we go."

Mark waved at the waiter for the check, then smiled at her. His heart was pounding. "I think I'd better run you home and give you a goodnight kiss on your doorstep."

She blushed and smiled into his eyes. "How quickly can you get that check settled?"

Chapter 9

Exactly as he had thought he would, Mark flew home to Illinois in a happy daze. He could think of very little but the evening out with Christiana.

Back in the office, he had to return to the cold present, trying to shake the lethargy from himself. Concentrating on the job at hand was almost impossible. But somehow, the Thursday and Friday ground their way to an end, and he left for the weekend to go to the Wisconsin retreat as he had promised Andrew. The late summer weekend was forecast to be fine and mild. The fishing would be good, the therapy excellent, but all Mark could think of was getting through another week before he could take the next Friday afternoon flight back to Washington. Before he left, he mailed a note to Feathers about the emails he had seen at the radio station, and added the email number of the office that had sent them. Then he forgot about faceless groups taking control of the USA. There were far more wonderful things to occupy his mind.

* * *

"Sarge, we got a fix on those prints!"

"What the killing of the hobo on Maine Street? You have?"

"Yeah. It's crazy, Frank."

"Why so?"

"Well, the FBI came up blank on any known criminal in the files. But it seems they automatically check through their data banks of military personnel. And that's when they found it."

"What, a serving military guy?"

"No, an ex-naval intelligence officer. Name of Mark Ashton. Present address right here in Evanston."

"That's nuts! This was a thrill-kill by punks if I've ever seen one. Naval intelligence officers don't go around doing that sort of shit."

"Sarge, you know better than I do, there's sickos everywhere, these days."

"Yeah, I know. All right, get a warrant out on this guy and pick him up. But it don't smell right. It really don't smell right."

* * *

Despite his wish to be somewhere else, Mark had enjoyed the two days. On the Sunday, temperatures sat in the mid-eighties, gentle cumulus clouds floated above the lake giving the odd patch of welcome shade as they crossed the lake where Mark lay lethargically, his fishing rod sprawled against the side of the boat. Andrew had been far more energetic, and had taken the Canadian-style canoe and paddled furiously around until collapsing exhausted a few yards away from the small boat Mark was using. At Andrew's request, Mark tossed a couple of cold beer cans from his cooler to the outstretched hand of his friend, then subsided into a sun-drenched stupor again.

Although entirely without interest in the subject, he had still managed to catch three moderately sized fish, and he unhooked them and stored them in the creel hanging from the side of the boat.

At four, they agreed to return to the cottage. Somehow finding the energy to unship the oars and row back to the jetty, Mark hauled the boat ashore and carried the creel with its unhappy occupants into the cottage.

For an hour or so, they drank quietly, enjoying the cool of the cottage. Mark rejected any more beer, already feeling the buzz of the three cans he had consumed, and stuck to lemonade, a pitcher of which had been located in the fridge. A few minutes before six, Andrew hauled himself to his feet.

"I'm the chef in this place," he said cheerfully. "I'll do the fish."

"Splendid fellow," Mark muttered, half asleep in the armchair. He stirred slightly to reach for the television remote control and tuned to the Chicago local station. For a few minutes, he gazed stupidly at the end of some unfunny sitcom, then sat up a little as the news came on. Half asleep, he sat through the world news, the happenings in Illinois and then the local news.

At that point, his life changed with a sickening crash.

"Police have announced a break in the case of the presumed thrill-kill of a homeless man in Evanston ten days ago," said the pretty Chinese newscaster. "The victim, who has yet to be identified, was believed to be in his late twenties. A clear set of fingerprints on the murder-weapon, a common household carving knife, have been identified. Police wish to interview Mark Ashton, an Evanston business executive and one-time Lieutenant in the US Navy. The police admit they can think of no motive for such a killing and hope to clear the matter up rapidly..."

Wide-awake, Mark switched off the television and coldly reviewed what he had just heard. The missing knife in his kitchen, that was the key. Someone had broken into his apartment in a highly professional manner and removed a weapon, which could be expected to carry his clear prints. A simple matter to kill some poor homeless man one night and leave the knife as undeniable incriminating evidence. Someone badly wanted Mark Ashton out of the way and silent. The somebody, or more likely, somebodies, must be the people Randy Crawford reported to. Mark realized that his attack on Crawford had resulted in upsetting more than just a lunatic fringe group. These people had money, they had influence, and they were afraid.

Despite the doubts expressed by the Evanston police, Mark knew that once he was in custody, pressures from influential people would ensure that he remained in custody, charged with first-degree murder. He could do nothing from inside a prison cell.

Quickly, Mark gathered up his clothes and threw them into his holdall. He washed his face in cold water to rinse away the last of the sun and the lethargy, and collected his car keys. He checked his wallet. Just over two hundred in cash. Four separate teller machine cards for accounts at two different banks. He could obtain two thousand dollars in cash as soon as he reached the town a few miles down the road.

Mark Ashton began his run.

He drove away from the cabin as quietly as he could, hoping to give himself as much time as possible before Andrew discovered his absence. A few miles down the road, he came into the town. In the early evening, the cash machine at the gas station was idle. Blessing the fact that the machine was separated from the eyes of the cashier by a line of shelves containing bags of chips, cookies, cans of beans and a magazine rack, Mark used all four teller cards to take the maximum amount he could, five hundred dollars per account to add to the cash he already had in his wallet. He sweated a little as the notes hissed from the machine, praying that there would be enough cash available.

"Thank God I had it," he mumbled to himself, getting back into the car. His pay check had been deposited only a week before, and Mark had been slow to pay his bills that week, what with the trip to Washington and the excitement of seeing Christiana. He had transferred money to an account he used for his mortgage payments and into two savings accounts, and he blessed his forethought in having teller machine cards for all four of them. He had no idea if and when the police would put locks on his bank accounts, or if they would trace his movements through his withdrawals and possible use of any credit cards.

He drove on, aware that he was utterly exhausted by the day in the sun and by the sudden, cataclysmic events of the early evening. As night fell, he stopped outside Milwaukee. Figuring that the police had not had time to issue photographs of him very widely, he called in at a drugstore, purchased some horn-rimmed reading glasses with the lowest possible power lenses, and some cotton-balls. Disguise should be the minimum, he had been told as part of his naval training in intelligence work. Forget beards, dyed hair, all the traditional techniques beloved of crime-writers. Work on the facial shape, the distracting details.

Back in his car in the safety of darkness, he stuffed some of the cotton balls into each cheek under the top and bottom gums. Looking at himself in the driver's mirror, he was satisfied that the slightly rounder facial shape he had achieved was a significant change. The glasses gave him a slight problem of focus, and also a headache, but he knew that he only had to wear them when dealing with others who might later be asked if they had seen a man answering a certain description.

Slipping the spectacles into his breast pocket, he drove on further into Milwaukee and found a small motel. The clerk at the desk barely looked up from his television as Mark signed the register with the name "Gerald Hornsby," entered an equally fictional registration number of his car, paid cash for one night and drove the Thunderbird to a spot shielded from the road. Finally, he retreated to his chalet. Trembling with the reaction of his sudden flight, he switched on the television, frightened but desperate to see if any more information about him was being broadcast. But the case seemed not to be a leader in the news from Chicago, and to his shattering relief, neither his name nor his picture were featured in the ten o'clock news.

He thought with some guilt about Andrew, wondering how he would have reacted to the mystifying absence of a man he had last seen slumped in an armchair, half asleep. He imagined Andrew returning from the kitchen with some sardonic comment, and finding the room empty, Mark's bag gone and the car missing from the front. Mark hoped that one day, he'd be able to explain to Andrew over another Chinese banquet. He prayed Andrew wouldn't think about informing the police, and would merely assume that something private had come up.

Despite the exhaustion, his sleep was dreadful, consisting only of catnaps interrupted by long periods of tense wakefulness.

* * *

Commander Banastre Featherstone was nervous. And furious. Something hideous was happening in his beloved America and he was baffled by it. His invitation to join Task Force Five had resulted precisely because other men and women had judged that his patriotism was not of the flag-waving, simplistic silliness of the people who called to fawn on Randy Crawford, but was a deeper, more genuine passion for the values that had made the country what it was in the first place. Those values were being threatened, he knew.

"There's something going on," he said firmly to the man on the other side of the desk. There wasn't a chair made that would allow Feathers to sit comfortably, and he shifted his legs to ease the cramps. The other man looked at him for a few seconds, then stood up.

"Let's sit down over there," he said, pointing at the dark brown leather armchairs surrounding the blue-slate-covered coffee table. "Can I get you a coffee, Feathers?"

"I'd like that, yes please," Feathers replied. The style of operations in Task Force Five was not easy for him after fifteen years in the navy. The man now settling into the armchair across from him had the presence and authority that simply demanded to be addressed as "Sir" but the instructions had been otherwise.

"TF5 has to work in a manner where everybody has equal voice," the head of the force said when Feathers met him for the first time. "*I* know I'm in charge, and *you* know I'm in charge, but if you have something to say about the way we work, the topics we tackle, the problems facing us, or anything else, talk to me. I will never, *ever*, criticize you for voicing an opinion. If we ever find that this job is beyond you, you'll be out before you can pick up your pen from your desk, but until that happens, *talk* to me. I'm just one of a group of people trying to do an impossible job. So bullshit and rank have no place in TF5. My real name is traditionally kept from you for security reasons. If you do learn my name, you're expected to keep the knowledge to yourself, even within these walls. It may be that I have to reveal it to you, in which case, the same applies. The group that controls us refers to me as "Taskmaster," or Task for short. You can call me that. If you really have difficulties with it, "Chief" will do."

Feathers had no idea who Taskmaster was. He was not a military man, because his name didn't appear in any services list that Feathers could call up on his computer, and Feathers had access to some astonishing data. He was not a politician, not now and not ever, as far as Feathers could tell. In fact, Feathers knew nothing at all about his boss, beyond his code name. Taskmaster was a short man, with energy radiating from him like a super-nova. His face was striking, with deep-set, dark eyes, and a mouth that had no difficulty in smiling. Authority sat all over him like the ancient statues of Egyptian Pharaohs.

The door opened and a young man appeared, carrying a tray. Like the two men in the office, he was dressed in simple slacks and plain shirt without a tie. Informality was the standard at TF5, Feathers had soon learned. But the young man was military, that was a sure bet for Feathers, who had seen the man before but not yet spoken to him. He had the taut, muscular look of a marine or a Special Forces man. Carrying coffee for the boss was not likely to be his sole duty. The young man placed the tray on the table between the two other men and walked out with that peculiarly soft, perfectly balanced walk of a ballet dancer or trained killer. Feathers took his coffee. TF5 had enough oddities without wondering about the identities and histories of the people around him.

"Talk to me, Feathers." Taskmaster looked calmly from his deep brown eyes at the big naval officer. He picked up his own coffee cup and sat back waiting.

"The best friend I had in the service was a guy named Mark Ashton," said Feathers. "I'm sure you know all about him."

"Of course. Mark Ashton, currently residing in Evanston, Illinois, employed as the Director of Information Systems by J.K. Hollingsworth, a multi-billion dollar engineering corporation. Drives a red Thunderbird, divorced from Alison after a one-year marriage. I trust you enjoyed your drinks with him the other night. I'm glad you killed the light when you told him about TF5."

Feathers stared at his boss. "Your man was the big guy with a Raiders' baseball cap?"

"Good," said Taskmaster with a nod. "What about Ashton?"

"A homeless man was found stabbed to death two weeks ago in a park a few blocks from Mark's home. The knife was in the body, and it had perfect prints of all of

Mark's right-hand fingers on it. The police are now looking for him since the FBI computer identified him."

"That makes no sense at all. Nothing in Ashton's psychological data would suggest that capability."

"Exactly," Feathers agreed.

"So?"

"So it's a set-up."

"And why is TF5 to be involved, beyond the fact of your friendship?"

"Because Mark had called Randy Crawford three times in the last few weeks and accused him of being an agent of some group working to overthrow the Unites States government. He visited the station where Crawford does his act a couple of days after meeting me, because he had something going with Crawford's producer. Two days later, I got this note from him."

Feathers reached inside his shirt pocket and extracted a photocopy of the note Mark had written. He passed it over the coffee table. Taskmaster picked it up and unfolded it.

"The emails go to over forty radio stations," said Taskmaster, reading aloud. "The number from which they are sent is below. And Simpson was not the only set-up. They seem to be a standard practice. And Feathers, old buddy, she's *gorgeous*." Taskmaster gave heavy emphasis to the last word that had been strongly underlined and smiled briefly. He put the paper down on the table again, and picked up his coffee cup. "Explain," he said.

"Mark had found at least sixteen talk-show hosts who raise the same topics every day. He deduced that some "dirty-tricks" group was issuing these after making up the sort of scandals and crap you hear every day from

Crawford. It sounds like someone told him the network was over forty hosts, and that the distribution is from some central office in Washington."

"And Simpson?"

"George Simpson was a seaman mechanic in San Diego. We both knew him, and it was no privilege. Mark identified Simpson's voice talking to Crawford claiming to be a Marine Captain during the Gulf War. The call was the standard 'I couldn't serve my country while that yellow-bellied, terrorist-supporting bastard is in the White House' crap that Crawford gets every day. Mark learned that such set-ups are common, but we don't know if Crawford is setting them up, or not."

"What sort of shape was Ashton in when you spoke to him?"

"Happy as a clam in a barrel. He'd been talking to Christiana, Crawford's producer, and had become very excited by the whole thing. The station manager had asked Mark to visit and perhaps be interviewed about his battle with Crawford, but he told me he was eager to see Christiana. That's the last reference in the note."

"Yes, I gathered that," Taskmaster said dryly. "He was not in the state you might expect of a casual killer who had just done another one?"

"No way in the world."

"And you think that whoever is behind Crawford decided that Ashton was getting too close and had to be removed."

"I'm sure of it." Feathers was adamant.

"Hmm." Taskmaster sipped his coffee and looked out into some deep space of his own. Feathers shifted nervously. This was the first time he had approached

185

Taskmaster with a lead to questionable activities, and he was worried about how foolish this might make him look.

"What do you think about Crawford, Feathers?" Taskmaster's eyes were firmly on the other man.

"He's an out-and-out jerk, telling a lot of lies about the president every day and definitely aiming to manipulate public opinion."

"Our First Amendment guarantees him that privilege, Feathers. The fact that Crawford is a living daily proof that any lunatic can spout any crap he or she wants is only evidence of the strength of our constitution. We owe Crawford a debt of gratitude for proving that to us so frequently."

"Yes, I agree." Feathers grinned for the first time. "But the philosophies he's spouting indicate a deep wish to replace American freedoms with a military dictatorship like a lot of other nasty little regimes around the world. I agree again, that such philosophies alone are not illegal. But if someone is so scared that Mark would make people begin to question Crawford's motivations and backing that they would have him put away, then I get frightened about who and what those people are and what they want."

"Sure." Taskmaster was lost in thought again, his coffee forgotten. Feathers drank his own, waiting for what he knew would be a decision.

"Okay, Feathers," said Taskmaster after a few seconds. "Go and see what you can find."

"Yes, sir." Feathers stood up.

"And can the "sir" crap, will you?"

"Sure thing, sir," Feathers said and grinned cheerfully as he walked out.

Chapter 10

Mark awoke with a sour taste of fear deep in his throat. For a few moments, he struggled to identify the horrible sensation and his location, then snapped awake with a jolt of appalled realization of his predicament. Hurriedly, he shaved and showered, dressed in his jeans and light shirt and carefully looked at the area outside his chalet before he walked into the cool open air. It was fifteen minutes before six o'clock. Nobody was around to see him gently start the Thunderbird and steer his cautious way back onto the road. He took the drive-through path at a McDonald's, purchased a large coffee, ignored anything to eat as the tension wrapped his guts into Gordian knots, and drove cautiously toward the freeway to Chicago's O'Hare Field. Once on the highway, he set his cruise control at a cautious sixty-eight in a sixty-five mile-per-hour speed limit. Too law-abiding, and he could attract attention almost as much as a speeder, particularly in a bright-red Thunderbird. Mark felt a slight trembling through his whole body. He was wanted for murder. The thought ran round in his head like a frantic mouse in a cage. After a few miles, he managed to lose himself in the driving, firmly keeping his mind off the dangers,

It couldn't last.

In his rear-view mirror, he saw a police cruiser about a mile behind him. Its lights were flashing and it was racing toward him at what looked like well over a hundred miles an hour. Mark's guts churned and he felt acid in his throat. Cold sweat ran over his chest and back and his hands became slippery on the wheel.

"Oh dear God," he muttered. "I've been found." The cruiser slowed and tucked in behind him, the lights still flashing. Trembling with the shock and the fear of what must be about to happen to him, Mark touched the brake and disconnected the cruise control. The Thunderbird began to slow. Mark could only stare ahead, seeing a prison cell, the horror of imprisonment while struggling to prove his innocence in an open-and-shut case.

* * *

"I know this is unusual, Sergeant, but the US Navy would be highly appreciative if you would give me some information. The man you're looking for is one of ours, after all."

Detective-Sergeant Frank Chenoweth almost ricked his neck looking up at Feathers from his mere five-ten.

"I don't think I can do that, Commander," he said. "This is a homicide, and I can't tell any guy off the streets about it, even if you are a US Naval officer. But if you know this guy, we need to talk. Will you come and sit down, for Christ's sake? I'm getting dizzy looking at you from this angle."

Feathers' laugh boomed through the squad room of the Evanston Police Department, causing faces to turn in his direction.

"It's a common problem, Sergeant," he said. "I hope your chair is strong enough."

Chenoweth grinned, and led the tall black officer to the coffee machine. "Can I buy you some of the Evanston sewage system while we talk? It's only seven-thirty, and I can't start the day without the stuff."

"I'm grateful," Feathers replied, and waited while the detective poured two cups of evil-looking black fluid into Styrofoam cups. Two minutes later, they settled down on opposite sides of a desk in a small office.

"How well did you know this guy, Commander Featherstone?"

"We'll do this easier if you call me Feathers, Sarge."

"Feathers? I like it! Call me Frank."

"Great. Mark was my best friend in the service. We trained together and worked in several areas of foreign intelligence. He speaks five languages."

"No shit? Five? And I suppose you can do that too?"

"Six."

"Hell, I don't think I could even *name* six languages, never mind speak 'em."

"And I haven't the first idea of how you conduct a homicide investigation. But the US Navy really would like to know something about this problem. Can I ask a few questions and see if you feel okay answering them?"

"We can try, but I make no promises."

Before Feathers could say anything, the door to the office opened. A tall, thin man in a neatly cut dark suit, light blue shirt and sober red tie leaned in. He studied Feathers intently for a few seconds, then looked questioningly at the man behind the desk.

Chenoweth stood up. "Lieutenant, this is Commander Featherstone, US Navy. He's helping us a lot with this case. He knew Ashton for some years. Feathers, this is Lieutenant Hobson."

The lieutenant came fully into the office as Feathers rose to his feet. The newcomer was only a couple of inches shorter than the Naval officer, and his handshake was firm.

"You knew Ashton, Commander?"

"My best buddy for some years, Lieutenant."

"You're naval intelligence like he was?"

"We worked together."

"What did you do that you can tell me?"

"Lots of stuff. We monitored a lot of radio and television from some real weirdoes running other countries, for one."

"Did either of you see combat?"

"Not beyond getting the crap beaten out of us by some military police after a crazy night in Manila."

"Is your friend a killer?"

"Not a chance, Lieutenant."

"That's what the man on the phone to the Captain just said."

Feathers and Chenoweth looked at each other for a second. A small grin appeared on the huge black face of Feathers, and Chenoweth spotted it.

"The Navy pulling strings, Feathers?"

"Sorta." Feathers looked at the lieutenant. "Sorry, Lieutenant, I don't like to use the political forces in your business. But there's some stuff going down here that made it important."

Hobson grunted noncommittally. "Okay. Here's the way it works, Commander. You and Frank can talk, but whatever he tells you, it's your ears only, okay?"

Feathers shook his head. "I'll have to report to my superiors, Lieutenant."

Hobson nodded. "Of course. I mean, nobody outside these circles gets anything."

"Sure thing, Lieutenant."

Hobson nodded and walked out if the office.

Feathers smiled again. "Nice to have pals in high places," he said.

"Damn right!" Chenoweth looked impressed. "Okay, open house. What do you want to know?"

"The fingerprints. There's no doubt they belong to Mark?"

"The FBI said it's conclusive."

"Does it make any sense to you?"

"Not a pile of dogshit's worth. If he'd come in and talked to us, we might have worked out some other explanation. People like that simply don't walk out a few blocks from their homes and knife some homeless bastard to death. He wasn't a combat vet or anything like that where you might have thought he was a trained killer who'd gone off the wall, or something. Like I said when I heard about it, it don't smell right."

"Any thoughts on how it might have been done?"

"How much of an imagination have you got?"

"A lot, Sarge. How about this? Someone wants Mark out of the way for some reason. They break in, steal a knife that's pretty damned sure to have a good set of prints on it, then kill a hobo and leave the knife. Simple, eh?"

"Too fucking simple for this poor cop. This sounds more like something out of a Tom Clancy book. Who wants your buddy Ashton out of the way? And why did he run?"

Feathers shrugged. The movement made the wooden chair he was in creak dangerously. "Mark's a hell of a bright man. If I could think of that idea after twenty-four hours since hearing about it, maybe Mark came to the same conclusion within minutes of hearing the news."

Chenoweth sipped his coffee thoughtfully. "And who's the mysterious bunch that would do that?"

"That I can't tell you," Feathers replied.

"Can't or won't?"

Feathers smiled at the cop. "It's a bit of both, but all I have a lunatic idea based on a casual conversation with Mark over a couple of beers a few nights ago. But I tell you this. That discussion took place a few days after the killing. If Mark had done it, he's the finest actor since Burt Lancaster and Lawrence Olivier combined, or he's a psychopath like this world has never seen before."

"And psychopaths don't make it through to a commission in US Naval Intelligence, eh? I wonder if great actors do? Tell me about that conversation, Feathers. What was Ashton doing in Washington? It *was* in Washington, I assume?"

"It was. He was on a business trip to Hagerstown where his company has a plant, so he'd arranged to come on into town first, and catch up with me. We hadn't seen each other for three years."

"And what did you talk about?"

"The real reason for coming to Washington."

"Okay Feathers, you got me. What was the *real* reason for coming to Washington? To see a girl, I suppose?"

"You got it in one. Her name is Christiana and she's the producer for the Randy Crawford show. Mark had called Crawford a few times and had struck up a conversation with the girl."

A look of distaste crossed the detective's face. "Crawford? That pig? You mean Ashton thinks Crawford's the savior of America?"

"Quite the reverse, I assure you. He'd ripped the crap out of Crawford quite successfully. I know, I was listening to all three conversations."

Chenoweth grinned. "I've just developed a good feeling about your buddy. I wish to Christ he'd come in and talk to us."

"Would you?" asked Feathers. "With a murder charge pending and evidence like a clear set of prints on the murder weapon? Would you surrender? Especially if you thought some influential nasties were behind it?"

"I suppose not," agreed Chenoweth. "Did he meet this chick?"

"He did. I got a note a few days later saying she was simply gorgeous. Mark was dead meat as far as she was concerned."

"Where was he going to meet her?"

"At the radio station. It's in Martinsburg, West Virginia."

Chenoweth looked thoughtful. "This sure as hell ain't the behavior of a casual killer, or a psychopath. And the victim, whoever he was, certainly wasn't the sort of person who could be causing Ashton deep problems like blackmail, or wife-stealing, or such-like."

"You don't think he did it either, do you, Frank?"

"That's not what I said. I just find the business a bit weird. But right now, there's a solid case against Ashton and we're looking for him. If he contacts you, it's your duty to let us know, right?"

"Sure." Feathers was about to ask another question when Hobson opened the door and walked in again.

The lieutenant leaned against the wall and smiled coldly. "The Streamwood police have just called me," he said. "There was a killing two nights ago. Woman named Sally Andrews, aged thirty, single, knifed in the parking garage of her apartment."

"My God, Lieutenant, you don't think Mark could..."

Hobson raised a hand, and Feathers subsided.

"Totally different MO, Commander. No weapon left behind and forensics said it was a stiletto or something similar, ripped her guts open. No, that's not the point of interest."

"What is, then?" Feathers was breathing hard from the shock of thinking Mark could have been involved in another killing.

"The odd thing is, that when they went through her things, they found a notebook in her handbag. The notebook has Mark Ashton's name and address in it."

The little office was silent for a few seconds.

"This is getting very weird, Feathers." Chenoweth broke the stasis. "Are you sure this has nothing to do with naval intelligence?"

"I wish to God I knew." Feathers stood up. "Lieutenant, do you think the Streamwood police would let us have a look at that book?"

"No doubt about it, Commander. They're waiting for Frank already. I'll give them a call and tell them to expect a navy spook as well."

Feathers tried to smile, but made a miserable job of it. "Lieutenant, I'm only a military snoop, nothing more. I just want to find my friend and make sure he's okay."

"Why are you still here, the pair of you?" Hobson asked.

Chenoweth pulled his jacket from a hook behind him. "We left ten minutes ago, sir," he said.

"I hope you signed out," said Hobson.

* * *

Mark passed a turn-off ramp and slowed even more, the sickness threatening to overwhelm him. His head thundered with the fear and the hideous realization that his life was over. He would not see Christiana again. Only the empty formality of destroying him remained. Prison, a brief trial, a life sentence. Maybe even the death sentence, years of agony on death row, every day a nightmare trying not to think about the moment when they came for him...

He slowed and pulled over to the side, looking in his rear view mirror at the lights flickering on the car behind him, imagining the triumph in the two patrolmen he could see. These were the last moments of freedom in his life.

To his stunned disbelief, the cruiser accelerated furiously up the off-ramp and vanished. The men in the car didn't look at him as they passed to his right.

Shaking uncontrollably, Mark let the car slow to a stop on the side, put the gear lever into neutral and struggled to control his breathing. The nausea slowly subsided and the sweat dried, leaving him feeling sticky and uncomfortable.

He regained his normal breathing and he stretched, easing cramped muscles. He put the car back in gear and carefully eased back onto the highway.

"Christ, Ashton," he mumbled to himself through stiff lips. "You're too young for a heart attack."

Fifteen minutes later, another police cruiser passed him, and once, he saw one waiting on the shoulder of the freeway. Each time, his insides lurched like an earthquake, and he knew that if he had eaten earlier, there would be an awful mess in his car. But after the first ghastly panic, he realized that the manhunt for him had not reached full intensity and did not yet include his car license plate number. He began to feel hopeful that he might survive the day.

Nonetheless, he knew that his car was too obvious and too easy to locate as soon as the registration number was broadcast. He took the I-94 fork east and drove carefully into the wealthy suburb of Highland Park. He was early enough to be part of the Monday morning commuter rush into Chicago and was able to find a parking spot. He stopped the Thunderbird in the station car park, as far from the rest of the vehicles as possible and spent five minutes inserting cotton balls in his cheeks again. Satisfied with his appearance in the rear view mirror, he carried his bag into the waiting room of the Metra commuter line, and bought a ticket, gratefully losing himself in the crowds of affluent executives and attorneys heading for their downtown offices in Chicago's Loop. He picked up a copy of the Chicago Tribune and waited as immobile as he could be.

When the train arrived, he joined the throngs climbing in and was able to find a seat in the upper level. Placing his bag under his knees, he worked his way through the paper. A small paragraph repeated the news item of the previous evening without further adornment. Breathing carefully, he tried to stay calm as he saw no photograph had been published.

Forty minutes later, he was in the crowds at Union Street Station. Glad of the throngs, he walked out, turned east and walked with the workers, sure that nobody would identify him in the morning rush. He walked down the steps to the underground line on Dearborn Street and bought a ticket. The train would go all the way into O'Hare Airport. He stood on the platform, the station smelling as always of old urine and disinfectant. A quartet of buskers played a neat version of *"Chattanooga Choo-Choo"* a few yards away. Mark dropped a dollar bill in the open guitar case and received a wide grin from the singer. A few minutes later, he climbed aboard the train and took a seat at the rear of the compartment. He buried his face in the newspaper again and tried to find some humor in the comics section.

He made it to O'Hare. Walking out into the bustle of the travelers, he located a bank of pay phones. He took a deep breath, picked up the phone and punched the numbers for Martinsburg, using his credit card number for the call. When the cheerful voice of the receptionist answered, he asked for Christiana.

"Sure," said the pert voice. "Who shall I say is calling?"

"Andrew Jackson," he replied, wondering if the young lady was familiar with America's history. She didn't seem to be, because she put him through without comment.

"This is Christiana Girard," said the familiar voice. Mark's heart almost turned over.

"It's Mark." He heard the indrawn breath of pleasure from her.

"I was wondering when you'd call." The warmth in her tones sent a wave of pleasure through him.

"Christiana, this is urgent. We don't have much time. Something nasty has occurred, and I need your help."

"Mark, what is it?" The alarm in her voice was a discordant note.

"I can't tell you over the phone," he replied. "But Christiana, promise me. Whatever you hear about me in the next few days, don't believe it."

"I don't understand," she cried. "What could I possibly hear about you, and from whom?"

"I'll explain later," he said. "I'm getting on a plane. I'll be there by this afternoon. I'm going to go to the hotel I stayed at last week, and I'll call you from there."

"This is serious, isn't it?" she said, calmer now. "What can I do?"

"I'll talk to you this afternoon. Christiana, I know I've only seen you the once, but I know I can ask you for help."

"Yes you can. I know I can trust you not to have done anything bad," she said. "So hurry up and get here."

"As fast as American Airlines can do it," he replied, and disconnected the call. He felt a thousand times better. She had not been hysterical, she hadn't demanded the details, she had accepted his statements and reacted calmly and without conditions.

"Ashton, if you get out of this," he muttered as he walked down the corridors to the ticketing counters, "the very first thing you do is find out if that incredible woman is ready to get married."

Ten minutes later, he paid cash for a one-way flight to Washington Dulles. Wearing the glasses for that time had given him a raging headache, and the cotton balls in his cheeks had made him speak slowly and carefully, but he decided that wasn't a bad idea. He had no choice but to present his driver's license as identification and have the ticket made out in his own name. But he had sounded like a foreigner and the ticketing agent would be even less likely to connect her memory of him with the picture and description of Mark Ashton, should the police ever ask her. And she was looking very flustered with the crowds around. He knew he had left tracks, but prayed that the manhunt wasn't in full operation yet.

He tried the teller machine in the terminal, his heart thumping in case his accounts had been blocked, which would mean that the police hunt had reached an unwelcome level of intensity, but he drew out another thousand dollars without a blip in the process, beyond sensing the irritation in the line of customers behind him as he used four different cards. Half an hour later, he boarded the Boeing 737 and sat near the back in a window seat. A large, bearded man sat next to him and read his copy of *"The New Republic,"* showing no interest in starting up a conversation. Nobody paid Mark any attention at all.

His silence and calm reflected nothing of the fury within him. Though frightened more than he had ever been before, Mark's rage was a wild, ravening scream. Only a few days before, he had been an affluent, successful man in his mid-thirties. Despite the loneliness and sometime the despair that had depressed him on occasions, his life had been a good one. And then Christiana had appeared and shown him a possible life that was everything he had wanted.

Now it was all threatened. Because he had challenged a political ideologue whose preaching bordered on the lunatic ranting of a Joe Stalin or Adolf Hitler, his life was at risk. Mark had no objections to Crawford's right to spout his nonsense. That was an integral part of American life, that freedom of speech in which he had always believed. But the abusers of that right were so aroused that someone had challenged them, perhaps laid bare the reality of the message being played over the airwaves, that they had chosen to subject him to becoming the victim of a police man-hunt, where the penalty was loss of freedom, perhaps even his death by lethal injection. Mark had no illusions about his position. He knew that his fingerprints on the murder weapon would convict him without any delay. A murder had been committed, enough evidence pointed to a killer, that would be enough for the police and the courts. Nobody would seek an alternative answer, and Mark's finances didn't run to top-flight defense attorneys.

Mark realized his life as he had known it was over. There was now only Christiana to believe in him, and maybe a gateway he could take elsewhere and hide.

Despite the calm exterior of the man in the window seat, Mark Ashton wept.

* * *

The Streamwood police station was a small building about half a mile from the crystal and glass structure of the municipal offices. Frank and Feathers sat in an interview room together with a muscular man in his forties. Detective-Sergeant Robert Welland had been curious about Feathers and his arrival with the other detective.

"He's helping us with our inquiries," said Chenoweth. "The navy had some data on Ashton that's proving useful. My captain's talked to your boss."

"Fine by me," Welland replied. "So long as the Chief has okayed it."

He passed over the little notebook that had been found with the body of Sally Andrews. Frank took it first and turned to the page that had been identified with a yellow "post-it" sticker.

"Mark Ashton's name okay," he muttered. "And his address. This looks like a post-office number in Roanoke, Virginia. I assume POB means post office box?" He looked at the other two men who nodded.

"That's what we assumed," Welland agreed. "We're getting a check on the owner of that number. Should have it by tonight.

"Virginia?" asked Feathers.

Chenoweth looked at him. "Didn't you say Ashton was going on to see some chick in Virginia?"

"In Martinsburg, West Virginia. Roanoke's in Virginia, but not all that far away."

Chenoweth studied the booklet again. "These numbers look like dates and times, maybe?" He slid the booklet over to Feathers.

"That's what we think, also," Welland said.

"Twelve-forty on June eleventh, and twelve-thirty-five on the twelfth," Feathers recited. "What the hell could that mean?"

"Beats me," replied Chenoweth. "What about your people, Bob? Any thoughts?"

Welland shrugged. "Nope. They're dates and times, okay."

"Who the hell would kill this little girl?" Welland muttered. "What did she have to do with Mark Ashton?"

"Who was she?" asked Feathers.

"Nobody unusual," Welland replied. "She was single, thirty, lived alone in an apartment here in Streamwood. She was killed in the basement parking lot of her building."

"Any signs of rape?" Frank asked.

Welland shook his head. "We're working on the assumption... belay that, we *were* working on the assumption, till this booklet turned up, that it was a simple boy-meets-girl, boy-propositions-girl, girl-says-fuck-off, boy-kills-girl. You know how much we get of that, these days, Frank."

"Right," Chenoweth agreed with a shake of his head. "What did Sally Andrews do?"

"She was a programmer with the cell phone company up the road," Welland replied. He looked at Feathers. "You say this Ashton guy was a friend of yours?"

"Yes, I did."

"Did he ever mention a girl he was dating in these parts?"

"I don't think so," replied Feathers. "When I saw him last week, it was the first time in three years. He'd just got divorced the last time I saw him, a year after his wife walked out."

"How long had he been married?"

"Just a year. It was a nightmare, from what he told me."

"A year?" Frank laughed without humor. "Longer than mine lasted, I can tell you. What about women since then?"

Feathers shrugged. "Nothing that I know of. We talked on the phone a few times and I got the impression that he hadn't had much joy with the opposite sex since then."

"A programmer with the cell phone company..." Bob Welland was looking at the blank wall and his words had been murmured softly, more like vocalized thoughts.

"What? What did you say?" Frank looked at the other detective.

"Sally Andrews was a programmer with a cell phone company," Welland repeated. "That's ringing a bell, for some reason..." His voice tailed off and his gaze resumed its sightless stare at the blank wall.

Feathers was about to say something, but Chenoweth, made an abrupt cutting gesture with his right hand, and Feathers stayed silent. Both of them watched the Streamwood cop as he sat silently. After a minute, Welland got to his feet and walked out.

"What the hell?..." said Feathers, and Frank grinned at him.

"Don't interrupt a man in the throes of deep thought," he said. "You of all people should understand that. I'd bet a million bucks you've wrestled with problems in your line of work, got a stray thought and hung onto its tail till it led somewhere."

"Poetically put," said Feathers. "And damn right, too. I hope he gets back here soon."

It was only three minutes before Welland returned carrying a sheaf of papers.

"Crime reports from other municipalities," he said, and sat down. "There's something in one of these that reminds me..." He began leafing through the sheets, then stopped, extracted a paper and stared at it. "Well lookee here," he drawled, and passed the sheet over to Frank. Chenoweth grinned briefly at Feathers then studied the sheet.

"Barrington, Illinois," he read out. "The body of Terry Seymour was discovered behind a gas station. He'd been knifed in the stomach with a sharp, thin blade, probably a stiletto. Same night that Sally was killed. Seymour was - get this, Feathers - thirty-five, a programmer with a cell phone company, not the same company that Sally worked for."

"Christ alive!" Feathers was stunned.

"Well done, Bob," said Chenoweth. "This has become highly interesting."

"Sounds like we should talk to their employers," Welland said.

"Damn right," Chenoweth agreed. "Let's split it. You arrange with the Barrington guys to go and see Seymour's company. The naval monster and I will tackle Sally's lot."

* * *

Feathers watched with considerable envy as Frank flashed his detective's badge and doors opened immediately. It would have taken him some time to organize the meetings that Frank had arranged within minutes.

"I'm the chief programmer." The small woman in a dark green, polyester pants-suit looked about forty, displayed a trim shape under the close-fitting suit, but her face had a down-turned mouth with thin lips in a permanent expression of disapproval. "My name's Janet Hampton."

Only a few moments had been taken when the meeting began for Janet Hampton to recover from any obvious grief and shock she was feeling from the murder of Sally Andrews. Feathers had the chilly feeling that the woman was more upset about the disruption to the project schedule than the snuffing out of a human life.

"Sally Andrews worked for you?" asked Frank.

"Not directly, no," the woman said shortly. "She was in the maintenance group under one of my project leaders."

"Maybe we should ask that person in?" Frank suggested.

"He's off sick." Hampton seemed to express distinct crabbiness at the fact. "You'll have to deal with me."

"Was Sally a good programmer?" asked Frank.

"She worked here for four years," Hampton replied. "Of course she was a good programmer."

"I understand." Frank gave a short glance at Feathers. The look seemed to say "Help!"

"What was she working on when she died?" Frank continued.

Hampton looked hard at Feathers for a second as if suspecting some communication beyond her comprehension and of definite insult to her had taken place then looked back at Frank.

"I'll have to consult her activity logs to get a precise answer," she said. "But it was mainly on accounts receivable, master file maintenance, that sort of stuff."

"Does your mainframe keep that activity log on-line?" Feathers chimed in. Hampton gave him a suspicious look, while Frank raised his eyebrows. Both seemed puzzled by Feathers' unexpected computer-wise question.

"Yes it does," the woman replied. "And yes, before you ask, I could search that log to see what she'd been doing." A tiny trace of warmth had reached Hampton's face, as if recognizing an intelligent question. "For what period?"

"From midday on July the twelfth through the close of her day on the twenty-fifth, when she died," Frank answered.

A tiny flicker of some emotion crossed Hampton's eyes as she turned to her computer keyboard on the edge of her desk. "This will take a while," she said, then seemed to wipe the two men from her awareness as she concentrated on the computer.

Silence ruled the office for five minutes before the woman spoke again. She turned the computer monitor about forty-five degrees so that the two men could see it.

"That's what she did on the system," said Hampton. She pointed at the top of the screen that displayed columns of data meaningless to Feathers. "These are the six programs she was working on," she continued. "As I'd expected, they're all accounts receivable programs, and the other figures are the times she logged onto the system to modify, compile and test them...." She pressed a button and a new column of data appeared. Hampton placed her finger at the top of the row and worked downward. "And so are these..." A third screen of data appeared. "And these... that's odd!"

"What?" Frank spoke sharply, as if he'd been holding his breath, and Feathers realized that he'd been doing precisely the same thing. The woman had a finger poised over a program with a shorter name than all the others on the list.

"That's not part of any program suite," Hampton replied. "That's an SQL program. I wonder what she was doing?"

"SQL?" Frank demanded.

Hampton nodded, as if she had only been half-listening. "It's a report program generator," she murmured. "We use it to write quickie, one-off programs if we want to extract data from files and produce a report."

"Can you see what the program was?" Feathers asked. His heart was pounding with the thrill of the hunter reaching the quarry.

"No, it's been deleted," Hampton replied, then suddenly smiled at Feathers. It was the first real sign of human warmth from her. "But I think I can find it for you. Don't go away."

"We're not moving," Frank assured her earnestly. She blinked at him, picked up the phone and punched four digits.

"Greg," she said after a few seconds. "Could you search the log for...." She looked at the screen. "For the twentieth. Look for an SQL program called..." She studied the screen again. "SALL1." Hampton spelled the five-character name out. "It's under Sally Andrews' Identification Code which is "ANDREWS" and her current password is "CRAWFORD." Call me back when you've got it and loaded it back on."

She looked at the two men. "Crawford?" she asked. "That's a weird password. Was that her boyfriend, or something?"

Feathers felt his heart go into double time. "No idea," he replied.

"Not that I know of," said Frank. He stared at Feathers and the look said clearly that the detective had linked Sally's password with the information Feathers had given him earlier that day, that Mark Ashton had established a relationship with Randy Crawford's producer.

"This could take half an hour, or so," said Hampton. "There's a canteen down the corridor. Why don't you get a cup of coffee or something and I'll call you when I've got that program back on line?"

The two men rose to their feet at the clear dismissal.

"Thanks," Feathers said and smiled. He received an expressionless look in return, and he followed Frank out of the office.

A few minutes later, they were seated at a vinyl-covered table in the cheerful, airy canteen overlooking the pleasant gardens of the office block. Each had purchased a mug of coffee and a donut and were looking thoughtfully out on the sunny scene.

"Good operator, that woman," Feathers murmured.

"All the sexual warmth of a hunting polecat."

Feathers nearly choked on his donut. "But competent as hell."

"Oh yes, all that," Frank agreed. "Like my ex-wife. I can just imagine having a good screw with her, collapsing back on the bed and listening to her give me a detailed and highly critical analysis of my performance."

"What a horrible idea!" Feathers laughed and drained his coffee mug. "I need another cup after that thought. You?"

"Sure," Chenoweth replied pensively.

When Feathers had returned, Frank looked at him. "Ashton had talked twice to Randy Crawford, you said?"

"Three times. I heard him call twice in two days, then again some days later. The last time was just a few days before he came over to Washington."

"He had a car-phone?"

"Yes, he did. And knowing Mark, he'd have used it, rather than use the company phone for a private call. He'd probably leave the office to ensure privacy, as well."

"You know what that program is going to be, don't you?" Chenoweth displayed a superior smile.

"It'll be a search on the call-files of cellular calls made on those dates between those times we found in Sally's book, to the radio station in Martinsburg, Virginia," Feathers replied dreamily. "And when they're found, the program will display the name and address of the caller."

"You're raining on my parade, Commander," Frank complained, struggling to contain the glee he was feeling at the inroads they were making on this case.

"I'm in Intelligence, remember? That's what we do."

"I'm glad my tax dollars are working so well," Frank replied, and reached into his jacket pocket, extracting a small cellular phone. "I'm willing to bet that little Sally was not supposed to write the details down when whoever-it-was that gave her the orders briefed her. But silly Sally did. I'm also betting that Terry Seymour was more obedient, 'cos there was no indication of those dates and times in his possessions anywhere. But Bob Welland hasn't got the computer expertise with him that I've got. Stand by."

He poked two fingers into his breast pocket and extracted the card that Welland had given each of them at the first introductions that morning. After a moment's study, he punched several digits into the cellular phone and waited a moment before speaking.

"Bob?" he asked. "It's Frank Chenoweth. How's it going? You are? Good. Listen old buddy, I think we have something here. You've got a copy of the page of Sally's notebook? Find out if Terry Seymour had done a search of the call-files for those dates and times. The top programming honcho should be able to find out for you. The one here is looking right now. Great! Call me back if you get anything."

He folded the little device back into his pocket and picked up his fresh cup of coffee. "I could use another of those donuts, if you're up to getting me one, Naval Intelligence."

Feathers grinned. "My expense account may be better than yours," he replied. "I think Uncle Sam can buy us a couple more donuts. He could even run to another coffee."

"Good for my favorite Uncle." Chenoweth's smile was thoughtful, distant. "This is a real shit-hot case, eh?"

"Shit-hot," Feathers agreed, and rose from his seat.

* * *

"What she did was to read through the billing data base, looking for long-distance calls made to this telephone number for two specific dates and within a specified time window," said Janet Hampton forty minutes later. She studied the lines of computer code on her monitor screen. "When she found a match on the date and time, she used the account code in the record to access the customer master file and extract the name and address. Her job gave her access to those files, so it was a simple search.

The information was displayed on her screen, not printed, as if she wanted to keep the information to herself."

"What was the phone number?" Feathers asked.

Hampton studied the screen. "An eight-hundred number," she said, and read out the seven digits. Feathers nodded briefly at his partner. It was the number for the Crawford studio.

"Can you print that program out for us?" asked Chenoweth.

"Sure." The chief programmer pressed a few keys and a laser printer behind her began to wheeze in an asthmatic way while sliding a couple of sheets into the waiting tray. "What the hell was Sally up to?"

"Miss Hampton, I can't tell you that, but this could be evidence in a homicide case," said Frank. "Would you sign those two sheets, indicating what they are, with today's date?"

"Of course." Hampton took the pages from the printer and scrawled over them, handing them back to Frank who filed them into his briefcase.

"We'll be going now," he said. "I just want to say, Ma'am, you're one hell of a professional."

The woman seemed astonished. "It's what I do," she said.

"Thank you," Frank replied, and opened the door for Feathers to lead the way out.

"Just like my ex-wife," Frank muttered as they found their way to the exit. "She couldn't take a compliment, either."

*　*　*

A couple of hours later, they found that Bob Welland had come away from his visit with two sheets of paper remarkably similar to those in Frank Chenoweth's possession.

"That number is the Randy Crawford show?" Welland looked baffled. "Why were these two kids looking for callers to that asshole?"

"Bob, I suggest you don't repeat that question outside this room," Chenoweth said gently. "Something dirty's going down, and you don't want to get hit by it."

"Fuck!" Welland looked shaken. It was the first expletive the other two had heard, and seemed to reflect his shock.

"We'll let you know what happens here," added Feathers. "But I agree with Frank here. Keep away from this for a while."

"It ties in with something from one of my interviews with Sally's friends, yesterday," Welland said, the shock still in his eyes, but apparently determined to continue his investigation. "I did an immediate check of her known associates once the body had been identified."

The other two men looked at him and waited for an explanation.

"She had only two friends at work," Welland continued. "They gave me nothing of any interest. But she had been dating some guy in another department for a time. I talked to him, and he said they'd broken up a few months ago."

"Did he say why?" Frank prompted, and Welland nodded.

"He said that Sally had called the Randy Crawford show, 'cos she thought that Crawford was an all-American hero and a true patriot. The guy said he told her that Crawford was a pig and a liar, and Sally had flown off the handle at him. That's when it ended."

"Curiouser and curiouser," said Feathers.

Chapter 11

"And a wonderful late summer's good afternoon to all you true Americans out there. This is Randy Crawford welcoming you to another three hours of putting right what's wrong with America today, and have we got some news for you." Crawford looked through the glass to the control room. Christiana was concentrating on the telephones, and Verity was standing behind her, his arms folded, staring fixedly at Crawford.

Oh, are we going to fuck up your day, Crawford glowed to himself. This was going to be the best thing ever, he felt, a chance to hurt those two little shits like they'd never been hurt before.

He watched as lines of data flickered onto his control screen in front of him. As usual, the screen filled up immediately, all six phone lines taken with eager callers, and more waiting. He felt in his bones that today was going to be one of those simply glorious events for him, in a lifetime of wonderful broadcasting memories.

"Yes, sirree, people," Crawford crowed, "this is a special day. Not only will we reveal some more of the appalling weakness displayed by that wimp in the White House, but we'll give you definitive proof of the sickness of the sort of people who call this station to attack patriotic Americans."

He saw Christiana's head snap up from her phone call to stare at him, and then look up to Verity. Crawford smiled at them, and saw the worry in both faces. *Oh yeah,* he thought, his heart thumping with delight. *Are you two pinkos gonna be sick in a moment.* It was the same sort of pleasure he had felt as he saw the fear and pain in the eyes of Monique Lamoureux when he first struck her. *I'll have to call that whore tonight,* he thought with another jolt of anticipation. *Jesus Christ, Randy, this is absolutely your week! Grab everything there is.*

"So we'll get to your calls in a moment folks," Crawford continued. "Don't go away, Hank from Seattle, Maureen from Albuquerque, Jim from Baltimore and all you other wonderful Americans waiting there in your homes and your cars, 'cos we'll be with you in a moment. First, I have to tell you just how sick the liberals are in this country."

He looked through the glass and could sense the tension in the watchers in the other room.

"Many of you may remember when we got a few calls recently from some loonie-toon individual who called himself Mark from Evanston," Crawford continued, feeling his power growing by the second. "That man claimed to be an ex-naval intelligence officer, which was obviously a lie in itself, 'cos people like that just don't get into this country's military service. You probably remember how he insulted one of our callers, a brave, patriotic American who had served his country as a Marine captain during the Gulf war, one of the finest men this country could ever produce. This sicko from Evanston claimed that our caller was lying, said he actually knew him, and that he was something other than what he claimed. Now, I know all you folks listening out there wondered just what sort of anti-

American would do such a thing, defaming a genuine American hero like that, but that's what liberals are, folks, they're communists, traitors to their country, and liars. And you probably wondered just how *twisted* this man was, calling me a communist and an enemy of America. *Me!* In saying that about Randy Crawford, he was, of course, saying the same thing about all you folks who call into this station, and who listen every day."

Crawford felt the adrenaline running wild. He was in the best form ever, he knew. There was nothing like some good, honest, all-out hatred to get the juices flowing, he decided and laughed outright as he saw the faces of the other two behind the glass.

"So listen up, folks, and Randy will tell you about this man. I got the news early yesterday afternoon from a wonderful, all-American police officer in Chicago who called me. This man, Mark Ashton, yes, that's his name folks, remember it, this Ashton is a common murderer! Yes, America, this communist, liberal lunatic killed a young man in Evanston a few days ago. He knifed a poor innocent in cold blood, a merciless, motiveless killing that has the Evanston police stunned. Not only that, he was too stupid to wipe the weapon down afterwards. He left his prints all over it. Just goes to show you, folks, you have to be incredibly dumb to be a liberal."

Crawford studied the reaction in the control room the way other men watch sex movies. He absorbed every movement, the shock registering on Verity's face, and the way Christiana put her hands to her cheeks. With delight, he saw the woman stand up, throw her headset off and walk to the door. She was weeping, he could tell. Verity immediately sat down in her seat, put on the headset and

216

took over. Crawford laughed out loud in the confines of the studio. *God, this is great!* he thought.

Crawford forced the door open and strode into Verity's office like an avenging crusader. As he expected, Christiana was there, the distress showing in her face. She had obviously been weeping.

"I thought I told you to knock before coming in here, Crawford?" Verity snapped. "Get the hell out of my office."

Laughing at him, Crawford took the other armchair and sat down, crossed his legs and put his hands behind his head, leaning back. "Your office?" he said with a smirk. "Listen jerk, you're going to have enough visitors here soon, that you might as well give up on that crap. The police are going to be in and they'll be reaming your asses out, asking why that little pig Ashton was calling on you so social and friendly-like. Maybe you're both accessories to that murder in Evanston?"

"No, we're not," Verity replied coolly. "But in another few minutes, they may be questioning me about the assault on a vicious, loud-mouthed talk-show host."

"You and whose army?" Crawford sneered. "Look asshole, you're in deep shit. That maniac is obviously a friend of yours, and the police are going to want to know why. And how about you, little girl? You fucking him?" He grinned at her, and made no effort to hide his stare at her legs and breasts.

She looked calmly back at him. "No," she said. "But as soon as I see him, I will. And it'll be just wonderful. Which is a hell of a lot more than I can say about you."

Crawford jerked back as if slapped in the face, and Verity laughed.

217

"And he won't be paying for it, the way you have to, Randy," he said. "Now, do you have anything important to say in that festering slime you call a brain?"

Crawford was breathing so hard in his rage, that a trace of moisture dropped from his nose. Verity saw it and dug the knife in deeper.

"For Christ's sake, blow your nose, Crawford. Didn't your mommy send you out with a clean hanky today?"

Crawford bellowed wordlessly and shot to his feet. Despite themselves, both Verity and Christiana flinched. Crawford stamped to the desk and leaned over it on his left hand, staring at Verity and shaking his right fist at him.

"Listen to me, you little faggot! The board will soon know that you and that felon are buddies and that she's fucking him. How long are you two going to last, eh? I tell you how long. A couple of days, that's how long! And I'm going to tell every American listening to my show why you two have been fired. Understand?"

Verity suddenly moved. His right hand shot out and clamped on Crawford's left wrist. He jerked it sideways and upwards. Crawford shouted in pain, then his face slammed into the desk top with a soggy crunch. Verity seized Crawford's hair with his left hand, lifted the head a few inches then thumped it down against the desk again. Christine jerked back at the scream that Crawford emitted. Verity released both the wrist and the hair and sat back again. Crawford collapsed to the floor, moaning, both hands against his face trying to hold back the blood, with little effect.

The door opened and a large, muscular man raced in. He wore a security guard uniform, and he was reaching for his gun at his side when he stopped as he saw the scene.

"Jesus Christ, Verity, what happened?"

Verity smiled. "Our all-American hero slipped when he was trying to show me something, Gerry. I think the floor in front of my desk is a bit slippery. You'd better escort Randy to first-aid."

The guard looked at the thick carpet on the floor. He glanced at Christiana, one eyebrow raised in question.

"Absolutely, Gerry," she said with a sweet smile. "That's a real death-trap that floor. Like an ice-rink. Randy really took a tumble."

"Yeah, right," the guard replied, bending over Crawford. "Come on, Mister Crawford, let's get you to the nurse." He hauled the tall man to his feet. Crawford staggered, dripping blood on Gerry's blue shirt. He mumbled something inaudible.

"Did he say something, Gerry?" asked Verity. He looked relaxed, sitting back in his chair, his hands behind his head the way Crawford had been a few moments earlier.

"I think he said he was going to kill you, Verity," the security man replied.

"Nah, that can't be right," Verity chuckled. "Not Randy Crawford, the gallant Knight of the Airwaves, surely?"

"I must have got it wrong," the guard agreed, a wide smile on his face. "No one would make threats like that against an old Special Forces man, now would they?"

"Not a chance," said Verity and watched as the two men departed.

Christiana let out a deep, shuddering sigh. "Oh God, Nick, this is awful! What's happening?"

"Has he called you?" asked Verity, ignoring her question.

She shook her head, not looking at him.

"Chris, we've been friends a long time," he said gently.

"He called this morning," she whispered, wiping her eyes. "He's on his way here."

He was silent for a moment, then reached into his desk drawer and pulled out a writing pad. He began to draw on it.

"About a year ago," Verity murmured, his head down over the paper, "I bought a cottage up in the mountains. Nobody knows about it except for Carolyn and John Power. It's small, but it's got all the things you need, including electricity, a stock of food and logs for the fire. There's no phone, but it's in the cellular area. Here's how you get there, and here..." he reached inside his briefcase by his desk, "...are the keys and the cellular phone. Now as soon as you can, get yourselves up there and have a honeymoon. I'll handle the desk for the Crawford show until something happens."

He selected a key from the ring he was holding. "This one is the front door." He touched a second. "That's the food locker. And this..." He took hold of the biggest key, a specialized one with multiple tines. "That's the gun locker. There's a shotgun and a bolt-action .762, with ammunition enough for both for a revolution. Also a .22 sporting rifle that little John Power will one day acquire." He passed the keyring over to her, smiling at her expression of astonishment. "There's a charging socket for the cellular in the kitchen. Leave the phone on from six o'clock every evening till ten. If anything happens, I'll call you then."

"Nick, I don't know what to say..." Christiana's voice tailed off as she took hold of the key ring and the map Verity had drawn for her. She put both into her handbag, then took the small cellular phone. "We're sheltering a wanted criminal. That's a federal offence. I'm getting you into deep trouble."

"Mark's not a killer. I'm willing to bet that pig Crawford knows this is a set-up." Verity's face was ice-cold. "Anything I can do to find out who or what's behind him, I'll do it and screw the federal offence."

"I don't know how I can begin to thank you..." she began, tears in her eyes.

"Then don't," he replied. "Push off now. I assume Mark's here somewhere and he'll call you?"

"He said he would," she said faintly. "I keep remembering the police are looking for him. Maybe he's been arrested already?"

"Let's hope not," Verity replied firmly. "Go home, Chris. If I hear anything, I'll call you."

She stood up, looking a little shaky. "What will happen with Crawford?"

"Leave that bastard to me," said Verity with not a trace of warmth.

* * *

By late afternoon, Mark reached Martinsburg. Refusing to tempt fate at Dulles airport by renting a car for which he would have to show a driver's license, he found the bus heading in the direction he wanted, and took a seat at the rear, gratefully removing the horn-rimmed glasses as he sat down. The bus was half-full, and he had the seat to himself.

221

In the town, he again decided to play safe, and didn't take a cab. Recognizing his location, he walked the mile or so to the motel he had stayed in before. Remembering his thoughts about his enforced speech using his cotton balls, he deliberately adopted a slight Spanish accent when he booked into the motel and paid cash for two nights. He felt that the risk of being recognized from his earlier stay was slight, and the clerk was not the same one who had checked him in the last time. He signed in as Gustavo Perez with an address in Monterrey, and thankfully closed the door behind him as he entered the small, comfortable room. It was just after five o'clock.

He waited for half an hour, then called Christiana at home. The pain in her voice was obvious as soon as she picked up the phone and answered it.

"Now you know what I mean about not believing anything anyone told you about me," he said.

She gulped. "Oh God, how did this happen?"

"Not over the phone. Will you pick me up at the hotel?"

"Of course I will. Give me five minutes."

"It will feel like a year," he said, feeling his nerves relax a little.

"You do say the loveliest things."

"Quick as you can," he replied.

"Bring your bag with you," she said, the laugh obvious in her voice, and hung up.

* * *

"Have the Roanoke cops got back to you with that post-office box number, Sergeant?"

"Yes, sir, but it's not a lot of help."

"What've you got, Frank?"

"It's registered to a James T. Wicklow, but nobody can remember seeing anyone ever use the thing."

"Anyone remember the guy who opened it?"

"Not a chance, Lieutenant. After six months, the people at the post office can't remember anything. The local cops questioned all the other box-holders. One woman said she thinks she saw a tall, thin guy, maybe thirty years old, get some stuff out of the box a few weeks ago, but she can't be sure, according to the report. They tried her with the police artist, but the old dear just got confused."

"Anything in the box?"

"Empty as a politician's brain, Lieutenant."

"Don't be sarcastic, Sergeant Chenoweth."

"Yes, sir. Or no, sir, as the case may be."

"Any more from that naval sky-scraper?"

"Nope. He said he'd get back to us."

"And any signs of Ashton?"

"They found his car in the parking lot at Highland Park Metra station, but nobody we've spoken to can remember seeing him, but it's obvious that he took the train into town and then switched to the "El" to the airport. The bank report says that he drew three hundred bucks out of each of four accounts at a teller machine in Fond du Lac, Wisconsin on Sunday evening and the same again at O'Hare the next morning. Then he flew to Dulles."

"Twenty-four hundred bucks? Who the hell has twenty-four hundred bucks available at any one time?"

"Certainly not detective-sergeants, Lieutenant. How about police lieutenants?"

"Jeez, you're a rude bastard, Frank! Where do you think he's gone?"

"Well, he ain't got family, according to Feathers. So I got to thinking that maybe he went to see his lady in Virginia, this Christiana Girard."

"Christiana? Now there's a sexy name."

"Apparently she's gorgeous, Feather said."

"Check up on it, Frank."

"What, whether she's gorgeous and sexy? Love to, Lieutenant."

"No, idiot! Whether Ashton's heading there."

"Already did. But no trace after he landed at Dulles."

"They're keeping an eye on this Girard broad?"

"They said they'll try, but they're very short of staff."

"Really? A police department undermanned? What in the world is police work coming to?"

"Don't be sarcastic, Lieutenant."

"Yes, Sarge. Or no, Sarge, as the case may be."

"Thank you, sir."

"Keep at it, Frank. And tell me if Feathers calls you."

"Sure thing, Norm."

* * *

Mark stood quietly in the doorway of the hotel and studied the traffic. Christiana drove a white Honda Accord, she had told him that magic night when they had dined together and the world had glowed with promise and new love. His eyes ached from the reading glasses and his mouth was dry and irritable from the wads of cotton wool in his cheeks. But he had to stay this way while people walked by and might give him a casual glance. He was sufficiently different from his normal appearance that only people who knew him would see the real Mark Ashton under his minimal disguise, but Mark had no reason to believe that anyone could suspect he was in this region of West Virginia. His old friend Feathers was the only one who knew about Christiana.

With a lurch of his heart, he saw the Accord slide into the kerb outside the hotel. Grasping his bag, he moved swiftly outside. He recognized the graceful shape of Christiana at the wheel and he wanted to laugh with delight. He opened the car door and slid inside, closing the door rapidly behind him. For a second, her face displayed shock and a touch of fear, then she recognized him

"Oh Mark," she murmured. "What have they done?"

He took her hand briefly, then took off his glasses so he could see her properly, and smiled at her. She returned it and immediately moved away from the kerb back into the quiet street. Gratefully, Mark removed the cotton balls, aware with delight that she had behaved in a disciplined, thoughtful manner, no hysterics, no embraces while in a public spot. Despite his belief that few people would know he was here, Mark was fully aware that he was in danger while he was in public. Christiana had recognized that fact, too.

"Christiana," he said, "thank God you felt able to trust me."

She took a hand off the wheel for a moment and grasped his. "I just knew I could. But you have to tell me what's going on."

"I will, as soon as get to a safe place. Where are we going?"

"Into hiding," she said firmly. "Verity's got a cottage up in the hills and apparently nobody knows about it. He gave me the keys."

"You mean, just you and me without a chaperon?"

She laughed. "I'll have you at my mercy," she said, and smiled at him. He took a deep breath at the prospect.

"Being on the run has just developed a couple of advantages," he said.

"Open my handbag," she said. "There's a map in there that Verity drew. And there's a map of the region in the glove compartment. Verity said it should take about ninety minutes to find this place."

It took a little more than that, but Mark forgot all the worries and the fear just at being close to Christiana and able to look at her as she drove with considerable expertise through the twisted roadways of the Appalachians.

"It's lovely!" she exclaimed, smiling through the windshield. The small log cabin was situated three-quarters of the way up a hill, one side looking over the valleys, the other backed by trees. The driveway off the track led up to the doorway. A massive stockpile of cut logs was neatly piled by one wall.

"Perfect," he agreed, sensing his excitement welling up inside him like floodwaters. She smiled, and reached for her bag in the rear seat just as he did the same. His hand moved to her shoulder, then up to her neck as her arm wound round behind his head. The kiss was long and sweet, and Mark could think of nothing but how exquisite was the feel of her mouth, of her hands on the back of his neck and the softness of her cheek.

They broke the kiss, and she lowered her head to his shoulder. He put his arms round her and stroked her face with his right hand, waiting for his breath to return to something like control.

"Being on the run has its points," she murmured into the side of his neck.

"I could get attached to it," he agreed softly. "And while this is awfully comfortable, do you think we'd be better off indoors?"

She chuckled and kissed his neck, pulling away. Mark felt a twinge of loss as cold air replaced her face, then followed her example and pulled both their bags off the rear seat. Christiana found the keys and followed him to the front door of the cottage. A few moments later, they were inside.

The cottage was simple and attractive. The walls had been lined with wood paneling, furniture was Spartan but effective, and the kitchen showed signs of a woman's viewpoint having been applied. A complete range of cutlery and crockery lay in the cupboards, together with pots and pans of greater application than most men would have chosen. A huge freezer seemed to be full of meats and vegetables.

"We'll be fine for a century or two," Mark said, standing up from his inspection of the freezer contents.

"I think so. Now move over, the lady is about to show off her astounding skills in the kitchen."

Mark smiled at her, and spent a happy half-hour watching her prepare a meal of pork chops, vegetables and salad. For a time he was able to forget the horrors that had invaded his life.

* * *

The reception at the massive Georgian brownstone was a typical Washington affair. Anyone who was anyone at all had come to the home of Senator Bryce Lombard to pay their respects to the new British Ambassador to Washington and his fair lady.

The police kept the traffic moving outside in the warm summer night, the fleets of limousines arrived like airliners landing at a major airport, and the watchers on the sidewalks goggled at the famous, the powerful and the supremely rich. When certain faces were seen climbing out of their vehicles, the gasps of excitement and applause rang through the crowd like Oscar night in Hollywood.

No gasps greeted the arrival of Charles Dansbury, nor that of Vince Jerome. The more discerning of the celebrity-watchers might have noticed that the police gave special attention as both the elderly gentlemen moved to the door of the house. They might have seen that the cops stared hard into the crowd during the short period of vulnerability between leaving the vehicle and entering the house, but most of the watchers were too concerned with spotting the headline-makers to care about two unidentifiable old men, one of whom used a heavy and ornate walking stick.

Inside the brownstone, it was a different matter.

The senator was in the lobby waiting for them, having been warned ahead of time that Dansbury and Jerome were arriving.

"Charles! Vincent! You both do my house great honor!" Senator Lombard greeted both men with delight and shook their hands firmly. His exceptionally beautiful wife added her own welcome with equal apparent joy.

"Senator," Dansbury said with a warm smile, "the honor is entirely mine, I promise you. Margaret, you always look lovely, but tonight, my dear, you glow like the Northern Lights."

Margaret Lombard placed affectionate hands on Dansbury's shoulders and kissed him on both cheeks. In her mid-fifties, she possessed the same brilliant presence and style that Jacqueline Kennedy had displayed, and her popularity in America transcended party politics just as the former First Lady's had. Her face on the cover on a women's magazine guaranteed increased circulation, even ahead of one graced by a deceased British Princess.

"Charles, you old sweetheart, this house is yours, you know that," she said with a sweet smile. "Any time you come here is a celebration for Bryce and me."

Dansbury touched her cheek lightly. "I should be thirty years younger, Margaret. Then young Bryce here would have problems with me."

She laughed and touched her husband's hand. "I bet you give the same line to my darling daughter, too!"

"Of course he does," Jerome agreed, receiving a similarly warm welcome from Margaret. "Believe me, Senator, I have to restrain this old roué every time Angela comes in!"

Lombard added his own chuckle. "I have faith in your ethics, Charles, my friend. Yours too, Vince. Angela continues to work well for you?"

"Simply couldn't manage without her," Jerome said with feeling. "The lady is an absolute treasure. Since you recommended her to me three years ago, the work has been made a million times easier. She is efficient, she is full of energy, and she is devoted to our cause."

The four of them walked along the elegant corridor to the ballroom where the sounds of the reception were indicating a successful party was in full swing.

"And she supports our real work, Vince?" Lombard asked softly so that nobody outside the four of them could hear.

"The New America depends on her," Jerome replied.

Margaret Lombard smiled, looking so like her daughter that Dansbury felt a wave of delight run through him. "Vince, and you, Charles, you two are the real architects of the New America," Margaret said. "Angela feels so privileged to be helping you bring it about. Her commitment is total, I know."

"We both know that," Dansbury agreed. "But she makes the path there so much more glorious for us two old warriors."

"You make my night," Senator Lombard said. "The party has found your help and support absolutely invaluable over these last years. It makes me very happy that I can help you in some small way by asking my daughter to work for you. Come, old friends, meet Baron the Right Honorable William Jason. I do believe that his lady is almost as lovely as my own."

"Quite impossible," Jerome chuckled.

"Thank you for that." The senator smiled at the older man. "At some time this evening, I hope you two gentlemen can join me in my study? We should review progress."

"Of course, Bryce," Dansbury replied. "Shall we say just after midnight?"

"The witching hour it is," Lombard agreed. "Now, come and meet the new British Ambassador."

The four of them proceeded through the crowded ballroom, exchanging greeting with the throng. Most seemed honored to be recognized by the two arrivals, and progress toward the end of the room where the British Ambassador waited was slow.

"Mister Webber!" the senator called at one point. A short, stocky man with red-brown hair turned from his conversation with a group of African dignitaries and smiled at the senator.

"Bryce! Great party."

"Colin," said Lombard, "have you met Charles Dansbury and Vince Jerome?"

"Of course I have," Webber replied. "Many times. The party thinks of you two as absolute pillars of our society. Charles, Vince, a massive pleasure to meet you again."

"Ours too," Dansbury replied as he and Jerome shook hands with Webber. Then the senator's party proceeded on to the Ambassador.

"I'll see you again," said Webber to the receding backs, but none of the four seemed to hear him. He turned back to the Africans, but found they had moved away and were now in discussion with a pair of Congressmen. Webber began to move back to the bar.

"Colin, good to see you here," said a voice to one side. Webber turned his head, then smiled.

"Senator! What a pleasure! I thought I might find you in this exotic gathering."

Morgan Eckhard shook his hand. "I think all of Washington is here tonight, Colin. The new Ambassador is popular. I think it must be his peerage and his relationship to the Crown."

"More likely, his adorable lady wife," Webber laughed. "She really is a doll."

"A Barbie-doll, perhaps," Eckhard agreed. "All of Washington is lining up to peer down her cleavage."

"If that's the only gap which exists between Britain and the US, then it will be a delightful task to work for closer ties," Webber chuckled. "How go the affairs of state, Morgan?"

"I worry for this country of ours," Eckhard replied. "The tide of liberalism flooding the country looks likely to destroy us. Even our efforts to raise the bulwarks after our last sweeping wins have not slowed the floods."

"If the country's will is to go that way, Morgan, what can we do about it? Though it was a move in the opposite direction, Germany's will in the thirties was to shift hard to autocracy. Could anyone have stopped it by any means?"

"At least that was a shift toward strength and self-determination," the senator replied. "For all the less attractive elements of the Third Reich, there was also courage, drive, economic expansion and powerful national pride. America could use some of the same, not this wishy-washy concern always for individual rights."

"The state is supreme, Senator? It should take priority over individual freedoms?"

"If it is a choice for national survival, yes, I believe so, Colin. We need strong leadership and commitment to *America*, these days."

"And who will provide this leadership? You, for instance?"

"I believe I have the qualities to help the country," Eckhard replied with dignity. "But also men like our host tonight. And the two you spoke to earlier, Charles Dansbury and Vince Jerome. They have been powerful friends to the party for many years now. They represent the very best of American philosophies, Colin. Self-made men who came from humble beginnings. They served their country in World War Two in the front lines of the battle, one a corporal, the other a simple private. And look at them now! Great Americans!"

"They are, indeed, extraordinary men," Webber agreed. "Do you think they would share your views?"

"I'm certain of it," said Eckhard. "They have become what they are by applying principle ahead of individual comforts."

"So I understand. But the philosophy interests me, Morgan. If such leadership is required, does that mean that you would remove anyone who opposed you?"

"The interests of the country must come first, Colin. Right now, I'm quite certain that dynamic leadership is essential to save ourselves. The current administration is failing us."

"This administration was voted in by democratic process, Senator. Would you replace it by alternative means?"

"You must remember, Colin, all the suspicions of a massive voter fraud. A second term was a foregone conclusion, given the economy at the time."

"So anything to return the administration to its rightful holders is fair game?

"America first, Colin, America first. I am, above all else, a patriot."

"It sounds very like revolution, Morgan."

Eckhard nodded. "This nation began with a revolution. Maybe a new and better direction will only be achieved with another one."

"This is possible, Morgan. I would support anything which would put America on a true, democratic path such as our founding fathers envisaged."

"Then we should talk further, Colin," Eckhard replied with a smile. "I believe I could show you some ideas a few of my colleagues have been developing which you would find interesting."

"I'd be fascinated," said Webber. "Please do call me when you can arrange such a meeting."

"I'll do that. Perhaps we should mingle further among this wonderful gathering?"

"I agree, Senator. Till the next meeting."

Eckhard waved and moved into the throng. Webber looked after him thoughtfully for a few seconds, then did the same.

At twelve, with the party cooling down and most of the visitors gone, Dansbury and Jerome moved casually down the corridor toward Lombard's study. Jerome opened the heavy oak door and let Dansbury enter ahead of him. The study was empty, but the two men were quite at home here, and helped themselves from the crystal decanters standing on the desk.

"A man of exquisite taste, you have to agree," Dansbury murmured as he sipped at his malt whiskey.

"In all things," Jerome agreed. "His home, his wife, his daughter, his gift for organization and conciliation, the man is a national treasure."

"Splendid presidential material," said Dansbury, moving to the bookshelves and casually scanning the titles.

"Perhaps the perfect candidate." Jerome poured a fine brandy into a balloon glass and sniffed the fumes with concentration. "He would sweep the polls from New Hampshire through to Election Day."

Both men chuckled.

"What a terrible thought," Dansbury murmured.

"A nightmare. That's the sort of thing that would undo years of our work."

"Just as well we've managed to persuade most of the party that Lombard is not a suitable candidate." Dansbury sipped delicately at his glass. "That little piece of information about Margaret's past indiscretions did the trick very well."

"I did it rather well, I thought. It was ugly, how eagerly people absorbed that tiny falsehood and believed it without a shred of evidence."

The door opened and Senator Lombard walked in with a smile. "Glad you made yourselves at home," he said, and advanced on the drinks decanters. He poured himself a brandy and moved to the elegant leather armchairs by the fireplace. "Make yourselves comfortable, my friends," he said, and put his nose in his brandy glass, inhaling the aroma.

The two older men did as requested, sitting in a semi-circle before the unlit fire. Jerome leaned his stick against the side of his chair, occasionally touching the silver handle.

"It's been a while since we last met," Dansbury commented.

"It is," Lombard agreed. "Gentlemen, I've been providing my support to you for some years now. Although my daughter is your assistant, she has obeyed your dictates of absolute secrecy, so I still don't know who your Council is. I believe it's time I was fully briefed so that I can provide the main resources and support from the rest of the party you will soon be needing. Who have we got supporting your project and where do we stand?"

"I agree, Bryce," said Jerome. "Charles and I had decided just this week that it was time to bring you fully into the picture. This is our team." He smiled. "I'll give you the identities of each, as well as their small weaknesses which allow us some measure of control over them."

"An unusual briefing," Lombard commented with a smile, "but clearly fascinating."

"Fascinating it is," Dansbury concurred. "Also a little disconcerting to realize the silly faults some of our leaders have." He shifted to a more comfortable position.

"Geoffrey Payne is the oldest-standing member," Jerome began. "He's highly competent and nicely focused on selling guns and little else. About three years ago, he discarded his delightful wife whom he married after Harvard Business School and acquired a trophy wife last year. She's quite bright, but her real attributes are more evident in her appearance on the front cover of a sports magazine some while ago."

"Is the marriage working?" Lombard asked with a cynical smile.

Jerome shrugged. "As much as either party seems to want it. Geoffrey has a beautiful accessory for his social and business events. He drinks far too much, so he's fast losing interest in the more sporting aspects of his lady as some serious problems begin to show with his liver. She's making up for it with a procession of muscular young men."

"So he's under control?" Lombard looked as if a bad smell had invaded his beautiful study.

"Oh, entirely," Dansbury said. "He knows we can remove him from his position at any time, and his drinking would make a new job difficult. However, he probably *doesn't* know that we have detailed evidence of the additional illicit manufacturing of small-arms being conducted at one of his plants, and the flow of the resulting income to a Swiss bank account. As things become more tense over the next few months, this information will be released to him to ensure his performance."

"Excellent!" said Lombard. "Next?"

"Grant Armstrong remains an unpleasant necessity to our team," Jerome continued. "He is deeply committed to the cause, but my God, Bryce, I have trouble dealing with the man."

"I understand," Lombard replied. "But he is essential?"

"He's the third most senior man in the CIA," Jerome said. "As the primary liaison with the Drug Enforcement Agency, he's the point man for the so-called war against drugs, so his commitment to us is absolutely vital. He provides the major income for the eventual crisis. By taking over nearly all the narcotics imports to the USA, he has provided us with billions in cash."

"Is he trustworthy?" Lombard looked dubious. "What's his little dark secret by which you control him?"

"That's our problem," Jerome admitted. "He has only one vice that we can find. No women, no little boys, no illicit use of his own captured stocks, money, nothing! He has never been married, he reads nothing but CIA briefings and Party literature. Do you know he collects jewelled Regency snuff-boxes?"

"Good grief, what does he do with himself on his off-duty time?" Lombard asked with a disbelieving smile.

"What little time he takes off, he plays with his boxes." Dansbury grimaced. "Most of those boxes he stole from homes during drug searches, many of which resulted from his own false tip-offs. This is not a healthy human being."

Lombard shrugged. "He fulfils his role, that's all we can demand. Let's move on."

"You know your senate colleague, Morgan Eckhard, of course," Jerome continued. "He has the public requisites of wealth, an adoring family, a suitably heroic record in Vietnam."

"Is there more to him than that?" asked Lombard. "You would surprise me if there were even that much."

"Less, in fact," Dansbury replied with a cold smile. "Much less. The money is all his wife's, the lovely Peggy Jo Asbury of old Atlanta stock, whom he married after his astoundingly average college career at Georgia State. His war record is less than the heroic appearance, also. His first tour was purely behind a desk in Saigon. He volunteered for a second tour and was sent into action as an infantry captain. What has never been published is the fact that in his one and only combat action, he was found groveling and weeping in a foxhole by his sergeant. The affair was hushed up by his family and the sergeant was given a field-commission and a rather enhanced pension fund."

"Anything else?" Lombard looked at his colleague. "Vince, I sense you're keeping something back."

"Indeed I am. We found out that he sexually assaulted his own daughter a few years ago, when she was fifteen. This kept on for over a year before she went to her mother."

"That's disgusting!" Lombard looked genuinely shocked, and both the other men wore looks of distaste.

"Peggy Jo refuses to divorce him in order to protect the family name, and all that nonsense, but the marriage, of course, is a sham," Jerome said. "Any sign of weakness on his part and we let him know that we know. And he's vital to us, after all. His wife's family money is enormously influential with his own party as well as with large elements of the other. Through him, we can exercise considerable authority over Congress."

"What we put up with for the cause," Lombard sighed. "And you're right as always, Vince. All the candidates now running for the party's nomination are thoroughly under the Asbury family influence. When one of them has the Oval Office, we're well on our track. Who's our military representative?"

"General Corley Rollings, US Air Force," Jerome replied. "He replaced Army General Whitmore a few years ago. Whitmore failed us in a few ways and had to be removed."

"Is General Rollings another flawed creature?"

"Not really," Jerome answered. "Corley is the nearest thing to a genuine patriot I have met. He has no political mentors and he's risen strictly on his merits. At the Air Force Academy, he was a track and field star, tried for a place on the US Olympic squad and just lost out. He flew

Phantoms in Vietnam, and was well decorated for it. His first wife, Gina, was killed by Arab terrorists in the Middle East and he married his second, Becky, about five years later, when she was twenty-five and he was nearly forty. The marriage is strained, and Becky has indulged in several affairs. What she doesn't know is that Rollings once killed a man for having an affair with Gina. The killing was covered up by Rollings' men."

"The air force doesn't know?"

"Not officially," Jerome replied with a smile. "They tend to look after their own."

"So what's the General's motivation?"

"Strictly a desire to have America the single, unassailable world power," Dansbury replied. "But he believes the citizens must be run like a boot camp to ensure security. He has little time for private lives."

"Admirable philosophy, if logically flawed," Jerome murmured.

"And the rest of your team?" Lombard prodded.

"I wish we could do without both of the last two," said Jerome. "But we can't. Tony Redman, or Antonio Scarlatti as he was once, is a pig, but an immensely powerful pig, one of the biggest and richest of the Mafia bosses in the country. He runs several large enterprises on the east coast, and a network of inter-related crime-organizations in the west and in Canada. All he wants is wealth and power. Oh, and young girls under fifteen."

"Ugly," Dansbury commented.

"As my elderly friend says, ugly," Jerome retorted. "But we need him to establish the break-down of law and order and to scare the population into demanding strong leadership. He scares *me* enough, so that should be easy.

The man is the coldest killer I have met. His personal score of bodies is into the hundreds, never mind those killed on his orders."

"And the last of your team, is he any better?" Lombard asked, and Jerome shrugged.

"Maybe the worst," he replied. "The Reverend Jackson Tarquin Vanderbilt is the power behind nearly all the top televangelists on our networks today. He no longer runs his own television program, finding that he makes more money behind the scenes. He lusts for wealth and power like other men lust for film starlets. He lusts for little boys, too."

"Oh, no." Lombard shuddered. "How awful."

"That's not all," Jerome added with a grimace. "He makes extensive use of a private service that supplies the boys, but he's also had a long-standing affair with one of his colleagues from his early years after ordination. The man died last year, of AIDS, naturally."

"Presumably he's of some use to our organization?" A look of distaste twisted Lombard's mouth.

"Oh yes," Jerome said enthusiastically. "His power over the other televangelists has not arisen purely because of his charismatic personality!" He smiled impishly. "Vanderbilt's intelligence operation is almost on a par with our own. His deep, accurate knowledge of the personal foibles of these people gives him considerable influence over them. In a similar manner, he controls many others in what is laughingly called the Religious Right. He serves us well, does the deeply devout Mister Vanderbilt. It is his influence which is destroying the education system in America and breeding a generation of uncritical, easily-led sheep."

"But we control him?" Lombard seemed curious.

"We do," Dansbury confirmed. "We have let the reverend gentleman know a little of what we have on him, with indications that we have a lot more, which we do, of course."

"So Vanderbilt is perhaps the most easily controlled by our knowledge," Lombard suggested.

"Vanderbilt or Eckhard, take your pick," replied Dansbury. "Neither of them would survive public scrutiny of their private lives. None of the team impresses me mightily, except perhaps General Rollings."

"Unfortunately, the dirty work of establishing our goals must be done by dirty people," said Lombard. "All right, gentlemen, our forces are in place, it seems. The timetable remains for one year into the next administration?"

"It does," Dansbury agreed. "The party will sweep the elections on a mandate for massive change, primed by our network of talk-show hosts led by Crawford. But they will get the same as they got before, lots of sizzle, but no steak, except poisoned meat. They'll be primed for revolution. Redman, Payne and their teams will spark it in a number of locations."

Lombard smiled coldly. "And then Corley, Eckhard and Payne will see to it that revolution is suppressed rapidly, but a state of emergency will be declared by the new president and all civil liberties suspended."

"Exactly," Jerome agreed. "The president will be one of our hand-picked men of little intellectual strength and even less moral baggage. He will do what we tell him."

"Good," said Lombard. "Vince, I heard about the young man who so embarrassed Crawford on air on three separate occasions. I take it you've had him removed?"

"Indeed yes," Jerome replied. "He's now the subject of a police hunt on charges of homicide. It should keep him occupied for some time. And when they catch him, I'll ensure complete silence and a quick conviction."

"Excellent!" Lombard beamed. "Margaret will be about to usher the last guest out of the doors. Why don't we join her for a drink before calling it a night?"

"That will be the pleasure it always is," Dansbury rejoined with a warm smile.

Chapter 12

Feathers was struggling to control his fury. He had been calm enough when he had walked into Taskmaster's office early in the morning, but his temper had risen as he reviewed what had been done to his best friend.

"It's a straight-forward frame-up," he said. "Those bastards located him, broke into his apartment, stole a knife with his fingerprints all over it, and murdered some poor jerk a few blocks away. Mark's wanted for Murder One and he'll be convicted in ten seconds flat when they get him."

"Located him, Feathers?"

"Chief, two separate computer programmers at the two main cellular phone companies in the area were asked to search the files for the calls Mark made from his cellular. One of them found the calls and sent the details to a box office number in Roanoke."

"And whose box number was it?" Taskmaster was calmly studying the other man's face and examining the data academically and without the distress that Feathers was experiencing.

"False name and address," said Feathers. "Nobody can recall seeing anyone using the thing. Police have watched it for the last few days, but nobody's gone near it, and anyway, it's been empty ever since they started watching it."

"And the two programmers?"

"Both killed on the same night a couple of days later. Similar murder weapon and technique."

"And all this information comes from your police contact in Evanston?"

"We talked an hour ago. He filled me in fully."

"Somebody's pretty set on leaving no traces behind, right, Feathers?"

"Damn right! And on silencing Mark, also."

"Okay, Feathers, why is this involving TF5? Why isn't it just a clear-cut murder by some crazies?"

Feathers sat back in his armchair and studied his boss. Taskmaster's clear gaze never left him, but Feathers could read nothing in the face across the coffee table from him.

"I find it highly obvious, Chief, that Randy Crawford was so upset by Mark's calls that he wanted him silenced. The only reasons I can think of for that are, either Crawford was so embarrassed by being made to look stupid to over thirty million Americans, or Mark was getting too close to Crawford's backers for comfort. To be honest, the first alternative isn't too far off the wall. Crawford's enough of a dumb-shit egotist that killing anyone who hurt him and his show is well within his capability."

"But you don't think so?"

"No Chief, I don't. This whole thing smacks of a major organization."

"So what conclusions would you make, if that is the case?"

"I'd conclude that whoever is behind Crawford has real reasons for worrying about Mark's calls. That means that Mark was near enough to the bull's eye in his accusations."

"Which were?" Taskmaster was still looking like an academic conducting a tutorial with a bright student.

Feathers counted the points off on his fingers. "One," he said. "Somebody is trying to destroy the basic American values of free speech, individual freedoms, and the democratic structure of this country. Two; big crime, one or more arms manufacturers and some far-right lunatics are co-operating to ensure the criminals have free reign. I believe the idea is to scare the American public to the point where they'll accept *any* solution to the crime problem. Whether the NRA actually knows it's being manipulated, I can't say, but they sure as hell have a lot of cash to throw away to pressure senior senators and congressmen to make sure anyone can buy just about any weapon. Three; this same group seems intent on killing any decent educational system in the country and so breeding a nation of half-wits. Half-wits will believe anything the authorities tell them, and it's a classic technique for ensuring controllable populations."

"That's it?"

"No." Feathers' smile was cold. "That's only the data. The conclusion to be drawn from this is obvious. Some mega-rich group is planning a violent overthrow of this country. A preliminary stage is the molding of public opinion to accept such a possibility. You may remember the first signs of that working, the number of lunatics who've tried to kill the President in the last few years.

Crawford and the others have essentially told them that this administration is so evil that destroying it by any means is the patriotic duty of all Americans."

"All those attempts failed, Feathers. Do you think something additional could be in the offing?"

"I keep remembering the approach Hitler used when he wanted to stir the Germans up to the point of demanding "strong" leadership, that is, leadership unconstrained by silly little considerations like morality, democracy, or human values."

"You're referring to the Reichstag fire?"

"Yes, Chief. Hitler's goons in the SS set fire to that lovely old building and then blamed the Jews. It was enough to tip the balance."

"And you think Crawford's backers are leading up to some American equivalent of the Reichstag?"

"I do, but I've no idea what that could be."

"It's all a bit thin, Feathers."

"The murder and the frame-up aren't imagination, boss. The searches for Mark's cellular calls weren't thin. And two murders of programmers to hide somebody's tracks are sure as hell not thin. Somebody's planning a coup in this country."

"And TF5 is therefore obeying its mandate by becoming involved in this, Feathers?"

"Fucking-A, sir."

"That means yes?"

"Damn right it does."

Taskmaster sat back in his armchair and studied infinity. The room became silent. After three minutes, Taskmaster got to his feet and went to his desk. He touched some location that Feathers couldn't see, and returned to his seat, looking firmly at Feathers.

A moment later, the door opened and the silent young man who had brought coffee into them on a previous occasion entered the room. Feathers had talked briefly with the man on two occasions, and learned only that his name was Paul, and he had been a Navy SEAL. That fact alone had earned Feathers' unconditional admiration.

"Paul," said Taskmaster. "Note the following instruction as a Class One Task Force Five bulletin. The police hunt for Mark Ashton is to be called off immediately. What's the next Operation name on the list?"

"Spartacus," the young man replied. The voice was calm and detached, the tones of a young military officer superbly trained at his task. Much like himself, Feathers realized with a small wave of amusement.

"Spartacus? Who the hell assigns these names?" Taskmaster muttered, then looked at Feathers. "Note for the record Paul, that Operation Spartacus is now in force at Level Alpha, under the field control of Lieutenant-Commander Banastre Featherstone. He acts with my full authority and can command any resources he feels necessary."

"Done," said the young man and looked at Feathers. "If you'll come with me, Feathers, I'll brief you on this."

Feathers looked at Taskmaster and received a small nod. He got to his feet and Paul turned to lead him from the room.

"Feathers?" said Taskmaster softly. The naval officer turned back.

"Do you know where Ashton is?" asked the man in the armchair.

"No. But I know how to find him."

"Bring him in from the cold, Feathers," said Taskmaster.

"Aye-aye, sir," snapped Feathers.

"And can that 'sir' crap. I've told you before."

"Yes, sir," Feathers retorted and delayed turning away long enough to see the shadow of a smile on Taskmaster's face.

As the door closed behind them, Paul led Feathers to a small office. "Sit down, Feathers," he said, and took his own seat across from the medium-sized desk. There was little in the room beyond the desk and two chairs. A filing cabinet stood in one corner, with a cactus plant atop it. A computer monitor sat on one corner of the desk. A poster-sized photograph hung on the wall to the left of Feathers. It showed the arrogant face of Saddam Hussein in full military uniform, surrounded by his retainers. The picture had the grainy quality of a small camera.

"I took it," said Paul. "From six feet away. Easy kill distance."

"And?" Feathers looked away from the photograph and stared fascinated, at Paul.

"Mission scrapped," said Paul shortly. "I had my pistol in my hand under the robe. And then the voice in my earpiece told me to come home."

"And you walked away?"

"Nobody knew a damn thing had happened," Paul replied, and for the first time in Feathers' experience, he smiled. "But that's history, Commander. You've got a Level Alpha mission of your own, now."

"What does that involve, exactly?"

"What do you want?"

Feathers looked curiously at the other man. "What can I have?"

Paul smiled. "You want a squadron of F-15s on permanent alert?"

"I could have that?"

"How about the Sixth Fleet moved across the world to shell Libya?"

"Seriously?"

"No." Paul smiled. "But the F-15s you can have. And a couple of platoons of Marines, too."

"And if I need them?"

"Call me."

"So what next?" asked Feathers.

"Give me ten minutes," said Paul. "Just let me organize the Ashton bulletin." He turned to the monitor and began typing in data. A few moments later, he looked up.

"The hunt will be called off," he said. "But it could take time to filter through to every patrolman on the beat. If he gets taken, and you find out, go to see the most senior police officer you can find. Keep pulling rank, or making a noise until you get to the station commander. Tell him that you're taking over Ashton and that the prisoner will be released into your custody. You show him your Intelligence Card and tell him it's a security code Alpha Nine. He'll look at you as if you're a man from Mars, but he'll go along with it."

"Power, eh?" Feathers was awed by Paul's words.

"It can corrupt, remember," Paul replied. "That's why we're here. We're the watchers."

"And who watches the watchers?"

"Don't ask," said Paul. "Don't even think about it. We might be the last thin line. Okay, Feathers, Operation Spartacus is running."

A little overwhelmed, Feathers began to plot his mission.

Verity regarded the police officer with suspicion. The patrolman was sitting across from his desk and looked uncomfortable.

"Verity, this is damned uncomfortable, I have to tell you," he said. "But the station sent me out to talk to you. Orders."

"Okay, Jim, so they've sent you. What do you want?" Verity was firm and unmoving in his coolness, despite the fact that he and the cop had known each other for some years and shot together at the local gun club.

"Where's Christiana?" asked the cop.

"No idea," Verity replied. "Why?"

"Somebody thinks she can help them locate Mark Ashton."

"And who's Mark Ashton?"

"For Christ's sake, Nick, lay off me, will you? You know I'd do anything to help you and Chris! When did I last give you a speeding ticket, despite the crazy way you race round the town? This is official."

"I know that, Jim. But when you come in here with that damned pistol on your belt, your peaked hat on your eyebrows, and arrest warrants hanging from your nuts, I get a tad uneasy."

The cop grinned self-consciously. "Sorry, Nick," he said. "Guess I got a bit excited about arresting Christiana. Thought maybe I could search her for deadly weapons."

"Arrest?" Verity looked hard at the cop. "Did you say arrest Chris?"

"No! No way," the cop replied. "Sorry, Nick, didn't actually mean that. No, the captain got a call from Chicago asking us to question her about the whereabouts of this Mark Ashton."

"I say again, who is this Mark Ashton?" Verity had adopted his cool, disinterested pose again.

"He's wanted in Evanston, Illinois for the murder of a John Doe."

"And why would he be here? Why would Chris know where he is?"

"Beats me, Nick," replied the cop. "I'm just a dumb patrolman. Ask me to count to eleven and I have to take my shoes and socks off."

At last, Verity smiled. "You shoot better that way, as well," he said, and the cop laughed.

"But this is for real, Nick," said the officer. "Do you know where she is?"

"No, I don't," Verity replied. "She asked me for a few days off, and she left yesterday."

"Bit sudden, don't you think?"

"Not really," said Verity with a shrug. "She's getting antsy as hell about working for Crawford, and he's been getting worse than usual these days. She wanted time away from him."

"Who wouldn't?" the cop muttered. "Ten minutes with that creep and I'd be reaching for my pistol."

"What, shoot that great patriotic, all-American savior of his nation, Randy Crawford?" Nick grinned cheerfully.

"In a New York minute," replied the patrolman. "So, you've no idea where she is?"

Before Verity could answer, the door swung open, and Crawford walked in. His face was bruised and both eyes looked red. The nose was badly misshapen and swelled way over its normal size.

Crawford didn't look at Verity. Instead, he stared down at the seated police officer. "I saw the patrol car outside," he said. "I suppose you're looking for that little jerk, Ashton?"

The police officer stared at Crawford for a second or two, then turned his gaze on Verity. "Am I?" he asked. Verity shrugged.

"You said you hadn't seen him, Nick," the cop complained.

"No I didn't," replied Nick. "I simply asked who he was."

"Has he been here?"

"Damned right, he's been here!" Crawford bellowed. "They were both in this goddammed office just days ago! So you can bet your life they're off together somewhere."

"Nick?" The cop refused to acknowledge Crawford and looked firmly at Verity.

"They were in here," Verity admitted. "Mark was visiting the station. Chris showed him round."

"And what happened after that?"

"I don't know," replied Verity. "I think they went to dinner together, and Mark returned to Chicago the next day."

"Not before he'd fucked her brains out," Crawford snapped, still standing by the door.

Verity smiled gently up at him. "Jealous, Randy?"

"Shut up!" snorted Crawford. "That murdering bastard and the foreign bitch are off somewhere together, and I hope they both get arrested. She's harboring a known fugitive."

"Verity, I have to ask you again," said the cop. "Do you know where they are?"

"Course he does," Crawford shouted. "Look, officer, take this bastard in! He's interfering with the operation of the law."

The cop studied Crawford intently for a few moments, then looked back at Verity.

"Who re-arranged his face, Verity?" he asked. "You?"

Verity smiled coldly. "Nasty accident," he said. "Randy fell over in front of my desk. You can see, it's very slippery right there."

"Jesus Christ!" grated Crawford. "Officer, I'm laying charges right now! I want this man arrested for assault."

Before anyone could say anything, the radio on the police officer's belt crackled into life. The cop touched a button on the microphone hanging from his tunic.

"This is Officer Weekes," he said.

"Cancel the APB on Ashton," the radio crackled. "Return to base."

"Acknowledged," the cop replied, and rose to his feet. He walked up to Verity's desk and studied the thick carpet. "Damned dangerous, that," he said. "Take care, Mister Verity, or I'll have to cite you for dangerous working conditions."

"I'll do that," agreed Verity poker-faced. "Do I understand you're no longer looking for Mark Ashton?"

"Correct," said the cop.

"What?" Crawford dripped saliva on his shirt. "He's a murdering son-of-a-bitch! He left his fingerprints all over the knife he killed that guy with. What the hell do you mean, you're calling off the search?"

The cop looked coolly at Crawford. "Which words didn't you understand, Mister Crawford?" he asked.

Crawford's face was red under the bruises. "Jesus Christ! I'll have you for insubordination!" he yelled. "And I'm laying charges against this bastard for assault!"

The cop stared firmly into Crawford's furious eyes, then looked back at Verity.

"Would you stand up, please, Mister Verity?" he asked.

Crawford grinned. "About damned time!" he said in triumph as Verity rose to his feet.

"What are you, Nick?" asked the cop. "Five-nine and a hundred and seventy pounds?"

"Give or take," Verity replied.

The cop turned to Crawford. "And you, sir," he said. "Six-four and two-twenty? You're sure you want to charge Mister Verity with assault? Going to look mighty silly in court, I think. And all the press there, taking photos of the two of you. Not good for the public image, I imagine."

Baffled and furious, Crawford could only stare back at the patrolman. The cop turned back to Verity.

"Get that dangerously slippery spot fixed, Mister Verity," he said, struggling to keep the laugh away. "Mister Crawford here might have another nasty accident any moment."

"Right away, officer," said Verity, not hiding his grin.

Crawford muttered something unintelligible and walked out, the door again refusing him the luxury of slamming it.

"What the hell's going on, Jim?" asked Verity when the door had finally closed.

"Dunno," the other replied. "Very unusual for an APB to be called off like that, unless they've found him. But Dispatch didn't say anything about finding him. I'll call you if I hear anything."

"Do that," said Verity.

"And you can call the two lovebirds and tell them all's clear," said the cop.

Verity looked astonished. "Me? How the hell would I know where to contact them?"

"Yeah, yeah." The officer sneered and walked out more calmly than Crawford had done.

* * *

"Detective-Sergeant Chenoweth!"

Frank Chenoweth looked up from his desk at the unusually formal mode of address from the Lieutenant. They had been friends for years, and ranks were only for special occasions or for sarcasm between the two of them.

"Yes, sir?" he replied, deciding to stay equally formal for safety. Norman Hobson looked dangerously upset.

"The Captain just called me into his office," said Hobson. "The APB for Mark Ashton is called off."

"Huh?" Chenoweth was astonished. "Called off? Who called it off? Have they found him in Virginia?"

"No, they haven't found him in Virginia, or any other fucking place," Hobson snapped. Chenoweth was almost as astonished by the expletive as he was by the news.

Norman Hobson was a devout Christian, a family man, and foul language was almost unheard of in his presence. The sergeant looked his puzzlement at his superior.

Hobson sat down wearily in the chair across from the other. "The word came down from somewhere so rarefied, the goddammed eagles would need oxygen," he grated, and leaned his elbows on the sergeant's desk. "Hands off Ashton. I'd say your sky-scraping Naval buddy had something to do with it."

Chenoweth sat back in his chair thoughtfully. "You're probably right," he said. "The whole shit-heap always smelled bad, I thought. I could never see Ashton doing that sort of thing, anyway, and if Feathers was here on official business, I'd say the Navy thought the same thing."

"Or someone who tells the Navy what to think," Hobson suggested.

Chenoweth looked startled. "Christ! That *is* high up! It's not just oxygen those eagles would need. They'd want a bloody jet engine, too."

A tiny grin sneaked over the lieutenant's face. "And a pressurized ass. C'mon, Frank, you owe me a beer."

"Yes, sir!" snapped Chenoweth with military precision. "But here's a thought. If we've got the whole of the FBI, the CIA, the National Security Agency and every spook from here to Alaska working on this, you can bet your ever-loving ass we'll have the bastard that actually did it, before too long."

"Not if it's another spook, we won't," Hobson replied with a gloomy expression.

"Right," Chenoweth agreed. "I think we need a scotch, instead of a beer."

"A scotch *and*, Detective-Sergeant Chenoweth, a scotch *and*."

"A scotch and, it is, sir," Chenoweth agreed.

"Two scotches and, Frank."

"You buy the scotches, sir, I'll buy the ands."

"Seems fair. Let's go. I think we're done with the Ashton case."

* * *

"Nick, there's a man called Featherstone here to see you."

Verity gave a puzzled look at his telephone. The receptionist's voice had an unusual note of excitement in it.

"Featherstone? Does he say what he wants?"

"No, just that it's important."

"Okay, why don't you bring him round?"

"Sure thing."

Verity replaced the phone and returned to the thorny problem of covering the production schedule with one less producer than usual. His nerves were tight. Since the astonishing news the day before that the hunt for Mark had been called off, Verity had been trying to call the cellular phone in the cabin and getting nowhere. The recorded operator's voice had calmly informed him that the phone was unattended or the vehicle had left the area.

"They're not in a goddammed vehicle," muttered Verity as he tried for the tenth time the night before, just after nine o'clock, and got nowhere. He was certain that he had told Christiana to switch the phone on between six and ten.

He forced his mind back to the programming schedule, and wished he could get Christiana back, if only to run the Crawford program. For all her distaste for the task, she was still the best at handling Crawford.

His thoughts were interrupted by the door opening, and he looked up. And up. One of the biggest men Verity had ever seen off the basketball court walked in. The man was a giant, but his bearing told Verity something. His visitor was military. Verity stood up and extended his hand.

"I'm Verity," he said, cricking his neck up to meet the eye of the powerful, ebony face of the other man. Verity saw intelligence in the dark eyes, and a smile on the wide, handsome mouth.

"Lieutenant-Commander Featherstone, US Navy," said the huge man. "You were a marine?"

"Special Forces," Verity replied, surprised and a little more relaxed by the obvious friendliness in the other man.

"Verity? Just Verity?"

"Just Verity."

"Okay. Call me Feathers."

"Feathers?"

"That's what Mark called me."

"Ah!" Verity completed the process of relaxing. "You knew Mark in the navy?"

"My best buddy. Bit of a dumb-ass, but not a bad dumb-ass as dumb-asses go."

Verity laughed outright. "And now you're looking for him?"

"I sure am. I got the hunt called off, 'cos there's no way Mark killed anyone. And there's something horribly smelly jamming up the works."

"*You* got it called off? How does a naval commander get a police manhunt called off?"

"Connections." Feathers looked firmly into Verity's eyes.

Verity studied the other man. "You're not just navy, are you?"

Feathers nodded. "Naval Intelligence."

"No," said Verity. "Not even Naval Intelligence gets a national APB called off before evidence has pinned the crime on someone else. Who the hell are you, Feathers? Or more accurately, *what* the hell are you?"

The massive face looked at Verity like an ancient Zulu warrior studying the opposing battle lines.

I don't want this man as an enemy, thought Verity with a small chill.

"I can't tell you any more," replied Feathers after a short silence. "But I guarantee it Verity, I'm on Mark's side."

"I really wish I could believe you," said Verity. "But you walk in here, making claims that are barely believable, and say you're Mark's friend. How can I risk the lives of two people who are definitely my friends without knowing more?"

"Mark and Christiana?"

"You know about Christiana?"

Feathers grinned. "The night before Mark came here the other week, he and I had a few beers in a bar in Washington. He was nervous as a rat at a cat-show about coming here and meeting her. A few days later, I got a note from him. He said the network of talk-show hosts was over forty, and a lot of calls were set-ups. I know about that, 'cos he told me how he recognized the voice of a seaman we both once knew, claiming to be a Marine Captain in the Gulf War. And his last words were that Christiana was absolutely gorgeous."

Despite his worries, Verity laughed. "Feathers, you almost convince me," he said. "But I still have two friends to worry about. Never mind a wife and a son called John Power."

"John Power?" Feathers looked amused.

"One hell of a positive name, I thought. Good for a kid. And I want him to play the organ when he grows up."

"So you named him after E. Power Biggs? The finest organist of the modern age?"

"Well, you may be a spook, Feathers, but you're an educated spook."

Feathers laughed, a mighty bellow that shook the office walls. "All right, Verity, I understand your problem, and I admire the resistance. Can you locate him?

"I'm trying to," Verity admitted. "Having a little difficulty, right now."

"Does he know the hunt's called off?"

"No way," answered Verity.

"When you make contact, tell him to call me. I'll give you a special number. You think you can describe me accurately enough?"

"Just about," replied Verity, not hiding the laugh. Despite his concerns, he felt great liking and trust for this huge naval officer. He took the card that Feathers passed across to him and noted the number. It had a Washington area code.

"Spooksville?" he asked with a smile.

"The Spooksville high rent district," said Feathers, and his grin lit up the office as if Verity had switched on the arc lights in the ceiling. "Call me there if you have any problems."

"I'll do that," replied Verity and stood up as Feathers rose to his feet like a giraffe reaching for a high leaf.

* * *

Vince Jerome studied the man in the other armchair thoughtfully, looking with interest at the bruises on the man's face. Crawford clutched his glass of bourbon and stared gloomily at the wall.

"When did you hear that the manhunt had been called off?" asked Jerome.

"This afternoon," Crawford replied. "I was actually in Verity's office when the cop came in looking for the Girard woman to ask them both about Ashton. The cop got the message on his radio right there and then."

"What exactly was said?"

Crawford looked embarrassed. "Just that the APB was cancelled. No explanation."

"And the patrolman just left?"

"Yes." Crawford wouldn't meet Jerome's eye. He took a sip of the bourbon and hunched in his seat, his long legs close together as if to ward off a blow.

"You think Ashton and this woman Christiana are somewhere together in hiding?" Jerome asked.

Crawford nodded and took another large mouthful of the whiskey. "Damn right," he muttered. "That bastard was in the studio a couple of days after the murder in Evanston, cuddling up to Verity and the broad as if they were having a threesome. You could tell, Ashton could hardly keep his hands off the woman." The anger in his

262

face made the bruises glow almost with an internal light. Jerome saw it and kept his amusement under control.

"But did you see Ashton return?" asked Jerome.

"No." Crawford shook his head. "But she vanished from the place the day I told my listeners about him. Those two are having an affair all right."

"Try and keep your personal jealousy out of this, will you, Crawford?" said Jerome softly. "Your animosity to the woman is based more on your frustrated desires than your concerns about our project, I believe."

Crawford's hand squeezed convulsively on his glass and he stared down at his lap like a chastised schoolboy. Jerome looked at him with contempt.

"However," he said, alleviating his tone of criticism, "you were right to bring this to my attention. We had decided Ashton's attacks on you were getting a shade too close and we initiated his removal. His disappearance is annoying."

Crawford stared at the older man. "You set it up? You mean Ashton didn't kill that guy?"

"Of course not," replied Jerome derisively. "What possible reason could there be for him to do so? No, one of our people acquired the knife from Ashton's apartment and found a suitable target."

"Jesus Christ!" Crawford finished his drink. "You people don't mess around, do you?"

Jerome didn't favor the comment with a reply, and Crawford looked embarrassed.

"I suggest you make no further mention of this affair on the program," continued Jerome. "But let me ease your mind on Ashton. I believe I know where he is."

"You do? How the hell did you...?" Crawford fell silent under the cold gaze of Jerome.

"This operation is thorough, Crawford," said Jerome. "Once you mentioned possible hostility from Verity and the Girard female, we investigated both. Verity acquired a cabin in the mountains about a year ago. We found the records in the land office files and I have the precise location. Action is being taken immediately."

"You're going to have him killed? Good! And her too, I hope. I'd give anything to be in on that."

Jerome gave him a cold smile. "Crawford, your function is to influence public opinion. Leave anything else to us."

Recognizing the danger, Crawford put his glass on the table beside him, and stood up. "I should be getting back," he muttered.

Jerome nodded. "Yes, you should," he agreed, and touched a button by his armchair.

Five minutes later, Crawford had been shown to the front door and was in his Cadillac on the way back to Martinsburg.

As soon as he had left the office, Jerome picked up the telephone.

"Something very curious has developed," he said when the soft voice of Charles Dansbury answered.

"Yes?"

"The manhunt for Ashton has been cancelled."

The silence echoed down the line for several seconds before Dansbury broke it. "I agree. That is very curious. I thought you had that tightly nailed down."

"So did I," Jerome replied. "I applied the normal pressures at Federal level and also in Illinois. There should have been no difficulty."

"And the source of this order?"

"Unknown. Can you make some inquiries? I'll ask my contacts."

"Of course. Call me tomorrow with any progress."

"I will."

Jerome replaced the phone. It had been many years since any conversation with Charles Dansbury had occurred without some mocking references to each other's relative ages. Jerome was more disturbed than he could recall. He picked up the phone again.

"Senator? It's Vince Jerome."

"Vince! An unexpected pleasure, old friend." Senator Bryce Lombard's tones were full of warmth. "What can I do for you?"

"I'm not sure, Bryce. I wonder if you know why the manhunt for Mark Ashton has been called off?"

"Mark Ashton? The man who gave Crawford so much distress on three separate occasions? I had heard something like that had happened."

"And do you know who initiated such an order?"

"No, Vince, I don't. But there's something odd going on."

"Odd? Can you clarify, Bryce?"

"I called friends in the West Virginia state legislature this morning on the subject. They advised me that the FBI had requested the cancellation of the APB for Ashton. But when I called our man at the FBI, he denied all knowledge of issuing such a request."

"And did you find any more?" Jerome's sense of disturbance was growing.

"Nothing. It's very odd. Have you any further information?"

"I don't. Bryce, if you find out anything, you will let me know?"

"Of course, Vince. As soon as I hear."

"Thank you, old friend."

Jerome hung up once more, and wondered why he should feel so unsettled by this small event. Nothing of importance happened in the United States that he didn't know of, or had a hand in implementing. A gap in his knowledge was profoundly worrying. He took hold of his walking stick and thoughtfully tapped the silver head with his forefinger.

* * *

The chill air of the mountains had recaptured the interior of the cabin after the log fire had expired soon after midnight. Mark and Christiana had no objections. They were cuddled closely together under the goose-down quilt of the capacious bed, Christiana lying on Mark's shoulder in the protective curl of his arm.

"I may be a wanted criminal," he murmured, still a little sleepy, "but I can't remember being happier."

"Me too," she whispered, and kissed his neck. "If this is what it takes to make these few days happen, I've no objections."

"I'm not sure how this happened," he said. "I was just hoping for a safe place to hide in. I didn't set out to get you into bed, attractive as the proposition was."

"I think it was just a cold night, and I felt sorry for you on the couch."

"No regrets?"

"None at all, silly man. Do I sound regretful?"

"Not that I can detect. But we have to do something about the mess in the outside world, sooner or later," he said, finally waking up. He sat up straight, a wave of worry running through him as he came fully aware of his situation. "Christiana, I'm still a man wanted for murder! Somehow I have to contact Feathers. He's probably the only one I can trust and who can do something positive. Is there any way of making a call other than one of us driving into town?"

"Oh God, I forgot," she murmured. "Verity left us a cellular phone. I was supposed to leave it switched on each evening in case anything happened."

"Okay, can you call him first? Then I'll try and contact Feathers."

"Let's have breakfast first. It may be a busy morning."

"Let's pray for something positive to happen." Mark smiled down at her, still snuggled in the eiderdown. He didn't feel as happy as he thought he should be, with this beautiful woman in his bed.

She reached out and touched his hand. "It will."

An hour later, however, they were dressed and finishing off the massive meal of bacon and eggs. The combination of the mountain air, the walks in the woods and their intensive athletics in the huge bed had given them enormous appetites.

267

"You're bad for me, Ashton," she complained with a wide smile, as she gathered up the plates. "I'm getting as fat as a heifer."

"Not a chance," he said and patted her rear as he stood up to prepared to wash up. "I plan to work you far too hard each night for that. It's excellent exercise, very aerobic."

"Very satisfying, I grant you that," she said. "If you're going to be all house-trained and do the washing up, I'll call Verity."

"Do that," he agreed, and poured liquid soap into the sink. She reached up and kissed his cheek, then walked out of the kitchen. A few moments later, Mark heard the beeps of the phone as she punched the numbers for the radio station.

She spoke briefly then re-appeared, carrying the phone. Her face was serious.

"You'd better talk to Verity," she said, and held the phone up to his face as Mark grabbed a towel and began drying his hands. Her clear eyes looked firmly into his as he talked.

"Verity? Hi, what's up?"

"Describe Feathers to me," said Verity. His tone was calm. Mark's heart missed a beat.

"Feathers? As in goose-down, or as in six-five and two-fifty pounds of naval intelligence?"

"Not goose-down," Verity replied. Mark almost heard the grin over the airwaves. "Friend of yours?"

"The very best," said Mark. He took the phone from Christiana's hand and touched her cheek. "He's called?"

"He came in two days ago, just after you'd left. I needed to identify friend or foe."

"Friend. Definitely friend. Any message?"

"Call him. Here's a number." Verity recited the seven digits, and Mark filed them into his memory, a trick he had learned as a child. He knew he would not forget those numbers.

"And he wants to know where you are," continued Verity. "Can I tell him?"

"Of course," said Mark. "What else is happening?"

"Crawford's face is like a Tequila sunrise. Chris will explain that."

"Your doing, young Verity?"

"Special Forces taught me a thing a two."

"Special Forces? Man, you didn't tell me!"

"You didn't ask."

"True. Anything else?"

"The manhunt for you is called off."

"What?"

"Feathers pulled strings, it seemed. You're clear to return."

"Nick, that's incredible!"

"Roughly what I said. Crawford is rather less pleased, for some reason."

"Can't imagine why."

"So when are you coming back down? Have you left any food in the place?"

"Couple of dried biscuits and a lamb chop or two."

"Healthy appetites, eh?" Verity's laugh was obvious. "Mountain air does that to you."

"It's not the air." Mark chuckled, feeling as light-headed as a child on its birthday. A load had been lifted from him, and he wanted to shout with delight. He wrapped his free arm round Christiana's waist and pulled her close. "I'll discuss it with this young lady here," he said into the phone. "We'll get back to you."

"Within the year, please," said Verity.

"Maybe," replied Mark, and switched the phone off. "The man-hunt's off," he said, put the phone down on the kitchen table and wrapped his other arm round her.

"Oh, thank God!" she exclaimed, and buried her face in his neck.

"We can go back to Martinsburg right away," he murmured.

"Do you want to?"

"Do you?"

"There's a lot of food still in the freezer," she said softly. "And I haven't had a holiday in two years." Her arms tightened round his neck.

"I'm glad you're thinking that way," he said softly. "We can manage a couple more nights here, perhaps?"

"I can probably stand it," she said. "If you can."

"I'll force myself," he whispered into her ear.

* * *

"Feathers? Verity."

"Hi there, Special Forces. The love-birds have called in?"

"They have. And Mark vouches for you. For some reason, he seems to think highly of you."

"Glad to hear it. Mark was always a man of great perception and wisdom. Where are they?"

"My cabin in the mountains. Got email access where you are?"

"Sure. You have the address."

"I'll send you a map. You'd better call on them. I don't reckon they're ready to see daylight for a while yet."

"Okay. Thanks, Verity. One thing more. Who knows about this cabin?"

"Nobody but my family."

"You bought it all legal?"

"Sure did. Why?"

"So they'll be some records somewhere?"

"In the county offices, sure."

"I just keep thinking of how some dangerous people traced Mark's cellular phone and located his address so that they could pin a murder rap on him."

"How did they do that, Feathers?"

"Another time, Verity. But it wasn't legal, and the results weren't nice."

"And you think the same people might be looking for him again?"

"Does Crawford talk crap on the radio?"

"I see your point. Look after my friends, Feathers."

"Me and a squadron of F-15s."

"What?"

"Forget it. Just a silly thought."

"Call me when you hear anything."

"You bet. Gotta go, Nick. Email me that map. Immediate."

"Three minutes."

* * *

"Where the hell's Jimmie?" Crawford demanded. "The meeting's supposed to have started ten minutes ago."

Janice looked nervous. "I don't know, Randy," she replied. "He got a phone call late yesterday, and took off without a word. I haven't heard from him."

"Shit!" swore Crawford. "How the hell am I supposed to run a program without my assistants?"

Janice didn't bother with a reply. She took a few papers from her briefcase and placed them on Crawford's desk.

Crawford looked as if he would sweep the papers from his desk in a rage, then subsided. "Okay," he said, "we'll just have to manage. What have we got here, Janice?"

Chapter 13 - The Appalachians

Christiana and Mark sat on wicker armchairs at the rear door of the cottage, gazing at the spectacular view across the valley. The low evening sun stretched the shadows of trees in a jet line over immense distances of hills. Fragile fingers of high cirrus cloud were like gold-tinted ferns reaching up to protect this scene from the rest of the world. Little reason to speak had occurred. Occasionally, they looked at each other and smiled, and once, Mark reached over and touched her hand. He could not remember ever having felt so happy and at peace with the world. His only question was how Feathers had called off the manhunt, but he had no doubts that Feathers and his TF5 organization were responsible.

The gentle silence was mildly scarred by the soft "wop-wop-wop" of a helicopter somewhere in the distance. It broke the hypnotic hold of the view.

"We should probably head back tomorrow," Mark murmured. He hated the idea.

"I suppose so," replied Christiana. "Even Adam and Eve had to leave the garden sometime."

He smiled. "Not for doing what we've been doing, I think."

"Apples were definitely the last thing on my mind," she agreed, and took his hand. "Mark, my love, this has been the happiest time ever."

"Yes, it has." He squeezed her hand. "Will you marry me?"

"Of course," she replied. "What other possible course of action is there for us, you silly man?"

"None at all. How long does it take to get a license?"

"I've no idea. The question hasn't come up before."

"Then that's the best reason I can think of for getting back. We can always come here again another time."

"We may never let Verity back in his cottage again," she said with a laugh.

Mark sipped at his beer, then put the glass down, sat upright and stared into the woods.

"What's the problem?" she asked.

"I thought I saw someone."

"Probably just someone out for a break, like us," she replied. "There must be other cabins around."

"Possibly." Mark felt the hair rising on the back of his neck. "Christiana, go with me on this. I'm feeling a little edgy. Let's go inside."

The alarm on her face was strong. "Mark?" she said hesitantly. But she stood up with him, and they moved back inside the cabin.

"Just a creepy feeling," he said, and touched her cheek. "Probably nothing, but I like to play safe. I keep remembering how someone traced me and stole a knife from my apartment. It's made me paranoid, especially with you here."

"You want the rifle or the shot-gun?" No sign of anxiety showed in her face.

He smiled. "You are, without doubt, dearest love, the most wonderful woman in the world. The shot-gun. And we'll get married next week, even if we have to go to Las Vegas or Reno, or somewhere like that."

She moved away from him and found her handbag with the keys as Mark stared out of the window. There! He was certain. Two men in combat greens moving through the trees. They had flickered in and out of his vision in the darkening scenery, but they were no tourists. Hunters, maybe, but Mark felt horribly certain that he and Christiana were the prey.

She was back by his side, holding the pump-action shot-gun. She seemed to display no hesitation or uncertainty in holding the weapon, and Mark looked a question at her.

"Farm-girl," she said shortly. "We lived on a three-hundred-acre property in the Eastern Townships. "I know guns."

"So I see," he replied, noting that the weapon was loaded.

"Staying in or going out?" she asked calmly, though her face was pale.

"You're in, I'm out," he said. "Stay away from windows. I'll just have a look around."

He moved to the front door of the cabin. The distance from the door to the trees was only a few yards. Mark stared hard at the woods but could see no sign of life. He chanced it and ran for the trees, stopping motionless as soon as he was in cover. After a couple of minutes, he moved deeper into the woods and began circling round the cabin. Every few moments, he stopped and froze against a tree, but he saw nothing.

His nerves began to tighten up. He was certain he had seen men in combat greens, and was equally certain they were not hunters. Fear for Christiana began to gnaw at him. He moved again, and through a clearing, saw the cabin about sixty yards away. Once more, he stopped and studied the area.

With a roar that almost stopped his heart, a heavy-caliber rifle exploded. One of the windows of the cabin vaporized as a shell slammed through and into the inside wall. A second and third bullet crashed into the solid log walls of the cabin, and the building shook from the impact. Mark felt his nerves constrict and a wave of panic hit him, as he thought of Christiana alone in the barrage. He fought to control himself, thought back to training school in the navy and told himself firmly that he had undergone basic combat training as well as his professional linguistic and intelligence studies.

He studied the general area from which the bullets had come and gradually delineated the outlines of the man behind a tree. Hatred ran through him like storm waters. He began to move toward the rifleman, taking incredible care with each step, ensuring no twigs lay underfoot to betray him with a snap, no leaves to rustle as his foot pushed them aside.

He and the rifleman saw each other at the same moment. In nightmare slowness, the other man's rifle swung toward Mark who flung himself toward the shelter of a tree and tried to bring the shotgun to bear on the target at the same time. The tree exploded into sawdust a foot from his head as Mark threw himself lengthways, rolled, and got off a shot. The gathering gloom in the clearing was flashed into brief daylight as the heavy shot-gun bellowed. But the other man had vanished.

Shaking with the shock and the brief, thunderous action, Mark moved as smoothly as he could to another spot, feeling his spine crawling with the possibility that the other man had him in his sights. But he made it to safety without another killing roar of the rifle.

Christ, he may be as shit-scared as I am, he thought, and took fractional comfort from that thought. He thought back to the shot he had seen crash through the window, and decided the trajectory had been too high to hurt Christiana, unless she had been standing by the window, and he was certain she had not. But the merest notion of her being hurt sent a torrent of wild, hate-filled rage through every vein and artery of his body. He tightened his grip on the gun and moved on. Dark was falling fast now, and the trees around him had merged into a gloomy background which hid killing danger.

He looked around him. The cabin was visible in the clear area about fifty yards away, still well lit in the last rays of sunlight. Mark could see no signs of life inside, and he blessed Christiana's coolness. She was staying well away from windows. He moved further round, staying the same distance from the cabin.

As he crossed a tiny clear patch, he barely had time to sense the danger, heard the tiny movement of a rifle muzzle brushing against a leaf, and the world exploded in red and gold fire. Completely without thought, Mark threw himself into the trees, his heart thumping and cold sweat breaking out all over him. He rolled into the cool undergrowth, mercifully aware that he hadn't been hit.

But he had no more time for prayers of thanks. A pair of hands seized him with a power that Mark could barely believe. One arm wrapped around the lower half of his face, another hand snapped on his left wrist, wrapped his arm into a painful bond that chained his body, and Mark was as helpless as a baby wrapped in swaddling clothes. Fear gushed through him with a wave of panic and grief that the game was over, the dreams of a wonderful life with Christiana had just died, and he struggled for breath against the steel arm against his mouth.

"Just relax, Mister Ashton," a soft voice said in his ear. "We're the good guys."

Mark's bones felt like they had turned to sand. He went limp in the astoundingly professional grip of his captor, and the pressure on his face eased a fraction. Mark knew that he couldn't move a muscle. Whoever was holding him had him like a boa constrictor crushing a pig.

"I'm going to ease off you a little, Mister Ashton," the voice whispered. "Now, you won't do anything silly, will you? Or say a word?"

The tiniest fraction of movement occurred in the hawser across his face, and Mark was able to shake his head roughly a millimeter.

"Good," said the voice, and Mark was free. He took a deep breath and slowly turned to see what manner of man had captured him with such astonishing force.

There was little to see. The other man was dressed in black, almost Ninja-like, though his face was uncovered. Dark stains covered the highlights of cheeks and nose. The man was only Mark's height, and Mark knew he was in the hands of a highly trained military expert, a killer without doubt. He carried no gun that Mark could see, or any other weapon. The lack of armaments in no way reduced the fear Mark felt. This man clearly needed no assistance.

"My name's Paul Kent," the man said in the softest of tones. "I'm a friend of Feathers."

Mark felt the breath go out of him as he had been holding it for hours. Remembering his promise, he didn't speak. Kent nodded in silent appreciation. He simply waved Mark with him, and began to move slowly through the woods. Not the tiniest of sounds came from the movement, making Mark feel as clumsy as a rhinoceros crashing through undergrowth.

Kent stopped, and touched Mark briefly on the arm, bringing him to a halt as well. Kent pointed. It took Mark a few moments to see what was ahead. About thirty yards away, two men were standing together. Mark could just make out the green clothing and the heavy rifles carried by both. Without Kent's warning, Mark knew he would have walked straight into them. He felt ashamed at his foolhardiness in venturing into the woods like this. The job was for professionals, and in comparison with Paul Kent, Mark knew he was a rank amateur.

He and Kent stayed in the shadow of the trees and watched the other two. He heard a minute whispering but could make out no words. A movement of Kent's hand directed Mark's attention to a spot to one side of the cabin. After a moment, Mark saw a third man slowly moving to join the other two. Like the others, he was dressed in combat greens, barely visible in the trees.

As the three came together, one of them raised his rifle and fired another shot at the cabin. The explosion lit up the three men for a fraction of a second and the bullet crashed through a front window. Mark tried to look at the men in the brief light and identify them, but as he did, a second shot bellowed from the cabin. The light of the explosion caused a short glow in what Mark knew was the kitchen then a scream was dragged out of one of the three men. The victim had been hit in the upper body and he sagged back against a tree. The other two jumped into the shadows, and Mark could just see the outlines of the injured man being pulled deeper into cover.

"The lady knows how to use a rifle," Kent whispered. Even in the barely heard tones, Mark detected the amusement, and finally relaxed, knowing he was with an ally.

"Okay, Mister Ashton," said Kent. "There are only four of them, and one is now *hors de combat*, courtesy of your lady. I want you to go back inside the cabin, making *very* certain that she knows who's coming in. I'll follow the bad guys for a while, see where they go. Okay?"

Not daring to speak, Mark nodded, and saw a small flash of white teeth. "Talk to you later," said Kent, and vanished. Mark had no idea of how he had moved so fast. Trying not to think about what Kent was really capable of, Mark moved cautiously toward the cabin. He reached the door, and called out softly, "Christiana, it's Mark! We're okay. Open the door."

From a window to one side, Christiana spoke. "When did you propose to me?"

Despite the shattering events of the last hour, Mark grinned happily. It was the perfect question to confirm his identity. Nobody else could know the answer. He decided yet again, that Christiana was simply the most incredible woman he had ever met. Such cool-headed behavior in the face of gunfire made her equal to any combat instructor Mark had ever met.

"About thirty minutes ago, sitting in the armchairs by the back door," he replied softly. "You called me a silly man for even questioning it!"

The door rattled, opened, and slid further apart. Mark still couldn't see Christiana, and recognized her wisdom in staying out of sight. She had no idea that the gunmen had moved on and were under the surveillance of the astonishing Paul Kent. He moved swiftly inside and closed the door behind him. Then Christiana was in his arms. He felt her tears on his neck, and stroked her hair like soothing a frightened child.

"You are really amazing," he whispered. "Are you really sure you want to marry some schmuck like me who gets you into this sort of stuff?"

Her body was trembling and she didn't answer for a moment. "You're not getting away that easily, Ashton," she finally said softly. "But you sure as hell add an extra dimension to the act of courtship."

"No point in making it too easy," he replied, sensing the enormous exhilaration of danger faced and overcome. He hugged her closer, and felt her own response. For a second or two, he almost surrendered to the temptations then common sense returned.

"There are friends of Feathers out there," he said into her hair. "Whoever the crazies were, you've smashed up one, and a man called Paul Kent is following them. I think his first name is really Clark."

He sensed the chuckle in her, and she moved a little so that she could look at him. Her tears reflected in the moonlight that was now growing and shone through the window.

"And who is this superman?" she asked.

"Damned if I know," he replied. "Feathers works for some super-secret intelligence group. Superman said he's in the same bunch."

"Somebody nasty and powerful is behind Crawford, aren't they? Verity and I decided this had to be the case when we realized how many similar lunatics were in the same network, all getting their instructions from somebody in Washington."

"I think that's what got Feathers involved," he agreed. "It must be some really high-powered people he's with."

He heard a soft call from outside. "Mark? Feathers. All clear, buddy."

Remembering Christiana's approach to identifying him, Mark released Christiana, moved to the window, stayed behind the log wall, and called out into the night. "How did I discover your first name?" he asked.

He heard the laugh, and knew it was his friend. Nobody else had that deep, bass voice. "In a lecture at the academy from Fred McCauley," Feathers replied. "He told us about Tarleton's men before the Battle of Cowpatch."

Mark laughed out loud. "Come on in, Feathers!" he called, and moved to the door to open it. He sensed the reaction in Christiana as the massive bulk darkened the door, and he reached out and took her hand.

"Miss Girard, you are one hell of a shot!" rumbled Feathers and closed the door behind him. He reached out a hand, and Christiana took it with her free one. "I'm real glad to meet you, Ma'am," said the big man. "You seem to have straightened out my little pal here." In the moonlight, his white smile was like that of the Cheshire Cat from *Alice in Wonderland.*

"I think the honor is mine," replied Christiana. "You guys run quite an operation, whoever you are."

Feathers released her hand and began to prowl round the cabin. "We can put the lights on," he said. "Paul and his group have those bastards well under surveillance."

"There were more of you?" asked Mark in astonishment, switching on the lights.

"Quite a bunch, apart from Feathers," said a voice, and Mark spun round, hearing Christiana's gasp of dismay. A man was leaning against the doorway, his arms folded.

Mark took a deep breath. "Paul Kent, I presume?"

"The only one," Kent replied and stood upright. He extended his hand to Mark who took it, then he turned to Christiana.

"Well done, Miss Girard," he said. "I wish everyone could keep a cool head like you did. Where did you learn to shoot like that?"

"A farm," she replied, uncertain about the dramatic appearance of the man.

Mark touched her shoulder. "Superman," he said, and her face relaxed.

"I could hit a running gopher at a hundred yards," she said with a smile, and Kent returned it.

"Or a wild snake at forty yards in the dusk," he replied. "You certainly hurt our friends out there."

"Who were they?" asked Mark.

Feathers shrugged. "We'll know for sure when our men get back. I'll let you know."

Mark nodded. "So what should we do now?"

"Bring you in out of the cold, like my boss said," replied Feathers.

"Task Force Five?" Mark asked and Feathers nodded.

"The police manhunt may be off, but somebody else still wants you," he said. "The boss said to take you in. You can help the action."

"What about Christiana? She's just as much at risk," said Mark with a worried frown.

"We'll look after the lady," Kent replied. "I think you can see that we know how to do that. Christiana, you can help us to flush out the baddies if you get back to your job."

Before anyone could reply, another man walked into the cabin. Like Kent and Feathers, he was dressed in black, black paint on the highlights of his cheeks and nose. Several badges were sewn on the shoulders and sleeve. He carried no weapon other than a pistol in a belt holster. He studied the group like a camera then looked at Kent.

"The area's clear, Commander," he said in clipped tones.

"Any further information?" Kent asked.

The other man nodded. "We tracked them for a while, got their direction then moved ahead. Found a car parked under cover, called in your tracker vehicle and waited. Four guys eventually got themselves to the car. One's dead, one wounded. We have the license plate number, and your man's following them."

"Thanks, Peter," Kent replied and smiled at the others. "Lieutenant Peter Drayson, US Marine Corps," he said by way of introduction.

Mark remembered the helicopter. "How many of you, Lieutenant?" he asked.

He received a cool look from the Marine. "Enough, sir," Drayson replied

Kent grinned cheerfully. "Better get those enough guys back home, Peter," he said.

Drayson nodded and vanished.

Kent looked back at the others. "I was saying we had a way of flushing out the bad guys," he said with a grin aimed at Christiana. "It needs Christiana's help."

"You have an idea?" she asked.

Kent grinned, a wide cheerful smile that almost matched that of Feathers. "I think you'll like it," he said. "It may not show all the nasties behind Crawford, but it will certainly drop the heroic Randy Crawford down the smelliest pit you could ever dream of."

"In that case," said Christiana with a laugh, "I want in. What do I do?"

"Got a beer in this place?" asked Kent. "This will take some time."

Chapter 14 - Frederick, Maryland

The tone of the meeting was volatile, little of the calm confidence that had characterized the previous session.

"Somebody's on to us," Redman snapped. "I thought you two knew everything that went on in Washington. What the hell's going on?" He was sitting in his customary spot at the end of the table. He had refused any refreshment from Angela, the first time this had ever happened, and his dark face glowed with fury.

"Sometimes things develop which we don't catch immediately," Jerome replied as soothingly as he could. "This seems to be one of those cases. But I have no doubts my agents will soon discover how the Ashton situation occurred."

"Jesus Christ, I hope so!" chimed in Geoffrey Payne. "This is the worst thing I've ever heard of! One whisper of this group's activities to the White House, or in Congress, and we can pick up our bat and ball and go home."

"Straight to the penitentiary, more likely," Charles Dansbury responded. His smile was ice-cold. "But have no fear, Geoffrey. The most likely explanation is that some regional police chief decided that the hunt for Ashton was of little value, and that the evidence against him was suspiciously obvious. This group is in no danger."

"I don't buy it, Charles," said Morgan Eckhard. His face was pale and his jawbones stood out rigidly. Tension was running high in the senator. "Vince, you said you located the probable hide-out of Ashton. Presumably you took the appropriate action?"

"I sent out men to take care of the situation, yes," Jerome replied. "I haven't heard back, but I believe we can say Ashton has been eliminated, together with the woman with him."

"What woman?" demanded Eckhard. "When did a woman appear in this?"

"She's the producer for Crawford's show," Jerome answered. For the first time any of the group had seen, Jerome looked unsettled. "She and Ashton had established a relationship. Crawford told me Ashton had visited the station and taken her out to dinner. She disappeared a few days after Ashton did."

"And what happens when the bodies of the two are discovered?" asked Corley Rollings. The General looked calm but his blue eyes were dangerously bright. "That will surely attract exactly the sort of attention to Crawford that we don't need."

"Discovered, General?" Jerome's smile was mocking. "What bodies? My people are professionals. The bodies will be removed and securely disposed of. The most likely conclusion will be that the two of them have left this part of the States and gone elsewhere. Without the police search for Ashton, nobody will be concerned. Crawford will find a new producer and everything will be as before."

"You should have asked me before you did any of this cops-and-robbers stuff," broke in Armstrong. "I could have circulated a story that Ashton was a known drug

287

importer. We could have raided him or set up a roadblock and killed him in a gunfight at any time."

Jerome nodded. "That would have been an excellent approach, Grant, and I commend you for the idea. I wish I had thought of it. But we are now faced with this problem and my men will settle it the best way."

Armstrong sat back with a shrug. "Okay," he said. "Think of me next time."

"I will," said Jerome. "Does this now clear the air?"

"No, it does not!" The Reverend Jackson T. Vanderbilt was irritated. Like Redman, he had refused refreshment and had not spoken to anyone until this moment. "I don't think you've explained anything at all," he said. His voice was almost a shout. "I don't think any police chief called off that hunt. Somebody at the top did it. Now, who the hell is it?"

"Reverend, there really is no group in Washington with that sort of power that I wouldn't know about," said Jerome. His tones were icy and his gaze fixed firmly on Vanderbilt. Most people in Washington would have recognized the danger signals and backed off. An angry Vince Jerome was lethal.

"How would you know if they existed or not, if you didn't know they existed?" Vanderbilt sneered.

"Because almost everyone in power in this country owes some sort of debt to Vince and Charles, that's why," Payne interjected. "Nobody in Washington, or anywhere else, for that matter, would form any sort of operation which could oppose them. It makes no sense."

"Well, I'm suddenly not so sure," murmured Eckhard. He glanced apologetically at Jerome and Dansbury. "It's never been worth mentioning till now, but I do seem to recall picking up some vague rumor of a specialist group who might just be the sort to tackle this situation."

"Tell us more," said Jerome. "What did you hear?"

"Almost nothing," Eckhard replied. "And I gave it no credence, then. I think it's supposed to be a group with complete independence from any party affiliations. I gather their mission is to protect the pure form of American ideals as they would term them. You know, individual freedoms, free speech, full equality of all, that sort of stuff."

"Sounds like a bunch of liberal activists to me," Vanderbilt growled. "Obviously a crowd of democrats. You can bet that bastard in the White House is behind this!"

"Reverend, I don't even know if the rumor I heard has any truth to it," Eckhard responded. "And I don't think the President has ever heard of it. I got the word even before the '92 elections."

"How the hell could such a group operate without the President knowing?" asked Payne. "Who could set up such an operation? And why keep it away from the White House?"

"For obvious reasons, Geoffrey," Eckhard replied smoothly. "A President will always assume that his motives and philosophies are pure-white and perfect. So any sort of super-protective group would be seen as a personal policy device. Imagine what Richard Nixon would have done with such a group had he been able to control it. If there *is* any such operation, which I personally doubt, it would have been set up as a private initiative with backing by a highly selective group of people in the military, Congress and private interests."

"And why the hell would they attack us, then?" demanded Vanderbilt. "Surely to God, we represent the purest, most patriotic motivations of all, to bring America under the rule of God's law and protect the country from her communist enemies?"

"I'm certain we all know that, Reverend," said Jerome. "But purists might disagree. After all, we certainly intend to suspend the Constitution, if only temporarily when we take power, and we will certainly discontinue some of the more liberal rules that we find to interfere with efficient running of the nation. Some might interpret that as being against the spirit of the Founding Fathers."

"Well those are exactly the sort of lunatics we have to get rid of," Vanderbilt shouted.

"As we will, Reverend, as we will," Jerome replied soothingly. "I assure you, that is high on the priority list. But meanwhile, we have to identify such a group, should one exist. Like the senator, I personally doubt it. But we must be certain."

"It was only a rumor." Eckhard looked worried. "I can't even remember where I heard it."

"Then I suggest, Morgan," said Dansbury, "you look very hard to find any evidence for such a group. And if you find it, we need to know who's in it and what their mission is. We're far too far along the path for anything like this to get in the way."

"I don't think I'll find anything," Eckhard protested. "It was just a rumor, and it died."

"Nonetheless, ears to the ground," replied Jerome with a friendly smile. "Like you, I'm certain it was just one of those idealistic rumors which fly around from time to time like urban myths. But we in this group need to be certain. Charles and I will do our own investigating, also."

Eckhard grunted. Jerome looked around the group again. "Is this matter settled?" he asked. "Obviously, if any of us hears anything to support this odd little idea, we will let the rest of know."

A small wave of agreeing murmurs rumbled round the tables.

"Good," said Jerome. "Anything else to be discussed?"

"I wish to raise an issue of national importance." Eckhard's face was tense as if he had been working up his resolve for some time.

"Certainly, Morgan," replied Jerome politely. "What is it?"

"The candidates for the presidential nomination," Eckhard continued. "I know that you have said consistently that I must not run, because the role will be so much smaller, but I've decided that I still want the position."

Jerome smiled. "There is far more important work for you do as part of this group, Morgan. The Presidency will be merely a figurehead when we've done our work. You wouldn't want that, surely?"

"I don't care," Eckhard replied hotly. "It's what I've worked for all my life! I could be more use in the White House than some birdbrain under your orders. I want to run!"

"No, Morgan, you will not run," said Dansbury softly. "We decided that some years ago, and the decision remains."

"And I want to know why not!" Eckhard shouted. "It's damned unfair!"

"You know why not," Dansbury replied. "The press will crucify you."

"Crucify me?" Eckhard was furious. "Why would the press crucify me? I've got nothing to be ashamed of in my past."

"Morgan, this is getting dangerous for you," said Jerome. "I strongly suggest you stop this line of discussion." He took hold of his walking stick and gripped it firmly.

"No, I damn well won't," Eckhard voice was sharp and defiant. "I want to be President!"

"Morgan, you are in this group for one reason and one reason only," said Jerome. The room went silent. "That reason is your wife's family, their money and their power over a lot of people in Congress and the Senate. We need that power to complete our aims. The Presidency is not for you."

"I know you need the Asbury influence," Eckhard replied more calmly. "I'm not stupid. But I can't see why I have to stay in the background. The White House has been my dream since I was a child. Why can't I take it? I know that the position won't be what it has been in the past, but I don't care."

"I'm sorry, Morgan," said Jerome. "I know how much this means to you. But the program demands that we have a puppet President after the next elections. You would lose the election, and that will set back our program."

"Why would I lose it?" Eckhard was angry again. "I've got the perfect image. My war record is good, I'm a family man, there's nothing to muddy up. Vince, I demand this for the last time. Either you endorse my candidacy, or I'll declare it myself this week. I can still run in New

Hampshire and I can raise the money I need without difficulty."

"I will not endorse your candidacy, and you will not run, Morgan." Jerome was icy. "Do you think that I would permit our sixty-year program to be ruined by you?"

"I'm intrigued, Vince," drawled Payne. "It sounds pretty obvious to me that the squeaky-clean, Vietnam hero, family-man senator may not be all that he claims, and you're the one that knows it. What's the real background?"

"This is not the time and place, Geoffrey," said Jerome, looking calmly at Payne. "And you should be the one to know that."

Payne shrugged. "I'm not perfect, Vince, I know that. I drink too much. But that's about all anyone could say."

"Not entirely," Jerome replied, looking irritated.

"Gentlemen." Dansbury's soft voice made the room go quiet. "I think we are all getting a little heated by the events of the last few days. Starting to draw blood from each other is the worst thing that we could do just as we reach the final stages of our long and successful program. Now, let us declare peace. We will have enough combat to suit even Geoffrey when our day comes."

Dansbury looked at each in turn and received a nod of agreement. He looked at Jerome last of all. "Back to you, Mister Chairman," he said.

Jerome smiled briefly. "Thank you, Charles," he said. "Your cool head and wise counsel is invaluable to us. So, gentlemen, is there any other business?"

"I may have a possible additional member to this group," said Eckhard, apparently over his temper. All faces turned to him. "I believe Colin Webber shares our views on the future of this country. I would like to explore the possibilities of recruiting him."

"Do we all know Colin Webber?" Jerome asked. A mixture of nods and shaken heads greeted the question. "Then let me summarize," he continued. "Webber is a man of extraordinary wealth, possibly in excess of fifteen billion dollars, gained from real estate, manufacturing industries, and assorted financial involvements. He has created at least four major corporations, built them up from behind a protective wall of cover-directors, then passed the running of them to others, always keeping himself out of the limelight. He is fifty-three years of age, married to the same lady for thirty years, but has no children. I am unaware of any political affiliation. He seems equally acceptable to all spectra of the political continuum."

"Sounds dammed suspicious to me," Payne growled. "If he's got friends among the liberals, he's no use to this group."

"I disagree," said Dansbury. "The man is a perfect case of an industrial power-house. He needs minimal interference in his business, access to government power when he wants it, and has no desire to be constrained by social considerations, trade unions, and the like. Webber would want the same America that we are striving for and would provide enormous power to our group. He could be a very useful addition, if he checks out clean."

"I agree," Redman concurred, looking a little less angry than before. "This is a self-made man. I imagine he's used unorthodox measures in the past to get where he is. I say we talk to him. We'll need management skills when we take over."

"No children?" asked Vanderbilt. "Is he a fag or something?"

"No more than you are, Reverend," Dansbury said with a soft smile. Vanderbilt's face went red for a few seconds, and he swallowed angrily. Redman laughed noisily, and Vanderbilt's glare turned on him. Redman was unabashed.

"Damn fool question, Reverend," the crime boss scoffed. "I've made lots of bucks out of your taste for little boys. Who the hell do you think has been supplying you, these last few years?"

A wave of scorn and anger ran round the table. Armstrong, Payne and Rollings looked with contempt at Vanderbilt. Rollings looked particularly disgusted.

"Gentlemen!" called Jerome. The room went silent. "This is unnecessary," Jerome continued. "As Charles said earlier, I know that stresses have suddenly been placed on us by the possible appearance of an opposition force, but we must still keep our cohesion. Personalities have no place here. We have our own mission, and that is the only thing that matters."

"It's just such fucking hypocrisy," snarled Payne. "I see this guy on the television acting like Jesus Christ returned, screaming about family values, and pretending to be a family friend of God's. Christ, he practically demands the death penalty for homosexuals and single mothers, and look what he is! He buys little boys from one of Redman's operations? Shit, what'll happen when the press discovers *that* little gem?"

"Geoffrey, that will do!" Jerome snapped. He glared at Payne like an angry father for a few seconds. "Let me remind you," he continued. "All of you here have things you don't want revealed. Starting to attack one another is the worst thing any of you want, I assure you! You can only loose."

"Do I understand that you have some sort of deep intelligence on each of us?" Payne demanded. "You intrigue me, Vince. I'd love to hear more about this select group some day. Especially why the honorable senator here is unsuited to be President of the United States, when he appears to be so popular and so admired throughout the country."

"I have nothing to be ashamed of," Eckhard insisted. "I'm the perfect candidate. I was prepared to stand aside in favor of Lombard, but since the press found out about his wife, I'm the next logical choice. I insist on it, Vince. I *will* run."

"It seems the good senator is determined, Vince," said Rollings. "I for one agree with him that he makes a splendid figurehead, and the delectable Peggy Jo Asbury could not be improved on as a First Lady. Why should he not run?"

Eckhard stared at the General for a few seconds as if trying to work out whether he had been insulted or not. "Yes, Vince," he said defiantly. "Why shouldn't I run?"

Jerome studied his lap for a moment in deep thought. He looked at Charles Dansbury as if asking a question. Dansbury shrugged.

"This is not a good idea, Morgan," said Jerome. His fingers beat an irritated tattoo on the head of his walking stick.

"I want to know," Eckhard insisted.

Jerome echoed Dansbury's shrug. "Colonel Gerald Hanley will report to the press, if asked persistently, that in your one experience of field combat, he found you groveling and weeping in a hiding spot, when you, as the officer in charge of the search-and-destroy mission, should have been leading and directing your men. The Colonel, who was then a sergeant, had to take over the skirmish and fight the action until the men could return to the base. His commission and a healthy cash settlement from the Asbury coffers were his price for silence. After thirty-five years, I'm sure he would talk if offered some sort of inducement."

"Which you would offer him, I suppose," the General said with a cold smile. He looked with contempt at the senator.

"Nobody would believe him," Eckhard snarled. His face was white. "They'd just assume he was looking for a fast buck."

"Maybe," Jerome murmured. "Maybe not. I won't risk it. And even if that didn't exclude you, I'm certain the domestic arrangements in your family would."

"No!" Eckhard shouted. "There's no way you could know anything!"

"Try me," challenged Jerome.

Eckhard was silent.

"But I want to know," spoke up Redman. "Just what 'domestic arrangements' would destroy the honorable senator? After all, we now know that the Reverend gentleman on my right likes little boys, and Mister Payne loses himself in bottles. I won't claim to be any paragon of virtue, either, so perhaps we should come clean with each other, Vince. Just who is in our little group of patriots who would take over the United States?"

"Let us say that Morgan took certain conjugal rights from his daughter that should have come more correctly from his wife," said Jerome coldly.

"Ah *shit!*" Redman swore. "Morgan fucks his own daughter. God's representative here fucks little boys. What the hell are we, this group of new Founding Fathers?"

"Let us not forget your own propensity for barely pubescent girls, Anthony," said Dansbury with a pleasant smile. "It rounds out the sexual excesses rather well, don't you think?"

The room was frozen. None of the men looked at each other except for Jerome who glared at each of them in turn. Redman stared back for a few seconds before dropping his eyes, but General Rollings seemed almost amused.

"What do you have on me, Vince?" he asked calmly. "I don't think there's anything in my record that I'm ashamed of."

Jerome looked back at him. "No?" he queried. "Does the name of Martin Walters mean anything?"

Rollings looked interested. "Astonishing," he said calmly. "I thought that had been well covered up."

"Who the hell's Martin Walters?" demanded Payne.

"A man I killed," Rollings replied. He smiled at Payne. "It was a long time ago," he added.

"No statute of limitations on homicide," Jerome reminded him. "A murder charge could still be brought. And we have authentic eye-witness reports which would finish you."

298

"Indeed," acknowledged Rollings. "Your intelligence system is admirable, Vince, I must admit. Perhaps we shouldn't test anyone else's resolve?"

Jerome smiled in genuine amusement. "Their secrets might be messier than yours, General," he agreed. "And rather less macho, too."

Rollings laughed. "Nasty, Vince, nasty. Should we move on, gentlemen?"

"We've not finished," Payne interjected sharply. "We have one more of our select group who has yet to be embarrassed."

Grant Armstrong seemed to awake from a long contemplation of the tabletop. His expression had never changed from one of boredom as the revelations had poured out.

"But we haven't finished with you, yet, Geoffrey," said Armstrong, his voice barely audible. "We haven't mentioned the long line of young men who visit your wife while you manufacture illegal arms and pocket huge sums of money from the private deals you make, without declaring it to the IRS."

Payne sat back as if stunned. He seemed unable to speak.

"Well, well," said Jerome with a short laugh. "Grant, you've been doing some of your own intelligence work!"

Armstrong looked at him without expression. "Of course," he said. "That's what I do."

"Of course," agreed Jerome, smiling. "And the amazing thing is, Grant, we seem to have nothing all that damaging on you."

"What could you possibly have?" Armstrong looked bored.

"Only your passion for jewelled snuff-boxes," replied Jerome. "Some of which, I know, were removed illicitly during contrived searches of several homes of people you happen to dislike."

Armstrong shrugged. "Perks of the job," he said calmly. "I believe the General had the right idea. Let's move on."

Jerome took the silence as agreement. Before he could continue, the door opened and Angela walked in. Jerome looked almost surprised for a second then recovered. He exchanged a swift glance with Dansbury who remained expressionless. Interruptions to these meetings were almost unheard of. Angela wore an elegant and expensive grey dress that clung beautifully to her generous curves and stopped some six inches above her knees. The scooped neckline revealed the beginning of her cleavage.

"A message for you, Mister Jerome," she said calmly. "May I speak with you outside?"

"Of course," Jerome replied and stood up. He took his stick and walked with Angela to the door, opened it for her and followed her out. Letting the door close behind him, Jerome looked at her.

"Jimmie called in twenty minutes ago," she said softly. "Last night's operation was blown. Badly."

"How badly?"

"They had protection," she said. "At least two men were near the cabin, possibly more. One of Jimmie's men was badly wounded by a shot from within the cabin which could only have come from an expert marksman."

Jerome was silent for almost ten seconds. "Does Jimmie indicate who they could have been?" he asked.

She shook her head. "Highly professional," she said. "Jimmie said he never saw anyone but Ashton, but Ashton disappeared after that. But so did one of Jimmie's men. They found him later, garroted."

"What happened after that? Was Jimmie followed?"

"He doesn't know for certain. But he thinks he shook off anyone behind. Obviously, he kept well away from here."

"And the dead man?"

"They carried him with them. I've organized disposal of the body, and I've called our doctor to work on the wounded man. He's seriously hurt, and he may not live."

"And Ashton and the woman survived?"

"As far as Jimmie could tell."

"This is trouble, Angela."

"Yes, sir, it is. I called my father a few moments ago. You'll need to talk to him."

"I will. Thank you, Angela."

She nodded and walked away. For a moment, Jerome watched the beautiful body then turned back to the conference room. As he entered, all eyes turned to him. He walked to the table and resumed his chair before looking at the others.

"The problem is greater than we thought," he said. "Ashton had highly professional protection last night. A team of four men attacked their cabin, but one was killed commando-style, another wounded by a shot from within the cabin that showed marksman capability. My men saw nobody, and they are experts themselves."

Silence held the room for several seconds.

"Why would anyone be protecting them?" Vanderbilt asked. "The police search was over. Who could they have been expecting?"

"The people who came," Corley Rollings replied. "Ashton obviously worked out the frame Jerome had tried to put him in with that murder, and deduced somebody was out to get him."

"I agree, Corley," said Jerome with a nod at the General. "But that doesn't explain who the protectors were."

"Obviously the people who called off the police search," Redman snarled. "Jerome, we've got a real problem, now. Somebody's on to us."

Jerome nodded again. "Finally, I must agree that some unknown agency is at work here. I think, gentlemen, that this time, we won't have lunch. Leave and go your own ways. Meanwhile, every one of us must search for any indications of who or what it is we are dealing with. I'm sure we all have connections of one sort of another. Farm them, gentlemen. Farm them intensively. Call me as soon as you hear anything."

Chairs moved back from the table as all eight men rose to their feet. All but Jerome and Dansbury walked to the door and left the conference room. As the door closed behind the last one, Dansbury resumed his seat and looked at Jerome.

"Well, old friend," he said softly. "After sixty years, somebody has finally produced a real problem for us."

"It seems so," Jerome replied. "Charles, I feel great concern. Who is it that wields such power that we don't know? Almost, this is an oxymoron. A power in

Washington that is unknown to us? How can this have arisen?"

Dansbury's face was expressionless. "I don't know. But it has. And we must find it and kill it like a scorpion. Talk to Lombard immediately, and get Eckhard working through his connections. I'll talk to the people at National Security, the FBI and the CIA. *Somebody* has to know if there's a specialist group hidden away."

He rose to his feet and moved to the door. "Call me when you have anything. I'll start work on my own investigations."

As he reached the door, it opened and Angela walked in. She smiled with warmth at Dansbury. "Leaving us so soon, Mister Dansbury?" she asked. "I was about to bring you a glass of Cardhu scotch."

Dansbury's eyes strayed unselfconsciously down the lines of her body, lingering at the neckline. "My dear," he replied, "you know that my visits here are simply to admire your lovely self. Unfortunately, as you also know, we have developed a small problem. I must start finding out what is going on, just as my young friend over there must do. So I have to leave you, Angela, much as it pains me. Please don't display your charms too much to Mister Jerome. He has work to do."

"Of course, Mister Dansbury," she said with a low chuckle. "I'll see to it that he starts work at once. Can I see you to the front door?"

"No, my child, I'll make my own way. I think young Jerome needs you more than I."

The door closed behind him as Angela came into the conference room and sat in the chair just vacated by

Dansbury. She crossed her legs. "The wounded man just died, Mister Jerome," she said calmly.

Jerome had his hands folded in front of his mouth and was staring at the table. After two or three minutes, he stirred and reached for the telephone on a stand behind him. He pressed two digits for a speed-dial call, and waited a few seconds.

"Bryce," he said. "This is Jerome."

"Vince, my dear fellow," said the strong voice of Bryce Lombard. "I was just thinking about you."

"Do you have any information as to who might have called off the Ashton search?"

"It's damned strange, Vince, but I can't find any trace of the order. The FBI denies calling it off, but everybody else seems certain that's who did it. The police organizations in Illinois, Maryland and West Virginia all believe that's where the order came from."

"Bryce, this is incomprehensible. How can such a thing be covered up?"

"This time, my friend, I'm defeated. I can only promise to keep hunting."

"There's another problem I've just learned about at our committee meeting, Bryce. Eckhard says he'd picked up a rumor years ago, that a special force exists, answerable not to the White House but to some unknown council. Its brief, if it really does exist, is apparently to protect against exactly the sort of program we have been conducting. Do you have any knowledge of such a group?"

Senator Lombard was silent for a moment. "That's odd, Vince," he said finally. "Somebody mentioned just the same concept to me a few days ago. I laughed it off, but the fact you've heard the same thing is disturbing. But no, I have never heard of any such organization. Could Eckhard recall the source of the rumor?"

"Not at all. Bryce, something very frightening is developing here. Somebody highly professional protected Ashton from our attack and our men got seriously mauled."

"So my daughter told me, Vince. This is a serious difficulty. We should lay low for a while."

"I'm not so sure," replied Jerome. "It may be that offence is the best form of defense. Maybe our schedule should be brought forward a few years?"

Lombard was silent again for a few more seconds. "That would be a risky course of action, Vince. Without a compliant president to declare a state of emergency and initiate the camps for dissidents, we may not be able to control the situation."

"However, I will consider it and put it before the committee for discussion," replied Jerome. "I'll keep you informed."

"Be very careful, Vince. This could destroy everything, going off before all plans are in place and without White House support."

"I agree. But it must be considered as an option, given this sudden and potentially severe threat."

"Okay, but please keep me well up to date."

"Of course," said Jerome, and replaced the telephone. For a few moments, he said nothing then raised his eyes to Angela.

"Angela, how can there be any group of people with such power that they can call off the search for Ashton, and yet not be known to Charles or myself?"

"It does seem terribly unlikely," she replied. "Particularly if my father doesn't know of any such group, either."

Jerome fell into a silent reverie again. After another minute, he spoke. "Charles and I have been working toward our New America for over sixty years now," he said. "In all that time, we have had many problems and hurdles to overcome, and finding suitable people to run the group with us has always been terribly difficult. But the problems have always been visible. We have known what the barrier was, who caused it, who to eliminate if necessary. But for the first time, Angela, I don't know what to do."

She stood up and moved over to him, sliding onto his knee with gentle familiarity. She pulled his head onto her breast and held him gently. "I'm sure it's not that bad, Mister Jerome," she whispered. "The whole thing really may just be a coincidence, somebody called off the search and the source of the order simply got lost in the confusion. You know how these things happen."

Jerome didn't speak. His left hand moved up Angela's back and slowly lowered the zipper of her dress. When the opening was at its widest, he moved his hand round her waist, then raised his other one to pull down the front of the dress. He cupped her left breast, while kissing the side of the right one. He slowly stroked the one for a few moments, then lowered his head a little more to take her nipple into his mouth.

Angela sighed softly. "That's nice, Mister Jerome," she murmured. "Just keep doing that, and everything will be all right, just you see." She began to rock slowly back and forth on his lap, crooning in a just-audible note, like a mother nursing a small child. "Nobody is going to stop us forming the New America."

* * *

Charles Dansbury climbed wearily from the limousine as it stopped outside the door of his manor house a few miles outside Frederick. The door opened as he walked up the steps and he nodded at the young man who held it for him. He retreated to his study, poured himself a crystal glass of fine scotch and sat in his favorite armchair. His mind wondered over decades as he sat, staring into an unknown distance. Who could ever have forecast this present? So much work had been done, but only a fraction of what was still needed. He prayed he could live to see the end of it. Things had been simpler once...

The morning began as it had begun for three weeks now, in ice-bound fear. At four, while the night still clamped its frozen mass over the Karelia Peninsula, Dmitri Alexandrovich woke in his tiny cot as a heavy hand shook his shoulder.

"Briefing in thirty minutes, Comrade Lieutenant," muttered the youth above him. The boy's uniform was completely invisible under the blanket he had thrown over him. The hand holding out the mug of coffee was streaked with oil and dirt, and the fingers were black with embedded filth.

Dmitri ignored everything but the mug of coffee. The dirt and the miserable cold seemed to have been for all of creation and all of time, even though his rational mind told him it was only three weeks. He pulled himself upright, huddling the blankets over him, just as the boy had done, and took the mug. He sipped it at first, and then gulped it as the bitter cold around him sucked the heat from the black brew. The boy moved off and began tugging at the shoulder of another of the squadron sleeping just two feet away from Dmitri.

Slowly, the twelve men in the room began to drag themselves upright. They didn't have to dress. In this awful winter, sleeping in tents, only a fool would remove any clothing. They slept in their uniforms, their coats, their boots and anything else they could find.

Shivering, Dmitri stood up and left the blankets on the cot. Rapidly, he rinsed his face in the basin of water that the servant had heated up for the pilots. Already, the water was cool. Wiping his hands, he walked out of the tent, clutching his heavy coat around him as the nightmare frost hit him. The blackness around him was broken by the fires a few yards away, where the mechanics were trying to loosen up the engines of the Polnikarpovs. They had been working since midnight, Dmitri knew. Since the evening sortie yesterday, the engines of the fighters had been drained of all their oil, covered with blankets and then the mechanics had grabbed a few short hours of sleep. At midnight, the fires were lit, the blankets heated over them, then re-draped over the engine cowlings. The oil, stored in the mess-tents where the temperatures managed to hover a few degrees above freezing, was returned to the engines, and the mechanics would play the dangerous game of trying to heat the solidly-frozen engine blocks with blow-torches, keeping the fire extinguishers close to hand. Then would follow a couple of hours of backbreaking work as the mechanics labored to turn the massive engines with the hand cranks and keep the oil liquid. After all that, the four machine guns had to be loaded. In temperatures falling as low as forty degrees below zero, Dmitri often felt that the pilot's life, for all its risk of death, was easier than the hell in which the mechanics worked.

In the mess-tent was some warmth. Miserably little of it, but an alleviation of the brittle misery outside. But there was some hot food, or as hot as it could ever get, which was something just above warm, and more coffee. Dmitri took a tin platter of some indefinable stew, dropped a slab of stale brown bread into it and ate hungrily. Around him, his squadron did the same, instinctively gathering close together for mutual warmth and comfort. Dmitri knew that there was every chance that not all of them would be back in two hour's time. *Those damned Finns,* he swore to himself. *Who in hell could have anticipated that they would put up this sort of resistance?*

"We should have been there by now," muttered Dmitri. "We should be in Helsinki, drinking vodka and dancing with the local women." Instead, they were in their frozen camps, still fifty miles from Vyborg. The Finns had managed to buy over four hundred aircraft from other countries, and the battles in the frigid air over the Peninsula had been vicious and unexpectedly short on Soviet success. A wave of fear rushed through Dmitri as he thought that in less than thirty minutes, he would be taking off again to do combat with those cursed Finnish thugs. He recalled the letter from Yuri he had received only three days ago. It had been brought to him by a new pilot who had been shot down within a mile of Yuri's Division to the north. The pilot had been almost dead of cold when the soldiers had hauled him out of the snow bank where they had seen him land with his parachute, but he was otherwise unhurt. Thawed out, he had been driven back to the squadron, but Yuri had been able to scrawl a letter and have the pilot risk carrying the uncensored note to the squadron.

"Who would have thought these primitive, ill-equipped Finns would have resisted the Red Army for so long?" said the untidy words on the dirty paper, a blank page torn out of a military text. "But somehow, they have held us. Our casualties have been terrible as those lunatics show no fear and attack us from all sides, all through the day and the night. We were supposed to be in Helsinki by the new year. But I still have total faith in our cause, dearest older brother. The rise of Communism cannot be stopped. The quicker we can complete this little skirmish and get on with destroying the Fascists to the south, the sooner the world will be saved."

"Little skirmish?" Dmitri smiled at the recollection of the words. Yuri had been captivated by the English style of doing things, ever since learning to read the language with fluency. Both brothers had kept up their English language training and were reasonably competent in their speech. But it was Yuri who seemed so taken with the ironic style of understatement that the British demonstrated so well. Although just eighteen, Yuri's strong party affiliations and the honorable reputation of their father had secured him a commission in the Red Army. He had come to Finland as an aide to Zelentsov and to gain his first experience of glorious combat with the Red Army.

"We are both following in your footsteps, father," Dmitri muttered. "I pray we will each be as great a warrior as you were."

Dmitri Alexandrovich was dragged into the frightening present as the flight commander cleared his throat. The sortie briefing was about to begin. As one of the pilots pulled back the covers from a map of Finland hung on the wall, the flight commander looked over his squadron. He was barely twenty-two, two years older than Dmitri, but a veteran of the wars already. The fatigue and lines of worry in his face made him look well over thirty, thought Dmitri. That was terribly old. He concentrated on the briefing.

"My gallant comrades," the flight commander began, "let me show you what our task is today." He turned and pointed to the map. "This morning, we must prevent bombing attacks on the 9th Army. These heroic troops are moving north-west on the road to Kuhmo to join up with their own 163rd Division under Comrade Commander Zelentsov." As he spoke, he pointed out the precise spots on the map. "The 81st and 662nd Infantry Regiments have already rolled through Juntasranta in a magnificent tactical drive, and they are now heading for the town of Suomussalmi in preparation for the triumphant liberation of Helsinki. They have not been slowed down at all by the cowardly sneak-attacks by the Finns, but we must save them from any unnecessary diversions by our mission today. We shall easily shoot down these Finnish thugs in their aircraft supplied by the British."

Not quite all the truth, thought Dmitri. The Red Army forces were being viciously harried, day in and day out, by the bombers of the Finnish Air Force. Yuri had told him in the letter that while the official word was that the glorious advance of the liberating Red Armies was free-rolling and without opposition, the truth was something less exhilarating.

"Dmitri," he wrote, "those damned British have supplied the Finns with Blenheim bombers. They call them *"Pelti Heikki"* which means Tin Henry, and they won't leave us alone. I wish to God you and your Polnikarpovs could come and help."

Today, we'll come, Yuri. Maybe I'll personally shoot down a Pelti Heikki for you.

Twenty minutes later, Dmitri was sitting in the freezing confines of the Polnikarpov's open cockpit, shivering from the cold and struggling to do up the straps. The engine had been started ten minutes earlier and the choking, stammering coughs of smoke had eased into a steady rumble. Finally sealed inside the aircraft, Dmitri followed the hand signals of the flight commander and taxied out onto the solidly frozen field. A few minutes later, as the first tiny glimpse of the sun could be seen and the impenetrable blackness around them eased into a pale dawn filled with cold and fear, the twelve Polnikarpov I-16 fighters lifted into the sky. Frowning at the idea of what would happen to them if any of Yuri's letters were to be found by the Party Commissar, Dmitri also felt a small niggling doubt in his mind behind the ever-present fear. *Maybe we're not supposed to be here,* he thought. *Why was Comrade Stalin so adamant that Karelia belonged to the Soviet Union? And how had the high command so under-estimated the resistance being put up by these ill-equipped Finns?*

Shaking his head at his treacherous thoughts, Dmitri stared through the ice-bound dawn to look for the enemy. His whole body was already trembling with the cold as air rushed by his cockpit at over two hundred miles an hour. The tiny bleed of heat from the engine to the cockpit was lost to the outside temperature that would be below seventy degrees below zero in the wind-chill.

He lost the sensation of cold as he saw the first aircraft in the distance. Waving a hand at his leader, he pointed, and received a small nod. The twelve fighters turned towards the enemy, and Dmitri was soon able to make out the shape of the Bristol Blenheim bombers. The Polnikarpov was only a little faster than the British machine, and Dmitri knew he had little time for an attack. He broke formation and began diving on the rear Blenheim. He unlocked his guns and prepared to fire. But as he did so, he saw the tiny shape up and to his right. He screwed his head round and saw the defenders. A flight of Fokkers! Recognizing the D.XXI low-wing monoplanes, a rush of fear surged through him. He broke off the attack on the bomber and turned to defend himself. The world became filled with noise, smoke and terror. Time and time again, he released a flood of lead from his machine guns at the Finnish machines. For one incredible moment of blood-racing delirium, he saw his target hit. The Fokker fluttered like a wounded bird as his machine guns raked the fuselage, then he twisted away as a new attack surged into him.

In bewilderment, he found the sky empty. It always happened like this. One moment, terror, noise, the sky filled so full of aircraft that his breath never seemed to move, so frightened was he of the collision that seemed impossible to avoid, the next second, nothing but blank sky.

Slowly, he found his orientation and position. The bombers had gone. So had the Fokkers. Around him, he was able to see five other Polnikarpovs. Gradually, they came together. The flight commander was missing. Without thought, Dmitri took command and waved the others into formation behind him. Seeing his fuel level gave him only another ten minutes of flight, he set course for their airfield.

The six were the only ones to make it home.

"Dmitri Alexandrovich, you are in command now," Colonel Malenkov said.

"We lost six men," said Dmitri, still stunned by the loss of half his squadron.

"But you survived, and got one of the damned Finns," Malenkov replied. "That is your second kill in three weeks. You are a Hero of the Soviet Union if you keep this up."

"Six men," repeated Dmitri. "Did the bombers hit our troops?"

"You need only worry about your squadron, Comrade Flight Commander," replied the Colonel. "More men and more aircraft will be sent from Russia in a few days."

Recognizing the warning, Dmitri saluted. *Oh God, Yuri,* he prayed, ignoring the rule of the Communist Party that there was no God. *I'm sorry. I will go to my knees later and pray that my little brother survived the day.*

Charles Dansbury snapped awake, a skill he had never lost since his flying days.

"I have my father to remember," he muttered. "The greatest hero of our country. And I still have to protect my brother from his own haste."

He stood up and began to remove his clothes. The massive bed looked like a haven to him this night, memories of his frozen bunk in Finland fresh again in his mind.

Chapter 15 - Martinsburg, West Virginia

Randy Crawford was feeling edgy and irritable. He had not exchanged a word with either Verity or Christiana when he came in that morning and his meeting with Janice had been a disaster. She had found few articles of value in the media, nothing to give him new ammunition for his task. Jimmie had still not shown up. He had been missing for three mornings and Crawford was badly upset. He depended on Jimmie and his network of helpers to keep the show exciting, because he could not rely on top-quality callers without salting them with some of Jimmie's ringers. Not that there was any shortage of people prepared to call in to him, but too many just wanted to fawn, lavish praise on him for his heroic patriotism and then revel for the rest of their miserable lives in the glory of once having talked to the great Randy Crawford. He wandered how many of them had recorded their brief bursts of fifteen-minute Warhol-fame and played them endlessly to friends, family and neighbors. Most of them, he decided. And he needed them, he knew, especially today. Without them, his program depended on his own monologues, and they could not keep the show alive for three hours. Janice was a competent researcher, locating the news items that he could use to pour retribution on the Democrats, liberals, feminists, environmentalists and all the other sub-human groups he hated so much, but she couldn't pull the golden callers out of the hat the way Jimmie did.

Where the hell was he? Crawford sat miserably in his chair waiting for the countdown to his broadcast. Christiana was at her control panel at the other side of the glass wall, and Verity was standing behind her, his arms folded and his eyes fixed unblinkingly on Crawford. The sight of them increased the nervousness that Crawford always felt just before air-time to the point of dread. Something was terribly wrong.

Christiana had returned the previous morning, just in time to take the producer's seat. Crawford had watched her come in a few minutes before air-time, watched Verity's delighted smile of welcome as he stood up and gave her a hug. The usual tug of lust had passed through him, watching her in her short skirt and light sweater.

"Shit!" he said loudly then swore again at himself as he saw the hated pair turn and smile at him. The intercom had been switched on.

"Something bothering you?" Verity's voice echoed from the loudspeaker. Crawford looked down at his papers. "No?" Verity asked. "Good. You have twenty seconds."

Enormous panic washed over Crawford. All his fears rose to the surface again, far worse than they had ever done before, even the day after Ashton had first called. He swallowed a deep gulp of water, refilled the glass from the flask of iced water he kept by the desk, and watched Christiana counting down the last seconds. He fought for his usual control and enthusiasm, and struggled to find even a part of it.

"And a great good morning to all you true-blue Americans out there," he boomed, louder than his usual tone because of the worries. "This is Randy Crawford coming to you from the heartland of American history, the beautiful state of West Virginia. I know there's a lot of you ready to call and tell me your ideas of how we're to win the next election, just a year from now, and believe me, I want to hear them all, 'cos like all of you, I'm sick to death of this bumbling fool that lives in the White House with that arrogant and questionable woman we have to take as our First Lady. First Lady? Hah! Now that's a corruption of a wonderful term, if ever there was, right folks?"

He looked through the glass. Christiana and Verity were watching him calmly. He knew that this had been a particularly vitriolic opening and he would have expected them to show disgust or anger. But they were just watching him without expression.

Christ, what the fuck's going on? he asked himself, and felt the worry almost overwhelm him.

"Now, I haven't pulled out anything particular this morning," he continued. "God knows, those two in the White House pull enough idiotic stunts every day to fill this program, never mind the combined stupidities of those liberal communists who daily disgrace the Congress and the Senate with their nonsense. As you know folks, we could fill a week of air-time with one day of these lunatics' carryings-on. But today I'll to leave it to you to set the tone and content, you, the real people of this great country, the loyal Americans who vote a straight Republican ticket, knowing that anything else is a foot in the door of the House for the communists in this country."

Crawford began to feel better. He knew he was pushing the envelope of propriety this morning, but the juices were beginning to flow and some of his depression was lifting. He looked at the computer screen on his desk.

"And so we go to... Ben, just up the road from here, in Washington. Hey, Ben, how's things in the nation's capital?"

"Say, Randy," a deep, bass and beautiful voice said from the loudspeaker. "I was wondering, what happened to that guy Mark Ashton who cut you up so badly a couple of times recently. Didn't you say he'd been charged with murder?"

God in heaven, where did this come from? Crawford took a breath. "I think you're mistaken about those times that lunatic called me, Ben. I showed without any doubt what a liberal fool he was. And yes, he *is* wanted for murder, a particularly vicious murder of a poor homeless man."

"Well, I tell you, Randy," said the powerful voice, "I listened to all three calls that Ashton made to you, and I'd say you're way off base. That guy made some strong arguments that make you a questionable American."

"Listen, caller," Crawford shouted. "You're being offensive. This is a show for true Americans to call in, not for fools to support a goddammed criminal! How dare you question my patriotism?"

"No guts, Randy? Going to cut me off?"

The challenge brought Crawford to his senses. "No, I'm not," he grated. "Do you have something sensible to say, or is this to be some more lunatic ramblings from simple-minded liberals?"

"I'd like to review some of the things Ashton said," the sonorous voice continued. Crawford was sure by now. The caller was black. Very few blacks called into this program, and Crawford's worries increased even more. If he cut this caller off, or was too offensive, he was leaving himself open to charges of racism. He clenched his fist and battled to keep his voice straight. This was by far the worst morning he had ever had. Not even a standard adulatory call to start the day.

"Go ahead, then," he said shortly. "What did that murdering criminal say?"

"First thing we'd better get straight, Randy ol' pal, is that last statement. Your listeners should know that all charges against Mark Ashton have been dropped. The police say there is nothing to warrant a charge."

"Oh yeah?" Crawford jumped on the opening. "He pulled in a few political favors did he? Or somebody he was connected to? One thing you can count on with these liberals, they'll always buck the responsibility to somebody else. His fingerprints were on the knife, fair and square. He killed that guy, whatever the police say."

"Better be careful of libel charges, Randy," the other voice replied, the amusement reverberating strongly. "The Evanston police have got good grounds for believing the knife was taken from Ashton's apartment and used in the killing to implicate Mark. Makes you wonder, doesn't it, Randy, how that happened just a few days after he accused you of betraying this country? Could there be some connection, do you think?"

Dear God in Heaven! Who in Christ's name is this caller? Crawford took several deep breaths. Verity and Christiana were watching without expression. Theirs were

320

the eyes of somebody who had just sprayed a cockroach and were coldly watching it die.

"Perhaps you should be careful about defamation yourself, caller," he said. "Those are serious charges to lay against a patriotic American."

"Yes, they are," the caller agreed. "If that's a true description of you. So let's press on with showing that perhaps you're something other than a patriotic American, like Ashton said."

There was no escape. Crawford remembered the instruction he had been given by Jerome. Let them talk. They'll wind down eventually. He said nothing.

"The first thing Ashton pointed out was that you had exactly the same philosophies as die-hard communists," said the man in Washington. "You hate anyone who opposes authoritarian government. You obviously hanker after just one-party rule, without those bothersome elections, and you call for freedom from the law for members of that party. Your passionate support of the religious nutcases who dominate the party these days seems to indicate that you strongly endorse the destruction of education for young Americans. So, just like Mark did, I'll ask you. Are you fronting some group that wants to overthrow our free America and replace it with a dictatorship?"

Crawford looked at Christiana. For the first time ever, he was begging for a commercial break. He drew his finger across his throat in the traditional "break" sign, but she shook her head. Verity continued to stare at him.

"That's such a stupid question, caller, that I'm afraid I *will* have to cut you off, after all," said Crawford, and pushed the switch to disconnect the call. "And we'll go to a short commercial," he continued, "while all of us get a breath of fresh air from that last example of liberal stupidity."

He made the "break" sign again at Christiana, but once more, she shook her head. For the first time, Crawford began to wonder if some specific action was being taken. She had never refused such a request before, and to do so was highly unprofessional, because any speaker on air had to be able to cut off in an emergency. But he was Randy Crawford. Nothing had defeated him before, and this day would be no exception, he decided, calling on every ounce of strength within himself.

"Well, it seems, folks," he continued, glaring through the glass, "my young producer has hit a snag and our commercial break will be a little delayed. As we're all finding these days, people, the quality of help has declined badly in recent years with all those liberals and communists dominating the education boards of this great country." He smiled coldly at Christiana. *Score one for Randy, you bitch,* he thought. *Try and screw me up, would you? Just wait. We'll see who's boss around here.* "And as you've all just seen, you can't trust people who've been trained at those artsy-fartsy schools of journalism and broadcasting, instead of learning the trade from the ground up, like I had to do. So if you had a chance to catch your breath after the unbelievable stupidity of that last caller, we'll go to the next one. And I tell you folks, I bet that last guy was one of those who couldn't organize a party in a brewery without an affirmative action program to help him." *There, you black bastard,* he thought in triumph. *Screw you and anyone who calls in to complain about racist remarks.* "And the next American on the line is... Paul, again from Washington. I hope I've got a real American on the line this time, Paul, and not some crazy liberal trying to score points off Randy Crawford."

"You've got a real American on the line, Randy, that's for sure," said the well-educated voice on the loudspeaker. Despite his detestation of such voices, Crawford felt a surge of relief. The words were typical of the most common type of caller, one who almost fell over himself with praise for Randy's war against the enemies of America.

"Well, thank God for that, Paul," said Crawford. "You're the sort of American that this program is made for. So tell the thirty million Americans listening to us something about yourself, Paul."

"Sure thing, Randy," the caller said. For a second, Crawford felt a streak of worry shoot through him. Had he detected a faint coloration of sarcasm in that educated voice? No, he decided, the caller's words fit the desired profile for his followers.

"First thing I should tell you all," continued the caller, "I'm an ex-Navy SEAL and I'm in a dedicated intelligence unit now, composed of people from several branches of the services."

"God bless you, Paul," said Crawford, looking to the ceiling in gratitude. This was undoubtedly one of his greatest supporters. "A real American hero who's served his country by putting his body in harm's way."

"And your worst nightmare," added Paul.

For a second, Crawford was unable to comprehend what the man had said. "My... *what?*" he stuttered.

"Your worst nightmare. I have that horrible characteristic that you hate so much, Randy. I tell the truth, not like you and a lot of your callers."

"What the hell are you talking about?" A wave of sickness ran through Crawford's bowels. He was losing control of this program and blind terror nearly overwhelmed him.

"You may well ask," the other man replied. "I know very well that many of your callers in the past have claimed to be military men with combat experience. Most of them were honest. But I know of a few who weren't."

"It seems this program is infested with damned liars, criminals and communists, today!" exploded Crawford. "Tell me just *one* of my callers who wasn't what he claimed to be."

"For sure. George Simpson, for one."

"And who the hell is George Simpson?" Crawford shouted, sweat breaking out on his face.

"He's the man who called himself Jake from Sacramento and called a few weeks ago, claiming to be a Marine Captain with combat experience in the Gulf War. You may remember, that Mark Ashton..."

"So that's it!" erupted Crawford. "You and that lying bastard who called before, you're friends of that murdering lunatic, Ashton! You're trying to set me up! It won't work. You're off the air, whacko!"

He slammed the switch to disconnect the call, and took a deep breath.

"As I was saying, Randy," Paul continued, "Mark Ashton told you the man was from Pittsburgh. And we caught up with *Seaman* George Simpson a couple of days ago, a man who never left the United States during his less-than-honorable service as a motor-pool mechanic."

Crawford stared in horror through the glass. Christiana and Verity hadn't moved since the program had gone to air. Christiana still studied him calmly, as if following his every order as she had in the past, Verity stood with his arms folded, watching the death struggles of the cockroach. Knowing that the over-ride switch had been altered, Crawford could do nothing but listen as the nightmare continued.

"Simpson confirmed the hoax, Randy. He told us he'd accepted five hundred bucks from a guy called Jimmie Wanlyn, an old school buddy of his, and one of your staff. Interesting, eh, Randy? So I wonder how many more of these heroic callers to the program were like that?"

Crawford forced words through his rigid throat. "And why aren't you just as much a liar, then? If one of my callers was a liar like you say, I can't prove it. The odd nut gets through the net. Maybe like you? Are you lying too, Paul?"

"I agree," Paul concurred. "You can't screen out the nutcases and liars. That still doesn't explain how it was that a member of your staff bribed this George Simpson to call your program and claim to be something he wasn't and could never have been. But you probably don't want to try and explain that, do you Randy? So let's show some of my credentials as a specialist intelligence operator. I have your life history in front of me, Randy. Want to hear some of it?"

"There's nothing of interest in my life history," croaked Crawford. He felt gripped in the worst horror that had ever visited him in his sleep. He couldn't switch off the torturer at the end of the line. He could walk away, he knew, but that would be the end of the career of Randy Crawford. Somehow, he had to stick this out and survive it, watching for any opening he could get to silence the dreadful voice that couldn't be silenced by any technical means at his disposal.

"That's mainly true, Randy," the caller agreed. "You're a particularly boring person. Except for your military experience, that is."

"My what? What are you talking about?"

"The military experience you claimed to have had when Ashton challenged you on it."

"So? What about it?"

"You were lying, Randy. Just as much as Seaman Simpson was lying. You never served a day in the military."

"You're a liar! How the hell could you know where I served?"

"Like I said, Randy, special intelligence services. I have a copy of the letter your grandfather wrote in July 1969, to the Secretary of the Army. He made reference to a psychiatrist's letter, which I also have right here, saying that young Randolph Crawford suffered from a nervous disorder which prevented him from completing military service."

Crawford's throat had seized up completely. He looked pleadingly at Christiana and Verity, but they didn't move.

"What's also interesting, Randy, is the letter the Army got from a certain senator, requesting your removal from the conscription list. The same senator who received a check for over a hundred thousand for his election campaign from your grandfather."

"That's a lie," Crawford rasped. "You've made up those copies. They don't exist."

"Well, I'll be happy to email them over to you, Randy old pal. But I think I'll leave it to your listeners to decide what's true. I'll wish you a pleasant good morning, now. Have a nice day."

The line went dead, and before Crawford could move, an advertisement for a national brand of coffee began. Crawford wiped the sweat from his face and poured some iced water into his glass. His trembling hand made the glass rattle against his teeth as he drank it, spilling a good portion down his shirt.

"Sorry about the over-ride switch," boomed the voice from the intercom. "I must have hit it when I was preparing your studio earlier."

Crawford raised his head, feeling it was as heavy as dead wood, and looked at Verity who was bent over the control panel to press the intercom switch and speak into the producer's microphone. Verity's face looked serious and sincere.

Crawford tried to speak, but the deathly weariness was too much. Sickness ran through his body as he realized he still had over two and a half hours of the broadcast. Normally, the time was too short, he loved every minute, revelled in every adulatory call from his more than thirty million fans, and felt disappointment when the three-hour mark rolled up. Now, the horizon of terror soared into the endless distance.

"Twenty seconds," said Christiana.

Oh God, no more of these calls, he begged, and looked at the monitor by his side. There were five calls waiting, none of them from Washington, he saw with a prayer of thanks. Maybe things were back to normal.

"We're back from the madness of liberal whackos, America," he intoned as he saw Christiana's count reach zero. "Whoever those lying lunatics were, I can assure you, folks, they were so far off the wall that maybe they've just been released from some asylum. In which case, their parole board should be inside as well." He began to feel better. The next bunch of calls would return the program to the standard he was used to.

"And so we go to... Alex in Phoenix, who's listening in through our new associate station WJKK, run by my good friend Jack Rylett. Talk to me, Alex!"

"Jesus Christ, Randy!" said a male voice. "Those were sure some whacked-out pot-heads calling you there! Communist agents, for sure!"

Crawford relaxed. Things were back to normal.

In an office in a nondescript building near the corner of M Street and 24th, Paul grinned widely at Feathers and Mark as he turned the radio up a notch or two to hear the Crawford broadcast. "Two down, one to go," he said. "I think our performances were almost as good as yours, Mark."

Mark laughed loudly, with a delight he hadn't felt outside of his times with Christiana. "Magnificent," he replied. "You got so far up that bastard's nose, you came out through his ass."

"I'd love to see how Crawford looks right now," said Feathers. "He must be in pain."

"Like a camel with hemorrhoids, I imagine," Mark agreed. "Having this straight-through line to Christiana is like fighting cavalry with a tank. The poor jerk won't know what hit him."

"Couldn't happen to a nicer guy," added Feathers. "Imagine his face when he found that Verity had rigged his cut-off switch!"

"Absolutely," Mark concurred. "Verity said he installed his own over-ride switch on Christiana's panel, so he could still leave Crawford with cut-off control if he wanted. So Crawford will never know whether his cut-off will work or not. It should drive him nuts! Christiana's going to mix him around to confuse him even worse."

"Lovely!" said Paul with a chuckle. "That lady's quick on the uptake, as well as a great shot."

"What happened to the guy she hit?" asked Mark with a look of anxiety. "Christiana's feeling dreadful about it, even though she fired in self-defense."

"The other three began to cart him away," Paul replied. "When the three got cut down to two, their task became tougher. But they made it to their car about a mile down the road."

"How did the three get cut down to two?" asked Mark.

Paul shook his head. "You don't want to know," he said. "But all four of them were in the car when it left. Just that one of them had no further interest in the proceedings."

"You killed him?" Mark felt unconcerned about the probability. One of the men had shot at him and another one had fired into the cabin where Christiana was. He had no wasted feelings about the death of any of the attackers.

"He's out of the game," responded Paul shortly, and turned back to the telephone. He handed the set to Mark. "Your turn, I think, Mark from Evanston. Talk to the man." He checked the direct phone number that Verity had given him the previous day, and dialed the digits.

Randy Crawford was regaining his composure. Two calls had come in since the catastrophic, nightmare attacks by the men in Washington, and both calls were highly-charged abuses of the Washington callers. The second pair had urged Randy to ignore the liberal-communist, nonsensical ravings of obviously deranged enemies of America and to keep up the fight for American principles. Randy began to feel better.

"And we're back, America," he said into the microphone. "We've had a weird day so far, eh folks? We began with two friends of a murdering criminal, an obvious fanatical enemy of this great nation of ours, both trying to defend their liberal buddy by attacking *me*, Randy Crawford. Can you believe the sick, twisted minds of some people in this country? Making up lies about letters from my grandfather to get me out of military service and about cash gifts to senators? If this is what these idiots are reduced to, then perhaps we're winning our fight for this country, my friends, because those calls were clearly the last gasps of desperate lunatics. You notice how that last caller claimed to be a military man? Well, he almost fooled me, I can tell you, sounding as educated as he did. But you know where his education came from, of course. Some liberal-arts college in California, or New York, where pansies like him learn *essential* skills like knitting and ancient Greek poetry. That guy was no more a military

330

man than my dog is. But at least the day picked up after that. We heard from two *real* Americans, who tagged those two previous lunatics like I'm sure the rest of you did."

He looked at the screen. Six calls waiting, none of them from Washington. Though still not filled with the crusading glow that usually ran through his body by this stage of his show, and still a little nervous about taking a call, he nevertheless pushed the receive button, taking a deep breath and mentally crossing his fingers.

"And I'm sure we're about to hear from another true-blue patriot who can tell the rest of us exactly what he thinks of those first two anti-American idiots. So we go to Jack in Palo Alto. Hey Jack, how's the sunshine in California?"

"I wouldn't know, Randy," said a familiar, dreadful and terrifying voice from the loudspeaker. "This is Mark Ashton calling from Washington. You seem to be having a little trouble controlling your system today, old buddy."

For one hideous moment, Crawford felt he was about to throw up. He fought for control, staring at Christiana, knowing he couldn't ask her to cut this call. He now understood that the entire program was set up to attack him. Verity had rigged the cut-off switch for control at the producer's desk, and Christiana was feeding false data into his control monitor, and preventing him from selecting calls as he normally could. He took a deep gulp of iced water to smooth his harsh throat and realized he was committing the worst offense in broadcasting. He had allowed nearly twenty seconds of dead air.

"You're a murderer, Ashton," he rasped. "I don't talk to criminals on this program."

"No? When do you talk to them? When planning to frame me for a murder of some poor homeless man? Or when sending gunmen to kill my lady and me at our cottage?"

"What the hell are you babbling about, Ashton? Your mind's gone completely out of control. Nobody framed you for a murder, it was all your own work. And nobody's been gunning for you, but I have to say, there are a lot of Americans out there right now who would like to do so. You're a lunatic, a killer, and America would be better off without you."

"Let me tell you a little of what happened these last few days, Randy. You might remember that I called you previously from a car phone with ID suppression. Now, the only way to trace a car phone call is to go to the computer records of the cellular phone companies. So, imagine the surprise of the police in two locations in Illinois recently when a young man and a young woman were killed on the same night, both stabbed to death, just a few days after I called you for the second time. They just happened to work for the two main cellular companies. Both just happened to be computer programmers. And at their offices, the police found a program written by each of them, that searched for the identity of the car phone on which I called you on the first two occasions. Are you following this, Randy?"

To Crawford, the world had shrunk to a frightening, evil place consisting of his studio, two impassive faces watching him, and the voice on the loudspeaker telling him facts which terrified him more than he could possibly believe. *There will be records in the computers of one of the cellular phone companies...* Jerome's softly-spoken words to him the time he had gone to pour out his worries about Mark's first call thundered into his mind like a heavy surf. He had been frightened then by the glimpse of the powers at the fingertips of Vince Jerome, but he hadn't considered that Jerome would clean up the traces of the hunt for Mark by killing the hunter's assistants. He wondered for a second who the victims were. Although he often asked for the contact addresses and numbers of the many people who called in and offered their help in the fight for America's traditions, he had never looked at the lists. That had always been the responsibility of Jimmie Wanlyn. Crawford had always assumed that was where Jimmie got his faked calls. A shudder ran through him. *Where the hell was Jimmie?*

Yet again he had let dead air occur.

"You've got a hell of an imagination, Ashton," he grated. "Typical of your kind, make up any story to avoid taking responsibility for your own actions. None of this took place. Now I have a suggestion. Hang up. Go to the police. Give yourself up. Take your punishment like a man. And I hope you get the electric chair, or whatever they use in Illinois. America will be a cleaner place when you've gone. Now get off the phone. You make me sick."

"You're forgetting something, Randy. You were in the station manager's office exactly at the time when the police trooper in there also was told to cancel the all-points-bulletin for me. You know very well that there's no murder charge on me. And I'm sure you might be thinking what a lot of the thirty million Americans listening breathlessly to this program are also thinking. A man was killed a few days after we talked the second time. Evidence suggesting my guilt was left on the body. But the police know I didn't

333

do it. So here are the questions, Randy. Who did it? And isn't it convenient that it happened just after I suggested that you were a front for some renegade group threatening the survival of America? Isn't it astonishing that two people who had called your program to offer you their innocent help had been used to locate me by illegal means, and then had been murdered also, to cover the traces of somebody that you clearly work for? Isn't it about time you asked yourself what you're doing, Randy?"

Crawford was frozen rigid. His mind whirled out of control as a tidal wave of panic washed over him like raging sewage water. He could barely breathe, and a sharp ache was pounding his chest as if a heart attack were threatening him. Transfixed, he watched the second hand of the studio clock flicker its soundless way round the dial. Twenty seconds... twenty-five... twenty-six...

The ambient hiss of the loudspeaker cut off, to be replaced by Christiana's gentle, cool voice.

"And we'll take a break from this historic Randy Crawford program while we play some messages and earn some money to pay our bills, ladies and gentlemen. Don't go away, my friends, we'll be right back with some more of your calls and the earth-shattering revelations of today. Stay tuned."

Music erupted as an advertisement for a national chain of discount electrical appliance stores shattered the icy atmosphere of the studio. Crawford knew that tears were running down his cheeks and the slow, sick waves of panic filled his innards. He pressed the intercom control.

"What are you doing to me?" he begged, staring for some signs of pity in the two cold faces through the glass.

Verity bent forward to speak into the producer's microphone. "Crucifying you," he said. "Like you did to Mark Ashton. How do you like it so far, Randy?"

"Oh God," cried Crawford. "I didn't know somebody had framed him for the murder! I really thought he'd done it. And I don't know anything about shots being fired at Christiana and him, honest! Please, you've got to believe me! I didn't know they'd do this."

"Who would do this? Friends of yours in Washington?"

"I don't know! For Christ's sake, leave me alone!"

"What about those Illinois murders, Randy? You have anything to do with those?"

"Jesus Christ, Verity! Do you think I'm a killer? For God's sake!"

"Not you, Randy. You're too gutless to kill for yourself. Somebody did it for you, though. You have twenty seconds."

"My God, Verity, you can't put me back on air! I can't handle any more of this! Please!"

"Fifteen seconds."

"Verity! For God's sake, man! I'll do anything! Don't go to air!"

"Ten seconds."

"Jesus Christ! Verity, I'll fucking kill you! Stop it!"

"And five, four, three...."

Crawford sat staring at the microphone that faced him expectantly, waiting for him to speak to thirty million Americans and damn himself in their eyes for ever. Dead air hissed through the speakers for ten, eleven, twelve seconds before he caught himself.

"Something insane is happening today, America," he said harshly. "It's clear that the liberal communists of this country have decided to come out of their smelly little caves and attack a patriot. And I have to remind you, folks, in attacking me, these bozos are attacking *you,* the true Americans in this country, the people who believe in the *real* American way, our liberties, our freedoms, and the rightful place of America as the leader of the free world. So this is what it's come to, today. Communist agents are calling in, friends of murderers, bleeding-heart liberals, with trumped-up stories and false allegations about me, trying to destroy my reputation and so silence the one man in America fighting for the truth. This is war, people, just like Pat Buchanan said it was back in 1992 at the GOP Convention, a war for the hearts and minds of Americans. And just like he said, there's no place in our America for liberals, homosexuals, bleeding-hearts and communists. And if you're any one of those, you're probably all of them, that's what I say."

Crawford felt the juices of his hatred begin to wake him from the frozen terror of a few minutes ago. His head lifted and he stared in triumph at the two silent faces beyond the glass. They remained expressionless. *Well, fuck you both,* he thought, *I'm Randy Crawford. Nobody gets the better of me. Nobody.*

"So here's what I say, my friends. The lefty lunatics have dominated this program so far with their cowardly, lying attacks on all of us true Americans. Let's fight back. Let's hear it from you all out there, the people who know what it takes to be an American."

He studied the board. "Let's go to... Frank from Houston." He pressed the selector button and prayed that it still obeyed his orders and hadn't been rigged by Verity. "What's the word in Texas, Frank?"

"I've been listening all morning," said the man on the line. His accent was slight but identifiably Texan. "I've never been so disturbed in all my life."

"And so you should be, Frank," Crawford chimed in. "This has been the most disgraceful attack on patriotic Americans that I've ever heard."

"That's not what I was thinking." The note of anxiety was evident in the caller's voice. "What scared the hell out of me was what they were saying, 'cos it started to make sense to me. The stuff you call for, all that rule of law, prevention of any environmental concerns, the way you've always implied that none of the people in Reagan's and Bush's administrations that broke the law, including the presidents themselves, should have been punished for their crimes. You know, Crawford, you *do* sound like one of those old hard-line communists. The way you call anyone who disagrees with the Republican party a communist and a traitor to America, that's goddamn disgraceful. So it's probably time you went home and retired, Crawford. And if you *are* fronting some lunatic group that wants to install a dictatorship in America, then I hope you hang."

The clatter of the remote phone being slammed down somewhere in Texas made Crawford sit up with a jerk. Without saying a word, he pressed the button for the next caller, not even reading the source of the call.

"Hello?" said a hesitant female voice. "Hello?"

"Are you going to be different from that last whacko, or do you want to say something useful?" snapped Crawford.

"I've listened to you for five years," said the woman, a note of rising anger in her voice. "Most of the time, I thought you were talking garbage, but it was interesting to see just what lies you'd tell..."

With a slam of his hand, Crawford cut her off. Just for a moment, he wondered how his cut-off had worked this time but not when he tried to cut Paul. But he had little time for thinking. Another voice was speaking.

"This is Mike in Jackson, Florida," said a deep, musical voice. "I'm like that lady you just cut off, I listen to you to see how far your lies will go. I get the newsletter from that guy in Chicago, *The Lies of Randy Crawford,*" and compare what you said with what the facts are. And man, you're one constant liar, Crawford. So now I understand why that guy gets death threats because of his letter. Is that your bunch of lunatics? Maybe the first callers were right. Maybe you *are* part of some group of right-wing lunatics. Like another caller said earlier, I hope you hang."

The cut-off worked again. The next caller was another woman.

"It's finally coming back on you, Crawford," she screamed, nearly overloading the loudspeaker. "Five years of telling half the population of America they were traitors to their own country! Hanging's too good for you, you jerk, I hope..."

The cut-off worked.

"Hammer time, Randy ol' buddy!" called a young man's voice. "Maybe we'll find out now that the real Americans are the ones you've been throwing dirt at all these years. I reckon you're a communist agent, you bastard..."

Cut-off. A woman's voice.

338

"So how many people have you killed, Crawford? Sounds like it's at least three, from what Ashton said. Is this the American way, Crawford? Kill anyone who disagrees with you or points out what a liar you are? You're getting your..."

His back drenched with sweat, and tears flooding down his face, Crawford jumped to his feet and strode out of the studio. He stormed down to his office, closed the door behind him and collapsed into his seat, dropped his head on his desk and wept.

From the control studio, Verity spoke gently into the microphone.

"This is the station manager of WNDY," he said calmly. "I regret to inform you that Randy Crawford appears to have become indisposed and left the studio. As I doubt he'll be back today, we'll play you a tape of a country music concert that took place here in Martinsburg just a few nights ago. We'll have Rita McNeil, Travis Tritt and more of your favorites after these messages..."

He disconnected his microphone as Christiana started the first of the commercials. She loaded the tape of the concert and sat back, her face expressionless.

"Goodbye, Randy," said Verity softly.

Christiana just chuckled in delight.

In the offices of TF5, Mark, Feathers and Paul let out a collective sigh.

"I never thought he'd get such a negative reaction," murmured Paul. "We've really let the dragon escape its cave."

"Like opening up Pandora's box," Feathers agreed. "At least from Crawford's viewpoint, we let out all the ills of the world."

"But we still don't know who's behind him," said Mark, looking distressed. "We may have killed the monkey all right, but who the hell is the organ-grinder?"

The other two men nodded.

"I think the chief is looking into that," said Feathers with a small smile.

"The chief? Who's the chief?" asked Mark.

"Nobody you know," Feathers replied. "Keep it that way."

"Oh my," said Mark with a grin. "We're playing with the big boys now, are we?"

"So big you'd never believe," said Paul. "So let's stay playing at our level, shall we. Let's think about Jimmie Wanlyn."

"Randy's gofer?" Feathers replied. "I have funny feelings about this man. You traced George Simpson neatly enough and he admitted Jimmie put him up to that dummy call to Crawford for a cash payment. What next?"

"Two things," Paul said. "My men followed the car after the incident in the mountains. They carried one body and one badly hurt man with them. They drove to a doctor's surgery in Frederick and dropped off the wounded guy. We're checking out that doctor right now. Then the car drove to a small field outside of town and dropped off the body. I've got men watching that field. They'll call any moment."

"Frederick?" Feathers and Mark spoke together. "What's special about Frederick?" continued Mark.

"A place where very rich people live," said Paul thoughtfully. "Lots of big, private estates, secure guards, that sort of place."

"And how about the car they followed?" Feathers asked.

"They followed it home," said Paul. "We know the owner."

"Jimmie Wanlyn?" suggested Mark, and Paul nodded.

"Got it in one," he agreed. He was about to say something else, when the phone rang on the desk. He picked it up and listened intently. He replaced the phone and smiled cheerfully.

"Wanlyn has received several calls from Frederick in the last couple of hours," he said. "A woman with a very sexy voice, but giving distinct orders. She was using references, so we don't know what she was telling Jimmie to do. But the calls came from one of those lavish estates. Home of a man called Vince Jerome."

"Never heard of him," said Mark. "Who the hell is Vince Jerome?"

"The richest man in America," replied Paul. "Something of a recluse, but immensely powerful. A real kingmaker with the party. I doubt that anything happens without Jerome being involved."

"Would he know about TF5?" asked Mark with real worry.

Paul shook his head. "I truly doubt it. I don't know exactly how TF5 was formed, or who the governing body is, but I believe that anyone with obvious party affiliations would not be involved."

The phone rang again. Feathers and Paul looked at each other.

"Put a bet on it?" said Feathers.

"No takers," said Paul and picked up the telephone. "Yes, Chief," he said. A question was obviously asked, because he nodded. "Mark's here," he said. "We ripped the balls off Crawford." Another moment of silence passed, and Paul looked at Feathers with a grin. "Vince Jerome," he said without further amplification. He nodded, looked at Mark, then back at the desktop. "He's ready, Chief. If not now, he will be in five minutes."

Mark felt a stir of anxiety mixed with excitement. He knew he had just been set up for something interesting. He waited until Paul had replaced the phone.

"So what do we do about this Jerome guy?" asked Mark.

"The Chief has some ideas on that," Paul replied. "How much vacation time do you have for this year?"

"Four weeks," Mark responded without thinking, then did a quick double-take. "Exactly what do you have in mind?"

Paul smiled. "Your reserve status is still valid, right?"

Mark looked with amused resignation at Feathers. "You guys planned this before?"

Feathers grinned openly. "You've just been activated, old buddy. Welcome back in harness, Lieutenant Ashton."

Mark looked concerned. "Paul, I'd love to help, but are you sure? I've never been the flag-waving, patriotic type. I joined the navy for what it would give me, not for what I could give it."

Paul stared him firmly in the eye. "Lieutenant Ashton, I believe you. But take a look inside yourself. This episode has changed your values."

Mark sat silent for a moment, evaluating the words. He realized Paul was right. The anger burning coldly inside him was not just rage at the injury done to him. Terminal damage to his country was being threatened, and he saw with startling clarity how much he refused to permit that threat to be carried out. He looked at Feathers and saw the sympathetic smile on the big man's face.

"Welcome to the club, little guy," said Feathers.

"Something you want me to do?" Mark asked.

"Damn right," replied Paul. "I think you'll find it interesting. But we'll have to get you into a more military shape, first."

"You're joking, of course," Mark objected. "I'm fit enough."

"Hah!" Kent's smile was derisive. "This is TF5."

"Yeah?" Mark felt intimidated.

"TF stands for Truly Fantastic," Feathers said. "And the Five is the multiplication factor. Believe me, little Mark, nothing you experienced in Basic Training is going to prepare you for the next few days."

Mark tried to sigh in resignation, then burst into laughter.

Chapter 16 - Maryland

"Colin, it was good of you to come!" Senator Morgan Eckhard was looking his usual self, aristocratic, self-possessed and authoritative, the perfect presidential image, standing several inches taller than the stocky frame of Colin Webber.

"Senator, who could resist an opportunity to discuss the future of America with such a distinguished man as yourself?" Webber replied with a smile. They were standing in the lobby of Eckhard's brownstone mansion in Georgetown. The telephone call to invite Webber to a meeting had come the evening before, and Webber had accepted eagerly.

"Are we meeting here, Senator, or are we going elsewhere?"

Eckhard smiled. "Elsewhere, Colin, but we'll have time to talk as we travel. The car is outside waiting for us. We can have a drink as we move, and lunch will be served when we get there."

"How mysteriously intriguing, Senator!" Webber laughed. "Whom do we meet?"

"People you know and admire, Colin, that I know. But we'll keep things hidden until we meet them. I know you'll understand. Some things must be kept from the ears of prying people whose interests are less favorable to America than are yours and mine."

"That I certainly understand," Webber replied. He moved to the front door under the direction of a small wave from Eckhard and followed him outside into the beautifully crisp, early fall air. At the kerb stood a black Cadillac limousine. As the two men walked down the steps of the house, the driver's door opened and a young man walked round the car and opened the rear door. The man was strongly built, his face immobile but with watchful eyes.

Webber climbed into the capacious rear of the limousine and sat in the red-pile cushions on the left side of the car. A dark glass screen separated the compartment from the driver's section. Eckhard followed him in and the door closed behind him with an elegantly subdued "thunk." The vehicle moved away gently and smoothly entered the light traffic stream. A few minutes later, Webber saw that they moved onto Wisconsin Avenue heading north.

"A drink, Colin?" Eckhard asked as he leaned forward to open a small cabinet in front of him. "I think we have everything."

Webber smiled. "Does the inventory run to a dry sherry, perhaps?"

"Naturally," Eckhard replied. He extracted a bottle with a gold label, drew out a crystal glass and poured some of the light, gold-brown contents from the bottle. He handed it to Webber, then busied himself pouring a scotch into a larger glass. After a moment, he leaned back.

"Your very good health, sir!" he said, and sipped his scotch.

"Indeed, Senator. Health to all of us," Webber replied and drank his sherry. It was a fine brand, he detected. Only the best suited the owner of this vehicle which, he suspected, was not the senator's. The limousine passed the Naval Observatory and continued north.

"The last time we talked, Colin, you indicated some interest in supporting the true strengths of this nation of ours," said Eckhard, breaking into Webber's observations of the route.

"I believe I did," Webber agreed. "I said I had always supported the ideals of our founding fathers."

"And yet you never entered politics? I have often wondered why."

Webber shrugged. "That was not the way I could best help my country." He took a thoughtful sip of the wonderful sherry. "My abilities lie in building private enterprise organizations and so providing jobs for my fellow-citizens. I did this rather well."

"Indeed!" Eckhard laughed. "Some thirty thousand Americans have cause to thank you for their employment. Yet few people know who is the man behind their good fortune."

"I have never sought the limelight," Webber acknowledged. "The limelight can be dangerous, after all. My way, I am free to do many things as a private citizen, which I could never do as some famous captain of industry. Do you know, Senator, I can even do my own shopping in the supermarket? I enjoy the experience enormously."

"Good God!" Eckhard seemed genuinely shocked. "I couldn't imagine doing that! Walking through a mass store, carrying one's purchases to a counter and lining up with so many people? It sounds terrible! I have never, ever done such a thing."

"Maybe you should try it, Morgan." Webber looked directly at the senator. "One hears the words of real Americans in the check-out line. I learn how small is the gap between being solvent and starving, how worried so many people are each and every day that they may lose their jobs, and so their homes, how terribly difficult it is to bring up children and pay for their education."

Eckhard was silent, staring thoughtfully into his scotch. "The country has suffered under the influences of those who care more for liberal ideology than for their country, these last few years," he finally said.

"Ideological passions and demagoguery have certainly damaged us," Webber agreed. "And we have suffered for too long under weak leadership which has reflected party loyalties rather than love of country."

"I do so strongly agree with you, Colin," Eckhard replied with enthusiasm. "This current administration has served the needs of the liberals, the weak, the bleeding hearts and the masses with little concern for the benefit of the true leaders of the greatest democracy on earth."

"So how do you think the country would be best served, then?" Webber sat slightly sideways so he could look at the senator, but could also watch the passing scene without too obviously following the direction. The limousine pulled left onto River Road and headed west.

"Leadership, Colin! Strong leadership, that's the solution!" Eckhard finished his scotch in a large gulp and leaned forward to refill his glass. "Special interests must take second place to the welfare of the nation! And law and order must always prevail over dissent against established rules. The will of government must be pre-eminent. America will grow great if we have the industrial strength such as you have built, uninhibited by silly concerns about environment, health and safety regulations and all that nonsensical equity hiring stuff. The business of America is business! I think Harry S. Truman said that, and I agree with him."

"I, too," Webber agreed. "And strong defense."

"Walk softly and carry a big stick," said Eckhard. "Harry S again. I never liked the man, but now and again, he expressed real American ideas."

"He certainly did," Webber concurred. "But how are we to change America to make such ideals live again? Is this what we're about to discuss?"

"We are. You and I and some others. We form a group which discusses such topics and suggests ways of achieving the objectives."

"A sort of think-tank? You debate the theories of *Realpolitik* and international strategies for power? Disciples of Henry Kissinger, Metternich and others of that breed?"

"We debate them, certainly." Eckhard took another large drink. "But we do more than merely talk. Another drink, Colin?"

"Certainly, thank you," replied Webber and allowed the senator to refill his glass while also topping up his own. Eckhard had drunk several ounces of scotch by this time. Webber took his glass back and sipped it lightly. "You were saying, Senator, you do more than debate these issues?"

"Like any good administrative team, we also plan contingency moves for varying scenarios."

"But to what ultimate end, Morgan? What is the face of America to which you would work if some of these scenarios were to come to pass?"

"The face which I believe our founding fathers saw when they first declared independence, Colin. This nation rebelled against the growing liberalism and weakness of Europe in order to establish a more pure form of democracy with firm government and leadership. I have never believed they wished a nation to emerge where industry could be stopped for such silliness as racial quotas, feminist propaganda, spotted owls and the hurt feelings of minority groups. Nor did they see a nation bowing to the terror tactics of lunatics elsewhere, and rejecting God in all places. They saw a nation where the will of the people was carried out by their representatives for the good of the whole nation, and law and order prevailed."

"I believe the last is true," murmured Webber. "And your group plans for a new America which returns to these old values?"

Eckhard looked closely at the other man. "A new America? How odd that you should use such a phrase, Colin. We tend to refer to it among ourselves the same way."

Webber smiled. "Not the most original of phrases. And is this the extent of your group's activities? You discuss theoretical scenarios and the possible outcomes?"

"Not entirely. We also consider how the group might react in such situations, and whether we could take an active role in restoring order."

"Then your group must include some influential and powerful people if you could consider actively taking control of this nation," said Webber with a piercing look at the senator. "Would you consider by-passing the existing constitution to achieve this?"

"Not at all," replied Eckhard with a passionate shake of the head. "Our constitution is a sacred document. Every one of the group is dedicated to its preservation."

"So you plan no changes to the essential structures of the country?" Webber persisted.

Eckhard made a vague gesture of disagreement. "No significant, *permanent*, structural changes, Colin, no. But we find, as I'm sure you do, that some of the liberal-inspired changes to the country in recent years have introduced inefficiencies in the way the nation works. So many considerations which must be made to the environment, to minority groups, to the masses, before anything of value can be implemented. As we discussed that night at Lombard's house, we find that these impede the path of progress."

"The price of democracy, Morgan," said Webber.

Eckhard shrugged. "Democracy is of itself a very inefficient structure. There are times when democratic principles really must be suspended if the nation is at risk. There is precedent for this, of course. We always restrict the rights of free speech, of assembly, and of movement during times of war. We have interned suspect nationals and dissidents in the past."

"And are we at war, Senator? Are you and your group suggesting that such liberties should be suspended now?"

"Don't you believe we are threatened, Colin? Can't you see the forces acting against the interests of America, both internal and external?"

"Very clearly, Senator. So clearly, that I am frightened sometimes, by the threats to our nation."

"Then you will find many commonalties with the thinking of my colleagues. We too, are frightened by the dangers we face, and believe that strong moves are essential to restore the true America."

"You said no permanent changes to the constitution, Morgan. Does that imply that your group plans on possible *temporary* alterations?"

"It would be essential, Colin. Restoration of order, removal of dissident elements which threaten the nation, these things could not be achieved quickly enough for success if we had to concern ourselves with individual freedoms and rights and the grinding mechanisms of the law courts. Such things should always take second place to the security of the nation, anyway."

"I certainly see your logic, Morgan. It astounds me that such a group appears to be functioning here in Washington. As I said before, there must be some powerful forces within the operation that makes such visionary thinking a practical possibility."

Eckhard smiled with satisfaction. "Such power as you would only dream of, Colin. When we have taken our rightful position as the leaders of this nation, the drive and strength within America will far exceed that of Germany in the thirties, but of course, with far more idealistic and positive aims."

"It sounds altogether wonderful, Morgan. And you think I might be able to join this select group of leaders?"

"Good heavens, Colin, you'd be a shining addition." Eckhard beamed. "America needs men of your strength, vision and accomplishments. Imagine what you could do if

351

you were unlimited in your resources! If you had access to the governing power, if you could forget the silly legislation which has hampered your business empire over the last decade, there would be nothing you could not achieve!"

"A fascinating idea." Webber smiled. "And we go to meet the force behind this group, I assume?"

"Forces. Yes, we do. I know that you are familiar with both men, because we spoke of them last time we met. Charles Dansbury and Vince Jerome are the powerhouses behind our organization. Both will be there when we reach Jerome's house."

"Somehow, this does not surprise me." Webber tapped his fingers on his empty glass. "I have always suspected these two men of being powerfully driven to lead the nation somewhere. I was just not sure where."

"To a New America," Eckhard replied. "And that vision becomes steadily clearer and more attainable as we follow a program which they began over fifty years ago."

"Remarkable. They could only have been in their twenties or thirties when they initiated this program. Such extraordinary far-sightedness."

"Considering their beginnings, remarkable indeed," agreed Eckhard. "Dansbury was an infantry corporal at the end of World War Two. Jerome was merely a private in the same unit. I believe they met in Berlin during the closing days of the war."

"And from there, somehow built business and financial empires worth billions. Astonishing achievements. One day I must ask them how they got started."

"I'm sure they'll be happy to tell you. We should be there in another twenty minutes, or so. Can I fix you another drink?"

"Certainly, Morgan, this is really a splendid sherry. You'll have another one yourself, I hope?"

"Rarely refuse scotch of this caliber, Colin!" Eckhard's words were a little slurred.

"Good." Webber waited while the senator poured two more drinks, spilling some scotch on the burgundy carpet of the limousine. The smooth road and luxurious suspension system of the car were not the cause of the spillage.

"The party prepares itself for retaking the White House, Morgan?" Webber resumed when the senator had sat back.

"A landslide, without any doubt, Colin," agreed Eckhard and burped slightly. "The purges of unsuitable people from the electoral roll are well under way again and what that doesn't achieve, the voting machines will. It will be done more subtly than before so there can be no public outcry."

"And will your name be among the Iowa and New Hampshire primary contenders?"

"I had considered it, Colin," Eckhard replied. "But I decided not to run."

Webber saw the small expression of discontent that ran across the senator's face and noted it with interest. "It's a terrible burden on one's family," he said in sympathetic agreement. "I would not want to place that load on such a lovely wife and daughter as yours."

"That's right," said Eckhard shortly, and stared out of the window. Webber studied the tense features for a few seconds, then shifted to his left to study the passing scenery also. The rest of the drive passed in silence.

"Morgan has certainly briefed me on your discussion-group," said Webber. He sat in Jerome's study, cradling another small glass of exquisite dry sherry in one hand. His taste buds felt clean and more than ready for the promised lunch.

"We might claim to be a little more than a think-tank or a discussion-group," Jerome replied with a small smile. "We do prepare theoretical action plans for possible scenarios as we develop them." He received a friendly nod of assent from Charles Dansbury. With Morgan Eckhard, all four men sat at ease in the leather armchairs of Jerome's study.

"I am truly fascinated," said Webber. "The overall philosophy, I gather, is to provide strong, well-focused leadership to this country in the event of a break-down of established authority?"

"Exactly," Jerome agreed. "I would say that we go further than theory, also. All the group members are in positions of power and authority with the resources to provide government should the need arise."

"So you would consider yourselves a sort of emergency government-in-waiting?"

"Yes." Dansbury nodded. "I think, Vince, Colin has finally expressed the concept for which we have been looking."

"Precisely," said Jerome. "And that's why we feel, and have felt for a time that your membership in our group would be advantageous to all of us."

"I thought I only mentioned Colin's name for the first time a few days ago," Eckhard objected. He seemed like a spoilt child trying to claim ownership of the class hero,

Webber thought, and suppressed the amusement that ran through him.

"I would say you finally expressed something which has been a developing relationship for a while," said Dansbury in a tone of conciliation. "Colin, Vince and I have exchanged such ideas on and off for a couple of years, Morgan. It shows your own perception in seeing the same strengths which we had detected."

Eckhard seemed uncertain as to whether to be comforted by the remark. He finished his scotch and rose to refill his glass. Webber estimated that the senator had drunk over a fifth of liquor since entering the Cadillac that morning.

"The question must surely arise, Vince, of how such a think-tank is perceived by the White House or by others on the Hill." Webber placed his half-empty glass on a small side-table. "Are you not seen as a threat, perhaps an upstart organization? Some might even question your loyalty to America and consider you a renegade group plotting a coup."

Jerome shook his head. "The members have been very carefully selected over the years, Colin. We recognize precisely the danger you mention, and none of us has any wish to be seen in such a negative light. Our motives are of the purest, as I hope you understand. So we have kept a flat profile and stayed away from any publicity or involvement with others in the executive, legal and legislative branches of government."

"Nobody knows about you, is what you're saying?"

"A small group of people in varying positions do know about us, but the number is tiny."

"And how have you selected the membership? Morgan said you had been preparing for over sixty years. Surely the group has not been the same personnel all this time?"

Both Dansbury and Jerome laughed cheerfully.

"No, Colin, hardly," said Jerome with a wide smile. "Only my geriatric colleague over there and I can claim the life-span to have been in this from the beginning. Every one of the existing team has replaced a previous member, but only after lengthy research into their histories and philosophies. Some positions are into their third generation. Yours would be a new position, should you join us, and your value lies in the enormous resources you can apply and your astonishing organizational skills. We need somebody to do precisely what you do best. That is, to provide strong guidance and management talent from behind the figurehead leadership without trying to take the limelight."

"You have obviously been looking into my history and private life intensively," said Webber. "I can't imagine an invitation to join such a group is being made just on the basis of our past discussions?"

"Naturally," said Jerome with a smile. "Even the knowledge of our group has to be severely restricted, or our existence would be threatened. We have been researching you for over three years."

"And what have you found?" murmured Webber. He picked up his glass again and sipped gently. His eyes were fixed firmly on Jerome.

"Nothing that would give us any doubts about you," Jerome admitted. "You are without any doubt, exactly what you appear to be, an outstanding executive and entrepreneur with no political ambitions whatever. You have never displayed any party affiliations, or shown any move to become involved in the executive management of the country. I find you unique, Colin. And of course, Senator Lombard speaks very highly of you. He has been our most reliable supporter over recent years, and a splendid conduit into the party. But, I'm sure you know that."

"You mentioned doubts? You have some sort of hold over your other team members?" Webber was coolly examining each of the other three men in turn. Neither Dansbury nor Jerome moved, but Eckhard shifted uncomfortably and took another mouthful of scotch.

"I happens that way," said Dansbury with a shrug. "We didn't intend that to be a mode of operation, but human nature is what it is and we discovered certain weaknesses in all our team. It does not affect their capacity to serve the nation, by any means."

"But perhaps enhances their capacity to serve you?"

Jerome seemed not to be offended. "That has always been a common form of ensuring loyalty and conformity to policy, Colin. We make no apologies for it."

"So you know about Morgan's fictional war record, I assume?" asked Webber without expression.

The room was silent with tension for a moment. Eckhard spilled a few drops of scotch on his tie. Jerome and Dansbury stared hard at Webber for several seconds.

"You continue to astonish us, Colin," said Jerome finally. "This is an unexpected aspect of you, I must admit. What else do you know about Senator Morgan Eckhard?"

Webber looked at Eckhard for a moment, then turned back to Jerome. "Any more, Vince, I would keep to myself."

357

Jerome nodded in acknowledgement. "And obviously, you have researched the two of us just as thoroughly?"

Webber finally smiled in genuine amusement. "Your histories are as blameless as my own, gentlemen. I know that neither have you has ever married since returning from the last battles in Berlin, but have concentrated on building your remarkable empires. If either of you has vices, you have kept them well hidden. No, the only oddity I find about you is that neither of you went home after the war. Vince, you have never been to Seattle, Charles has stayed so far away from Los Angeles, one might almost suppose you have both avoided your old homes like the plague."

Beyond a slight widening of the eyes, Jerome showed no reaction. "We were both changed men after our experiences in Europe, Colin. Returning to our childhood haunts simply wasn't an option for either of us. Our friendship became a business partnership immediately, and we decided to concentrate our efforts here in the east."

"I understand," replied Webber. "Sometimes one must make the break with the past completely."

"Exactly." Jerome rose to his feet, taking hold of his walking stick. "I believe lunch will be ready. Shall we go to the dining room?"

The other three men followed his example and walked out of the study up the stairs to the ground floor. Jerome led them into the dining room, a beautiful, spacious room with light green walls, furnished with highly polished, antique furniture. The floor, like the furniture, was burnished to a high glow. Windows looked out onto the perfect lawns of Jerome's estate.

As the four men entered, Angela smiled at them. She was in a black dress that clung to her like a passionate lover. The neckline was low enough to display the tops of her beautiful breasts, and although the hem came to her knees, as she moved to take a wine bottle from the cabinet, the split up one side reached the top of her thighs.

"Good afternoon, gentlemen," she said with a glowing smile. "I would like to welcome you to this house, Mister Webber. I have been looking forward to meeting you."

"The pleasure is entirely mine," Webber replied and took her outstretched hand, bowing over it in an old-world fashion. "I have already seen how Vince likes to surround himself with beauty. You complete the pattern to perfection."

"You're as bad as Mister Dansbury," she said laughing at him. "Now, sit down, and I'll organize lunch." She returned to the cabinet and began to open the wine bottle.

"The vision's name is Angela," said Jerome with a fond smile in her direction. "She has been my personal assistant for two years, and every bit as important to our group as the committee members. I depend on her completely."

Webber looked in admiration as Angela came to pour wine for each of them. She smiled at him again then concentrated on filling his crystal goblet.

"It's an Australian wine," said Jerome. "I discovered the remarkable qualities of that country's wineries some years ago and developed a great liking. This is one of the finest clarets in the world, a Penfold's Grange Hermitage."

"Then I drink to your health, gentlemen." Webber took a sip of the ruby wine.

"To the New America," said Dansbury. "I believe we should welcome our newest member."

Webber smiled back at the old man, and gestured with his glass. "To the New America," he replied. "I shall try and serve it faithfully."

"Wonderful," said Jerome. "Now, no business while lunch is served, gentlemen, but afterward, we must brief you fully on our group, its aims and our program."

"And will Miss Lombard be part of that discussion?" asked Webber innocently.

For a second or two, a silence rang in the room.

Then Jerome laughed. "I think we have made a splendid choice in you, Colin. It would be far better to have you as a friend and part of our group than an enemy."

"Better believe it," Webber replied, and took another drink.

* * *

Some hours later, discussions over, Webber left for the ride home with the senator, and Dansbury was driven to his mansion in the rolling hills near Sugarloaf Mountain. Vince Jerome was dozing in his armchair, the glass of wine by his side forgotten. He was in a long-ago yesterday of unsurpassed tragedy.

The cold was even worse than he remembered from the devil's climate in the Karelia Peninsula. Once, he had thought that nothing could ever be worse than trying to fight, sleep, think and somehow stay alive in the permanent deep freeze of that murderous winter of three years ago. But in that brutal, three-month war, he'd had food most days, he had weapons and ammunition and he had clothing that gave a degree of protection against the vicious cold.

Now it was even colder. And they had few weapons, little ammunition, and dreadfully inadequate clothing with which to defend themselves against the Wermacht. The problem of food was even greater. Yuri woke each time from whatever few moments of nightmare-filled sleep he could take when the German artillery eased, or the sentries could see that no attack was imminent, wondering if this would be the last time he would open his eyes, aware of the pain in his stomach.

"Stalin had promised us that the Germans would never get this far," he muttered to himself through chattering teeth as he stared out over the Russian plains where the Nazi hordes were camped. The sight was something worse than any nightmare of hell. Where once had been rural country was now a devil's stew of torn-up earth, craters, shattered remnants of the hulls of tanks and other vehicles, and many hundreds of bodies still littering the place. Neither side was able to collect their dead. Neither trusted the other to allow a truce long enough. So the bodies rotted where they had fallen, and in the summer, when the wind was in the wrong direction, the smell of carrion flesh drifted over the ruined city of Leningrad. At least something could be said for the forty-below temperatures of this January - the bodies didn't rot and stink the city out.

"My brother would not like to hear me say things like that," he said, smothering the words in the deep grey wool of his heavy scarf, the white swirls of his breath smoking out of the wrapping. Even in the pain of his hunger and the cold, Yuri grinned, his flesh around his mouth stinging as the unfamiliar creases pulled at his skin. He wondered if Dmitri had lost any of his adoration, even idolatry for the Soviet leader and the cause of international communism after the three years of constant warfare, agony and fear through which they had lived.

"And to think," he muttered, his breath smoking again, "I came back to Leningrad for some rest from the war! A man comes home to see his mother, and look what I fall into!"

The Germans had been thundering across the Russian plains, looking as unstoppable as they had been in Poland and everywhere else, when Yuri had come home on leave. But Joseph Stalin had said that the invaders could never reach the Russian cities, and Yuri had believed him. Even after the Finnish fiasco and the serious doubts he had developed about the fighting qualities and leadership of the Soviet forces, Yuri had not thought it possible that the Germans would attack the prime cities of Mother Russia.

But they had. And soon after his twenty-first birthday, Captain Yuri Alexandrovich Kutasov found himself trapped in his beloved Leningrad as the German guns opened up and began to shell the city.

The time was just after one in the afternoon. At two, he knew the German guns would open up again, timed to catch the workers leaving the factories. The workshops had tried staggering hours, but German Luftwaffe spotters were always able to tell the artillery what was going on. Yuri pulled off the Nievsky Prospekt toward his home. His mother was in dreadful shape, but so was everyone else. Food was so scarce that a dog or a cat was worth a month's wages. The daily bread allowance was down to three ounces a person. Yuri knew that many of the civilian workers organized hunts for rats and cooked them also when they could get some heat started. But the factories continued, and the tanks rolled off the assembly lines straight into combat. They had stopped the Germans at the city boundaries and the enemy had never come into Leningrad. It had been three days since Yuri had been able to get away to see his mother and bring her whatever tiny rations he could find.

He picked his way along the battered crater that had once been a broad, beautiful street. A group of women and children were digging through the road at one point. It had become a common method of locating water, because the pumps had failed. So they dug, and they drilled, and they opened up water mains and drew the water from them. Some of the children in the work-party were probably no more than ten, as far as Yuri could tell through the heavy coats and blankets they had around them. Members of the Komsomolski Youth, the children's organizations, he saw. These women and children had been some of the toughest weapons the Party Leaders had available to keep the city going.

Yuri waved at the group. "It is time to be off the streets, Comrades. The pigs will be shelling again, soon."

Even before any of the working part could reply, the shells began.

Damn the German swine, thought Yuri, racing for cover. *They can't even keep a schedule. Nine hours a day they shell us, every day. One day, I will take my own little revenge for what they've done to us.*

Two hours later, he crawled out of the deep ditch in which he had taken shelter. The shells had stopped, and a cloud of oily black smoke hung over the city. Yuri looked around him. The water gatherers lay dead around the hole they had been digging. Some of the bodies had been blown into unrecognizable lumps of bleeding flesh.

"We must survive," swore Yuri. "The world needs to know what we lived through and what the Germans did to us." *And also what our glorious leader Iosif Visarionovich, now known as Joseph Stalin caused his people,* he added internally. *That raving madman has caused most of this, first by gutting the army of its best leaders in his insane purges, and then by trying to come to terms with that other madman, Adolf Hitler. They were two of a kind. May they both rot in hell for all time.*

Consumed with fear for what may have happened to his mother, Yuri turned and ran toward his old home, clutching the small packet of food he had rescued from the miserable meal in the army camp earlier that day.

The whole road was flattened into rubble. Yuri caught his breath when he turned into his old street. Not a house was standing. Not a wall stood more than a foot high.

Frantically, he raced along the road, trying to identify which were the remains of his house. He stopped, recognizing not the house, but the shattered furniture. It was the old armchair his babushka had adopted as her own, old white leather now burned and torn, but still a familiar object. He gingerly worked his way through the rubble, already knowing what he would find.

He had been much later returning home than he realized, he saw as he found his mother. She had not been killed by this latest bombardment, but by some earlier one. Her head was shattered under masonry, her arms trapped under other boulders, her legs still hidden under remnants of a brick wall. The worst sight was her arms and torso, already half-gnawed away by the rats of the city.

"Oh my mother," whispered Yuri. "What have they done to you?"

For only a minute, he stayed, looking for the last time at the corpse of his mother. Then he turned and walked away back to his unit.

"Somebody has to pay for this, Dmitri my brother," he mumbled, as he worked his way through the shattered buildings of Leningrad. "Somehow, some day, this insane world will pay. Wherever the hell you are, elder brother, and if we ever see each other again, you and I will make the world pay for what has happened."

Vince Jerome spluttered as he woke from his dream. The taste of ancient evil was bitter. He blinked, stared round his room and returned to the warm, comfortable present. He picked up his glass of wine from the table by his side and took a mouthful, swirling it around before swallowing.

"Somebody has to pay," he muttered and drained the glass.

* * *

Randy Crawford's entrance to the studios of WNDY was worthy of a news story. The thirty or more reporters camped outside the red building in Martinsburg obviously thought so too, because they besieged him as he parked his Cadillac, opened the door and got out.

Crawford looked stunned at the sight, and he raised his hands to protect his eyes from the flash of the cameras and the glare of the television camcorders.

"Are you going on air as usual today, Randy?" a reporter called. Crawford refused any answer and began to push his way to the doorway of the studios.

"Is there any truth to the allegations made by Mark Ashton, that you work for some group planning a political coup?" a large, beefy man bellowed, holding his camera almost into Crawford's face.

"Will your listeners continue to support you?" shouted a young woman. "And will the station put your program out today?"

Crawford ignored everything until he reached the doorway, then he turned. His tall frame gave him a commanding appearance, and he raised his hands for silence. The mob in front of him obeyed.

Crawford glared at them, then smiled into the watching television cameras. "I'm sure you all understand what happened yesterday," he said. "It's obvious that I've really upset the liberals and communists in this country and they got together to attack me. How anybody can believe that crap is beyond me, but they tried. If I got a little distressed yesterday, I'm sure you all understand how that can happen. I'm a true, patriotic American, and when enemies of this country attack me like that, I get sore. Now, I've got a program to do, and I'm going to do it, so if you'll excuse me..."

He turned to the door, but another voice called out. "What about your military service, Randy? Was that caller correct, that your grandfather got you an exemption from call up?"

Crawford glared. "No, it's not true," he snapped.

"So where in the US forces did you serve?" the reporter persisted. He was a man in his forties, well dressed, with grey hair, wearing a light brown suit.

"None of your business," said Crawford.

"Did you serve at all in the US armed forces, Mister Crawford?" shouted the reporter. The other members of the press fell back, listening to this exchange and watching. The reporter stood next to a camcorder held by a muscular young man with a beard and a ponytail. The glare of the radiant beam killed the sun's shadow and caused a second one.

"Yes, I did," growled Crawford. "But the details are not for release."

"Mister Crawford, yesterday, my station received an email of the letter from your grandfather to the Army board. It appears to verify what that caller said."

"Then it's a forgery!" Crawford was fighting for composure.

"How about the fact that two people were murdered in Illinois?" the reporter continued. "Is it true that both of them had run searches on their companies' computers to locate Mark Ashton, the man who had called you and first laid these charges against you?"

"I have no knowledge of any murders," said Crawford. He swallowed nervously. "As far as I know, that's just a lie made up by the caller."

"What about the claims that many of your callers are set up by one of your staff, Jimmie Wanlyn?" The reporter was calmly reading his notes. "Is this Wanlyn guy one of your people?"

"Jimmie is a loyal American, and yes, he's on my staff," Crawford admitted. "But the claim that he sets up false callers is garbage. Look people! Can't you see what a tangle of lies these people have been telling you? It's just a liberal conspiracy to destroy a loyal American who simply wants to tell the truth to his listeners. Now if you'll excuse me, I have a show to do."

He turned and walked inside the building.

In the lobby, the receptionist stared at him but said nothing. Crawford stamped down the corridor to his office and walked in. To his astonishment, both Janice and Wanlyn were waiting for him.

Crawford stared at Jimmie. "Where the hell have you been?" he demanded.

"Occupied, cleaning up your mess," replied Wanlyn. He looked white and haggard, his eyes hooded with weariness.

"What the hell are you talking about?"

"You know damn well what I'm talking about." Wanlyn looked briefly at Janice. "Ashton was becoming a major embarrassment."

Crawford walked to his chair and slumped down in it. "You mean... those shots Ashton was talking about? That was you?"

"The idea was just to scare him off," replied Wanlyn. He looked again at Janice, and her face reflected utter horror.

"But how the hell did you know where to find him?" Crawford looked shattered. His mouth stayed open after he had finished speaking, and his face had grown pale.

"I was told," said Wanlyn shortly.

Crawford stared at him. "Well you didn't seem to scare him off all that successfully, did you?" he snapped. "The bastard was on the line the next day."

"He had help," Wanlyn retorted. "Somebody was protecting him."

"What the hell do you mean, somebody was protecting him?"

"Look, Crawford! Two of my men were killed! Does that answer your question?"

Crawford fell back in his seat. Wanlyn had never spoken to him except in deferential terms as junior to superior. This animosity was startling. "Killed?" he stammered. "Two of your...? Jimmie, what's going on here? What men?"

"That's not your concern," retorted Wanlyn. "Right now, we have a show to do and your career to recover. I've been busy overnight rounding up callers, and I've got enough here to give you support and wipe out the negative ones. With luck, we'll pull through."

Crawford studied his assistant. There was something going on beyond his comprehension, he knew. He felt dreadfully disturbed at the realization that Wanlyn had another boss. It was obvious to him that the other boss was Vince Jerome. He took a deep breath, recognizing that Jimmie had spoken a major truth. He had a career to recover. He took a deep breath.

"Okay, Jimmie, let's have those callers. Who are they?"

Wanlyn took a sheet of paper from the inside pocket of his dark jacket. "I've got fifteen," he said, and slid the sheet across the desk.

Crawford picked it up and studied it. "More of your friends?" he asked sardonically.

"Just be grateful," Wanlyn replied. A tiny buzzer sounded, and Wanlyn reached inside his pocket again and extracted a tiny cellular phone. He flicked it open.

"Yes," he said, his eyes concentrating on some distant place. He was silent for a few seconds, then his gaze focused on Crawford. "Yes," he said again. "By tonight." He closed the phone and replaced it in his pocket. Crawford looked a question at him.

"Just another one for your list for tomorrow," said Wanlyn. "Let's get into today's program."

Crawford lowered his head to the paper again. "Okay," he replied. "Tell me about these people."

At seven that evening, Crawford was sitting in the lounge room of his home, cradling the fourth in a series of large whiskies. One partial bottle of Jim Beam had been emptied and another brought from the case in his kitchen. The show had gone adequately, he felt. Every caller had been supportive, almost like the old days, but Crawford's nerves were shot. Every time Crawford had pressed the button to take a call, his fear had threatened to overwhelm him, so frightened was he that the caller would turn out to be Ashton or one of the other two unknown men who had ripped into him the day before. But none of them had.

Verity had not stood watching the show, much to Crawford's relief. Christiana had not spoken except to count down the time between breaks for advertising and resumption of the program. At the end, Crawford had stood up, feeling his bones creak as if he were a man in his seventies, instead of his early fifties, stretched and walked straight out to his car. When he opened the door to the outside, his heart lurched with shock as he realized he had forgotten about the horde of reporters from the morning. But the parking lot was deserted. Crawford climbed into the Cadillac and drove home, feeling as if he had put in a night at the mine coalface.

At home, he took a shower, changed into light trousers and shirt, and put the television on. When the six o'clock news came on, he was furious to see his own face in a story from the encounter in the parking lot that morning. But after a few moments, he relaxed. He felt that he had handled himself well and put the blame where it should be, on a group of liberal activists out to destroy him. He worried about the references to his military service, however. *Damn,* he swore. *Who would have thought that one day I would be caught by that? All I can remember of that day is the wonderful relief that I wouldn't be going into the army and probably to Vietnam. I called Grandad and thanked him. Shit, thirty years, and it's back to haunt me. Who the hell were those guys who called me? And how come one of them was able to find that fucking letter?*

He finished his whisky and reached for the bottle to refill his glass. He intended to finish the second bottle tonight. Tomorrow was another day, with a new program and the same excruciating panic every time he pressed the button to take another call, that the caller would not be the name displayed on his computer monitor, but one of those terrifying men in Washington or Mark Ashton himself. He needed spiritual sustenance to handle the prospect.

At ten, his schedule on the bottle contents having fallen behind, Crawford was asleep in his armchair. The television flickered in front of him with unwatched scenes

371

of carnage as a popular movie star mowed down hordes of yellow soldiers in a mythical version of the Vietnam war in which Crawford had taken no part.

The door opening into his lounge room made him twitch, but only when the door slammed close did Crawford wake up. He lifted his head and looked dimly at the intruder.

"Jimmie? Jimmie, what the hell are you doing here?" he mumbled and rubbed his eyes. He looked at his watch. "Jimmie, it's ten o'clock! What are you doing here?"

Wanlyn sat down in the other armchair across from him and smiled. "Sorry, Mister Crawford, but I thought I'd better run down tomorrow's program with you. I got some more callers, but a few of them will need a briefing for you. Better do it tonight." He was dressed in blue jeans, black sneakers and a black, long-sleeved shirt. Crawford saw a folded piece of paper in the breast pocket of the shirt. A pair of thin gloves hung out of Jimmie's back pocket.

"Christ alive, Jimmie!" Crawford muttered. "If you say so. Let me just go and have a piss and wash my face. Afraid I've been into the booze a bit."

"That's okay, Mister Crawford." Wanlyn seemed to be back in his usual respectful manner, thought Crawford as he stood up and weaved unsteadily to his bathroom. Five minutes later, he returned, looking a little fresher.

"How the hell did you get in?" he asked, sitting down again.

Wanlyn smiled. "I tried knocking, but you were obviously asleep. I found the back door open and walked in. You'll have to watch that, Mister Crawford."

"Yeah," muttered Crawford and tried to make his mind function. "What's this about the list of tomorrow's callers?"

"That can wait a while," said Wanlyn, and crossed one ankle over the other knee. "Couple of things I have to tell you first."

"What, about the program tomorrow?" Crawford felt fuzzy and confused. *He was certain he'd locked the rear door...*

"In a way." Wanlyn looked around the luxurious room. "You know, Ashton was right," he said with a wide grin.

"Like hell he was," snapped Crawford. "We're doing everything we can to get the right party back in the White House. So what the fuck's so startling about that? It's what America needs. We've had those liberals in power for too long."

"Of course, Randy," said Wanlyn. He seemed to enjoying himself, and it irritated Crawford.

"Jimmie, there's something I have to tell you," he said, swallowing the taste of sour liquor on his tongue.

"What's that, Randy?" Wanlyn asked. He sat back in his seat in a relaxed manner.

"What we're doing, Jimmie, it's a bit more than just getting a proper president elected," said Crawford. "It's time you learned this. I'm working for a very powerful group of people. When the time is right, they're going to take over this country and run it properly, without any interference from liberals. We've got to do this to protect the place from the communists. Those people could be back in power in Russia at any time, and we have to be prepared."

"Hell, I know that!" Wanlyn laughed. He seemed to be relaxed. "That's what I said about Ashton. He was right about that and about the other bits, too."

"What other bits? What the hell are you talking about, Jimmie?" Crawford was confused. The bombshell he thought he was dropping on Jimmie had been a wet squib. *Jimmie already knew?*

"I killed those two in Illinois, you know," Wanlyn replied. "They had to be silenced after they'd been asked to locate Ashton. Pity really, the young woman was quite a doll. Wouldn't have minded having a bit of a play first, but I was running low on time and I had to do the other guy as well."

Crawford struggled to get his mind working. He was having dreadful trouble understanding what Wanlyn had said.

"The guy Ashton was supposed to have killed, I didn't do that one," Wanlyn continued. "Not enough time. Had to get a contractor in to steal the knife and slice up the hobo. Glad about that. My friend said the old tramp smelled like a week's garbage."

Finally, Crawford began to make sense of the words. "Jimmie! You killed those two...? Dear God in Heaven, Jimmie, what's with you? What the hell's happening? Who told you to do that?"

Wanlyn laughed. "You don't know a damn thing, do you, Randy?" he chuckled. "You think I've been working just for you these last four years? Hell, no! I've reported to Mister Jerome the whole time."

Astounded at the confirmation of his thought earlier that day, Crawford could only stare at his assistant.

"Mister Jerome told me to look through our files of all the people who've offered to help you, and find somebody who could locate Ashton. When they did that, I killed them. And setting up Ashton, as well, I arranged that. Always on the orders of Mister Jerome."

"So it was Jerome who told you where to find Ashton? He told me he'd located them in a cabin up in the mountains."

Wanlyn nodded. A look of rage crossed his face and his voice was tight. "I went up there with three men. But somebody was ahead of us. Somebody professionally trained. One of my men was garrotted when he couldn't have been more than six feet from me. The other one was hit by a shot from the cabin."

"What did you do?" stuttered Crawford. He felt more terrified than he had ever done in his life before. The murderous force in the man across from him was burning the air between them. Crawford saw that he had never known Jimmie before. The man in the other chair was not the familiar, respectful Jimmie Wanlyn.

"We buried the dead guy," said Wanlyn. "Angela arranged a doctor for the other one, but he died."

"Dear God," Crawford mumbled. "I never knew any of this..."

"There was a lot you didn't know," sneered Wanlyn. "Your job was just to keep everybody happy while the big boys took over the country. Pity you won't be able to do that now, Randy. The country's gonna miss you."

"What are you talking about?" Crawford's mind cleared more, and a wave of hideous fear ran through him. Wanlyn looked utterly remorseless and cold.

"You blew it," said Wanlyn. "You completely screwed up with Ashton and those other two. You've lost your credibility."

"Fuck that!" Despite the fear, Crawford was furious. "I'm the best, damn you! Nobody does it like Randy Crawford! I've got thirty million Americans who follow my every word! Look at today's program! Even after those loonies had done their worst yesterday, every call was in support of me!"

"That's because I set them up, Randy," sighed Wanlyn. "And I had to work my buns off to find those callers. I can't do it every day."

"You don't have to," Crawford grated. "Americans will call me, anyway."

"No, they won't, Randy. Not any longer." Wanlyn stood up. His right hand moved behind him and he pulled out the gloves from his rear pocket. Carefully, he slipped them onto his hands, taking considerable pains to ensure a close fit. "The best role for you now is that of a dead hero, a martyr to the cause."

"A what?" Crawford began to tremble. His eyes fixed in disbelief on Wanlyn's gloved hands.

"A martyr, Randy. A dead hero." Wanlyn reached into his trousers pocket and pulled out a metallic object. It clicked and a long, evil blade appeared.

Crawford screamed and got to his feet. "Jimmie! What the hell! There's no need for this! Please Jimmie! Don't do this! For God's sake..." He backed away from Wanlyn, his eyes wide open. Spit burbled on his lips.

Wanlyn's long arm reached out so fast it was almost a blur. His hand seized a clump of Crawford's hair, pulled his head forward and down and dragged Crawford toward him. As the two men closed, Wanlyn pulled Crawford's head back up so that their faces were level. Crawford's face was green-tinged and his mouth was wide open as a scream of horror seemed locked in his throat.

"Think of it this way, Randy," murmured Wanlyn. "We'll make sure you're remembered as a real patriot, a hero for the nation's kids to look up to. We'll tell the world that you were murdered by a group of liberal activists."

His right arm moved with a swift jerk and Crawford froze. His eyes widened even more as he stared into Wanlyn's smiling face. His torso trembled and shook, and a gasping rattle of pain came from his open mouth, like a fish being removed from the hook. His eyes went dull and moved their focus from the face before him into some infinite distance. His body went slack.

Wanlyn gently lowered the dead man back into his armchair, removed the knife with a sharp tug and studied the corpse. He wrinkled his nose at the smell erupting from Crawford's loosened sphincter.

"It was a pleasure working for you, Mister Crawford," he said. He moved to the washroom and rinsed the knife under a tap before carefully wiping it, folding back the blade and replacing it in his pocket. "I'll look after Janice for you."

From his breast pocket, he took the single sheet of paper and unfolded it. He read the contents with a smile on his face and shook his head. Then he dropped the paper on the floor and walked out, stripping off the gloves as he went.

* * *

Jimmie Wanlyn stood on the steps of the studio WNDY in Martinsburg and looked out over the crowd of television cameras and reporters. A Gordian knot of microphones had been placed before him, containing an alphabet soup of network call signs. Wanlyn's face was pale with grief and he appeared to struggle for self-control.

"I have a statement to make," he said. "But you'll excuse me if I'm not able to answer too many of your questions. As you have heard, Randy Crawford was found dead at his home this morning when police were dispatched there after Mister Crawford failed to show up for his regular broadcast to the nation today. He had been stabbed to death, and the rear door showed signs of a break-in. A note was left by the body, and I have a copy of that document here. The police gave it to me after examining the original for prints. Here's what the note says."

He unfolded a sheet of paper and looked at it for a second or two, then began reading.

"Randy Crawford was just a loud-mouthed pig who trumpeted the lying, bigoted garbage the Republican Party preaches. He was a traitor, a liar, a bigot, and an enemy to all real Americans who believe in freedom. We killed him to protect civil liberties in America. Long live the ACLU! Long live all liberal democrats! Down with the Republican Party!"

Wanlyn raised his eyes to the crowd. "As you heard," he said, "the crime was obviously committed by a bunch of insane liberal activists who thought that by silencing the strongest, bravest voice in America, they could forward their own communist agenda. Well, I want them to hear this. Randy Crawford was the finest man I have ever known. He fought relentlessly for the truth in this country, never flinching despite the many threats he got from cowards like these."

He gesticulated with the paper. "Randy may be dead," he continued, "but his voice will continue. Other men with similar love of their country, a passion for truth, freedom of the individual and a delight in the free enterprise system which made this country the greatest nation in the world, other men like Randy Crawford will come forward and fill his shoes. Now if you'll excuse me, I have to get back to work."

He quickly moved inside before any of the press could catch their breath and shout questions to him. Inside, he found Janice looking at him with a glow in her face.

"Oh Jimmie!" she said. "That was wonderful! I know Randy was a hero, but you are too! Oh Jimmie, I'm so proud of you." She clutched his arm and followed him along the corridor to Crawford's office. Wanlyn smiled at her and stroked her hand on his arm.

"Janice, you're a delight," he said. "Perhaps you and I should go out to dinner tonight?"

"Oh I'd love to," she squeaked. "But why don't you come round to my place and I'll cook up something special for us?"

"It's a date, Janice," he said, and tried not to stare too hard at her breasts.

From the end of the corridor, Verity and Christiana watched the couple thoughtfully. Nick Verity ignored Janice and watched Jimmie Wanlyn like a boxer watches his opponent climb into the ring.

Chapter 17 - Frederick, Maryland

"Yes, I had him killed." Jerome looked round the spacious conference table. Tension showed in each of the faces staring back at him. "His value to us alive had ended," Jerome continued calmly. "Dead, he still had a role to play, and he's doing it extremely well."

"Sounds like a side of beef," General Rollings retorted, receiving a smile of amusement from Jerome and a black glare from Charles Dansbury.

"That was about his intellectual level," Jerome murmured. "His performance declined sharply once Mark Ashton decided to wage war against him, and you saw the effects when two other strong intellects attacked him in concert. Crawford's time had ended."

"Obviously, those two men were part of the mysterious group we've been trying to identify," Geoffrey Payne said harshly. "I can't believe that the people in this room have been stymied by this task. Doesn't *anyone* have a glimmer about this bunch? What about you, Colin? You're the newest one here. Can you throw any light on this problem?"

Webber shook his head. "Good Lord, Geoffrey, I'm not a Beltway insider! I wouldn't know about mysterious intelligence groups like that!"

"I'm still unconvinced that any such group exists," said Jerome firmly. "As Geoffrey implied, the fact that nobody in this room, nor any of our extensive contacts can identify any such counter-intelligence operation in Washington, speaks for itself. There *is* no such operation."

"Regardless, Vince, I still say that having Crawford killed was rather impulsive," said Dansbury. The usual friendly tone was missing from his voice. Dansbury sat one seat away from Jerome's left, instead of his usual place immediately next to him. Redman had occupied his normal chair at the far end, the others had spread themselves around the table giving each other maximum space. The air in the room crackled with tension.

"Yes, Vince, it was," Redman agreed. "But you never do things impulsively, I know you well enough for that. So come clean. *Why* was Crawford killed?"

"I'd like to know that too," Morgan Eckhard added coldly. "He may have been a buffoon, but he brought votes into my party by the busload. He'd have got over the last couple of days' misadventures."

"I think otherwise," Jerome replied. "If his support staff had not gone to extraordinary lengths to round up compliant callers the day after the triple-headed attack from Washington, Crawford might have collapsed. The small recovery he made was insufficient to carry him for more days of hostilities. Had he been left in place, our cause would have been badly hurt. In fact, I'm sure the backlash would have started to reflect in increasing support for the opposition."

A moment of silent thought hummed round the table.

"So what do you plan, Vince?" Webber asked. "Is Crawford to be replaced, or will others take up the slack?"

"For the moment, the latter," replied Jerome. "But that slack must be pulled in tight. I want the pressure increased dramatically. Every other member of the talk show network must start to call for retribution against Crawford's killers and step up the pace of far right preaching. In the meantime, young Wanlyn performed as I asked him to, by initiating the rumors that liberal conspirators murdered Crawford. Several newspapers have picked up that story, as well as a number of our radio hosts and captive television stations. The news is well on its way round America and Crawford sympathy will soon be running high again."

"Vince, this sounds dreadfully like the early stages of the plan's implementation phase," called out Rollings. "Just what are you doing here?"

"Yes, Vince!" Dansbury snapped. "What the hell *are* you doing? This phase is not supposed to start until a year into the next administration."

"I suggest to all of you, that we must bring forward the plan start date," Jerome replied coolly. One finger tapped the handle of his walking stick.

"What?" Several of the men shouted out together. Redman and Payne rose to their feet, followed by the Reverend Vanderbilt who had been staring in confusion at Jerome. Only Grant Armstrong remained quiet, watching the proceedings in complete calm.

"I think it's essential," said Jerome quietly. "Sit down, all of you, and I'll tell you why."

He waited for the few moments necessary for the room to settle down again, the whole time staring eye to eye with Charles Dansbury. The fury in the older man was palpable. When the room was silent, Jerome moved his eyes back to the group.

"As I already said," he began, "the backlash against Crawford and all he had stood for over the last few years was a real danger. Add to that, the threat posed by this actual or non-existent group which is causing havoc with all of you, and I see a real danger that we would lose our way. There is nothing sacred about waiting for a pocket president before we move. In fact, I believe the time is better now than it will ever be. The killing of Crawford can be used to trigger a huge public outcry by the middle classes and the undecided voters. We always have planned for such a trigger, as you know, but the precise details were to be left until nearer the date. Well, now we have it. Let's use it."

"Vince, that's only one bolt in the whole works," Payne objected. "There's a shit-load of other stuff that needs doing as well."

"Agreed," Jerome concurred. "But the only difference between now and our planned schedule, is the presence of the current president in the White House, instead of our trained puppet. I'll address that problem in a moment. Right now, if all of you performed your functions, we could bring about our New America before Christmas."

"Jesus Christ!" Rollings exploded. He received an offended glare from Reverend Jackson Vanderbilt and an uncharacteristically wide grin from Jerome.

"Appropriately put, General," said Jerome. "It takes your breath away, doesn't it, when all the academic plans suddenly take concrete shape?"

"Fucking-A," Rollings swore, staring into an infinite distance.

"So let's review our state of readiness, shall we?" Jerome continued. "Let's start with the civil uprising. Morgan, can your network start raising the level of intensity of their output? Can they generate the fury and discontent with the present administration to the point where almost any change will be seen as an improvement?"

"I think so, Vince, but without Crawford, I'm not certain." Eckhard appeared calm and interested. "I'll talk to our dirty tricks team immediately and get them started. Certainly, with the radio stations we own, we can install really extreme speakers and heat things up well."

"Do that," said Jerome and turned to Vanderbilt. "Jackson, your people. They must start preaching utter hatred against the administration and raise the fear level about Geoffrey and Tony's work to a level beyond rational restraint. Remember, Tony will incite massive riots in the ghettos of all the major cities. Geoffrey will arm both his irregular forces and the ghetto forces from his stockpiles and send them into battle against each other and initiate armed conflict throughout America. Your network of preachers, Reverend, must make more millions get to the point of reaching for their guns to defend their homes against anyone who shows their face in the neighborhood and so join Geoffrey's forces to destroy the under-classes. Can they do that?"

"Of course," Vanderbilt replied. "Just as soon as I give the word. Every one of them has their parts prepared and rehearsed."

"You see, gentlemen," Jerome said with a smile. "It's looking simpler, already."

"The question of presidential compliance still has to be raised," Dansbury growled. "That one is not some simple question of speeding things up."

"I agree," Jerome replied with a polite nod. "But please bear with me for a moment. General, let's turn to you. You can guarantee that each of the state National Guards in the areas where Geoffrey, Tony and Jackson will incite rioting will hand control of the action to your military groups?"

"Damn right," said Rollings. "Every one of the commanders knows that he'll get special treatment from the Pentagon when things settle again, providing they've followed my orders completely. Their roles will switch to taking control of the radio and television stations. My people will continue to broadcast panic news until they get the word from me, at your indication, that we tell them things are cooling down. I'll have every one of those selected cities totally under military rule within three days. If necessary, I'll bring in the Air National Guard to conduct bombing runs of the ghetto areas. The destruction and death rate will be monumental and that will give even better reasons for the military presence. We're ready."

"I expect nothing less," said Jerome with a smile. "Geoffrey?"

"The same," replied Payne. "I have nearly sixty thousand paramilitary troops ready to take weapons from the caches round the country and follow orders. They'll attack the ghetto rioters with everything they have. I think I've recruited every Ku Klux Klan whacko, racist, skinhead and neo-Nazi shitbrain in the country. They're raring to go. I think you're right Vince. Sooner, rather than later.

My people are ready to crack heads and lynch a few niggers."

"Exactly," Jerome murmured. "And Anthony?"

"As with Geoffrey," Redman agreed. "I have people in every one of the selected slum areas and ghettos. They'll whip up a storm that'll make Los Angeles look like a christening service. If it's necessary, my own men will fire into the crowds here and there, then incite revenge against Whitey. Whitey, of course, will be Geoffrey's teams."

"And I won't weep if they take out the majority of those guys," said Payne with a cold smile. "They may be of use right now, but the country will be cleaner when they've gone, I tell you."

"And less of a problem with running the place after, as well," Rollings added. "I don't want us following Hitler's path and letting the thugs take over the government."

The Reverend Vanderbilt looked angry. "One thing I'm going to see about when we're in power," he snarled, "is that this country stops pouring dirt on Adolf Hitler. We should have fought with Germany and destroyed the Soviet Union back then, not allied with the godless heathens in Russia and destroyed a fine man who built his nation and did great works."

"Yeah, yeah," drawled General Rollings. "Always knew you were a Nazi at heart, Reverend. Amazing how many of you Jesus-freaks are."

Vanderbilt slammed his fist on the table in fury, but he was interrupted before he could speak.

"Gentlemen, will you get it into your heads that we're about to go to war!" Jerome spoke loudly, a rare event. "The last thing we need right now is this sort of bickering. Reverend, we'll consider your proposed educational agenda when we have the country, not till then. Now then, Grant. You have everything ready?"

"Of course," Armstrong replied. He had not looked at any of the speakers as the last contention broke out. "I have only to email a code number to the banks for the money to be transferred to several suppliers around the world. Over a hundred thousand Kalashnikov AK-47s with ammunition will be delivered into Geoffrey's arms caches within two days after that, to provide the evidence that the ghetto rioters are being supplied by revolutionary countries. Customs posts in Los Angeles and New York are prepared to pass through all the crates marked with a code sign and expedite delivery immediately. After things are in our hands, money will be transferred without any fuss to the accounts you and Charles control to handle as you need."

"And Colin will be the administrative force managing the whole thing," said Jerome with a nod at Webber. "Colin will also be managing the military rule for the first six weeks, especially the setting up and running of the concentration camps in New Mexico, Utah, South Dakota, Alaska and Nevada. Once peace has been restored, it will be Colin's mandate to set up the apparent return to democratic rule with elections. But of course, as there will not be an opposition party at that stage, we will create whatever we want."

"You still haven't addressed the question of the President," said Dansbury. His normally soft voice had picked up a strident note that sounded like a discontented whine.

Jerome turned to him. "Then let us do so," he said. "I see no problem, even though he is not the puppet we envisaged. When hell is let loose on America, he will be so confused, frightened and helpless, that I have no doubts he will agree to do what we want. That is, declare a state of emergency throughout the nation so that the existing laws regarding detention camps can be enacted and the constitution suspended. We will overwhelm him with pressure groups from those senators and congressmen who depend on us and the Asbury influence to remain in power. In the almost impossible circumstance that he still resists such a move, then we simply speak to him privately. We will tell him that his family cannot be protected any longer, and that we cannot even be certain that the Secret Service corps assigned to protection duties does not contain enemy agents committed to killing them both unless he follows our will. He will get the message. As a last resort, we will repeat our triumph of 1963 and remove him."

The silence in the room lasted nearly a minute before Anthony Redman broke it.

"You seem to have things covered, Vince. I say we go."

"I second that," said Geoffrey Payne enthusiastically. "Let's do it!"

"For God's sake, yes!" the Reverend Vanderbilt shouted. "We've been waiting too long and we have let evil triumph in this nation. It's time to bring God..."

"Give it a rest, Reverend," snapped Armstrong. "You're in this for the same reason the rest of us are. You want power, and the irritations of democratic procedure are too much for you. Jesus and God have nothing to do with it. Your preaching gives me the shits. Now stop it."

Astonishment hung in the air as all the men in the room stared at Armstrong. Vanderbilt's jaw had dropped and his mouth was open. Finally, Redman laughed out loudly.

"Well, talk about still waters, Grant!" he chortled. "It's time somebody pricked that blown-up windbag lover of little boys. Well said."

"That's enough, gentlemen, for the last time," said Jerome, and the room fell silent. "We have yet to poll all of you. Colin, what about you? Go or no go?"

"I believe the final decision can wait," replied Webber. "I suggest the following. Let Eckhard's army of talk-show hosts step up the vigor of their rhetoric. Let us see what the results of that are in ten days. Let Vanderbilt's people do the same and build up the tensions among the religious right. Geoffrey should start to mobilize his army of whackos as he terms them, and Grant should have the banks and weapons dealers ready to move on a moment's notice. In ten days, if the signs are right, then I propose you give the word, Vince."

Jerome looked steadily at Webber for a few moments, then nodded. "That seems eminently sensible, Colin. I support that idea. General, what about you?"

Rollings seemed lost in thought. "You were right, Vince," he said finally. "It's a bit overwhelming when all these years of planning in a rather academic manner come to the point of taking reality. I have to remember that I'm going to break my oath as an officer in the United States Air Force and be part of a move to change the face of the nation by altering the democratic principles, maybe even conniving at the assassination of my Commander-in-Chief, the President."

"Corley, I hope you're not having doubts about your role in all this?" said Jerome urgently. "I trust you're not considering backing out?"

Rollings smiled. "What, and face one of your young men with a pistol when I try and walk out of here? No, I think I want to live a bit longer, Vince. And no, I'm not backing out. We have to put the country back on the road, and if a benevolent dictatorship for a few years is going to do it, count me in. I just have to trust you that you do indeed plan to restore the constitution and democratic, multi-party rule some time down the road."

"Why should we not wish to, Corley?" said Jerome smoothly. "We're not communists. We're Americans who believe in the American way of things. But a rebuilding is necessary, we all know that, and it can't be achieved on the existing political swamp that is America today."

Rollings nodded. "Okay, Vince, you have my support and my vote. Let's do it."

"Thank you, General," said Jerome. "And finally, Charles, I know you have reservations about this. Your opinion?"

Dansbury was staring at the table top in deep thought. After a second or two of further deliberation, he looked up. "I think this is too early," he said. "I believe we would have more distinct success if we waited until after the elections and had total control of all branches of government. But I have listened to you all, and I must agree that an unpleasant and unforeseen development has occurred with Crawford's public embarrassment and the possible backlash that might result, and with the fears about this mysterious group that might be opposing us. I agree with Colin. Let us start the preliminary activities and review the situation in ten days. But I don't like this at all. Sixty years of planning are in jeopardy."

A rumble of assent ran round the table.

"Good," said Jerome. "Those of you with assignments to complete, begin them as soon as you leave here. We'll meet again in ten days. Now, gentlemen, pass me your note pads, and then we'll go to lunch."

Each of the men with the exception of Dansbury rose to their feet and brought their notepads to the head of the table. As Jerome began feeding the pads through the shredder, the others walked out, leaving only Dansbury and Jerome in the boardroom. Neither of them spoke as Jerome completed the destruction process, then sat back with a small sigh.

"Yuri, little brother, what is it that you're doing?" Dansbury asked softly. "I thought I knew you, but this sudden move on your own without consulting me has frightened me."

"Am I supposed to consult you on everything I do?" Jerome flicked an irritated look at his brother.

"Don't be silly," Dansbury retorted. "We have never needed to refer our every action to each other. But this is not some incidental part of the plan, Yuri, this is *The Plan* you have initiated without talking to me. Surely, you should have talked to me?"

"I had no time," replied Jerome. "The events surrounding Crawford were too rapid. His incredibly stupid performance when he faced the three-pronged attack was the end, and he would have seriously damaged our structure if he had continued. I had to move at once."

"And when we have achieved our aims, Yuri, what then? Why is it that I suspect you of having different plans than we first developed after Berlin? What is it that you want to do, my little brother?"

"Exactly as we have always done, Dmitri. We will control America and run it our way."

"That was only a means, Yuri, not the end, you know that. We would use our power to bring about something else."

"Then maybe I've grown up, Dmitri. The something else you have always dreamed of no longer interests me. I will be perfectly happy with the first phase of our plan, controlling America. You promised me as we stood in the ruins of Berlin, that we would become the richest men in America. Well, we have, Dmitri. We are so rich that I cannot count fast enough to keep pace with the rate at which the money increases every second. We have power no King or Emperor or Tsar could ever have imagined, greater even than that old lunatic Joseph Stalin had. Why would I want anything else?"

"Because a true communist wants not just power, Yuri, but to achieve great things with that power. He wants equality and fairness. He wants the people to have the power over their government. He wants the ordinary workers, the men and women who produce the wealth to say how their lives should be run."

"Communism, Dmitri? You will give away all this, all these billions you have salted away in banks around the world? To whom will you give it? Will you stand on some street corner and give it away to every man and woman who passes by? Or will you write a check for what, seventy, eighty billion and give it to the IRS? And then what will you do? Live on a state pension in some apartment block in Baltimore?"

Dansbury stared at the other man for over a minute, studying Jerome's face with great care.

"You betray our agreement, little brother? For what? To hold onto this immense power and wealth for what purpose? What else can you possibly want out of life? You have everything. No, I do not plan to give it all away and live like a common worker in some apartment block. After all these years, I realize that some of the theories of Marx and Lenin do not match up to human nature. I will certainly hand over my corporations to the state, because we must make all commercial ventures the property of the state, but I'm human, and I have every intention of remaining rich and comfortable for my last years. As would you, and all our council and their supporters. I do not pretend the hypocrisy of pure egalitarianism. But the fact still remains, Yuri, the country is almost destroyed by the greed and disparity of wealth. We have always used the argument for our cause, 'A house divided against itself cannot stand.' If we are to bring Lenin's dream back to Russia, we must first make America strong again. And that means healing the damage that the last few decades have wrought and returning some equality to the people. This nation is about to collapse. I believe we will build something greater from that collapse. But not just to make ourselves richer and more powerful. We will do it to make a better world. We have that chance, Yuri."

"What chance have we to make it a better world, Dmitri? The world is rotten to the core. Look at the cesspit of greed, lust and corruption with which we have surrounded ourselves to form our council. These are the men to run our New America? How many of them are interested in making a better world? The religious pig will use his position to get more little boys brought to him. The Mafia filth will have more little girls. Our bloodless CIA moron will steal more snuffboxes and Geoffrey Payne will drink himself to death in a year. Rollings will buy more expensive toys for his friends and God knows what Eckhard's wife will let the simpleton senator do. Webber will have the time of his life running America like he used to run his businesses. It will just be a bigger and better factory to tune up."

Dansbury nodded. "I have no argument with any of that, Yuri. We used the resources we had to for our own ends. But there are another three hundred million Americans out there who are less fortunate. Our task begins with them, and then one day, with our old fellow-citizens in Russia."

Jerome sneered. "Ordinary Americans? What do you think they care? They are as much simpletons as Morgan Eckhard. Leave them with their idiot game-shows on televisions and their gladiatorial contests on the football fields, give them beer and pop-corn and nothing to disturb their minds, throw a war against some small country every year or two, and they'll be happy. If we rebuild the slums, the slums will come back, because the pigs who live there will make their habitat just as they were before. They don't *want* to change, Dmitri. They love their cities as they are, they love to kill each other almost as much as those maniac Arabs in the Middle-East do, and they know in the deepest hearts that this the finest country in the world where everything is perfect so long as a Republican is in the White House, regardless of whether he has a brain or not. Why on earth should we bother with improving their condition, big brother?"

Dansbury seemed to droop in his seat. "When did you begin to hate this country so much, Yuri? You have got so much from it, and yet I hear a detestation that frightens me. What happened to you?"

"What happened, dear elder brother, was the war. When I froze almost to death in Finland, when I looked at our mother's body half-eaten by rats, and when I walked with you through the rubble of Berlin, I learned that wars are fought by eager young men on behalf of megalomaniac old men. I decided then that I wouldn't be part of that stupidity. America is just a place where it was easy to make money, particularly when we started with the millions we brought with us from Berlin. But this country is full of megalomaniacs just the equal of Joseph Stalin, Saddam Hussein or Adolf Hitler. Its old men go to war and kill its young men for personal aggrandizement just as easily as any of the others do. I want no part of it, Dmitri. I will help you in this current project because it suits me to do so and because I can make America pay for what happened to us. But if you want to bring Marxist-Leninism to America or return it to Russia, do it without me."

Dansbury looked steadily at him. "But will you interfere, Yuri? Will you do anything to stop me?"

Jerome shook his head. "Why should I interfere with your hobbies, Dmitri? If you want to make America the new workers' paradise, do it with my blessing so long as you take nothing away from me that is mine. If you want to take that glorious struggle back to Russia, I know you'll have enthusiastic support from our little council for an invasion of the old Soviet territories. They will be as ignorant of your real plans as they are today. Vanderbilt will pretend he's returning God to the Communists, while what he really wants is a supply of pretty young Slavic men. Rollings will love it, because he can finally justify everything the Pentagon has represented for the last sixty years. It will be the biggest war-game of his life and that of all his brass-brained friends. Geoffrey will sell more guns and Redman will have whole new territories to exploit with drugs, protection rackets and women. Leave me out of it, though. I want to enjoy the last years of my life without more crusades for ideological paradise."

Dansbury was silent, lost in thought. "I'm deeply sorry about this, Yuri," he said at last. "We had an amazing dream, you and I. We were going to change the world like no other has ever done. The fact of doing it with my brother was always the greatest source of delight and pride to me."

"But we did do it together, old friend." Jerome spoke softly and with warmth. "We became the richest men in the richest country on earth. We are about to complete a program we set running over sixty years ago, and we will succeed. It's just that you can put the finishing touches to the plan yourself. I admire your courage, your persistence in sticking to principles I abandoned long ago, but I became tired of war. I want a vacation that will last for the remainder of my life. There's a world I haven't seen yet, Dmitri." He grinned, looking almost like the young warrior of half a century before. "And I want to see it before you convert the whole world to your workers' paradise."

At last, Dansbury laughed. He rose to his feet. "All right, my young and foolish brother, I accept those conditions. Work with me through this phase and I will take it on from there. Now, shall we join our New Founding Fathers for lunch?"

"And Angela," Jerome added with a warm smile. "Never let us forget Angela."

"What man in his right mind could ever do that?" Dansbury responded dryly and moved to the door.

* * *

The Reverend Jackson T. Vanderbilt sat back in his leather armchair and drank half his bourbon and branch water with a noisy gulp. Across from him, the Reverend William Boxmire, president of Children of Christ Networks sat stiffly, cradling a glass of mineral water. Seated in a hard wooden upright chair, the Reverend Hugo Shipman of the Shipman Ministries held a large brandy balloon. Both of Vanderbilt's guests looked uncomfortable.

"So here's what you're gonna do," Vanderbilt proclaimed and belched. "I want the crusade stepped up. I want every one of your flocks ready to pick up their guns and kill anyone who even looks cross-eyed at them. You're gonna tell them that the liberals and communists in this country are arming themselves to destroy our institutions and wreck the churches. The niggers are pouring out of the ghettos and gonna rape our women and kill all of us. And man, I tell you, they really are! Count on it!"

"But Jackson, how can you know that?" Shipman looked alarmed. His narrow-set eyes were wide open and his pale face was even whiter than usual.

Vanderbilt looked contemptuously at him. "That's outside your territory, Shipman," he said. "But you can take this to the bank. It's gonna happen. And if you want the Christian, God-fearing, white people of America to live through this, you'd better prepare them. Tell them the anti-Christ is rising. Get them scared out of their fucking wits. Believe me, it's for a good reason. When it's all over, America will be ours. The rule of our ministries will be the rule of the land. This will be God's own country again, and all the niggers, kikes and spics will be dead or back in their own smelly little countries."

Boxmire sipped his mineral water. "What about abortion?" he asked. "Can you assure me that we'll finally put a stop to that?"

"Damn right!" Vanderbilt snorted. "We'll finally be able to make it a crime to have one, to do one, or to know about one and not tell the law. It'll be the death penalty for any doctor doing one, and years in the slammer for any bitch who gets one done."

"Hallelujah!" said Boxmire and lowered his head reverentially. "God's law will finally be enforced."

"Yeah, yeah," Vanderbilt agreed impatiently. "Can you do this? Get the people really steamed up?"

"Of course," Boxmire replied. "Can I tell them that the president has finally been revealed as a worshipper of Satan?"

"That sounds good," agreed Vanderbilt. "You too, Shipman. Tell them that."

"But Jackson, I'm still very uncertain," Shipman protested. "These are lies! We have no way of knowing any of this. What are you trying to do?"

Vanderbilt glared at him and pointed a long finger at Shipman's nose. "Now listen, Shipman," he growled. "Do I have to *make* you do this? You won't like it if I do, I assure you. The IRS will love to hear about all those millions you've salted away into private accounts in the

Caymans, and I'm sure your parishioners who sent all that money will forgive you, won't they?"

Shipman closed his eyes as if in prayer for a few moments, then opened them and looked at his glass. "I'll do what you ask, Reverend Vanderbilt."

"Glad to hear it," replied Vanderbilt. "How about you, Boxmire? Need any pushing to do this thing? Maybe some words to the press about that secretary you're boffing after services each Sunday and Wednesday? Or the money you siphon off from the contributions by pensioners and the cripples?"

Boxmire shook his head. "Not at all, Jackson. I am God's servant and will do His bidding. If this is to restore the rule of God to America, there is nothing which can be deemed wrong about what we do."

"I'm sure the Lord appreciates your efforts," said Vanderbilt sarcastically. He was about to say more, when the telephone by his elbow rang softly. He picked it up.

"Yes," he said, and listened for a few moments. "About ten minutes," he said, and replaced the phone. He looked at the other two.

"Any more questions?" he asked, and received two silent head shakes. "Good. Get on with it on your next broadcasts. I want to see results within five days."

The two men placed their unfinished drinks on the coffee table in front of them and rose to their feet. Vanderbilt didn't bother standing up to see them off. His mind was clearly elsewhere. When the front door closed behind the departed televangelists, Vanderbilt rose to his feet and went to his bathroom. He brushed his teeth and sprinkled some after-shave on his face and neck, looking happily at his reflection in the mirror.

A soft tap came on the front door. Vanderbilt walked along his corridor to the entrance and opened it to the dark night. A young boy was standing outside. He looked about fourteen, thin and fair-skinned. His face held an almost angelic beauty to it, and the boy's eyes were dark and dreamy.

"Come in, my son," said Vanderbilt in a warm, friendly tone, then caught his breath as the boy came under the hall light. The child's beauty almost overwhelmed him. He began to feel warmth spreading through his whole body.

He led the boy along the corridor and showed him into the lounge room from which his visitors had just left. He placed both hands on the boy's shoulders and smiled. The boy's eyes seemed blank and distant, the influence of a drug showing in the enlarged pupils.

"You are really a very handsome young man," said Vanderbilt, and bent to kiss the boy full on the mouth. "Come, I think the other room will be more suitable."

Geoffrey Payne sat in a gloomy bar outside Baltimore. The place reeked of stale beer and urine, and Payne was uncomfortable, despite the automatic nine-millimeter pistol near his armpit. The weapon was one of his private designs. It held eighteen bullets in the magazine and every test so far, in all conditions had resulted in a faultless performance. The weapon had never jammed. Payne had another .22 pistol strapped to his right ankle, but he still felt threatened in his surroundings. Four grossly large men were playing pool in a few feet away from where he sat with another man at a table in the corner. Several more men sat at other tables, some in groups, some sullenly drinking alone. A massive, dangerous-looking man in one corner wore a Raiders' baseball cap over black hair tied in a ponytail. His table held four empty beer cans and he sat alone.

Payne's conversation partner was tall and thin. His head was shaved bald. He wore a black, sleeveless leather jacket over in a black shirt, also without sleeves. Both forearms were covered with tattoos. Amid the swirl of colors and patterns, a small swastika nestled between a rose and the name "Maureen." The man held a beer can between long, prehensile fingers.

"We'll be declaring open season in about two weeks," said Payne. "After that, anything goes."

"Great!" said the other man. Payne knew him only as Jensen, and they had met three times before.

"When do we get the guns?" Jensen asked.

"As soon as I get the clearance, I'll email you the codeword "Foxfire" followed by the code number for the city where the first action is to take place. You'll also get the address of the arms store and the date and time to get there. As soon as you arrive, I'll have people ready to open up the store and you can take what you want. One of the men there will identify himself to you as Adam Smith. He'll tell you where to head to meet the blacks. There'll be a crowd of them, probably with weapons, also."

Jensen's eyes gleamed in the dim lights of the bar. "Just more niggers to kill," he said. "How's it going to happen?"

"Largely up to you," Payne replied. "A mob out of the ghetto will be advancing on a demonstration. You'll be placed to stop them. Nobody's going to interfere. The cops and the National Guard will both be kept out of there, so it's your call."

"Sounds too good to be true," said Jensen. His smile was cold. "How come we're being given shooting rights on niggers all of a sudden, Mister Payne? Who's okayed this?"

Payne shrugged. "You don't need to know. But let's say that the powers-that-be have decided to do some spring-cleaning. The ghettos are overflowing and threatening to go crazy. Your job is to cull the herds, so to speak, but it can't be seen as official policy, obviously."

"And what about cities after that? We're gonna get more spring-cleaning duties?"

"Of course," replied Payne. "I'll send the same codeword and city details as soon as we want the next place cleaned out."

"It's gonna be a blast, Mister Payne, I promise you. And you're certain that there'll be no crackdown by National Guards or the military? We have complete freedom of action?"

"Burn the place to the ground, if you want," replied Payne.

"And all the niggers in it as well, eh?"

"If that's what you want. It will help to clear the areas. We'll have to bulldoze the places afterward, anyway."

"What about the Jews?" Jensen persisted. "When do we get a crack at them?"

"In time. But it will have to wait. We need the ghettos cleaning out first. Don't get ahead of yourself, Jensen, or I'll take away your toys."

Jensen raised the beer can to his lips, threw his head back and drained the can. He crushed the can in his hand and tossed it carelessly behind him. It clattered into the far corner. The large man under the Raiders' baseball cap looked briefly at the flight of the can, then at the two men, and resumed his own thoughts.

Jensen grinned. "Foxfire, eh? Followed by a city address? And then I get the final details from somebody called Adam Smith?"

"Right."

"He wrote *'The Wealth of Nations,'* I recall. Well, he's sure gonna improve the wealth of *my* little nation, that's a fact."

"Jensen, you surprise me," said Payne with a smile. "I didn't even know you could read."

"You don't know me at all, Mister Payne," Jensen agreed. "I have a master's degree in physics from Minnesota."

"Adolf Hitler's mantle has been passed to a worthy successor," replied Payne, and walked away from the table, hearing the laugh behind him.

Grant Armstrong smiled at the ledger book. The final figure at the bottom of the eighth page was a few hundred over fifteen million dollars. It represented the balance in an account in a bank in the Cayman Islands. Other than the bank employees, only Armstrong knew of the existence of the account and the code numbers that could access it. Accumulating the sum had been the easiest project Armstrong had ever undertaken. Every drug haul he had supervised over the last two years had resulted in a few kilos of the powder being hidden away and later sold during the period of pent-up demand following the shortage caused by the CIA action. He could have taken so much more, he knew. When the money started to flood in from sales of subsequent imports of narcotics, now under the control of groups set up by Armstrong and his team, he could have siphoned off millions, even billions with little risk of detection. He had complete control of the bank accounts that would fund the New America coup. Armstrong had his own version of ethics. He would never steal from his employer. It was just that the stolen heroin and cocaine did not belong to Jerome and Dansbury at the time of the theft.

Smiling, he placed the ledger back in his safe, and opened another drawer. He took out a wooden case and opened the lid. Inside, the tiny gold snuffbox gleamed at him. Rubies and diamonds lined the lid, and a delicate frieze of sapphires circled the base. Armstrong had found the treasure in the home of a wealthy industrialist when the DEA had conducted a strike as a result of an anonymous tip that the industrialist had been importing narcotics from Mexico. The squad had turned the house over and found nothing. Armstrong, who knew what the result of the search would be beforehand, because he had furnished the tip-off himself, was more interested in the man's store of treasures like the one now on his desk. He had read about the snuffbox collection in a magazine and determined to own it. The industrialist had not taken action to recover the missing item. He had no wish to be targeted again by the DEA.

Armstrong held the box in the palm of his right hand and fixed a watchmaker's glass in his eye. He spent the next two hours crooning over his latest acquisition.

Finally, as midnight came, he took a book from his sparse bookshelf, and prepared a series of emails on his portable computer. They were carefully coded, using the unbreakable "Private book" code. The messages were a series of triplets of numbers. Each triplet represented the page, line and word number from a book. Only Armstrong and the recipients knew which one of fifteen pre-selected books it was, and the title was specified by a dummy number at the beginning of the message. Without that knowledge, the message was unreadable.

Armstrong connected up his telephone line to the computer and sent out a series of emails to locations around the world. One of them was a bank in Geneva, initiating a transfer of over six hundred million dollars to an account for which only Vince Jerome had access. Armstrong knew that Jerome would be spending heavily in the next few days, preparing crucial people and organizations. The emails sent, Armstrong replaced the copy of Tom Clancy's *'Clear and Present Danger'* on the shelf and went to bed.

"President? My dear man, I do hope you're joking!" Peggy Jo Asbury's disdain was monumental, and Senator Morgan Eckhard shriveled beneath it.

"I only suggested I was as good as anyone to have in the White House," he protested weakly. "I also said you'd make a perfect First Lady."

"Hah!" Peggy Jo resumed her reading of *'War and Peace.'* She sat in the silk-covered wingback chair of their home in Atlanta. The room was furnished with exquisite taste, all at Peggy Jo's direction and design. Cream curtains hung over the massive bay windows, lime-green carpets like a tropical sea held a number of beautiful and rare antique pieces of furniture. If the room was beautiful, Peggy Jo Asbury put it in the shade. She was tall, slender, graceful, the shape and presence every international model dreamed of having. Her flawless complexion framed startling green eyes, and dark red hair flowed like a waterfall to her shoulders.

She turned a page with an elegant hand and looked up at her husband. "Morgan, my dear, how could you possibly run for President? One whiff of your real war record would destroy you, never mind what would happen if the world ever heard of your taste for your own daughter."

Eckhard flushed crimson. "Dammit, Peggy Jo, I wish you could let me forget that. It was a long time ago."

"And she was very young, for that precise reason." Her voice was like a glacier. "And anyway, Morgan, I have no wish to be First Lady. Bowing and scraping before you and turning adoring looks on you like that awful Reagan woman did with that Ronnie person would turn my stomach for a start, and having to look like the perfect couple for so many hours in the day would stretch my capacity for acting. No, dear, Vince was quite right. Forget it. Be content with working on the Council."

Eckhard struggled to control his rage, knowing very well that he could never injure his wife in verbal combat. Before he could say anything, the door opened and a younger version of Peggy Jo came in. Deborah Anne looked coolly at her father, and advanced on the twin of her mother's wingback chair, seating herself with a graceful motion. Both women looked at Eckhard.

"The rule, Morgan, remember the rule," Peggy Jo said, closing her book. "You may not stay in the same room as Deborah unless there are at least three other people with you."

Stifling his rage, Eckhard rose and walked out of the room, painfully aware of the cold glare from his daughter. He walked down the corridor to his own study and entered it. He prowled the room restlessly, touching the bookshelves with his fingers. Eckhard had never read a book from cover to cover in his whole life and was bewildered by the capacity of both his wife and daughter to read so much. He had no duties to prepare for the coming rebirth of America. His job had already been done. He had supervised and generally guided the dirty-tricks group that sent out the emails each day to Crawford and the others in the network of controlled talk-show hosts, and he had been a conduit between Jerome and the Asbury family. That evening, after returning to Atlanta, he had called the head of his email-creators in Washington and ordered an intensive upgrade in the level of vitriol aimed at the administration, and now Eckhard knew he was redundant, probably permanently. He took a bottle of Jim Beam and a glass from his cupboard, poured out several ounces and sat down before the television. He used the remote control to switch it on then surfed through the channels before settling on a movie on HBO. Sylvester Stallone appeared to be single-handedly destroying the entire North Vietnamese army with a machine gun that fired several thousand bullets without requiring a new magazine. Eckhard watched sullenly. From time to time, he wiped away a tear.

General Corley Rollings was busy. The headset he wore to leave his hands free while calling had been on his head for nearly two hours. His conversations had been circumspect and in code, for he could not use the phones in the Pentagon for this purpose. Instead, he was in the study of his home in Bethesda. He called the commanding officer of each state National Guard where the coup could be initiated and spoke similar words each time.

"Cliff, the party could be starting sooner than planned," he said. "Maybe two weeks. I know that's ahead of schedule, but we decided to celebrate early. You know how it is."

"What brought this on?" asked the man at the other end of the line. He was like most of the others Rollings had on his list, a combat veteran from Vietnam and Iraq, now working as a senior executive in a corporation with strong defense connections.

"The boss may decide to quit early," Rollings replied. "I'll call you when I have the details. But the arrangements stand? You'll let my people organize things once the party starts?"

"Sure thing, Corley. You'll deliver the goods when the party's over?"

"It's a deal. I'll call you soon. But you'd better get the party hats and the streamers ready."

"Okay, Corley. I'll hear from you."

Six times, Rollings made such a call. After that, he contacted each of his subordinate officers who were part of his undercover operation and gave similar advice. The military operation that would strip America of its legitimate government and replace it with an effective dictatorship controlled by two ex-Soviet military officers had begun, though Rollings was unaware of the histories of the two men he considered the finest Americans alive.

When he had made the last call, Rollings sat back in his seat and saw his hands trembling. "My God, Corley," he said aloud, "in a couple of weeks, you could be the top commander of all American armed forces everywhere in the world. All you have to do is stand by while somebody suspends the constitution you took an oath to defend and maybe shoots your commanding officer, the President of the United States of America. Simple, eh?"

He stood up and went to the small stock of liquor he kept in his study. He poured a large helping of scotch and went to stand by the window. He looked out over the long garden that gave him a degree of privacy, and sipped thoughtfully at his drink.

"You'll be a hero, General," he said. "They'll all say you saved America from the liberals and communists. You returned power to the people who know how to use it, not the bleeding hearts who worry about trees and whales and spotted owls. They'll say you helped return America to being the world's greatest military power, so that all those dirty little bastards around the world won't be able to hijack American ships and aircraft and take our people hostage in our own embassies. Yessirree, General, you're a real hero."

General Corley Rollings threw his glass of scotch hard against the wall. It splintered to fragments and a couple of ounces of single-malt whisky made a stain like a bomb blast.

* * *

Tony Redman lay luxuriously on his king-sized bed at his home in New York. After getting home from La Guardia airport where he had landed in his Gulfstream jet, he had taken a long hot bath together with two of his favorite nymphs that he had pulled from other duties at a nightclub on Lexington Avenue three weeks ago. They had claimed to be eighteen when they came asking for jobs, but the club manager had an eye for these things. "No more than fifteen," he said when he called Redman to tell him. "You should see these two. Best bodies I've ever seen." Redman had driven round within an hour and appropriated the girls for his own household.

The two now lay cuddled up, one on each side of him. All three were naked. Redman shifted slightly and took a deep breath. Recognizing the signaled instruction, one of the girls drifted down the bed until her head was level with his thighs. She lifted herself up and Redman relaxed with a sigh as he felt her lips close gently over him. He shifted his left hand to cup the breast of the other, who rolled her back against him. He pulled her up so that she was lying on her back on his chest and he clasped a hand on each breast, squeezing hard.

"Okay, little one down there, up!" he gasped, and grinned as the second girl sat up and moved herself astride him. As she rode him, squealing loudly, he grunted and groaned, rubbing his hands hard on the slight breasts of the girl on his chest. He roared his release at some moment and bucked hard. The girl on his thighs fell forward on top of the other.

"That's nice," Redman whispered, and watched hungrily as the two girls kissed and stroked each other. Ten minutes later, he fell asleep. The two girls slid off him and did the same.

* * *

"The problem, Admiral, is that we know Jerome is starting the process, but I don't know where. All I know is that we have probably ten or twelve days before it happens."

"You've not been able to get copies of the council members' procedure manuals?"

"No, Admiral. There's only one copy of each, except for the master copy Jerome has, and each member has been strictly bound to secrecy with his own copy. Apparently, Jerome had one of them killed in front of the others a few years ago when he discovered that the guy had shown his copy to one of the others. Rollings is the replacement for the dead man. It was General Whitmore."

"Whitmore? Jesus Christ!" The Admiral's face showed disgust. "His name had been on a short-list for Chairman of the Joint Chiefs."

Taskmaster sat comfortably in the armchair of the Admiral's house. The Admiral wore jeans and a tee shirt and looked like a retired businessman. He smoked a pipe that he used to make emphatic gestures when he spoke. He had refilled and relit the pipe three times during this meeting and the air of the study was blue and fragrant with scents of honey and spices. Taskmaster saw the tobacco packet on the table by the Admiral's side. It was called *Yachtsman*, which Taskmaster felt was appropriate. He wondered if the Admiral smoked it because of the name or because of the unusual fragrance.

"So what's the general procedure, Task? What's happening right now?"

Taskmaster looked across at the third man in the room. "They've been persuaded to take ten days to step up the campaign and make preparations before having a go/no-go decision. This has given TF5 a chance to follow each of the members and see who their contacts are. My men are occupied with that right now, Senator. I had to weigh up that opportunity against the risk of what might happen as the New America Council propaganda gets hot. I know that we have to expect some outbreaks of violence between the so-called left and right before the lid is taken off fully."

"Any progress reports?"

"Few, Senator. Vanderbilt had a meeting with Boxmire of the Children of Christ broadcasting network and Shipman of the Shipman Ministries. He'll be telling them to step up the preaching of hatred and fear of black uprisings. We'll monitor those broadcasts carefully. Vanderbilt will be meeting with others of that nasty little breed over the next few hours, and that will let us identify each of Vanderbilt's trained hypocrites. We'll find out every one of them."

"Have you been able to get pick-ups into his home?"

Taskmaster shook his head. "Not yet, Admiral. Every one of those people has serious security facilities in their homes. I haven't had a chance to plant all the bugs everywhere, yet."

"Any others, Task?" asked the senator.

"Eckhard went home and made one call to Washington, which we were able to monitor," Taskmaster replied. "It was to the home of Helen Pierson, a journalist from some trashy publication. Eckhard just said, "step it up by a factor of ten," and hung up. Then I assume he settled down to a warm evening of tranquil domesticity with the loving Peggy Jo and Deborah Anne."

The senator grinned at him. "I imagine he needs surgery and a blood transfusion after that."

412

"And de-icing, Senator. Couldn't happen to a nicer guy. However, Senator, assuming that this Pierson is the leader of the bunch of little hyper-imaginative, morally-challenged composers of emails, be sure that the old Crawford vitriol will pale into insignificance beside what we're going to be hearing over the next few days. I suggest that we look into the management of stations channeling that crap and see where their money comes from. It might etch in a few more details in this whole filthy picture."

"Any others of that sick bunch you followed?" the Admiral asked. His expression was one more in keeping with finding excreta in his pipe rather than the fragrance he expected.

"Payne went home," said Taskmaster. "He made one call to a number in Baltimore and obviously set up a meet. I've got a man tracking him. I'll let you know the details when I get them."

The Admiral grunted and picked ashes from his pipe.

"We had more luck with Armstrong," Taskmaster continued. "A series of electronic transmissions were made from his home, obviously emails to banks and arms dealers around the world. We've logged the numbers and should be able to identify some of them over the next few hours. However, many of them, even the banks' emails will be unlisted numbers, so we have to enlist foreign security forces on our side. It's not always easy."

"I'll call in some debts with the National Security Council and the CIA," said the Admiral. "There are still *some* people there I know I can trust."

"Thank you, Admiral," Taskmaster replied.

"How about Redman?" asked the senator.

"Redman just went home," Taskmaster answered. "I have nothing on him at all. No calls, just sounds of horny passion picked up by the FBI monitors they'd placed there a year ago. And General Rollings made lots of calls. Knowing what he was talking about, it was clear that he was doing exactly what he was ordered to do, preparing the national guard units and his own teams for a three-year advancement of the program. Again, we logged the calls. We'll identify each Guard unit."

"I'll fly his balls from a B-2 bomber when this is over," the Admiral growled. "The man took an oath to protect the constitution against all enemies, domestic and foreign."

"I hope you get the chance, Admiral," said Taskmaster.

"That's for the future," the senator said. "Meanwhile gentlemen, we have a problem. We know that an uprising is being planned, and we'll have maybe a day or two's notice of it. But for now, we don't know where it will be. We can't do anything before it happens."

Taskmaster nodded. "And because of the strict personal security among the team members, I have no way of knowing where Payne's arms stores are. We should be able to identify the leader of his irregular forces soon, but that doesn't help us know where the bastards will strike."

"Maybe we should worry less about the law and more about what's going on," said the Admiral with a wide sweep of the pipe. "We should just arrest every one of those traitors and hang them tomorrow."

Taskmaster and the senator looked at him in silent sympathy, and the Admiral smiled sadly. "But of course, that's exactly what we're defending, isn't it? They've not yet broken any laws, and our constitution gives them the right to stir up any old shit they like, particularly the religious shit. Even conspiracy to commit treason would be damned hard to prove. Until this thing breaks, we're powerless."

"That's our problem, Admiral," agreed Taskmaster. "Whatever we do, a lot of Americans are going to die when this happens. All we can do is minimize the damage when it actually breaks."

"But they *have* broken laws," the senator interjected. "We know for sure that the attack on Ashton at the cabin was conducted by Jerome's people, led by that awful little prick, Jimmie Wanlyn. It seems Wanlyn murdered the two in Illinois. That makes Jerome and the entire council guilty of murder by association."

"Legally, yes, Senator, I agree," Taskmaster replied. "Trouble is, to indict Jerome and Dansbury would bring the whole affair into the public domain and it's too early for that. And if we did, can you imagine the army of high-priced attorneys Jerome would send into the field? All of them backed up by the most senior members of both parties, and the Asbury family. They'd tie us up in legal knots for the next decade and we'd get nowhere. Just as the Admiral said, even conspiracy charges would give us the same problem."

"Damn, you're right," the senator agreed. "It has to wait."

"Yes, it does," the Admiral concurred. "When we get them on high treason charges, then you can bet all the little political puppets will run a mile and the Asburys will show a dignified and remote silence."

"But we know that this President won't issue a series of pardons like his predecessors did," said Taskmaster.

"True," the Admiral agreed with a thin smile. "There's still some unfinished business from that era with a certain marine colonel that I'll be looking into when this is over."

"Task, what about the bunch of jerks sending out the emails to the talk-show hosts?" asked the senator, changing the subject.

"Much the same problem," Taskmaster replied. "First amendment rights. They can send out any lie they want and the talk-show lunatics can spread it like cow-shit. The only recourse there would be a defamation suit by the President or First Lady, but that would be political suicide and they've got more sense. However, I may just apply a little non-constitutional pressure there, but you never heard me say that."

"Say what, Task?" said the Admiral with another smile. "All I heard was silence, don't you agree, Senator?"

"Absolutely, Admiral. Task, in the absence of the other three members of this council, we must act alone for a while. You'll keep us completely informed as soon as you hear anything?"

"Naturally, Senator. I'm going to follow up an idea that came to me recently, but it will be done diplomatically. Gentlemen, I should go. I have people to assign to a number of duties."

* * *

The telephone rang on the desk of Paul Kent. He looked at the faces of Feathers and Mark as he picked it up, and smiled at the eagerness displayed.

"Yes, Chief," he said, and waited while the caller spoke. "Yes, Chief," he said again. "He's ready." He replaced the phone and looked at Mark with an expressionless face. "Want to come for a ride to visit some people?"

"Of course," Mark answered with a wave of excitement. "Who?"

"People you helped us locate," said Kent with a tight smile.

"Get the man a gun, Paul," said Feathers.

"All taken care of." Paul stood up. "Let's go visiting."

The ride was short, barely twenty minutes. Mark sat in the rear seat with Paul, while Feathers folded himself into the front passenger seat. The driver was a young woman who didn't speak a word and was not introduced. Mark was conscious of the nine-millimeter automatic pistol in its shoulder holster. The weight was cumbersome and unfamiliar, despite the intensive practice with a variety of weapons in the last few days. Currents of nervous tension ran through him at short intervals. The early afternoon traffic in Washington was heavy, and Mark estimated they could have walked the distance in not much more time than they had taken by car.

They stopped outside an office block. Mark hadn't followed the course, and was uncertain where he was. He shifted across the rear seat and followed Paul onto the sidewalk. Feathers hauled himself from the front seat and joined them.

"Sixth floor," said Paul and walked into the building. They waited by the elevator shaft. Nobody joined them, to Mark's relief. The concealed weapon made a bump like a small mountain on his chest, he felt. The three moved into the elevator car and rode silently up the six floors. Mark's heart was pounding. Feathers and Paul seemed unconcerned, as if visiting a business for some innocuous purpose.

"Six-one-nine," said Paul as the door opened. In front of them, a small sign indicated the direction of the office numbers. Paul walked off to the right, the other two followed silently.

The door to office number 619 was plain wood, uninformative. It was unlocked and Paul walked in. Mark followed him, and Feathers closed the door behind them. The lobby was tiny, barely large enough to hold the three men. A single door faced them. Paul turned the knob and the door opened without hesitation. He strode in.

"Good afternoon," he said. Mark walked in behind him, followed by Feathers. A circular table stood in the center of the room, with four chairs around it. The table was covered with newspapers and note pads. More newspapers littered the floor. Three men and a woman sat at the table, looking with blank astonishment at Paul. Mark moved round the room to stand against the wall opposite from the doorway. Feathers moved in and took a position in the middle of the wall to Mark's left, near a large filing cabinet and a table with a telephone and a desktop computer standing on it.

"Who the hell are you?" demanded one of the men. He rose to his feet. He was portly, in his forties, and heavy glasses framed a round face. He wore light blue trousers, with his tie half undone and his shirt unbuttoned at the top. The jacket to his suit lay over the back of his chair.

"Editorial division," Paul answered.

"Cut the crap," the woman said loudly. "Explain this."

Mark looked at her. She was about thirty, he estimated, smartly dressed in a black skirt and white blouse. Her hair hung to her shoulders and her face was strong, with good features. An attractive woman, but cold, Mark thought.

"Miss Pierson, the series of emails being distributed from this room stops here and now," Paul said firmly. "They contravene FCC obscenity regulations."

The woman looked astounded at being addressed by name. All four people at the table looked at each other for a few seconds. The other two men appeared to be in their twenties. They didn't speak.

"Bullshit!" said the portly man. "Now, explain who you are or I'm calling the cops."

Paul shrugged. "All right then, we're the anti-pollution squad. Either way, the untreated sewage emanating from this room has to stop."

"That's enough, I'm calling the cops." The man moved away from the table and toward the phone. Feathers moved a step nearer the table and the man stopped. Feathers towered threateningly over him. The man turned back to the table and looked helplessly at the others.

"What the hell is this?" For the first time, somebody showed anxiety. The woman's voice had risen a notch. "Who the hell are you people?"

"Like I said, ma'am, anti-pollution." Paul was polite. "But it really doesn't matter. Those emails stop. Now."

"Like hell they do!" Pierson replied in anger. Her face was flushed an angry red. "You can't do this. We're breaking no laws. What are you? Friends of the President, I suppose."

"No, ma'am, we're not. We're his subordinates, but we're acting illegally, just like you said."

"What?" The woman seemed almost breathless.

"This is illegal," Paul repeated. "Nonetheless, your operation stops here."

By the table, Feathers was ignoring the man and studying a pile of papers. He leafed through them, reading them quickly. After a moment, he stood up, holding one of them, and nodded with a smile at Mark. It was clearly a printout of one of the emails sent to Crawford.

The four seemed to realize something above their heads was going on. But the woman persisted.

"Get the hell out of here," she demanded. "There are a lot of powerful people behind us. You'll regret this!"

"I know about your powerful friends, Miss Pierson," Paul replied. Casually, he took his weapon from its holster and examined it carefully, then replaced it. Four sets of eyes followed the movements with fascination. "Believe me, lady and gentlemen, your friends are running out of steam. Illegal as this action is, it's still going to stand. What you've been doing is rather more complicated than you believe. At some stage, the people behind you exceeded any boundaries set in a democratic nation. I have no doubts each and every one of you here believes themselves to be a loyal American. The people behind you are not. Please believe me, regardless of the illegality of my actions here, if you persist in this operation, I'll come for you again. And on that occasion, you will not receive the considerate and painless attentions such as you've received so far."

The portly man moved again, reaching for the filing cabinet. Mark watched him carefully. Feathers continued to read through the pile of emails on the table. The man opened a file drawer.

With a flash of fear that churned his stomach, Mark saw the man's hand start to emerge with a gun in it. Feeling as if fighting through molasses, Mark reached for his own weapon and drew it out. "Stop right there," he said, his voice an embarrassing croak, not the calm, authoritative tones of Paul Kent.

The man's head twitched sideways and he saw Mark's pistol pointed at him. With an audible gasp, he froze. The thump of the pistol falling back into the drawer was like a hammer stroke in the silent room. Feathers lifted his head and blinked at the sight of the gun in Mark's hand.

"Close it," Mark ordered, his voice more under control. Silently the man obeyed.

"Tisk, tisk," said Paul.

The four were silent. The woman seemed to understand first. She picked up her handbag from the floor by her chair and stood up. She nodded with understanding at Paul.

"We can just go?" she asked.

"At this point," Paul confirmed. "As can all of you."

The woman looked carefully at Feathers, at Mark, then back at Paul. Surprisingly, she smiled. Her face became beautiful under the change.

"Then that's what we'll do," she said. She looked briefly at the other three. Her expression seemed to reflect dismissal and farewell in one glance. She walked past Paul and out of the door without another look. Quietly, the two younger men followed, leaving the stocky man pulling up his tie and lifting his jacket from the chair back.

"Can I get my gun?" he asked uncertainly, looking at Mark.

"Wait," said Mark. He opened the drawer and pulled out the weapon, a Heckler & Koch automatic. Without thinking, he unsnapped the magazine and removed it. Rapidly, with practised movements, he removed the bullets from the magazine and handed them to the man who placed them in his pocket. Mark replaced the magazine and handed over the gun. Looking pale, the man followed the others out of the room.

"Neatly done," said Feathers with a smile.

Mark realized his friend was right. He had handled the weapon with surprising dexterity. The few days of intensive training had been effective.

"I think we're done here, guys," Paul said as the last man left.

"Agreed," murmured Feathers. "Let's get back."

By the time they were back at TF5's office, barely an hour had passed since they had left. Paul's phone was ringing as they walked in. Paul picked it up, listened for a few seconds, and directed an astonished look at Mark.

"Yes, Chief," he said. "He's ready." He replaced the phone and looked at Mark with an expressionless face. "Got your passport?"

"Huh?" Mark looked startled. "No, it's at home."

"And how's your Russian?"

"A little rusty. Paul, what the hell is this?"

"The Chief wants you to do a little research," said Paul. He picked up the phone. "Get your jacket," he said to Mark. "Feathers will run you to catch a plane."

"It'll take some time to get a flight to O'Hare, collect my passport and get back here," Mark complained, rising to his feet.

Paul shook his head and paused with his fingers on his phone. "This is TF5," he said. "We do things our own way." He pressed two digits and spoke quietly into the phone. "Commander, this is a Priority Sigma Two. I need you to get a man to the Glenview Naval Air Station in Illinois and bring him back. Very fast."

He listened for a few seconds and replaced the phone. "He's got twenty minutes, Feathers," he said. "Ever flown an F-14, Mark?"

Stunned, Mark could only shake his head.

"It's a hell of a ride," said Paul. "Don't upchuck your cookies. Move!"

"Where am I going, once I get my passport?" Mark pleaded as Feathers ushered him out the door.

"St. Petersburg," said Paul. "I'll have the visa by the time you get back."

"Florida? What the hell do I need a passport and visa for in Florida?" Mark's confusion overwhelmed him.

"I think he means the one in Russia," Feathers murmured. "You heard the man, buddie. Let's move ass! You're part of TF5 now!"

Chapter 18- St. Petersburg, Russia

The heat was blistering. Sweat rolled off Mark in streams. Combined with the thunderous speed of his transition here, he felt as if he were on some alien planet.

Feathers had raced through the city, stopped briefly at the gates of a military base then rushed Mark into a building by the side of an airfield. Two men calmly packed Mark into a flight suit, fitted him with a helmet and bone-dome, then walked him out to an F-14 Tomcat sitting a few yards out on the concrete surface. A pilot looked down from the front seat and gestured a brief wave of greeting. The two men guided Mark into the rear seat and busied themselves with the complex connections between man and aircraft. A few moments later, the engines began to thunder as Mark tried to settle into the seat, the straps binding him firmly, the helmet tight on his head.

"Flown one of these things before?" said a disembodied voice in his ears.

"No." Mark tried to sound cool.

"Enjoy," said the pilot.

Mark did. Despite the massive "G" forces that slammed him into his seat, he felt a raging flow of exhilaration as the Tomcat howled into the air, climbing in what seemed a vertical ascent till the sky turned deep blue. He had only a short time to enjoy the sight of America distantly below him, then his stomach went into some different orbit from the rest of him as the F-14 began a dramatic descent. He barely had time to recognize Lake Michigan, tried to spot Evanston, then the wings opened from the dart-like high-speed geometry to the lower-speed landing formation. A squeal of rubber on concrete, and he was at the local naval base, a few miles from his home.

"Fun, eh?" said the pilot. Mark couldn't answer, as the canopy was already open and somebody was hauling him from his seat.

A white police car was waiting, the roof lights already flashing. Mark was hustled into the back and the car roared off. Nobody asked his address, but the cop in the passenger side gave him a curious look. Mark was breathless.

Thirty minutes later, it happened again. This time, he managed to say thanks to the pilot before he was pulled from the Tomcat's rear seat. He got no reply.

An hour later, he was sitting in the business section of a United Airlines flight to Moscow.

He tried to sleep, and failed. He didn't open the briefcase that Feathers had given him before he left. The rushed briefing in the car on the way to Dulles International Airport had been clear on that. "Open it when you're alone," Feathers had said. "You'll be met in Moscow, transferred straight to St. Petersburg, taken to an office. Here's a bag with three days of clothing. Be back before you need laundry. But find the answers."

Mark looked at the man across the desk from him. He was a General in the Russian Army. The summer was at its height, and the room had no air-conditioning.

"I have physical descriptions," said Mark, working hard to oil his Russian after the years of disuse. "And fingerprints."

"Difficult," said the General. "Our records not computerised."

"But you will have them?"

The General shrugged. *"Vozmorszhno.* Possibly," he said. "It was long time ago and period of some confusion. Come."

He rose to his feet and Mark followed him through a door and into a warehouse, nearly staggering under the combination of heat and jetlag.

"Some confusion?" he thought to himself. Maybe the General had a sense of humor after all. World War Two in what was then Leningrad had been more than confusing. He walked through the door and stopped, stunned.

"This whole place is full of your personnel records?" he said, struggling to keep his voice from echoing his despair. The warehouse was huge, and crates seemed to occupy the entire space. "There's no way I can work through this in three days."

The General waved to a woman standing against the far wall. "You have help," he said.

Mark watched as a line of young people flooded into the room.

"Give them physical description," said the General. "I will make copies of those you have and give to everyone. They will find those that match ones you seek. Then you will have to check fingerprints."

Shaken by the size of the task in front of him, Mark did as he was asked. Four hours later, the first sheets of paper were placed on his desk by a woman who looked like an untidy version of Audrey Hepburn. Within another three hours, the table was covered with foot-high piles of such sheets, and four of the large squad of helpers were re-assigned to checking the fingerprints against the charts which Mark had brought with him. Two more tables were brought into the warehouse and rapidly covered with piles of papers taken from the endless lines through the warehouse.

A trolley arrived at some time, and Mark wolfed down a sausage sandwich and a mug of tea.

Sixty-eight hours later, having sat at the table in the warehouse the whole time except for a brief pair of naps on a cot in the office, rising only to go to the washroom, eating sandwiches as he worked, he found the answers for which TF5 had sent him. Photocopies of two sheets of paper from the hundreds of thousands which had been unpacked, examined and repacked by the army of willing helpers were placed carefully in his briefcase. He fell asleep in the car to the airport, and had no recollection of being transferred to the United flight at Moscow. He slept throughout the flight to Washington.

Chapter 19 - Chicago, Illinois

Mark felt cheerful. Wednesday morning of a lovely Fall day in early September, and Christiana was due to come to Chicago on the Friday. They planned a long weekend, as she had arranged two day's vacation with Verity and would not return until the Tuesday night. It would be the first time she had come to Chicago to stay with him, and Mark felt almost breathless at the idea of the entire four days alone with her. She would drive out the ghosts of Allison permanently, he knew. He had begged Paul for a few days off from his new TF5 duties, both to prepare for Christiana, and also to clean up some tasks at his office in Chicago. His complete exhaustion after the three non-stop days of over-heated, tension-filled labors in St. Petersburg, and the streaking rapid-transit travels before and after, guaranteed him the result. After consultation with the Chief, Paul had agreed, warning of possible fast recalls if anything happened.

At eleven-thirty, as a meeting in his office came to a close, Mark remembered with a satisfied smile that he had often prepared to listen to the Randy Crawford show at this time. Since returning from Washington after his last, destructive attack on Crawford together with Feathers and Paul Kent over a week ago, he had not tuned in, as Verity had told him that the three-hour period once filled with the vicious attacks of Crawford and his followers was being reshaped and nothing permanent had yet been arranged. The return to work had been hard, also, and Mark had not reached home either evening before nine o'clock, too tired to watch the news or do anything but play some music and go to bed by ten. Beyond reading the newspaper quickly over a hurried lunch, American and world events had passed him by these few days.

Press reactions to the professional demise and physical death of Crawford had been mixed. Most of the newspapers that Mark had read expressed relief that the Crawford vitriol had ended. Though they had never said it while Crawford was alive, something that interested Mark considerably, the editorials seemed pleased with the result and gave considerable attention to discussion on the identities of the two men with Mark in that last, explosive telephone call. Other newspapers were less friendly. Several issued editorials of thundering rage against the cowards and liberals who had murdered the voice of conservative America. They also raised the question of Mark's associates and implied a conspiracy was brewing among anti-American forces within the country, warning of possible retribution for Crawford's death. For two days, Mark left the telephone answering system on and refused to pick up the phone unless he recognized the caller. Each evening when Mark got home, he found numerous messages left by reporters requesting interviews. Mark took pains to call each one back the next day, but refused to be interviewed by any of them, and within two days, the topic had almost died.

Checking the time, Mark decided to switch on his radio and see if the local station that had carried the Crawford program had replaced it in any way. At fifteen minutes before noon, he found out. The shock was unpleasant.

"I tell you, my friends," said the baritone voice emerging from the radio speaker in Mark's office, "one of the finest men in America, that voice of freedom and strength, Pat Buchanan, said it right in 1992. He said then, that there's a holy war going on, a war for the hearts and minds of Americans everywhere. And the despicable, cowardly murder of Randy Crawford last week represents the worst terrorist tactics imaginable by those who would destroy America. It's typical of the approach by liberals in America today, my friends. They display the nastiest form of cowardice. Not only do they demand that the press and the media support their communist, anti-American ideologies twenty-four hours a day, but they murder anyone who expresses opposition to their craziness by telling you the truth of what is happening today in America."

"Jesus Christ, who is this?" Mark muttered. The unknown voice didn't enlighten him.

"I think this is a watershed time in America," the speaker continued. "The liberals and their communist friends have allied and are they taking the war right to your door-steps. I know that I can expect attacks on my life after this, because I've taken the decision to carry on the great work of that fine American, Randy Crawford. But I tell you, all you loyal Americans listening to me out there, I'll keep going, regardless. But you all had better take heed also. The liberals are on the warpath. They killed Randy Crawford, they may be able to kill me, and they'll be out to get anyone who doesn't support their communist ideology.

So hear this, and hear it good. I understand from my sources in law-enforcement agencies round America, that massive shipments of AK-47 automatic assault weapons have been illegally imported into this country. We all know who makes these *Kalashnikov* guns, don't we, and we all know who uses them, right? Russians make them, and you can bet your little lives, those Russians still hanker after a return to communism, and terrorists around the world use them. Well, there's a few hundred thousand of these *Russian* weapons now in the country, they've gone to stock-piles everywhere, and you know who's gonna be using them and against who, don't we? Damn right we do. Liberals, communists, enemies of this country are going to be shooting loyal, true-blue Americans. We know that the underclasses, the unemployed, the so-called homeless, all those people who have rejected the real spirit of America, are going to be egged on and armed by their liberal masters. So you'd better watch out, my friends. Get *yourselves* armed, I say, regardless of what those bleeding-heart liberals say, those hand-wringing wimps running the councils of villages like Wilmette, where they banned honest home-owners from having guns, ignore the rules, get a gun! Get one, keep it by you, and be prepared to use it. This could be the last battle for the real America before the communists take it from inside."

Mark felt a cold shiver run down his body. Something dreadful was happening, and he began to understand what it was. "Dear God, the bastards are warming up to something," he muttered, and reached for the phone. But when he got through to the TF5 office, he could only talk to an unnamed young man who remained uninformative.

Mark could not identify the voice as anyone he knew at TF5.

"Commander Featherstone is not in the office," the cool voice said.

"Paul Kent, then," said Mark. The other man was silent for a few seconds, and it occurred to Mark that Paul's name would be known to few people, certainly not to somebody who called in by public telephone.

The man in the TF5 office was obviously uncertain about this. "Mister Kent is also out, sir," he said. "May I ask who's calling?"

"This is Mark Ashton."

"Ah, I see, sir," the TF5 operative replied. "Is there something I can help you with, Mister Ashton? I was with you in the mountains the other day."

Mark's anxiety and desperate need to tell Feathers what was happening relaxed a small amount. He was dealing with an ally. "Then I'm talking to a friend," he said with a smile. "I owe you several drinks some day."

"I'm sure I'll collect on that debt, Mister Ashton. What should I tell Feathers?"

"Just tell either of them that Crawford's replacements have stepped up the poison. They're just about telling people to shoot any liberal they see. That's here in Chicago, at least."

"The same thing has been happening round the country for a few days, Mister Ashton. We were expecting it, in fact, despite your operation last week. The Chief is onto it."

"Then I hope I can buy the Chief a drink as well, one day."

"That I very much doubt, sir. He's not a sociable animal."

"Then add it to yours. Thanks, my friend."

"Good day to you, Mister Ashton."

Mark hung up feeling a little better, but still sick with fear at what was happening. Despite closing the "dirty tricks" group in Washington, the network of hatred was still raising its level of virulence.

In Baltimore, a man named Jensen was making violent love to a woman on his bed in a small apartment. Her legs were clamped tight round his thighs, her arms equally firmly gripped his neck as his shaven head lay alongside her red hair, and she was gasping with the efforts of his powerful thrusts. When the ringing tone began on his email machine by the bed, Jensen stopped moving, making the woman moan slightly. He lay still for a few seconds as the fax machine whirred and hummed then began to slide a sheet of paper into the output tray.

Jensen reached across and took the page. Beneath him, the woman was nuzzling his chest. He smiled as he pulled the paper to him.

"Wait a moment," he said gently, and read the paper. The message was short.

"Foxfire," it said, and gave a date and a code that he mentally interpreted to give an address on South Halstead Street in Chicago. Jensen dropped the paper and lowered his head again. A few seconds later, the woman began to gasp even harder than before.

Mark returned his attention to the radio. The nameless man had not stopped pouring out venom.

433

"What happened the other night in Virginia was disgraceful," he intoned. "It followed on a day of intensive, personal attacks on Randy's character by a group of obviously well-rehearsed terrorists determined to spread lies and dirt. They even sent a forged letter to the newspapers, knowing full well that the liberal, communist-inspired media of this country would accept it without question. You may have seen that lying piece of dirt in some of our liberal newspapers. That letter purported to be from Randy's grandfather, asking for him to be excused military service. Well, I know that Randy has been reticent about discussing his military service in the Vietnam days. It's what you expect of a hero. Not for him the great tales of slightly exaggerated heroism. No, he was just a quiet man who got on with doing what he had to, like a lot of other valiant young Americans of that day, and certainly *not* like those whackos who called him up and claimed to have served in military intelligence. If they were military intelligence, they sure as hell weren't *American* intelligence, that I can assure you. Whoever those two loonie-toons were with that murderer Mark Ashton, they were traitors to this country. Now, we know that Ashton had already killed one man with a knife, regardless of that nonsensical claim that one of them made, that charges against Ashton had been dropped. And Randy Crawford was killed by a knife. There's something to make you think, isn't it? So if you're listening, Mark Ashton, that's two we know you've done. Any more you want to tell me about? No, I bet you don't. Criminals like you are liars as well."

Mark felt a raging torrent of fury run through him. He reached for the phone, determined to call this maniac, and then stopped himself. Whatever was happening was clearly part of a plan being carried out over the country, according to the young man at TF5. To call in and stir up this intense, vicious speaker might do more harm than good. Calming himself, Mark left the phone alone. He turned off the radio, sickened by what he had heard and frightened by what might be happening in America.

Anyway, he had four days with Christiana to look forward to next week. Nothing was going to be allowed to spoil that.

* * *

Jensen listened to the sounds of the shower, then reached for the telephone. He dialed a long-distance number.

"City number twenty-three in the chart," he said, when a voice answered. "Get the boys there and alert the local crowd. Meet me at the airport tomorrow, seven o'clock. The party's been brought forward a few days. It's on Saturday."

* * *

General Rollings made eleven quick calls. "Next Saturday, city number twenty-three," he said each time somebody answered.

Tony Redman made six similar calls. He was as terse as the General, and gave the same message.

An hour later, Taskmaster made a call to a Washington number from his secured phone at TF5 headquarters.

"It's next Saturday, Senator," he said. "But they're referring to the location by a code which I can't identify. The kingpin seems to be a man called Frank Jensen. He's a known white-supremacist, neo-Nazi lunatic. Payne met him a few days ago in a bar in Baltimore. One of my men watched them. We'll follow him, and see how quickly we can find out where he's heading.

"Keep me informed," the other man said tersely.

"Naturally," said Taskmaster, and hung up.

* * *

Deeply worried by what he had heard that morning, Mark went home at a more normal hour of five o'clock. Even at that early hour, his red Thunderbird was still almost alone in the parking lot as he walked out of the building. Lost in thought, he drove the short distance home with almost no recollection of the drive.

Once in the apartment, he came to a conclusion; the evening would be spent in research. Immediately, he turned on the radio and tuned to the station that had carried the terrifying broadcast of earlier that day. The AM station was an all-talk program and as he tuned in, Mark heard a strident voice from a telephone caller.

"I think Don was talking a great deal of sense, this afternoon," said the loud male voice. "There's absolutely no doubt that we're at war, just like Pat Buchanan said, and it's a holy war, all right. This is a Christian country, and only Christians should live here. The liberals are out to take over the country and they killed Randy Crawford, like Don said. If you're horrified by what Don's been saying all week, then you're a wimp, a liberal, and one of those bleeding hearts. Don was right, and I'm not going to be caught defenseless. I've got a handgun in the house, and I'm getting a rifle. When those pinkos start walking up my street, they're not going to know what hit 'em."

"Don't you understand what he *said?*" demanded the host, a woman to whom Mark had occasionally listened in the past. "He was telling you to be prepared to shoot *Americans!* They could be your neighbors, maybe even your friends or family! You mean you're ready to kill an American because he or she disagrees with the right-wing zealots? This is the action of Christians?"

"Damn right it is!" the caller shouted. "These people are liberals, not Americans, and not Christians! Randy has always said that liberals are just communists under another name, and he was dead right! They don't deserve to live." The dead sound of the line being disconnected echoed from the loudspeakers.

"I can't believe what's been happening this week," said the host. Her voice held a note of deep distress. "Five days ago, this station put on this incredible man, Don McAdam in the Randy Crawford time-slot and he's done nothing but howl and scream that the liberals and the poorer, less privileged people of this country, meaning, of course, Hispanics and African-Americans, are about to launch armed offensives against the rest of us. He has absolutely no evidence for this sick piece of imagination, but most of the people calling this program actually *believe* him! I've tried asking the station management just what's going on, but I have to tell you, I got the brush-off in no uncertain terms. I was told to leave the topic alone. Which means without any doubt, people, this is my last broadcast.

"So in the remaining hour of my slot, assuming management even allows me that hour, I'd like to hear from anyone out there who believes like I do, that Don McAdam is a rabble-rousing, lying jerk with an agenda all of his own. Is there anyone left in Chicagoland who *doesn't* believe that they have to get a gun and be prepared to shoot it out in the next few days with anyone who still believes in democratic principles in America? I pray that there is, and I pray that you call me, because I tell you, people, I'm losing heart here in this studio. Already, there are hostile faces staring at me from the glass window in the producer's studio. I doubt they'll cut me off before the end of the hour, that would be just too obvious. But if they do, then you'll know that dissent is no longer tolerated in this new America, the land of the free and the home of the brave. So you have one hour left, you voices of the real America. This may be the last chance you get to express opposition to the views of Don McAdam, Randy Crawford and the rest of the slavering pack of so-called patriots. You know, I reckon that guy Mark Ashton was right. There *is* a conspiracy to take over this country. I don't know if the whole GOP is behind it, but they sure as hell seem to have some nasties in there. And I can't tell the difference between those nasties and the same smelly little anus-droplets who ran Germany in the thirties and forties, or between them and Joe Stalin's bunch of hooligans. We'll take a short break, and if I'm allowed to carry on, we'll take more of your calls in a few moments."

The woman's voice cut out to be replaced by a loud, aggressive male voice urging listeners to borrow money from a bank branch in Cicero. Mark turned the volume down, feeling the sickness rising again in his throat. The propaganda had stepped up beyond all belief. Obviously, this station was one controlled by the same people who had controlled Randy Crawford. Mark had no idea who they were, and it was the one topic on which Feathers and Paul Kent had been silent. Almost without breathing, Mark waited out the advertisements to see if the woman was still broadcasting. Two minutes later, he found out that she was.

"She probably got them with that statement of being too obvious," he muttered to himself. "I wonder if the producers will let anyone through who wants to side with her?"

He decided that he would try and call the station. As always, the line was busy, and he spent fifteen minutes alternating between pressing the cut-off and re-dial buttons. When he got through, the conversation was short.

"The Kathie Roberts program," said a male voice.

"I'd like to add my piece to this debate," Mark said.

"You agreeing with the other callers or not?" the voice demanded.

"I think somebody should speak up for Kathie."

"Tough," replied the other man, and the call was disconnected.

Appalled at the crude censorship taking place, Mark replaced the telephone.

By the end of the hour, Mark knew that either the producers were blocking other supportive calls as they had his own, or there weren't any more. He listened for the last few minutes of the program to make sure, but nobody called except to attack the host in varying degrees of viciousness. For the last five minutes, the woman was struggling with tears.

"This is no longer the America I grew up in," she said, fighting to control her voice. "This is no different from

Communist Russia or Nazi Germany. It seems only one viewpoint is tolerated and that's in favor of authoritarianism, religious extremism and one-party military rule. This isn't America any more. I don't know what's happened, but it terrifies me. I know I won't be here to take your calls tomorrow night, and frankly, if the calls I've had this evening are any guide to what's coming, I don't want to hear them. So my last words are these; please try and remember what this country stands for. Don't shoot your fellow citizens. Try to believe that once we stood for the rights of free speech, tolerance, the right to dissent and freedom both *of* and *from* religion. I don't think that any of the Founding Fathers would support the view of America that I've been hearing from Don McAdam and the other lunatics who have taken over the airways. It's coming up to seven o'clock, and this is the end of the line. I don't know if Peter French is following me on this station, or whether he's already been dumped in favor of another ideological lunatic. I won't be here tomorrow night, so I'll just say this. God bless you, *including* those of you maniacs who called me tonight to say they're preparing to kill their fellow-citizens. I pray that whatever this madness is that has afflicted America these last few days, it will be healed before the bullets start to fly. I'll echo a fictional talk-show host I once watched on a television series. Good night, America, wherever you are."

A moment of silence hung over the airwaves before a blast of music heralded an advertisement for a car dealership. Mark took a deep breath and went to his bedroom to strip, take a shower, and prepare to discover what other evils were flying in the air over Chicago that night.

By ten o'clock, he had found out, and the discovery was frightening beyond anything he could have ever dreamed.

One of the two religious broadcasting channels showed a service by the Children of Christ Broadcasting Network. Mark had never watched such a program in his life before, and the experience was not edifying. The preacher, a Reverend William Boxmire, was a stocky man of middling height, narrow-set eyes and a pasty complexion. His lips were thin and the mouth seemed set in a permanent curve of disapproval. His blue suit sat beautifully on his frame. Mark estimated that at least two thousand dollars worth of tailoring draped this self-proclaimed representative of Jesus Christ.

Boxmire prowled the stage of the auditorium like a restless dog. Behind him, a phalanx of blue-clad singers, male and female watched him.

"Oh my fellow-worshippers of our Lord Jesus Christ, a great evil has struck America and the world," Boxmire shouted. "We have incontrovertible proof that the President, yes the *President* of this great nation is a follower of Satan, that unspeakable acts of devil-worship take place regularly in the White House, attended by this evil man's wife and his family. Blood is spilled, my friends, yes, Blood Is Spilled in the rooms where great men, predecessors of this enemy of the nation, fine men like Presidents Reagan and Bush once tried to give this country back to God."

"Hallelujah," sang the choir. As they did, the camera panned closer to the ranks of the singers and Mark was certain that a number of faces wore expressions of worry and discomfort. Whether that was because of the awful

441

things they were hearing about the President or because they were horrified by the obvious lies Boxmire was spilling into the air, Mark couldn't tell.

"And because evil will always attract followers, we know that this President has corrupted much of the citizenry of this nation," Boxmire continued. "We fear for America, brothers and sisters, we fear for the very cornerstones on which this nation was built. Word is coming to us, at this very church, that terrible things are about to happen. The masses of the unbelievers, the enemies of God, the killers of Christ our Lord, all of Lucifer's flock will soon take arms against the country that has nurtured them."

Mark's breath was drawn in sharply. "Ye gods, they've resorted to blatant anti-Semitism as well," he muttered. "Who else is he going to blame?"

"And with the Christ-killers are allied the Children of Ham," Boxmire shouted. "The ungodly, those who so offended God that He burned their skins black and gave them the sign of Satan, these are the enemies of the Lord who will rise up against us all. They are armed with dreadful weapons, brothers and sisters, dreadful weapons provided to them by the ancient enemies of America, the Communists, those who denied God and sent their messages of hate against all Americans everywhere in the world. Communist weapons are in the country and they are to be used against *you,* my friends, *you,* the followers of our Lord Jesus Christ. And we know what these devil-worshippers will do, don't we? They want to kill us, to wipe the country of the godly, the worshipful, the Christians of America. They want to pillage and loot and burn and *rape,* my friends, that's what they want."

The choir's "Hallelujah" was fainter, and Mark saw the glare of rage that Boxmire directed against them. Mark was certain now. Many of the choir members were appalled at what they were hearing, but it was disgust with the lies, not the fear of the ungodly that was causing the expressions of dismay. The African-American choir members had picked up on the reference to the Children of Ham.

"The same message," Mark said aloud. "The Jews, the blacks and the under-privileged are being armed with AK-47s to attack the rest of America. God Almighty, this is dreadful."

Boxmire was still prowling. His expression had become ugly with rage. "A great man, a man of God, an American patriot said it before, my brothers and sisters," he called out, pointing a finger into the air. "Some years ago, he said there was a Holy War in America. I tell you truly, my friends, Pat Buchanan was right! There *is* a Holy War. It's a fight for the spiritual health of the whole world, a fight between those who stand for God, for Jesus Christ and America, and those who fight on the side of Satan, the communists, the anarchists, the Christ-killers. It is up to each and every one of you now, to prepare for this final conflict to save God's country. Be prepared, brothers and sisters, be prepared."

In disgust, Mark switched off the television. He walked into his kitchen and poured himself a stiff scotch. For a few moments, he stood still and silent, breathing in the aroma of the scotch, trying to kill the ugly smell of racial and religious bigotry from his mind. It didn't work. Taking a drink of the fine liquor, he walked to his radio and switched it on. He found his newspaper and checked the radio frequencies. There was a black talk-show host he had occasionally heard and enjoyed. The man had wit and intelligence and had urged tolerance and understanding. Mark tuned his radio to the station. A new voice was shouting. It had the richness and color of the man Mark had once listened to, but it was not the same voice. A note of stridency and anger tainted every syllable.

"And you know it's the *Man* who's telling everyone that we here are gonna rise up against them. It's the *Man* who's claiming that we got guns from Russia. It's the *Man* who's telling you we're gonna shoot our way out of the South Side and rape all those white women and children. Ain't that the truth? But I ask you, where does the *Man* get these facts from? Do *you* know anyone in your neighborhood who's gonna get an AK-47 and head north to shoot up Whitey? I don't. Do *you* know anyone planning on raping and pillaging up there on Michigan Avenue or in those nice, new *changing* areas where the poor folk are being moved out and sexy new condos being built for those rich white men and women? Well, I don't. What I *do* know, is that when the *Man* starts talking like this, we black folk gotta watch out. That's *lynching* talk, brothers and sisters, *lynching* talk. The *Man* is warming up to something, and it ain't good for black folk, *that* we can take to the bank. So you'd all better be asking yourselves the obvious question? What's Whitey up to, this time? Who's he gonna lynch? And how are we gonna stop it happening? Well, I *tell* you how we stop it. We *prepare*, brothers and sisters, we *prepare*. And if Whitey comes marching down to our side of town, we *know* what he's aiming to do. But he *ain't* gonna do it, brothers and sisters, he *ain't* gonna do it, because we're gonna be *prepared.* And you wanna know how to be prepared? Well, here's how. My people are gonna be round the south side over the next few days. They'll be in blue vans with the call letters of this station. Just go and talk to them. They'll tell you how to be prepared."

Mark found he was sweating in the cool air of his apartment. If he was correct in his analysis, agitators on both the poor sides of Chicago and the affluent, middle-class suburbs were stirring up rage, fear and a killing anger that could explode at any moment. This agitator on Chicago's south side was clearly telling his listeners how to obtain guns.

"God, maybe they've got stock-piles of weapons ready to hand out to both sides," Mark muttered. "That would work. Stir up the sort if shit I've heard here among the black suburbs and in the ghettos and get guns to them. Whip up all the old fears of blacks coming to rape and kill the white, middle-class people and have them ready to shoot when they see a black face. Christ, all it needs is a few hundred neo-Nazis with assault weapons primed to get in there and you've got the makings of a first-class shooting war."

He dialed Christiana's home as he did every evening. Even a day without talking to her was painful, and he couldn't miss it. Despite his worries, the sound of her soft voice was magic to him.

"You're a much sweeter voice than I've been hearing this evening," he said. "I need some therapeutic touches."

"Wait till Friday evening," she chuckled. "Therapeutic touches all round are on the menu."

445

"Dearest Christiana, it's almost impossible to wait till then. But I'm worried. Have you heard the sort of stuff that's fouling up the airwaves?"

"Oh God, have I!" she replied. "It's happening all over the country. Verity and I have been checking around. It's bad, Mark."

"Christiana, maybe you shouldn't come to Chicago this week. If things are going to explode anywhere, this is the sort of place that's most likely. Small towns in Virginia might not be so obvious."

"Listen, Ashton," she said, "I've been on a Mark-free diet all week and it's not good for either of us! I need to break the diet this weekend. And if things are going to explode, I want to be with you, not on my own here, worrying frantically about you."

Mark felt warmth run through his body. "You do put things so expressively," he laughed. "But we'd better be careful. If we go into the city, we'll have to watch how things are. Any signs of tension, I'm getting us as far away as possible."

"Do you really think we could see outbreaks of violence?" she asked anxiously.

"Sweetheart, there are people on the national and local airwaves pretty well demanding it," he replied. "The local loonies are screaming for war between black and white, with a pogrom thrown in. It's really scary."

"Then than settles it," she said. "If the world is coming to an end, I need to be with you. And as I said, if it did blow up and I was here, I'd go insane worrying about you. Anyway, it means it could be my last chance to see the Art Institute and go up the Sears Tower."

"I'll be at the airport an hour before you get there," he said with a smile.

"I expect nothing less," she replied warmly.

The next hour was intensely personal, and Mark let the memories of the inflammatory radio and television broadcasts slide from his mind.

Work pressures skyrocketed for the rest of the week, and Mark was too tired to listen out for any more when he got home each evening. And anyway, his mind was more fixed on Christiana's arrival in Chicago on Friday afternoon.

* * *

"Mark, it's lovely!" she exclaimed, turning in a slow circle in the middle of the lounge room. "This is such a nice place to live!"

"I'm glad you like it," he said, carrying her suitcase through to the bedroom. He came out again and joined her in the middle of the room. "I have every intention of living here for a while longer, and with you."

"Seems a splendid approach," she said and touched his cheek. "Let me look around a bit more."

"Of course," he agreed. "The second bedroom is across from ours, and will be the nursery for our twelve children. The kitchen is thataway, where I expect you to spend most of your time, barefoot and permanently pregnant, when not in my bed being put that way."

She blew a raspberry at him, and went to examine the large, spacious kitchen. "It has its points," she agreed. "I could probably concoct the odd sandwich and make tea in this place."

She came back into the lounge, gesturing at the two large book shelves against one wall. "An impressive collection of books. I like a well-read man."

"I hide the bottles from the cleaning lady behind them," he said.

She chuckled, examined his two oil paintings and some framed photographs of Mark in his naval uniform, then pointed at a corner of the room. "What's that strange object?" she asked, walking across the carpet.

"My boomerang. Got it on my trip to Australia a few years ago."

She picked the object up. It was about three feet long, with one arm twice the length of the other, heavy, with sharp edges burned into the wood. She hefted it. "Can't imagine throwing this thing and making it come back," she said with a doubtful look.

"You couldn't," he said. "Nor could anyone else. Contrary to popular wisdom, not all boomerangs are supposed to come back. That's one that doesn't."

"It doesn't?"

He shook his head. "It's not a toy, or a tourist's souvenir made in Taiwan. That's a real killing weapon. The aboriginals use them to bring down kangaroos. They throw them level with the ground, and it breaks the roo's legs."

"Ugh!" She put the boomerang back in its corner against the fireplace.

"Could kill a man," he commented, then put his arms round her. "I'm glad you're here," he whispered into her hair.

Her arms tightened round his back. "Were you saying something about us both living here for a long time?" she murmured.

"Starting anytime you're ready," he replied. "About now might be quite a good idea."

The warm breath of her laugh gently fanned his neck.

"You haven't shown me our bedroom yet," she said.

* * *

"Actually, I'm not sure I even want to get up," she murmured lazily, the next morning. She lay snuggled in the crook of his arm, her face on his chest.

"You said you wanted to see the Art Institute and go up the Sears Tower," he replied, holding back a laugh.

"You're an art form enough for me, Ashton," she said. "And talking of towers..."

"Disgusting woman," he retorted. "I must tell you, you've corrupted this innocent American boy beyond all redemption."

"And you've enjoyed every second of it, haven't you?"

"Absolutely. In fact, some more corruption right now seems like a good idea."

"Agreed. Do you think we'll get to see Chicago today?"

"Lunch at the Art Institute at noon," he said firmly.

"That gives us four hours," she murmured, shifting slightly to look at his clock radio. "Do you think we can get in enough corruption in that time?"

"No. But we do have this evening and all day tomorrow."

"And Monday to build up some reserves to last till the next trip," she agreed. "This seems a reasonable schedule.

Now, am I going to corrupt you this time, or is it your turn?"

"My turn," he said firmly. "If the maiden isn't going to the tower, then the tower..."

He changed position, and she gasped.

Despite the enjoyable delay, they were walking along Michigan Avenue toward the Art Institute by soon after noon. Mark's Thunderbird had been left in a parking lot a few blocks north, just off the "Golden Mile" of some of the most expensive shops and apartment buildings in North America. They strolled in the gentle Fall warmth past the glamorous shop windows, looking at the displays, the tourists, and, a lot of the time, at each other. Forgetting the worries of the growing tension around the country, Mark felt happier than ever before.

As they approached the Art Institute, the glow of the day began to fade. Mark felt the coldness and the silence in the normally bustling street. He squeezed Christiana's hand gently and she sensed the message with the almost psychic communication they had developed. They stopped, watching, horrified at the sight.

Walking east along Madison Street from the direction of Wabash Avenue came a massive file of men. They marched in step, eight abreast, silent and intense. The line of men stretched back at least to the junction with Wabash, as far as Mark could see. Most wore combat-green jackets and trousers. Many wore fatigue caps, some wore black military-style peaked hats. A lot were bareheaded, most of those with shaved scalps. The sight of such a threatening group was itself frightening. What made it so much worse was the heavy automatic assault weapon hanging from the shoulder of each of the men.

Mark had seen such weapons before. They were Russian-made AK-47s.

"We have to get out of here," he said firmly to Christiana. She nodded, her face white, and they began to move back up in the direction from which they had come. Around them, the crowds watching the scene were silent. The press of people had become severe, and movement was growing difficult.

"Where are the cops?" said Christiana in puzzlement. Mark looked around him, aware as she spoke that he hadn't seen a police patrol car since arriving in the city.

"They've been pulled off," he said, beginning to understand what was happening and the extent of the power in the force behind these events. "That means that here's where it's going to happen. We're in the middle of it."

"Oh God, Mark, look!" she cried, terrible distress in her voice.

Mark turned his head to where she was looking, south along Michigan Avenue. The road was full of people. A huge crowd was advancing up the avenue, spilling over into the greenery of Grant Park. As far as Mark could tell, every face was black. The crowd was nearly all men, but here and there, a few women could be seen. Just like the army of quasi-military troops coming out of Wabash Avenue, guns were the predominant sight. In the one look Mark could give the north-moving masses, assault weapons were standard issue.

The day promised to be bloody.

"We have to move," Mark said in growing fear. "Hang onto my hand, I'm going to try and push through."

But he couldn't. The wall of humanity was impenetrable. Combined with the silence, Mark found it becoming the most frightening thing he had ever experienced, even worse than the terror he had felt outside the cabin in the Appalachians as unseen men fired at Christiana and him.

The two masses of opposing armies had stopped advancing and fanned out to block the entire avenue as they stared at each other. Mark looked around and upward. On the tops of several buildings, he could see men. They seemed to be spotters, for at least two of them that Mark could see were talking into radios or cellular telephones. Mark wondered if he and Christiana were the only ones in the crowd who understood the extent to which the affair was being choreographed by other forces. A lot of people would die in the next short while, he knew. There was little he could do at the moment to stop Christiana and himself being part of that tragic group.

Frank Jensen calmly studied the crowd about fifty yards away from him. "Look at that lot," he said clearly to the young man standing by his side. "Just down from the trees a couple of generations ago, and they think they can handle *us?*"

The young man shifted nervously, and Jensen laughed. "Hey man, it's nigger open season, and there's not a cop in sight."

The other man stared at him. "Christ, Jensen," he said. "This looks dangerous. The goddammed national guard will be bound to be here before too long. Maybe we should just pull back and wait. I never expected to see so many of them with guns."

"That's a fact," Jensen murmured, looking hard at the crowd before him. "Now where the hell do you think those niggers got the same guns we've got, Hans?"

"God knows," replied the other, white-faced. "But it scares the hell out of me, man. You told us it would be like shooting fish in a barrel. Those niggers are armed, man, and angry."

"You may be right," Jensen conceded. "This ain't what I thought it would be. Pass the word along. Keep it quiet. Something's wrong."

"Yeah, it sure is. That National Guard had better be here soon, man, or we've got a war on our hands."

"There's no National Guard coming, sonny," said Jensen. "The man told me we'd have a clear shot at the coons."

"What man?" The man called Hans turned to look at Jensen. "What man, Jensen? What the fuck's going on here?"

"None of your business," replied Jensen. "Now, get the word moving. No fast movements, and start backing away."

"Damn right," Hans snarled and muttered a few words to the man on his left. Orders received, the man began moving softly through the ranks of combat troops, talking to each man in turn. Others followed his example.

Fifty yards away, Isaac Condell studied the masses of armed men bunched up on Michigan Avenue near Monroe Street and swallowed nervously.

"Man," he swore. "Whitey's armed to the fuckin' teeth."

"Fuckin'-A," agreed his lieutenant. "I thought you said we'd be able to shoot the shit out of those white dudes."

"That's what I'd been told," said Condell. "That's what the brothers said when they told me where to get the guns. Fuck, man, looks like Whitey's got the same stuff we've got."

"You gotta tell everyone to back off," said the lieutenant. A tremble shook his voice. The two armies were close enough to hear voices in the other ranks, and every man on both sides appeared to be armed with an assault weapon. The potential slaughter on both sides was terrifying.

"Tell ya' man, we need the National Guard right here and right now," said the lieutenant.

"Ain't gonna *be* no National Guard," said Condell. "That was the fuckin' *idea,* man. Whitey was gonna come lookin' for a lynchin', and he'd find a thousand niggers armed with AK-47s. We was gonna ram it up his white *ass,* man, and *nobody* was gonna stop us."

"Jesus Christ, I hope nobody lets off a round, man," the lieutenant quavered. "We need to get the word round, boss. *Cool* it."

"Get goin' then," said Condell. "And do it quiet. Keep the brothers calm, whatever you do, and start backin' away."

"Got it, man," said the other.

On the roof of a building overlooking the scene, Tommy Lugano spoke into his cellular phone. "Nothing's happening, boss. They're just looking at each other."

"That's what I expected," said the cool tones into his ear. "Neither side expected to find the other guys armed like that. Okay, kid, you know what to do."

"Sure, boss," replied Lugano, and switched off the phone. He touched the shoulder of the man next to him and pointed into the middle of the crowd which had come up from the south side. The other man nodded, cocked his rifle and took careful aim. Lugano lifted his own rifle, shifted position so that he was looking down at the crowd of skinheads, and pointed the weapon at the front line. Both men fired at the same time.

The heavy .762 bullet hit Isaac Condell one inch under his heart. His chest shivered as if a miniature earthquake had struck it, and his back erupted like a volcano belching out blood and flesh in an obscene baptism of gore of his immediate neighbors. Condell's body fell against several men behind him, including one whose knee had been shattered by the bullet leaving Condell's body. A moment of disbelief and shock passed immediately, then screams of horror and fear emitted from several lungs. Before the first ten seconds had passed, three more heavy bullets hit men in the crowd, throwing blood and dreadful gouts of flesh over more. The crowd shook like wheat stalks in a cyclone. Most of the men fought to reach the shelter of the buildings on either side of the road, but there was too little concrete and too many bodies.

Others of the men, especially those who had seen combat in Vietnam, or other, more recent American wars held onto their minds. They unslung their AK-47 assault rifles, released the safety catches and began firing methodically into the crowds of whites only a few yards away.

Tommy Lugano's bullet from the building rooftop hit Frank Jensen in the left shoulder. The entire joint was blown away, leaving his arm hanging only by skin and a small shard of bone. For the first few seconds, he felt no pain, only a numbing shock to his whole body which dimmed his vision and took away all control of his muscles. As he sank to the floor, he partially heard the scream of pain from Hans as the bullet that had removed Jensen's shoulder took the younger man in the stomach. The already-distorted bullet struck Hans as it rolled and wobbled, ripping out his entire bowels and intestines and passing through his body, hitting his spine as it exited, destroying every single bone between his hips and the bottom of his ribcage. Hans collapsed like a rag doll thrown by an angry child, and mercifully died the same moment.

The agony ripped through the numbness in Jensen a few seconds later. Sobbing with the pain, he tried to lift himself up on his one good arm and then to sit up, desperate to signal somehow to the men to open fire. But no signal was needed. While most of the army raced for the buildings, some did as their opposite numbers had done a few yards away. As men died screaming around them, a select few methodically unslung their assault weapons and opened fire at the other army. Jensen tried to drag himself to cover, swearing furiously at his stupidity in having been misled so badly by Geoffrey Payne, and feeling his overwhelming hatred for blacks rise like a bore well of acid.

"Fuck you all," he grated then died as another shell hit him in the right eye.

The sudden, violent movements of the panicking crowd gave Mark the opening he needed. Clutching firmly to Christiana's hand, he began to drive for the shelter of the street corner. Feeling as he were in the middle of a broken field attack in the football games he played at university, he withstood thunderous collisions with screaming, galloping people, and pulled Christiana to him, standing close to the wall.

"Dear God," he gasped, as he folded his arms round her. "We're out of the direct line of fire, at least."

She was sobbing, her face pressed tight against his chest. There was little he could do but let the madness swirl around them as he heard the shrieks of pain and the rattle of gun fire from just a few yards away in the killing ground of Michigan Avenue. Then that stopped, too. The silence seemed to roar as loudly as the echoes of the warfare of just a few seconds ago had done. Not looking round the corner to see what had happened, Mark began to lead Christiana away, keeping well away from the sight lines of the combat area, moving a block east to provide a safety barrier for them. Despite the racing crowds, there was enough space for the two of them to work their way north to where Mark had left the car. Gratefully opening the door, he made sure Christiana was inside before he climbed in and moved off. There was nobody at the exit to collect any money, but Mark had no compunctions in driving away and heading up the lake shore drive toward Evanston.

* * *

Charles Dansbury looked at his brother with a mixture of pain and anger. "Yuri, I find it impossible to understand! I thought we had agreed to wait until the next meeting to make the decision. Why, in God's name, did you set things in motion without consulting the rest of us?"

The two men stood in the middle of the dining room, a few feet apart. Jerome held his walking stick in his right hand, but put none of his weight on it.

"Dmitri, why consult?" Jerome looked coolly back at his brother, his blue eyes without expression. "They would have done as we asked, anyway! The whole bunch of them, the corrupt, venal, amoral group of loyal, patriotic Americans would have been so eager to set off the destruction of their country, you know that! Why bother asking them?"

"And me, Yuri? Is my opinion as worthless as that of our committee?" Dansbury was furious, his eyes glaring.

Jerome retreated a little. "No, Dmitri, of course not. But the timing was perfect. I knew you would have backed me up in this. Dammit, Dmitri, it's what we've worked toward for over sixty years! It *had* to be started!"

"No, Yuri, it did *not* have to be started. The risk of failure is enormous. You have set off a chain of delicately prepared events without ensuring that all the connections were fully in place. The current president is not as malleable as the plan calls for. The country itself is not completely ready for what we have to do. I'm really not sure that today's Americans are yet ready to accept concentration camps, or one-party rule. I suspect there is something else behind your precipitate action, little brother. What is it?"

"Nothing, Dmitri, I assure you. What else could there be?" Jerome looked away from Dansbury. The older man studied him carefully and grunted.

"I know you too well, little Yuri," he said. "You're hiding something. Tell me, Yuri, what do you really want from this destruction of America? Not the installation of our socialist state, I think."

Jerome turned sharply on his brother like a cornered tiger. The fury in his face was powerful, his eyes burning with rage.

"The socialist state, Dmitri?" he snarled. "I don't give a rat's testicle for your socialist workers' paradise! I never have done! *This* is what I want. This, the horrors I have let loose on this sick, stupid country today, this is *it!* This is my culmination of sixty years of dreaming, Dmitri, the death, the destruction, the fear, the punishment, Dmitri, the *punishment!* At last, this country is paying for its crimes. And I'm the judge and the executioner, just like I always promised myself."

Dansbury recoiled in shock. "Punishment, Yuri? For God's sake, what punishment? What has this country done to you, Yuri, that you should hate it so much? We came here with a few million dollars and now we're worth over a hundred billion each. What in God's name is wrong with you?"

"Nothing is wrong with me! My hundred billion dollars are just part of the price this country has had to pay! It was just the down-payment. Now it's paying with its blood and its people." He thumped his stick on the floor, and it gave a soft thud on the polished wood.

"Paying for what? Yuri, the madness is taking over you! Paying for what?"

"For the death of our country, Dmitri," Jerome shouted. "For the death of fifty million of our people in that monstrosity of a war. For using our Russian people as a battering ram in its economic battles with Germany and Japan. For the..."

He stopped and turned away, his arms tightly against his side. He turned to the window and stared out of it.

Dansbury moved so that he could study his brother's face. "For what, Yuri? For *what?* That last thing, what is that? This has nothing to do with America's part in the war, has it? It's something else. Tell me, little brother, what is this one thing that has eaten away at your soul so much that you sentenced America to death today?"

There was silence at the window. As Dansbury watched, a small tear appeared in Jerome's right eye. Furiously, Jerome wiped it away.

"Yuri?" Dansbury whispered. "The crime, Yuri, what was the real crime? What is America paying for today with its people and its innocence? For what, Yuri, *for what?*"

Jerome was silent for a second or two longer, breathing deeply. Dansbury waited. Something was about to happen, he could tell from all the signals he had learned to detect in his brother.

"When I walked away," said Jerome in a voice so soft that Dansbury could just hear. "When I walked away, I swore then, that somebody would pay."

"Walked away from what, Yuri?"

Another pause lasted a few seconds.

"The rats had eaten her arms, Dmitri. I looked down and I saw the bones of her elbows and forearms. Her hands were gnawed away so that just the fingers and tendons were left. Her head was shattered under a rock. But her arms... Her arms were just blood and flesh, like some scrap meat off the butcher's block."

Jerome moved away from the window and sat down in one of the armchairs, dropped his stick and put his head in his hands. When he spoke again, his voice was blurred by tears.

"Our mother, Dmitri, our mother. Somebody had to pay for our mother."

Vince Jerome broke into helpless weeping, his body shaken by the sobs of more than sixty years of suppressed rage and agony.

Charles Dansbury could only stand and watch.

In a small apartment in St. Louis, a telephone rang with the distinctive tone of the fax machine. The apartment was a one-room studio in a working-class area. The walls were painted in an attractive dove-grey, the windows outlined in deep blue. Cream carpeting gave a final touch of elegance and careful design to the room. An Escher print hung on one wall. On the other, was a black-and-white photograph of Adolf Hitler standing on the balcony of his mountain home. Eva Braun smiled with love at him from a few feet away as Herman Goering saluted his *Fuehrer*.

The man reading in the armchair looked up expectantly as the machine rang, and placed his book on the coffee table. He was in his late thirties, tall, lean and muscular, dressed in plain jeans and black shirt. His head was completely bald. When the machine began to grunt delicately and slide a sheet of paper from within itself, the man rose to his feet and walked over to read the words as they appeared.

The message was short. "Foxfire," it said, followed by a date and an address in the dockland region of the city. The man smiled and reached for the telephone.

* * *

Christiana lay tightly enfolded in Mark's arms on the huge bed in his apartment. They had been this way ever since reaching home and locking the door behind them. Her weeping had subsided and she was quiet, except for the occasional shudder that ran through her. Mark stroked her back gently, and after a hour of peace in the darkened bedroom, they both felt they had recovered a little from the horrors of the afternoon.

Mark reached out his right arm and switched on the bedside radio. It was tuned to the station that had carried the talk-show to which Mark had tried to call and been rudely turned away. The voice coming from the radio was unfamiliar to Mark.

"What happened here today proved one thing, people," said the voice. "Law and order has broken down completely in this country. As you know by now, the National Guard was unable to reach the city before the slaughter occurred. Instead, the military has been called in and a number of units are now stationed in and around the city. We are now effectively under martial law, and I for one, am grateful for that. You will see armored personnel carriers in the streets from now on, soldiers on patrol, even tanks. Be prepared to be stopped by troops and your car searched..."

Mark switched off the radio. "It's well on its way," he murmured.

Christiana stirred. "Then thank God I'm here with you and not back home frightened silly about what's happening."

"I agree. Of course, there's not a chance in hell you'll be able to get a plane out of O'Hare on Monday evening."

"You're right. You're stuck with me, Ashton."

"Maybe you should just email your resignation to Verity right now?"

"I think so," she agreed. "Think I'll be able to find a job around here?"

"I'm not so sure we'll be staying," he said. "If this thing isn't beaten soon, this country won't be liveable."

She tightened her arms around his neck, and he felt tears on her face again.

"I hope to God Feathers and his boss are doing something about it," he murmured.

He discovered that they were, thirty seconds later, when the telephone rang.

"I hope you weren't downtown this morning, buddy," said Feathers' deep voice.

"We were part of it," Mark replied. "Nearly didn't survive."

"Christ! You both okay?"

Mark could hear the worry in his friend's voice. "We're both here."

"Not for much longer. You've got another hot ride."

"How long?"

"The Tomcat's landing at Glenview about now, pal. Get your ass over there immediately. There's people to do and things to meet."

Mark replaced the phone and started trying to explain his departure to Christiana.

Chapter 20 - Washington, DC

The President of the United States looked up from his desk as the small group of men filed into the Oval Office at just after eight o'clock in the morning. He looked tired, eyes puffy from lack of sleep. He was dressed informally in light slacks and a dark-green, short-sleeved shirt. He signed another in a pile of documents and nodded at the young woman who hovered at his right elbow. She picked up the pile and walked out with a brief look at the new arrivals.

"Gentlemen," said the President. He sat back in his seat. There was no sign of welcome in his face, and he did not rise to meet his guests, or lead them to the seats round the coffee table a few feet away. "You said this was urgent. I've left the National Security Council meeting downstairs to hear what you have to say. You have fifteen minutes."

"It's urgent," Senator Eckhard confirmed. He took a seat across from the famous desk. The Reverend Vanderbilt did the same, sitting on Eckhard's right. Moving more slowly, Charles Dansbury took the seat to the senator's left.

The President looked coolly at the three men. "This is an unusual grouping," he said. "Senator, we deal with each other regularly, of course. But the Reverend Vanderbilt..."

He looked at the televangelist with unconcealed distaste. "You, Reverend, I see only sitting on the Party bench, mouthing hatred for other Americans, or on television when you announce some new and startling revelation about my disgraceful misdeeds." He smiled without warmth. "I must thank you for those, Reverend, they give my wife and me endless amusement as we ponder on exactly who made them up for you."

"God tells me of them," Vanderbilt replied.

The President ignored him, looking instead, at Dansbury. "Mister Dansbury, what brings you here in this odd association of embittered failures? Hardly your chosen companions, I imagine?"

Dansbury smiled at the furious faces of the other two men then looked at the President. "No, Mister President, not my elected friends, but associates in a vital matter. They have served my purpose."

"And exactly what is that?" asked the President. Clearly, the two other men had become irrelevant. Dansbury was the leader and the President recognized that fact.

"To obtain your support in our plan to end the unrest that has erupted in the last few days, culminating in yesterday's horrors in Chicago," Dansbury said calmly.

The President looked at him for a few seconds. "Let me ask you this, Mister Dansbury," he said. "Have you and your associates had a hand in generating this unrest?"

Dansbury did not manage to hide his surprise, but it showed only in a slight widening of his eyes. Vanderbilt and Eckhard were more obvious, and both men grunted with shock. The President looked at them in disgust for a second or two then returned his attention to Dansbury.

466

"It seems that perhaps you have," he murmured. "So, Mister Dansbury, now that you have succeeded in stirring up the population of America so that they kill each other with less compunction than they spray cockroaches, what is your suggestion for restoring order? And what is your price?"

Dansbury nodded in acknowledgement. "I have always had the greatest admiration for your intelligence, Mister President. Of course, I cannot agree with your conclusions as to responsibility. But we have suggestions, and naturally there will be a price."

"Of course," the President agreed sardonically. "Just as there will be implications of retribution if I don't follow your recommendations. Let's start with the suggestions. What have you in mind?"

"You will recall, Mister President," began Dansbury, "that in yesterday's affair in Chicago, the National Guard failed to appear. To replace them, a few hundred armed troops arrived, fully equipped for riot suppression. They have now taken over the city under full martial law."

The President looked coldly at him. "Yes, Mister Dansbury, as Commander-in-Chief of the armed forces, I could hardly fail to notice that certain detachments took action that I did not authorize, and that several military bases have since become inaccessible to the Pentagon. It has been the topic of heated discussion all night with the Security Council. We have found that among the only officers with the sort of authority to issue such orders, one has since gone missing and beyond any contact. General Rollings is part of the same group as these two loyal Americans with you, is he?"

Dansbury nodded with a small smile.

"And the divisions of troops which have since sealed their bases from any communication, these are now answering only to Rollings, I assume?" the President continued.

"It can no longer be stopped, Mister President," Dansbury agreed. "Another city will experience similar events this afternoon, and neither you nor I nor anyone else can prevent it."

"You will kill another three thousand Americans, Mister Dansbury?"

"And three thousand more the next day, and five thousand every day after that, if necessary."

"And their deaths will be on your head," Eckhard suddenly shouted. "It's all your fault anyway, for carrying out those stupid, liberal policies all these years."

The President turned weary eyes on the senator. "Oh, do shut up, Morgan," he said gently. "Or I'll tell Peggy Jo and she'll give you a good spanking." He turned his eyes back to Dansbury, ignoring the red face and fury of Morgan Eckhard.

"You must want something very badly, Mister Dansbury." The President's voice was expressionless. "What is it?"

"Suspend the Constitution, Mister President. Authorize the start-up of the concentration camps for dissidents for which the law already allows. Establish martial law throughout the nation and start arresting anyone who stirs up trouble. Put them in the camps, and things will begin to quieten down."

"On your orders, I suppose?" The President seemed calm, interested in what Dansbury was saying.

"I will arrange that," Dansbury agreed with a pleasant smile. He could have been organizing a business lunch with a friend, for all the tension that seemed to exist between the two men.

The President turned to the other two men. "How about you two?" he asked in a friendly manner. "Are you here just to see the Oval Office, or is there something you want to enforce on this administration?"

"This must become a truly Christian nation," Vanderbilt blurted out. "I want prayers back in schools, I want abortion stopped, I want people to be *Christian,* or..." He stopped, in some confusion and embarrassment.

"Or what, Reverend Vanderbilt?" the President prodded. "What? Burning at the stake for Jews and Muslims? Ecclesiastic Courts for heresy charges? Maybe citizenship should be open to Christians only? Shall we enforce church attendance, maybe? And with what penalties for failure to comply?" His tone had become razor-sharp, and Vanderbilt shifted uncomfortably.

"Of course, you'll want the current trends in education accelerated, won't you, Reverend?" the President continued. He turned back to Dansbury. "Is this your man?" he asked. "Is this the prime mover in dumbing down the American mind over the last few decades? Is he one of yours, one of you mysterious people who have caused Americans to become sheep, following their leader?"

"One of the series," Dansbury admitted. He seemed uncomfortable. The President was not reacting as he had expected.

"My God, Dansbury, what has this country done to you that you should hate it so much?" asked the President.

"Look at you, perhaps the richest man in the world, certainly in America, and you want to destroy it? You want to make it a military dictatorship, something just like Hitler's Germany or Stalin's Russia?"

"Not Stalin's Russia!" Dansbury snapped, more loudly than he had intended. "That man betrayed his nation..." He stopped, uncertain, angry at himself for revealing emotions he was not ready to show to the world. He felt some confusion, hearing an echo in the President's words of those he had spoken recently to his brother.

The President looked at him curiously. "Well, Mister Dansbury, what an odd reaction! What could you possibly have given away, just then?"

"Merely my shock that you should consider I would wish to imitate a communist tyrant, Mister President," Dansbury replied, taking control of himself. "But we are forgetting the reasons for this meeting. Our demand of you is that martial law be imposed on America immediately, and that the constitution be suspended."

"Why?" asked the President. Again, Dansbury felt a sheet of worry run through him. Something was not going properly. Furiously, he cursed Yuri for precipitating the plan three years ahead of schedule. Their trained-dog President would not be behaving like this if the meeting had been held three years from now.

"Because that way, we can restore order," Dansbury replied.

"And after that?" asked the President.

"After that, you'll be out," Eckhard grated. "The elections will be held soon after things have settled down, and we'll have one of our own in this office. Then we can run things properly."

470

The President laughed. "And will you be my successor in this office, Morgan? Will you and Peggy Jo invite me to your swearing-in and treat me nicely?"

Eckhard flushed red again, and Dansbury laughed softly.

"No, Mister President, Morgan will not be the next President of the United States. Even with the reduced needs of the role after the next election, Morgan could not be the man."

Dansbury raised his hand at Eckhard's fury. "Not now, Morgan. This ground has been covered already."

"Reduced needs, Mister Dansbury?" The President looked interested. "Now, I find that fascinating. Do you mean that the country will be run by you, instead? Or by a council of you and your appointees? Presumably, the enforcement of your will is to be the responsibility of General Rollings and his military?"

"Accurately put," Dansbury agreed.

"And will there still be a permitted opposition in the House and Senate?" asked the President. "Or will we not have those institutions any more?" He seemed to debating a political question in a classroom and Dansbury felt a rush of worry.

"It's not an efficient manner of operation, Mister President," he replied. "A single party will control the nation and the means of production, thus allowing concentration on solving the country's problems instead of wasting so much effort and time on being re-elected every few years."

"Vladimir Ilich Lenin is a hero of yours, Mister Dansbury?" The President seemed amused.

Dansbury remained in control of himself. "About as much as Adolf Hitler is a hero of Reverend Vanderbilt's," he replied. He smiled at the expression of horror on Eckhard's face then turned back to the President.

"So, Mister President," he said. "Your decision? Suspend the constitution, declare martial law, and things will settle down. In fact, the results will be so good that you will be a hero to the nation for the last months of your administration. You can retire to a popular and well-regarded life with a rich future and the history books will declare you to have been a strong, courageous leader."

"And you will write them, of course," the President murmured. "And if I fail to follow your *suggestions?* What will you do?"

Dansbury shrugged. "Then I'd have to tell you that nobody can stop the carnage in America except for the military. And once order has been restored through those rather forceful means, it would be hard, perhaps impossible to return to the old ways. Nor could we be certain any longer of the loyalty of your protection squads. Who will know when one or more of the men might decide that they no longer believe in you, and turn a gun on you? Or perhaps on your wife, or even worse, your children? Then it will require your Vice-President to make the same decision."

"With the same conditions, I take it?" the President retorted. "And if he doesn't follow orders, what then? Execute everyone until you find someone who will agree?"

"The succession path goes down to the Speaker of the House," Dansbury replied. "Should it get that far, I am quite certain that *he* will agree."

"I have no doubts," the President agreed dryly. "What if nobody in the protection corps loses their sense of rightness, Mister Dansbury? Will there then be a man with a rifle in a book repository and backup gunmen nearby, to shoot my head off?"

Dansbury shrugged again. "Anything is possible, Mister President. I urge you to accept our recommendations."

"And how long do I have before you start enforcing those recommendations?"

"Twenty-four hours, Mister President."

"And will the action in the next city still continue as scheduled, regardless of my decision if I gave it to you immediately?"

"Regrettably yes. Nobody can contact General Rollings any more until that event is complete. But please don't worry, Mister President. The event will only underline your strength and leadership in declaring martial law."

"Another three thousand or more deaths, and you see it only as a gesture, Mister Dansbury? Maybe you're more like Joe Stalin than you care to admit?"

"Those who will die are scum, Mister President," Dansbury replied calmly. "Skinheads, neo-Nazis..." He ignored the gesture of rage from the Reverend Vanderbilt. "... welfare layabouts, criminals, drug-users, black trash from the ghettos, *disposables*, Mister President."

"*Americans*, Mister Dansbury."

Dansbury merely stared back at the President and said nothing.

The President looked hard at each of the three men in turn. "An interesting group," he murmured. "You, Morgan, a United States Senator, a man who has taken an

oath to protect this nation, a man who has sex with his
daughter, depends on his wife for his means of support,
and you come here to make me run the country according
to your standards of moral leadership?"

Morgan Eckhard looked at the desktop, his face white.
The President passed on.

"And you, *Reverend* Vanderbilt, what shall we make of
you? A homosexual pedophile, tax cheat, blackmailer, and
a man of God? And you want *your* standards of morality
imposed on the country?"

Vanderbilt shot to his feet. "You're a liar!" he
bellowed. "You're a fucking liar! God will damn you to
Hell for eternity for those lies!"

"Reverend, be quiet!" Dansbury snapped. "The whole
of Washington knows of your propensities by now. We
have more important things to be getting on with." He
glared at Vanderbilt. "Sit *down!*" he said. Authority
crackled in the air. Vanderbilt stood for a few seconds
glaring with hatred at the President then slowly subsided
in his seat.

The president smiled at him. "The FBI is quite good at
what it does, Reverend," he said. "Almost as good as
Mister Dansbury's people, I've no doubt."

He turned back to Dansbury. "And of course, General
Rollings who swore an oath to protect the nation and obey
his Commander-in-Chief, he is one of yours. And you,
Mister Dansbury, I cannot understand at all. Is this the
total membership of your Cabal to run the United States,
or are there other, even more unsavory characters among
you?"

Silence greeted his words, and the President stood up.
"Well, gentlemen, you've had your time, and a very

interesting session it was. I must return to my other meeting with people rather more concerned with keeping the country whole." He moved from behind his desk, and to the door. As he opened it, he looked back. "You'll have my answer tomorrow," he said, and walked out.

Another door opened, and a young man walked in. "This way please, gentlemen," he said, and led the way out.

In the corridor, the three men looked briefly at each other. Eckhard was still pale with anger and Vanderbilt's fury was obvious.

"That bastard!" Eckhard swore. "If he thinks he's going to survive this, he's got another think coming! I'll kill him! I'll have him impeached!"

"Be quiet, Morgan," said Dansbury as if remonstrating a child. "This is no time for a temper tantrum. We have problems."

"Don't you tell me what to do," Eckhard hissed. "God *damn* you, Dansbury, I'm sick to death of being ordered around by you and Jerome as if you were God, or something..."

Dansbury glared at him, and the senator subsided as if gagged.

"Dansbury, what was that he said about admiring Lenin?" broke in Vanderbilt. "What the hell did he mean? You don't admire Lenin, do you?"

"Indeed I do, Reverend," Dansbury replied. "Lenin had perhaps the finest mind in history. He showed us how a country could be run fairly and well, with peace and prosperity for all. Of course I admire him. I intend to emulate him as much as possible when this country is mine."

"But he was a communist!" Eckhard stared wildly at Dansbury. "How can you say we'll run America as a communist state?"

"Don't be more stupid than you have to be, Morgan," said Dansbury. "We'll run it as we've always said we'll run it. Who could possibly tell the difference?"

"You're crazy!" Eckhard squeaked. "I'll tell Jerome, I'll tell..."

"Be quiet, Morgan," said Dansbury firmly and stared into Eckhard's eyes until the senator went quiet again.

"Something was wrong at that meeting," Dansbury continued, forgetting Eckhard's outburst immediately. "The man wasn't reacting the way he should have been. We can't contact Geoffrey, Tony or Grant until after St. Louis. I'll get Jerome and Colin Webber and we'll go and see Lombard. He may know something more." He looked at his watch. "Things will be starting in St. Louis in a few hours. We're all due to meet at Jerome's house tomorrow morning at eight for a progress review. Things will be clearer by then, and presumably, we'll have heard back from the President."

"Er... there's something else, Charles," Eckhard muttered. He looked frightened.

Dansbury looked coldly at him. "Something you forgot to tell us, Morgan? Is it somehow connected with the unexpected reactions of the President just now?"

"Probably," Eckhard replied. "A few days ago, somebody walked in on the group that sends out the emails. They were three men, one of them a huge black guy, all of them armed. They ordered the group to disband."

Dansbury was silent for a few moments, but his breathing was harsh as he struggled to control his anger. "And you just decided to tell me now?" he demanded.

Eckhard's face was white. "I..." he stammered and fell silent.

Dansbury looked furiously at him then turned on his heels. The three walked along the corridor until they reached the outside. Dansbury climbed into his limousine without bothering to offer the others a ride. As the vehicle moved off silently, Vanderbilt and Eckhard looked at each other in baffled rage, then set off to walk to the gates to find cabs.

* * *

"Bryce Lombard has been our strongest and most consistent support for the last ten years," Charles Dansbury said as the black limousine slid through Washington's streets on a beautiful Fall Sunday. The time on the clock inset into the partition said five minutes after eleven.

"A powerful ally," said Colin Webber. He glanced at Vince Jerome who had barely spoken since Webber had joined the two men in the luxurious rear cabin.

"Indeed," Dansbury agreed. "His contacts and influence within the party are quite remarkable, even though he has never sought the leadership. He would have made the country's finest President, I'm certain, had it not been for regrettable and surely false stories circulated about his wife's amorous adventures some years earlier."

"I think so," Webber concurred. "I was deeply upset when he pulled out of the presidential race before even the primaries. Lombard has always seemed to me to represent the best of America's leadership."

Jerome shook his head, as if waking up, and joined the conversation. "Not for our purposes, Colin. We needed to start drawing the angers and frustrations of this country to a head. It served our purposes best to set up a three-way presidential race. It gave a free rein to Crawford and his like to build up a headwater of anger and hatred. That way, we knew that we could get a compliant and not-too-bright President in the coming election. Lombard could not have played that role and he agreed to stay out of the race."

"You mean you undercut Lombard's position?"

Jerome nodded.

"Does Bryce know this?" Webber seemed amused and Dansbury smiled at him.

"I sincerely hope not," he replied.

"I'm certain he doesn't," Jerome added. "He could hardly have helped us so much over the years if he had known. He asked his daughter to work for me several years ago, and she has been splendid. No, Bryce Lombard is our greatest support, as Charles said."

"And what do you expect from this meeting?" asked Webber.

"Something rang false in our meeting with the President this morning," said Dansbury. "I need to know what it was. If something is happening which we don't know about, Bryce will know. The mysterious attack on our email group which that fool Eckhard finally got round to telling me about, is a serious worry which Bryce may be able to explain. And it will be a good place to be when events start happening in St. Louis in about half an hour."

"Bryce can also check with all the power sources within the party during the afternoon as events unfold," Jerome added. "Somebody may have more news."

"I see," said Webber as the limousine pulled up outside Lombard's brownstone mansion. He climbed out first and waited for the two older men to join him before walking up the steps to the door which opened as he arrived.

Lombard's greeting was subdued. "Good afternoon, gentlemen," he said, standing in the lobby of the house as the others entered. He extended his hand to Webber who took it. "Welcome to our group, Colin," said Lombard. "I know you will be most valuable in our project."

"I hope so," said Webber, and waited while Lombard met the other two, then led the way to his study.

"A volatile situation," Lombard said when all four had settled in armchairs in the comfortable study. "I wish you had not precipitated the action so early, Vince. We really were not ready for this."

"I felt it necessary," Jerome said shortly. "Factors fell into place which made an early start essential." He held his walking stick by the handle, one finger tapping an irritated rhythm.

"Could you not have told us?" asked Lombard. "Surely, even telling us where the first confrontation was to take place would have done no harm?"

"I deemed it too risky." Jerome refused to look at any of the others in the room. Lombard saw the glare of anger from Dansbury, and exchanged a look of understanding with Webber.

"Bryce, is there anything you can tell us?" Dansbury asked. "Morgan's news about the email group is particularly disturbing. And I got the strong sensation this morning that the President had some information that we did not. Either that, or the young man has greater composure and courage than I had ever dreamed"

"You may certainly have underestimated him," Lombard agreed. "I may argue with most of his policies, and I have great distaste for his personal life-style, but I have never had anything but admiration for his strength and vision. He has more moral courage than many in my own party, I have to admit."

"But do you know of anything that may be interfering with our plans?" Dansbury persisted.

"A few things," said Lombard. All three of the other men looked at him. "I have to confirm that your suspicions are correct, Charles. There *is* a specialist group in existence, set up to look for and counteract exactly the sort of activities the New America Council has been conducting. It's called Task Force Five."

"And is it this Task Force which demolished our email group?" asked Jerome. He appeared to be more alert and involved than a few moments before.

Lombard nodded. "I believe so."

"Does the President know about it?" Dansbury persisted.

"He knows of it, but has no authority over it."

"Then who controls this group?" Jerome demanded. "Who could be trusted to direct the work of such an operation without misusing it for their own ends?"

"I hear that it's a small governing council of five people drawn from the military, Congress, the Senate or the public service," Lombard answered. "I understand that nobody may serve more than two years. The group advises the President, but he has absolutely no say in the group's composition or directives."

"Do you know anyone on this council?" The worry in Dansbury's face was twisting his mouth.

Lombard shrugged. "I only know that there is a senior officer of each arm of the services, and two senators, one from each party."

In the worried silence that hung in the room, Colin Webber spoke up softly. "It's about time something should be happening in St. Louis. Why not put on the television and see if anything is reported?"

"A good idea," Lombard agreed and touched a button on the arm of his seat. A screen began to move up in one wall of the study, revealing a large television monitor. It flickered on as the screen reached the top, and the channel changed to the CNN network. It was exactly noon, an hour earlier in St. Louis. Lombard kept the volume low as the news program started. The news reader, a dark, attractive woman was reading from papers in front of her, and behind her, scenes of the carnage in Chicago flickered on and off.

The room was silent, and the tension grew as time passed.

"Something should be coming through any moment," Jerome muttered. "Payne said he had set up the confrontation for eleven, local time. Somebody will start shooting at any moment. It's already five after."

As short silence occurred as the four men looked at the television monitor.

"You know, gentlemen, we've known each other for over a decade, but we've never really talked about ourselves," Lombard said in a conversational tone.

481

Dansbury looked at him in astonishment. "Is this a good time to open up personal confidences, Bryce?" he asked. The strain was showing in the tightness of his vocal chords.

Lombard shrugged. "It may help us to keep cool while we await events in the mid-west. For instance, Charles, I understand you were born and raised in Los Angeles?"

"Yes, I was," Dansbury said curtly. His eyes stayed fixed on the television screen.

"An ugly place," Lombard commented. "I try and stay away from it as much as possible. As I understand you have, Charles."

"What? Yes." Dansbury seemed irritated. He looked at his watch. It was nine minutes after twelve.

"In fact, you've never been back there at all, since you returned from the war, somebody once told me."

Dansbury looked sharply at him. "No," he said. "I never wanted to return there. My childhood was not happy. The place has no fond memories for me."

"I understand," said Lombard with a nod. "But what of family, Charles? Is there nobody back in L.A. that would remember you?"

"Nobody," snapped Dansbury, and looked at his watch again. The news reader was relating another in the series of the non-stop stories about the previous day's massacre in Chicago. There had been little other news in the US since that event.

"Such a shame," murmured Lombard. "One should have friends and family to give one roots. Horrible not to have them, I would imagine. I was born in Seattle, you know. The same city as you, Vince."

"I know that," said Jerome coldly. The tension in the room was climbing by the second, but Lombard seemed not to notice it.

"Yes, a lovely city," he said. "I would have been about nine or ten when you went off to war to serve the United States, Vince. It's funny that we've never compared notes on our home town. We might have found that our two families knew each other."

"I doubt it," Jerome said sharply. "We were not a wealthy family like you. Your father was a merchant banker, I know that. We wouldn't have moved in the same circles."

"My step-father," corrected Lombard. "No, my real father was a clerk in a factory, and my mother struggled to raise her two sons. Did you know I once had a brother?"

"I didn't," muttered Jerome, and looked at his watch. It was sixteen minutes after twelve, and the news had not touched on any events in St. Louis.

"He was ten years older than I," Lombard said cheerfully. "That would have made him about your age, Vince." He seemed oblivious to the atmosphere in the room. Webber watched all three men like a hunting owl studying the movements of a mouse on the ground.

"So when America entered the war after Pearl Harbor, he joined the infantry," Lombard continued. "Ended up with the US First Division. Wasn't that your old group, both of you?" Lombard smiled pleasantly as the two men turned their eyes from the screen and looked at him. Neither spoke. It looked to Webber that the two old men had finally realized that Lombard was not just making idle conversation. Something was seriously wrong.

"So you may have served with my brother in the war," said Lombard. "I wonder if you knew him. I miss him badly, because he never came home from Europe."

"Killed?" asked Jerome. His blue eyes were bright, searching Lombard's face with intensity.

"Apparently not," Lombard replied. "The records show that he was discharged a few days after the fall of Berlin, but he never came home. Actually, Vince, it's odd that you never met him. He had the same name as you."

"What?"

Both Jerome and Dansbury jumped with shock. Jerome was nervously tapping his stick on the carpet.

"Yes," said Lombard softly. "Didn't I mention that? My father's name was Henry Jerome. He died when I was just three, and my brother was thirteen. He named his elder son Vincent, and his younger son Bryce. Of course, I changed my family name when my mother married Greg Lombard a couple of years later, but my brother didn't. He was more attached to it than I was."

The silence rang in the air like a giant's bellow of pain.

"Problem is," said Lombard, "according to the records, there was only one Vince Jerome in the US First Division. So here's my question to both of you. Vince, Charles, who the hell are you?"

As the silence continued to roar, Lombard smiled and touched the button on his armrest. The television went off and the screen started to lower. It sounded like the rumble of a freight train in the still room.

"Might as well, gentlemen," said Lombard. "Nothing's going to happen in St. Louis, or anywhere else. Corley Rollings decided his oath as a United States Air Force officer was more important than the New America."

Chapter 21

For over a minute, silence gripped the study. Webber almost held his breath as the other three men stared at each other. Dansbury's face was pale, almost greenish. Jerome's was harsh, the blue eyes blazing with fury and frustration.

"Bryce, I thought you were our friend," Dansbury croaked. "For ten years, we have worked together."

"Only on the face of it," said Lombard calmly. "In fact, the hardest thing for me over those ten years was to pretend to be a colleague and admirer of the men who almost certainly murdered my brother. There were many things I failed to tell you, even lied to you about. One of them is that I am one of the five councilors for Task Force Five."

Dansbury froze. "Then who is the leader of this group?"

Lombard turned his eyes to Colin Webber. "We call him Taskmaster," he said. Webber found himself impaled on the stares of Dansbury and Jerome.

"Sorry," Webber said, and smiled. "Your research investigators must have blown this one."

Jerome ignored the pleasantry. "It was Rollings who failed us?"

Lombard nodded. "Rollings went directly to the President late last night. The President called me immediately."

"It's a pity Rollings couldn't have seen the light earlier," said Webber with cold anger. "Over three thousand people in Chicago need not have died. Your system worked very well, Vince. With each person only knowing his own functions, I wasn't able to prevent Chicago, even though I knew all your team, when it would happen, and who the ringleaders were. And with Vince precipitating the action without your group consensus, not even that knowledge was able to give us any warning."

"When the armies went to their weapons supplies in St. Louis this morning, there was nothing there except the National Guard," said Lombard. "The Commander of the Guard had been replaced an hour earlier and is now in custody, as are a number of his opposite numbers around the country. The crowds were dispersed without fuss. So there was nothing for CNN to report, as you see."

"And the military units were withdrawn from Chicago this morning, also," Webber added. "The clean-up is in process. But there are still over three thousand dead on your conscience, gentlemen. If you have one, that is."

The two older men ignored him.

"Of course," Webber continued, "your colleagues are now totally confused. Tony Redman's rooftop spotters had nothing to spot. Geoffrey Payne only knows that his weapons stocks remain untouched. Vanderbilt and Armstrong will have done as we did, watched the news to see how it was going, and will be vastly disturbed to see nothing of interest beyond endless stories of the Chicago killings. Nothing to excite any of them. The General is still undergoing a rigorous debriefing by the President and the Security Council in the White House, much as he was when you visited the Oval Office this morning. It promises to be an interesting session tomorrow morning, when the New America Council meets for a review of progress. It's a pity you'll have to miss it."

Dansbury flicked a glance in Webber's direction, then turned to Lombard. "And you have been watching us for ten years, Bryce? I commend you for your diligence." He smiled through the pain in his eyes.

"Of course, Charles. You see, I saw the remarkable Vince Jerome many years ago. It was clear to me that he was not my long-lost brother." There was a savage look in Lombard's eyes as he flicked a glance at Jerome. "When I learned of this extraordinary recluse, and his close association with the equally mysterious Charles Dansbury, I began to study you both. Imagine my surprise when I found that Charles Dansbury had done the same as my brother, abandoned his home town and never, ever travelled there."

Lombard rose to his feet and went to his liquor cabinet. He poured himself a scotch and returned to his seat. He issued no invitation to anyone else to help themselves.

"It was no surprise, therefore," he continued, "when I discovered that the entire squad of men led by Corporal Charles Dansbury had gone missing in Berlin. When a group of bodies was discovered, four of them had the dog tags of First Division GIs. Two had no dog tags at all. All six had been shot through the head at close range. It was some years before that information became available to me. It was one of those oddities of war that were kept hidden because of the strained politics of Berlin for so many years."

"Please, Bryce, may I get a drink?" Dansbury's voice was weak and dry. Lombard shrugged, and Dansbury took it as assent. He rose and poured two large brandies, passing one to Jerome who took it with a subdued smile.

"How long have you known this?" Jerome asked.

"Six years," Lombard replied. "Once the Berlin Wall came down and the USSR collapsed, more data became available. Even with my connections, it was some years after those events however, before I learned these details. With those details I began to go back to your early histories after your return from Berlin."

He sipped his drink thoughtfully. Webber looked at him, and saw the grief in his face.

"Eventually, we traced the icons you sold and discovered their history. Some of the gems you so carefully unloaded for so many millions also had identities, and these we found as well." Lombard seemed to fall into a deep reverie.

"Which left us with a couple of questions," said Webber, picking up the action. "One of them was the one Bryce just asked; who are you two people? The other one, of course, was what were you up to?"

The two Russians turned to him. Their faces were expressionless.

"The answer to the second was quite easy," Webber continued. "Astonishingly easy, in fact. Bryce got close to you, made all the right sounds of admiration, and you eventually sounded him out on the New America concept. He led you by the nose all the way. Despite all the intensive background research, you missed the vital

488

history of his childhood under another name. Amazing, Vince. You obviously only studied his record as an adult."

Webber looked at the drinks cabinet, seemed to ponder for a few moments, then rose and poured himself a scotch, adding nothing to it. He sat down again, crossed his legs and took a thoughtful sip. "Your identities were harder," he continued. "But the source of your initial wealth was a good pointer, and Bryce has touched on the key event which allowed us the breakthrough, the fall of the Soviet Union in the summer of 1991. Once we had established some semblance of co-operation with the FSB, the old KGB, things got easier. Of course, they had your fingerprints on file, as they had with all military officers. We got the information only a few days ago."

Jerome stirred uneasily, and Dansbury downed his brandy in one gulp.

"Dmitri Alexandrovitch Kutasov, and Yuri Alexandrovitch Kutasov, you are now both under arrest as enemy agents acting against the interests of the United States of America," said Webber formally.

Jerome said nothing but stared into his brandy glass. Dansbury let out a long sigh and seemed to shrink within himself "Over sixty years and it ends like this," he whispered. "It hardly seems possible."

"You almost succeeded," said Lombard softly. "Perhaps the thing that strikes me with most horror, is how close you came, how many Americans would have welcomed the sort of military rule you were about to impose on us, how many believed that one-party rule was good for the country, how many who saw the lunatic religious theocracy favored by Crawford, Vanderbilt and the others as being truly American. These things frightened me beyond belief. It was only in recent weeks, when we were able to get Colin into your confidence after five years of efforts, that we were finally able to see what you were doing and how you were doing it. You were as astonishingly brilliant in your ways as you had been in your financial dealings."

"Yes," agreed Webber. "And your strategy of using the far right to front your Communist take-over was quite amazing. I congratulate you."

Jerome sneered. "That was an obvious ploy! The far right has always tended towards acquisition of power without concerns about how it was acquired. It was easy for us to cause the party to abandon morality and ethics as they have in recent years. It just took money. The liberals were far too diffused, too many agendas, too little obsession with power. Of *course* we used the far right and its Republican allies!"

"Sadly, I have to agree with you," said Lombard. "I shall make it my mission for the future to try and return the party to some old standards."

"You'll fail!" Jerome snapped. "They'll brand you as a liberal activist! You won't survive the next election."

"Possibly true," said Lombard with a nod. "But as President, I may stand more chance."

"President?" Jerome laughed. "With Margaret's reputation? Forget it!"

"Ah, yes. Those stories that mysteriously circulated about Margaret. Something I have here which might interest you."

Webber couldn't see what Lombard did, but the hiss of a recording began in an unseen loudspeaker. Words came out loudly, with crystal clarity.

"A man of exquisite taste, you have to agree," said the voice of Dansbury. A tiny sound of chinking of ice in a glass was the background to his words.

Webber watched the two Russians. They seemed frozen rigid as the recorded words came back to them.

"In all things," said the voice of Vince Jerome. *"His home, his wife, his daughter, his gift for organization and conciliation, the man is a national treasure."*

"Splendid presidential material," said Dansbury. His voice fluctuated as he apparently moved around the room.

"Perhaps the perfect candidate," said Jerome's voice. *"He would sweep the polls from New Hampshire through to Election Day."*

Both men chuckled, the recorded sound conflicting sharply with their present expressions.

"What a terrible thought," murmured Dansbury's voice through the speaker.

"A nightmare," Jerome agreed. *"That's the sort of thing that would undo years of work."*

"Just as well we've managed to persuade most of the GOP that Lombard is not a suitable candidate," said Dansbury. *"That little piece of information about Margaret's past indiscretions did the trick very well."*

"I did it rather well, I thought," said Jerome. *"It was ugly, how eagerly people absorbed that tiny falsehood and believed it without a shred of evidence."*

The sound of the door opening punctuated the recording, and Senator Lombard's voice came through clearly. *"Glad you made yourselves at home,"* he said. The sounds of ice being added to a glass and the pleasant *"glug-glug"* of a bottle being poured took up a few seconds.

"Make yourselves comfortable, my friends," said the voice of Lombard.

The senator touched a button and the recording stopped.

"Perhaps you remember that conversation, gentlemen?" asked Lombard. His face was cold. "I'm sure you could understand how easily I could refute that story now?"

"Bryce, I am most terribly sorry," whispered Dansbury. "Surely you see how we were working toward a plan that truly would have benefited America?"

"Benefited America?" Lombard laughed without humor. "A puppet President following the orders of a council of perverts, criminals, religious fanatics and alcoholic arms-merchants? This is your view of America?"

"Is our proposal any different from the way things have been in recent years with your system?" retorted Jerome. His blue eyes flashed. "At least, Bryce, our council would have been led by Charles and me, with our proven abilities in commercial development. Could you say the same about the leaders of your last administrations?"

"I can't deny what you say, Vince," Lombard acknowledged. "But as you admit, some of the blame for that decline in morality and competence lies at your own feet. You caused it."

"Indeed we did," agreed Dansbury. "But how can you disagree that we would have run a far more efficient America than your present system seems to do?"

"Efficient?" Lombard laughed again. "I think we saw just how efficient a state-run economy is. Your old country is hardly a blazing example of your proposals."

"We had no intention of implementing such a stupid system," Dansbury countered. "You miss the point, Bryce. What Stalin did to the ideals of Lenin was as much a crime as your party has committed with the ideals of Lincoln and Washington. We were not about to copy that insanity."

"No," said Lombard dryly. "You were simply about to implement one-party rule under a puppet leader."

"Can you deny it would have been more efficient than your present insane method?" Dansbury demanded. "Your so-called representatives spend more time being re-elected than in doing their jobs. That is, when they're not feathering their nests with corrupt agreements. We'd change that dramatically for the better. And we had no plans to nationalize all your industries, merely the defense corporations. Again, how much more effective it would be to tell companies to build what they're best at, and ignore all the rigged tests and trials and political lobbying. This way, we could have had an advanced fighter to replace your ageing squadrons ten years ago, instead of still waiting."

"Unfortunately," replied Lombard, "we Americans have a quaint preference for choosing our representatives and their varying philosophies, and throwing them out when we tire of them. Nor do we like to hand major defense contracts to companies without some form of competition."

"Such rubbish!" Jerome sneered. "Look at the popularity of such men as Crawford and his like! It was clear that the majority of Americans had no time for such silly ideas as an opposition party. They would have been perfectly happy with one-party rule. And as for competitive defense contracts? You make me laugh,

Lombard. Just how many weapons systems have been foisted on the taxpayer despite their inability to satisfy their contracted mission? Your so-called competition has not prevented these farces."

Lombard nodded. "The system has its deficiencies, Vince, you know that. You created many of them and have taken advantage of all of them. But we'll stick to it and try and improve it. And one of the points of our freedoms is that any idiot may propound any alternative, even one which would remove the very freedom they are abusing. Winston Churchill once said that democracy is the worst system in the world except for all the others. We'll keep trying with what we have."

"We would have improved on it," insisted Dansbury.

"It doesn't matter any longer what your intentions were," Webber broke in. "They will not come to pass. Perhaps we should concentrate on your own futures?"

"What futures are they, Colin?" asked Dansbury with an amused smile. "Will you not just take us out and shoot us? After all, any trial will be an enormous embarrassment to you and your party. I doubt you'll bother."

Webber nodded. "You're right, Charles. I prefer an older approach."

"And what is that?" Dansbury seemed barely interested. Jerome studied his glass. Lombard appeared to have detached himself from the discussion, and his eyes were focused on some remote, distant past.

"The Romans had the right idea," said Webber. "It allowed for retirement from public life with honor, dignity and grace, regardless of the crimes committed against the state. It avoided exactly the sort of embarrassment you mentioned."

"What? You suggest we go home and slit our wrists while lying in a warm bath?" Dansbury seemed stunned.

Webber shrugged. "The precise method is your own choice. The one you mention seems unfair on your domestic servants, however. Something cleaner and neater, I suggest. I can even give you something to assist, if you wish."

Jerome stirred and looked up from his glass. "And if we choose not to follow such a barbaric suggestion?"

"Then I shall ensure the same result," Webber said coldly. "But then you'll have no choice in the timing or the method."

The two Russians stared at him. Dansbury looked hard at Lombard as if begging for some assistance, but Lombard seemed unaware of the plea.

"One of my men will drive your limousine home," said Webber softly. "Another will accompany you in the vehicle. It's done, gentlemen. You failed. You have just been tried, convicted and sentenced to death. We must now clear up the debris of your efforts."

As if walking into a funeral parlor to pay their last respects to an old friend, the two Russians walked from the house under the gentle but firm guidance of Colin Webber. Jerome seemed to putting some weight on his walking stick.

At the foot of the stairs, Mark Ashton studied the trio. "Good afternoon, Chief," he said to Webber, receiving a nod in return. "Your limo, gentlemen," he continued with a touch of irony, and held the door open while Jerome and Dansbury climbed in like weary, arthritic men. When they were in, Mark pushed the door against the latch, and looked back at his boss.

"Feathers is at the wheel," he said. "The driver is with the police. Something to do with an expired license, I understand."

Webber gave him a smile. "You have tomorrow morning planned, Mark?"

"Paul and Feathers have everything under control, Chief. Looks like a busy day."

"When it's over, you and I need to talk, Mark. TF5 needs you."

Mark looked firmly at Webber. "I'm getting married in a few days, Chief. Married men aren't useful to you. We won't take the risks."

Webber shook his head. "It's not all combat stuff. I need people who can see the trouble spots coming. Just like you did with Crawford. I need people to research, analyze, conclude and advise me. I need people who care about this country."

"Sounds boring, Chief. Count me in."

"That's what saving the country's all about, Mark. All work and no play. Boring. See you tomorrow."

Mark waved cheerfully, re-opened the door, and climbed inside. He nodded courteously at the two men as he made himself comfortable. "I believe my boss was discussing ancient Roman rituals, gentlemen," he said. "Is there anything further I can tell you on that subject?"

Only silence greeted his words. The two old men stared sightlessly ahead.

"By the way, did I introduce myself?" Mark asked. "No, I thought not. I'm Mark Ashton, and I'm very pleased to meet you, gentlemen."

The two men turned their heads and stared at him. Mark smiled back pleasantly, but his eyes were savagely cold.

* * *

Nick Verity swore as he drove into the parking lot of the radio station. The day was flawless. Temperatures had fallen overnight in recent days enough to make the leaves start to lose control of themselves and erupt into the joyous, flaring madness of color that looked as if some careless giant had left strands of lights wound round all the trees through the mountains. Fall was Verity's favorite time, the days when he took Carolyn and John Power tramping through the woods around the cabin, breathing in the smoky, wine-scented air, made so sweet by the tiny twinge of sadness for the end of summer and the advent of winter.

But this Sunday, he had to work. The dreadful events yesterday in Chicago had to be followed for possible after-effects, the police investigation tracked, and questions asked about the sudden, shocking, military take-over of the city. At least, his fears for Christiana and Mark had been eased temporarily after a phone call from Mark last night. But it didn't make up for the missed walk with his wife and son this glorious Sunday.

He fumbled for the key for the side door, inserted it, twisted it and halted. The door wasn't locked. Verity stared at the door then looked around. There were no other cars in the parking lot. Nobody was here working on a late story or tidying up the accounting files. The station was usually empty on a Sunday, as no live broadcasts took place. Feeds from other affiliates kept the wavelength occupied.

"What the hell?" he muttered and opened the door. "The cops would have checked the place overnight, so it's not just somebody forgetting to lock up when they left." He moved quietly into the corridor, but he could hear nothing inside the building.

Softly, he began to move along the corridor. As he passed the lobby, he cautiously looked in, but saw no signs of life. The building seemed empty, but some psychic sense told Verity that animal life was present. The hairs on his neck rose.

The smell of gasoline was the signal. Verity realized that something hideously wrong was under way. The smell was not strong, but it was out of place, and every warning bell in his mind went off. He followed the smell, walking along the corridor past Crawford's old office, past the conference room, Jimmie Wanlyn's office, then the line of two studios, and stopped outside the computer room. The smell of gas was emanating from there, and that was obviously the least appropriate odor from a computer room, Verity knew well.

He stopped, uncertain. He heard a small sound from within the room, and the door opened. Jimmie Wanlyn walked out, and Verity understood what all this was about.

"Well, good morning, Jimmie," said Verity softly. "After the emails, are you?"

Wanlyn went rigid. "What the hell are you doing here?" he demanded.

Verity laughed. "Now there's a damn fool question, if ever I heard one, Jimmie. You've come to get all those emails from your little bunch of fantasy-merchants in

Washington, and the last thing you wanted was to see me, wasn't it?"

"Then give them to me, Verity, and nobody will get hurt."

"What happened, Jimmie, rifled through all the files and couldn't find the copies?"

Wanlyn's silence confirmed Verity's question.

"So you've decided to burn out the computer room instead?"

"Give me the emails, Verity, I'm warning you." Wanlyn put his hand inside the pocket of his trousers and pulled out his stiletto. With a small, evil click, the blade flickered out.

"Well now, I have a problem with that," Verity replied, his eyes ignoring the knife and staying fixed on Wanlyn's face.

"Don't mess with me," grated Wanlyn. "I want the originals of those emails, *now*."

"You didn't hear me," replied Verity. "I have a problem with that. Not only would I never give them to you, ever, but they're not here."

"What do you mean, not here?"

Verity sighed. "You really are a technical ignoramus, aren't you, Jimmie? The emails get written to a computer disk on the machine. We take backups of those files every day and store a series of them in a secure vault. There *are* no originals of the emails, you turkey."

Wanlyn smiled. "Then there's no problem, is there? The computer will be a pile of burning rubbish in a few minutes, and there go the emails."

"Not even then, you idiot," replied Verity. "Didn't you listen to what I just told you? The computer disks are

499

backed up onto other disks every night and those disks go to a secure location. We've always got copies stored securely."

Wanlyn seemed confused then he grinned. "You're lying, Verity. Don't expect me to swallow what you tell me."

Verity laughed. "If you'd had a classical education, Jimmie, you'd know my name means Truth. Believe me, those emails are safe from you and your cover-up attempt."

"Bullshit! This computer goes up in five minutes and your emails with it. And then I'm out of here, safe and sound."

"You have to get by me first, Jimmie," said Verity.

Wanlyn smiled. "That'll be my pleasure. It's time you paid for everything you've done to us."

He began to move carefully toward Verity who seemed to gather himself like a cat about to jump to a window ledge. Wanlyn moved closer, the knife held with the blade pointing forward, the point moving in a regular cyclic motion. Verity kept his eyes fixed directly on Wanlyn's.

Wanlyn moved like a cobra striking. The knife flickered out and traced a path across Verity's chest. Verity seemed hardly to move, but he leaned backward a minuscule amount and the knife missed him by a fraction of an inch.

Wanlyn sneered. "Lucky, lucky, Verity. Next time, your guts are on this carpet."

Verity said nothing, his eyes not moving from Wanlyn's face.

Wanlyn struck again, the blade flashing to Verity's eyes. Verity moved his head fractionally, and the knife missed again. Wanlyn snarled and moved fast, driving the blade directly at Verity's stomach. Verity's right hand moved so fast, it made Wanlyn look like a sloth. One hand clamped tightly on Wanlyn's right wrist and pulled him off-balance. Verity's left knee flashed upward, straight into Wanlyn's groin and Jimmie screamed in a high-pitched screech of agony. Verity twisted the wrist he was holding and slammed it against the wall. The knife dropped. Verity pulled Wanlyn's arm round behind him, over Wanlyn's head, then shoved him hard against the wall. The top of Wanlyn's head hit the wall with an audible crunch, and Jimmie folded gracelessly to the floor, immobile.

Ignoring him, Verity moved to the computer room, opened the door and looked in. The stench of gas was overwhelming. A large plastic container lay on the floor, obviously the carrier for the fluid. Then Nick saw a familiar sight. A box lay on top of the computer. A small red light pulsated on it. Nick knew a timer when he saw one. Not bothering to check further, Verity turned and ran, raced for the door and flung himself out into the parking lot. He ran for the car, fumbling for his keys, unlocked the door and got in. As fast as he could, he started the machine and pulled away, heading for the open road and reaching for his cellular phone.

As he reached the road, he saw the glow in his rear-view mirror. Flames belched from the computer room window then the wall blew outward. Smoke billowed into the air as bricks crumbled to the ground, covering the parking lot with rubble.

"Oh shit," said Verity, came to a stop at a safe distance, and called the fire brigade. For a second or two, he thought about Jimmie Wanlyn, incinerated in the holocaust of his own making, then wasted no more time on that matter.

Chapter 22 - Frederick, Maryland

The light was fading as the limousine rolled through the countryside to Vince Jerome's house. Mark sat silently, studying the two men with fascination, but they seemed nervous under his gaze and refused to look back at him after the first startled recognition of their one-time prey.

Not a word was spoken in the car for twenty minutes. Dansbury and Jerome sat staring out at the darkness, the stasis broken only when Dansbury reached forward to open the drinks cabinet. Mark flinched slightly, his hand flickering to the gun holster at his shoulder, but Dansbury merely brought out a bottle of scotch and poured two tumblers, passing one to his brother without a word.

Both men sipped dreamily at their drinks for a few minutes. Charles Dansbury finally broke the heavy silence.

"We had your country's best interests at heart, Mister Ashton," he said softly.

Mark was startled then took control of himself. "Three thousand dead people in Chicago would disagree with you, Dmitri Alexandrovitch," he replied in Russian. It seemed appropriate to him. He was unwilling to converse with the two men in the language of the country they had tried to destroy. "And when your gangsters were shooting at me in the hills a few days ago, the notion that this was good for America somehow escaped me."

503

"Great progress is always costly," Dansbury spoke in Russian, also. "Your own nation's freedoms were purchased at a dreadful price."

"But it was *our* nation. We made our own way. It was not to serve the grandiose dreams of megalomaniacs."

Dansbury seemed to hunch up in his seat as if to avoid a blow.

Jerome smiled coldly. "You know, Dmitri, he reminds me a lot of you, sixty years ago," he said. He turned his eyes from his brother and studied Mark in detail. "Be careful, Mister Ashton. I see the same strength and commitment in you that my revered elder brother used to have. Be careful what you wish for. You will achieve it."

Mark almost smiled. For all his horror at what the two men had done to his country and to himself, he recognized the charismatic strength within them. They were, after all, the two richest men in the world. The aura of power radiated from them, despite the events of the last few hours.

"No, Yuri Alexandrovitch," he replied. "If reaching for my dreams will cost the world what you have cost us, I'll stay where I am."

Jerome shook his head. "Impossible, Mark. Men like us cannot stand still."

"Then I will choose another direction. World domination is not my choice."

Dansbury stirred and raised his head from his chest. "Just as well," he replied. "Mister Ashton, is it your task to see that we follow Webber's suggestion?"

Mark was silent for a moment. The directness of the question startled him. "It mustn't come to that," he replied.

"Yes, Dmitri," Jerome broke in. "That is his task. And he will do it without hesitation."

Mark looked at him, startled to realize that Jerome had read him so well, and how much he had changed in the last few weeks. "Yes, Yuri Alexandrovitch," he said. "That is my task."

"You see, Dmitri," said Jerome. "He is just like we were in Berlin."

Not another word was spoken during the ride.

When the car stopped, the two Russians left their glasses sitting on the small ledges by the windows and meekly followed Mark into the house.

Paul Kent opened the front door, looking fit, rested and well-dressed in a smart grey suit. He nodded briefly at Mark and carefully watched the two Russians as they entered.

"Where would you like to go, Mister Jerome?" Mark asked politely, reverting to English.

Jerome ignored him, and walked to the doorway leading to the conference room. Mark exchanged a signal with his colleague who returned to the front door as Mark followed the two old men. Jerome walked in, Dansbury followed and shut the door firmly behind him. Mark smiled to himself in the corridor and prepared to wait for whatever would happen.

"We were too precipitate, Yuri," said Dansbury. He moved slowly to his customary seat at the side of the table next to the chairman's position. Jerome remained standing, his walking stick in one hand.

"Don't you mean *I* was too precipitate, elder brother?" said Jerome. "It is clear that you all blame me for this result."

"Not I," Dansbury replied. "I was not in a position to make that decision. I have always left you in command of this adventure. You had the qualities of a leader that I did not. Had it been my decision, I don't know whether I would have done the same as you. The question is meaningless, now."

"Why is that?" Jerome snapped. "Do those fools think that just because they have discovered the overall plan, that we have been stopped?"

"Yuri, it's over. We failed. There is no way we can take over this country when so much of our resources have been removed. We lost the military. The plan is impossible without that element."

"And you want to give up?" Jerome demanded with contempt. "You just want to retire gracefully and say, 'Sorry, America, we tried to give you the country you wanted, but it was too hard'?"

"Yuri, don't be silly!" Dansbury remonstrated. "It can't be done. The dream is over. Maybe Colin was being dramatic about the Roman retirement style. Perhaps they'll leave us in peace, just two old men with their memories."

"Maybe *you* can say goodbye to your dream, Dmitri. After all, you wanted to bring socialism to America and return Lenin's theories to Russia. Remember, I had different dreams all these years. I can still achieve mine."

"What, that dream of revenge, little brother? Your need to make this country pay for the death of our mother? Surely you don't still believe you can do that? And why

506

would you want to? The idea is infantile." Dansbury's contempt was sweeping.

Jerome banged his stick on the floor with a dull thump. The anger in him made his voice shake. "Don't treat me like a child, Dmitri! It was always your way! You were always the superior, the elder brother with his so-ethical sense of protection for his little sibling! It's got on my nerves for seventy years, and it still annoys me."

"Then you won't have to be annoyed for much longer," Dansbury replied icily. "Clearly, we need have no further dealings with each other. Our only relationship for sixty years has been this New America. With that dead, we can go our separate ways."

"Don't be a bigger old fool than you are," Jerome shouted. "You think Webber was joking about our suicides? Like hell he was! He intends us to die tonight. If we don't do it, we already know the job of that young man who came home with us. After what we did to him, I'm sure Ashton would love the task."

"You know, Yuri, when you show this stupid side of your nature, I wonder if I failed with you. Perhaps I'll welcome the peace that Colin's suggestion will give me. I'm tired of this nonsense. You should consider the same thing."

"I will not kill myself obediently," replied Jerome. "If that's your idea, then perhaps you're right, you're too old to keep going. I'm not. I can still achieve my dream."

"Your blood-lust for revenge, Yuri? Just how do you propose to accomplish that?"

Jerome turned to the telephone by his seat at the head of the table. "They may think they've pulled our teeth by arresting Rollings and blocking today's events. Do you think I've left all my eggs in this puny basket, Dmitri? No, of course I haven't."

Dansbury looked alarmed. "Yuri, what the hell are you talking about?"

"Call it my Plan B, Dmitri," Jerome snapped. "I can still initiate uprisings all over the country. I have access to Geoffrey's weapons stocks, and I have the people who would love to use them. I don't *need* our New America Council, not for *my* goals."

He picked up the phone and began dialing a number.

Dansbury rose to his feet in alarm. "Yuri! For God's sake what are you doing? This is insanity!" He put his hand on Jerome's forearm and pressed down, pushing his hand from the number keys. He pressed down on the disconnect switch and cut off the call.

With a shout of rage, Jerome pushed his brother hard on the shoulder. Dansbury fell backward, grabbed at his chair but failed to stop his fall, and landed hard on the floor. Jerome began pushing the buttons on the phone again.

Dansbury got painfully to his feet and stared at his brother. Determinedly, he strode forward and pushed Jerome, considerably harder this time. His stocky, muscular body was not as weak as his age might have suggested, and Jerome was sent flying against the shredder cabinet, the phone dropping on the table with a clatter. Dansbury replaced it carefully.

"This is not the way, Yuri," he said, breathing hard. "There is no point in destroying the country just for that purpose. Give up this silliness."

Jerome's face was white with fury. He walked carefully back to the table, his eyes fixed firmly on

Dansbury the whole time. He stooped and picked up his walking stick that he had dropped in the collision. "Dmitri, be careful," he said, his voice a hiss of fury. "I *will* do this! Neither you, nor Lombard, nor Webber's Task Force Five will stop me. Now, get out of the way, or I'll have to hurt you."

Dansbury looked shocked. "Yuri, what are you saying? In nearly eighty years, you have never threatened me! What in God's name has..."

He stopped in horror. Jerome had twisted the head of his walking stick and pulled out a wicked-looking sword blade nearly eighteen inches long. He dropped the wooden scabbard and directed the needle point at Dansbury.

"Dmitri, move away," he said. His voice was cold, almost metallic in its lack of human quality. He moved a little nearer.

Dansbury flicked his hand over the back of the chair nearest to him, and threw the chair directly at Jerome. It collided hard with his hip, sent him staggering against the table. Jerome kicked the chair away furiously and lunged. The point of the sword entered Dansbury's throat, slid through and came out at the back of his neck.

The old man rasped a cry of pain and stared in horror at his brother. Jerome stood rigidly as Dansbury gasped for air, his face turning blue. Blood drained down his neck, stained his shirt and ran over his jacket. The rasp of agony faded, his eyes went blank, and Dansbury collapsed on the floor, pulling the blade out of Jerome's hand as he fell.

Jerome seemed not to notice. He moved back to the table, picked up the phone and, yet again, began to enter a number.

"I can't let you do this, Mister Jerome," said a voice behind him. Astonished, Jerome turned back to the door into the room.

Angela stood in the doorway. Instead of her usual sensual style of dress, she wore blue jeans and a light sweater. She held an automatic pistol in her right hand, the muzzle pointed firmly at Jerome's chest. She moved a few steps closer.

"Put down the phone, Mister Jerome," she said clearly.

Jerome stared at her, his eyes wide. "Angela?" he said uncertainly.

"Put it down," she repeated.

"I should have realized," Jerome said, almost to himself. "When your father revealed himself this afternoon, I should have thought about you. You've been monitoring us all this time?"

"Of course, Mister Jerome," she said. Her large eyes looked sadly at him. "This way, it was easy for us to keep an eye on you until you started putting the plan into effect. But much as I like you, I can't let you damage my country."

"Angela, you know I've loved you from the start," he said, his eyes fixed on the pistol. It never wavered.

"I was just your assistant," she replied. "Now, Mister Jerome, put down the phone."

"You can't shoot me, Angela," he said. Some of the patrician stance had come back to him, his eyes were clear and cold again. "I've taken your clothes off you, loved your breasts, played with that beautiful body. You can't shoot a man who's done that."

"It was a necessary part of the act," she replied. "It kept you from thinking too much. For the last time, Mister Jerome, put it down."

510

He smiled. "Not a chance, Angela," he said, and pressed the last digits of the number. The ringing tone came through clearly enough for Angela to hear.

A voice spoke on the other end, and Jerome took his eyes off Angela. "This is Jerome," he said firmly.

The shot thundered in the room. The bullet hit Jerome in the chest, though he kept his feet and his hold on the phone as he staggered. His eyes flashed back to Angela in complete bewilderment. Then he looked down at his chest. Blood was seeping through his white shirt.

Jerome seemed to gather himself and draw on hidden strength. He lifted the phone back to his face, his eyes fixed on Angela. "This is Jerome," he said again, his voice almost as firm and strong as before.

The gun bellowed once more, and the bullet hit Jerome under the nose. His face seemed to melt and distort as his head snapped backward and his body shook like a torn flag in the wind. The phone dropped from his hand and Jerome's body folded to the floor.

Angela walked to the table, picked up the phone. She spoke clearly into it. "Wrong number," she said, and replaced the phone in its cradle.

"Of course, we'll trace that number," said Paul Kent. He stood leaning against the doorway. Mark stood just behind him.

"I know," she said, looking down at the body of Vince Jerome. She moved to look at Charles Dansbury then stared again at Jerome for a few more seconds. Then she placed the gun on the table and walked toward Kent.

"Dammit!" she cried, tears flowing down her cheeks. She leaned against him and he put his arms round her. "God dammit, Paul, I loved the old bastard!"

For five minutes she wept while Kent held her silently. Finally, she stood away from him, wiped her eyes and sniffed.

"I sure made a fool of myself there, didn't I?"

"It's permitted," he said gently. "There's nothing else for you to do tonight. Why don't you take the rest of the day off? We still have work to do tomorrow."

She nodded. "You'll get this mess cleaned up?" She gestured at the two bodies.

"I will. Go home, Angela."

She touched his cheek in gratitude and walked out, smiling briefly at Mark as she passed him.

Mark walked in ahead of Kent and surveyed the sight in the conference room. "Thanks, guys," he said. "I really didn't want to have to do that to you. I wonder why the hell you two couldn't have been satisfied with what you had?"

* * *

Geoffrey Payne arrived at fifteen minutes before eight o'clock, driving his dark blue Mercedes. He parked outside the front steps of Jerome's mansion and climbed out, pulling his jacket from where it hung over the rear seat. The morning air was cool. Payne looked unwell, a greenish tinge to his face, with dark eyes seeming dull and listless. He looked much older than his forty-five years.

"Who the hell are you?" he demanded as a young man walked down the steps.

"I'm Mister Webber's assistant," replied the man calmly. "The regular man is off sick, today. Mister Webber asked if I would park your vehicle, sir."

512

Payne seemed reassured by the mention of Webber's name. He waved at the driver's seat. "The keys are in," he said. "What the hell's going on, do you know?"

"Sir, I'm just an assistant," the young man said as he climbed into the Mercedes. "Mister Webber will tell you everything when you go inside."

"God, he'd better," muttered Payne and set off up the steps. He stopped as he reached the door, seeing another vehicle arriving. He waited while the black limousine slid to a halt and Tony Redman climbed out of the rear seat. As he did, the young man who had taken the Mercedes walked round from the side of the mansion and approached the driver's window.

"Tony!" Payne called. "Come on in. Things seem to be a bit confused this morning."

The young man stood up, having finished his parking directions to Redman's driver, and smiled. "Not at all, Mister Redman, just a few staff changes. If you'll follow Mister Payne, Mister Webber is inside."

Redman glared at him, looked up at Payne, and shrugged his shoulder. At the top of the steps, he looked at Payne. "What the fuck happened, yesterday?" he snarled.

Payne recoiled at the fury. "Damned if I know," he retorted. "I hoped you could tell me."

"No, I can't," Redman snapped, and stamped inside the house through the open front door. Another athletic-looking man was waiting for them.

"Good morning, gentlemen," he said cheerfully. "Mister Webber will be with you in a moment, if you would go into the conference room. There's coffee inside."

"Webber? Why the fuck is Webber suddenly running everything?" demanded Redman. "Where's Jerome? And where's Angela?"

"Angela is making some final preparations for the meeting, sir. Mister Webber will explain," the man replied and moved to the entrance where another vehicle was arriving.

His face angry, Redman walked rapidly to the conference room, followed by a confused-looking Payne. Inside, the room looked as it normally did. A table against the wall was covered with a white cloth. A large coffee pot emitted smells of fresh coffee, and several plates of pastries stood in a row. A jug of orange juice and six heavy, crystal tumblers sat on a silver tray. Both men poured themselves a cup of coffee and sat down, Redman at his usual position at the foot of the table, Payne half way up the table on his left side. Neither spoke.

Grant Armstrong was next. He walked in, studied the two men in the room and went to the coffee pot. After pouring a cup, he sat down two seats from Redman's right and calmly drank his coffee. He did not speak. Nor did he look up when Vanderbilt slid into the room.

"What in heaven's name is going on?" Vanderbilt demanded. "Angela's not here, there's a whole bunch of new faces parading around outside, and Webber suddenly seems to be running things. And what the hell happened yesterday?"

"That's what we're all here to find out," Payne replied.

"Yeah?" sneered Vanderbilt. "Well, you three should know, if anyone does. Where the hell were you?"

"We were there," said Redman. "Now shut up until everyone's here."

"Don't tell me to shut up, you fucking wop!" Vanderbilt shouted.

"What's up, Jackson, couldn't get a little boy last night?" asked Payne with a cold smile.

Vanderbilt turned to him like an angry cat. "Listen you..." he began. Redman stood up and glared at him. Vanderbilt turned to him, seemed for a moment as if he would attack the crime-boss then thought better of it. He moved to the coffee pot and Redman sat down again, still glaring at the preacher's back.

Eckhard walked in, followed by Colin Webber. The senator stood for a moment looking at the room, then sat down without taking any refreshment, taking a place two seats away from Payne's left. He didn't speak a word.

Vanderbilt turned to the table with a cup in his hands and saw Webber. "Well, thank Christ for that!" he said loudly. "Now perhaps someone can tell what's going on! Webber, what are you doing running this meeting? Where are Jerome and Dansbury?"

Webber took the chairman's position. "Both send their regrets and have asked me to chair this meeting," he said with a pleasant smile. "Good morning, gentlemen. Shall we begin?"

"We're one short," said Payne. "Where's Corley?"

"General Rollings has been detained at the Pentagon," Webber replied. "Gentlemen, we have some serious matters to attend to this morning, so let's get started."

"Damn right we have!" Redman said loudly. "Webber, what happened in St. Louis, yesterday."

"Nothing," replied Webber.

"Nothing?" Payne rose to his feet. "Good God, Colin, we were supposed to have a repeat of Chicago. I had everything in place, but nobody came for the guns. The guys had been briefed on both sides, Redman's people were in place. What do you mean, nothing happened?"

"Let me be more accurate," Webber replied. "What actually happened was that the bunch of white lunatics arrived at their weapons store as expected, and the bunch of black lunatics arrived at theirs. Both of them met a sizeable military contingent who told them to go home like good little boys and not to be a nuisance."

"What?" Payne's gasp was barely heard, but Webber smiled at him.

"General Rollings decided he could not face another three thousand deaths on his conscience, not on top of his treason," he said.

The room went as frigid as a polar night. Nobody moved.

"That got you, didn't it?" said Webber softly. "Let me explain."

"Yes, Colin. Please explain." Redman's voice was a harsh whisper from the end of the table.

"Remember that mysterious group of people we were discussing a few days ago?" said Webber. "It does exist. It's called Task Force Five. I'm the leader."

"Dear God!" Payne whispered. His face was white. "We're dead."

"More than likely," Webber agreed. He looked round the table. Apart from Armstrong who was studying his hands intently, the others were staring at him in shock. He smiled at each of them.

"Webber, where are Jerome and Dansbury?" snarled Vanderbilt. "I want *them* to tell me what's happened."

"Unfortunately, they can't be with us today," Webber said. "But I'd like to tell you a story about two remarkable men."

"A story?" grated Redman. "What the fuck are you on about, Webber?"

"The story begins with a man called General Alexandr Kutasov," said Webber as if nobody had spoken. "A dedicated fighter for the communist cause, a great Soviet patriot, if ever there was one. He fought with the Russian Army against the Germans in World War I. He fought alongside Stalin, Bukharin, Trotsky, all of them, in the 1917 revolution that swept out the Romanovs. Then he fought against the White Russians who tried to reverse the revolution, and four years later, he died of wounds sustained in that conflict, a decorated Hero of the Soviet Union. He left two sons."

Webber looked round the table again. Everyone was watching him like a mouse watches the cat.

"The two sons were war heroes, also," Webber continued. "They fought in the Karelia Peninsula against Finland, one as a fighter pilot, the other as an infantry officer, and distinguished themselves greatly. Both were dedicated believers in Marx, Lenin and the cause of communism, though they began to feel betrayed by the path taken by Joseph Stalin. But they kept up their war against the Germans, eventually meeting up in Berlin in those cataclysmic days as the Third Reich collapsed."

"Webber, what the hell...?" began Vanderbilt angrily, but Webber raised a hand, and Vanderbilt subsided.

"In the middle of the rubble of Berlin, these brothers made two finds," Webber said. "One was a cache of jewelry and icons worth about ten million dollars in those days. The other was a small group of lost American troops. The young Russians shot the Americans, took the identities of two of them and eventually made it to the United States. The rest, of course, is history."

"Sweet Jesus, Dansbury and Jerome are Russians?" Morgan Eckhard gasped.

"Indeed so, Morgan," replied Webber. "But, as I said, Russians with a dedication to the communist cause. They had a mission, gentlemen, a mission astounding in its size and scope. They were going to take over the United States and make it the communist paradise that Stalin had ruined in Russia. Then they would return to their old homeland and reverse the Stalinist wrongs, returning pure Marxist-Leninism to its place of honor. But first of all, they had to control the United States. That's where you all came in."

"You mean..." Vanderbilt's face was green. "All this time, we've been helping a couple of communist bastards....."

Webber nodded in sympathy. "Congratulations, gentlemen," he said. "You bunch of patriotic, conservative Americans have spent your recent years facilitating a communist take-over of the United States. I hope you're very proud of yourselves."

"Christ, I'll kill them!" shouted Redman as he rose to his feet.

Webber smiled gently at him. "Sorry, Tony. You're too late. By about twelve hours."

The room echoed with silence for a few seconds. Payne finally broke it.

"They're dead? How?"

Webber waved away the question. "It's no longer important. What is really important is what to do about this New America Council."

"Do, Colin?" asked Payne. "There's nothing you can do. Apart from your testimony against us, there's no evidence of any wrong-doing. It's no crime to discuss possible military coups, and that's all we have done."

"That's why we left you alone for so long," said Webber agreeably. "Just as all those funny little para-military groups can play with their assault weapons and dress up in jungle greens at weekends, providing nobody gets hurt. But when they bomb city blocks and kill a few hundred people, the situation changes. Just as it did with you after the events in Chicago."

"It's just your word against ours that we had anything to do with it," replied Payne.

"You're forgetting the word of General Rollings," said Webber.

"Still no solid proof," Vanderbilt sneered.

"Yes, I thought you might say that," Webber said pleasantly. He sat back in his seat, his fingers laced together on the table.

The hiss of a loudspeaker infiltrated the shocked air of the room. It was a recording.

Jerome's voice broke the silence. *"Gentlemen,"* he said, *"I give you the New America."*

"The New America," replied a set of other voices.

"By God!" said Senator Eckhard's voice. *"You're right, Charles. This is the nectar of the Gods!"*

"Tell that to my young friend here," came Dansbury's voice. *"He insists on drinking that French soda pop."*

"You may all want a note pad, gentlemen," said Jerome's tones again.

"Jesus Christ!" exploded Grant Armstrong, the first words he had spoken that morning. "It's that meeting in here a few weeks ago!"

"Yes it is," agreed Webber. "Listen."

"Good," came the voice of Jerome again. *"Our quarterly meeting of the Council is now opened. We have little new business to discuss, but we must review the status of current projects. Grant, perhaps you will start?"*

Armstrong stirred in his seat, looking round the table as if seeking escape. "This room is swept for microphones," he mumbled. "How did you get that recording?"

"A moment," said Webber with a smile. "Just to confirm, this is your voice?"

"Imports of all narcotics controlled by my group are now averaging just over a billion dollars per month at street value," came Armstrong's voice through the speaker. *"In the last three months, CIA and DEA agents have destroyed six more major importers and we have taken over their delivery systems effectively. That increased our income by fifteen percent."*

"Excellent," said the voice of General Rollings.

"Indeed," said Geoffrey Payne. *"Well done, Grant."*

Webber looked round the room. "Do we need any more, gentlemen? I have the entire meeting on tape. I fact, I have *all* your meetings for the last two years on tape."

Stunned silence greeted his words.

"How?" Armstrong insisted loudly.

Webber stood up, walked to the table and took one of the heavy crystal tumblers used for water and other drinks which Angela had carried into the meetings each time before they began. "Look in the base," he said, and passed the glass round the table. Armstrong took it and studied the glass intently.

"A microphone in the glass," he murmured. "Just a filament, looks like the curve of the base. And Angela always brought in the glasses after the room had been swept. Brilliant."

"Angela?" Eckhard gulped. "She's with you?"

Webber nodded. "A member of TF5 for a few years now."

"But that means Lombard..." Eckhard stopped. He looked ill.

"One of TF5's councilors," confirmed Webber. "So you see," he continued. "I've got you cold. All agreed?"

The air seemed to leak out of all of them like a punctured balloon.

"I asked before," said Payne. "What now?"

"I think it's pretty obvious," Webber retorted. "Public trials would be a dreadful nuisance, not to say highly alarming for the population. That's even if we ignore the horrific embarrassment it would cause to the Party, possibly destroy it. You are all such shining examples to it that perhaps we need to suppress this. Unlike you, I believe that two effective parties is the absolute minimum."

"You're just going to kill us?" Payne looked terrified, but Webber laughed.

"Not a lot of point in your case," he replied. "I've seen your last medical report."

Payne didn't speak.

521

"Your liver may last another year, at best, Geoffrey," said Webber.

"I have a transplant scheduled," Payne said defiantly. "I've spent a lot of money to ensure I get the next available liver."

Webber shook his head. "Livers are scarce. Your operation has been cancelled. The liver goes to a more deserving cause."

"You can't do that!" shouted Payne, getting to his feet. His illness seemed to have worsened, and he had aged many years.

"It's already done," said Webber. "Don't look for alternative sources, Geoffrey. You won't get one. Better get your personal affairs in order, instead."

Payne subsided into his seat, his face seeming to crumble. There was no sympathy in Webber's look at him then he changed his attention to Vanderbilt.

"Much the same with you, Reverend," he said. "I've got the blood-test results from your last check-up. You haven't seen them yet, of course. But you've got AIDS. Very badly." Webber gave a cold smile. "Unfortunately, it seems to have resulted from an error during the check-up when you accidentally became infected with tainted blood. Dreadful mistake. Can't imagine how it happened."

Vanderbilt's jaw dropped wide open. He tried to speak, but couldn't.

"We can't let you infect anyone else, given your rather *active* life-style," said Webber. "My people are going to take you straight to a government hospital, a secure one, and we'll keep you there. You'll be well looked after, I assure you. About a year, the doctor estimates, with a rapid decline as infections take hold and find no resistance. Unfortunately, the press seems to have got hold of the details, Reverend. Can't imagine how that happened, either. I think you'll be better off out of the public eye, and I don't imagine you'll want to see any newspapers for a few months to come. They won't be kind to you."

His eyes lingered for a few moments on the horror-stricken face of the Reverend Vanderbilt. His smile was cold.

"Which brings us to you, Grant," he said. Armstrong's eyes flickered up to meet Webber's gaze then returned to their study of his hands.

"Every nickel comes back, Grant," said Webber. "The thirty-seven billion or so in the foreign banks, as well as the sixteen million in your accounts in the Caymans and Switzerland. We have the account numbers. You can cooperate and bring it back yourself, or we can take a couple of years while the White House puts pressure on the governments involved, but it *will* come back. Your choice."

Armstrong nodded. His face had turned the color of wet blotting paper.

"And the snuff-boxes get returned also," added Webber.

Armstrong nodded again.

"You will be arrested on charges of drug-dealing," Webber. Continued. "Open and shut case. Thirty years, I imagine, less if you cooperate."

Armstrong didn't move. His eyes were closed.

"And so to the big crime-boss." Webber looked down the table at Redman. "Tax evasion, of course. Also carnal knowledge with minors. Should hold you for a while.

Though you probably know about the cultural climate in America's prisons, don't you?"

Redman was frozen rigid. Webber smiled around the table.

"No, I doubt that you do," he said. "The one thing hardened criminals, murderers, thugs and drug-dealers all hate is a sex-offender. Especially if the offense is committed against children. Those people seem to have a short life in prison. I wish you every chance, Tony, but I doubt you'll emerge from your ten-to-fifteen sentence."

Redman pushed his chair back from the table. His face was almost purple and his hands shook, but he said nothing.

Webber stood up. "That leaves us just the Honorable Senator Morgan Eckhard. You know, Morgan, I had trouble thinking about what to do to you. Then I realized what the worst thing in the world would be."

He began to walk to the door.

"What?" Eckhard whispered. His hands were trembling and his whole body shook with occasional tremors.

"I'll just leave you to the tender care of Peggy Jo and the Asbury family," said Webber with a chuckle. "And may God have mercy on your soul."

He opened the door and stood aside. Paul Kent walked in together with Mark, Feathers and Angela. All four were armed with nine-millimeter automatic pistols.

"Tony, Reverend Vanderbilt, Grant, you will go with my operatives," said Webber. "Please don't bite anyone, Reverend. They'll shoot you first."

He turned to the door. "Morgan, Geoffrey, you're both free to go. But you'll be under observation. Don't do anything stupid."

Webber walked out of the room. Feathers grinned at the shocked faces in the room and pushed Mark a little ahead of him. "Hi, guys," he said. "May I introduce you all to Mark Ashton? Mark, say hello to all these nice people who tried to kill you."

Chapter 23 - Evanston, Illinois

Mark pulled the paper bags of groceries out of the car and kicked the door shut. He walked to the door to the lobby and, with difficulty, managed to unlock it and walk to the elevator doors. A cool snap had hit Illinois as the Fall had progressed, rain was coming down heavily, and Mark was happy to be back inside. He felt good about the prospect of finding Christiana in the apartment, preparing dinner for the evening. Though neither barefoot nor pregnant, she was happy to demonstrate her refined culinary skills to an appreciative Mark.

When Verity had called them with the news of the burning of the station building, they had talked for a long time, but her resignation had not been the problem for Verity that it might otherwise have been.

"I know you kids will be happy," Verity said. "Make sure you both come and see us when we're back on the air."

"I'm just so glad you got out in time," whispered Christiana.

"Rather me than Wanlyn," Verity agreed.

"God, yes!" said Mark on the extension phone. "He was just plain scum. You know he killed Crawford? Feathers gave me some of the details that Rollings provided. What those people were up to is beyond belief!"

"It's a closed book," Verity replied. "Anyway, I need to find some sort of replacement for Crawford's program, and organize a new location. Send me the wedding invitation. I'll bring Carolyne and John Power."

"That will be wonderful," said Christiana, the warmth in her voice very obvious.

Mark smiled at the memory of the conversation as he reached his apartment door. He put down the bags, unlocked the door, picked up the bags again and walked inside.

The sight that met his eyes brought him to a stop as if he had walked into the side of a tank. A heavy silence numbed his mind for a moment and he heard the thunder of his blood rolling through his veins. He fought the dizziness, feeling the sweat on his hands dampen the paper bags he was carrying.

Christiana sat naked in one of his Italian chairs. Her arms were bound to the ebony armrests. A strand of rope tied below her breasts bound her against the white silk back-rest. Her clothes lay in ripped piles around her feet. Heavy bruises covered her left cheek, one eye was partially closed. A broad strip of duct tape was plastered across her mouth. Her head was slumped toward her right shoulder.

Mark dropped the bags of groceries, his heart freezing with fear. He moved down the entrance to the apartment toward the dreadful scene. Christiana lifted her head from her shoulder and stared at him. Mark was about to speak when a shape lifted itself off the settee against the wall.

"Good afternoon, Mister Ashton," said a harsh, rasping voice. "You really should have left things alone, you know."

527

The man standing next to Christiana was a dreadful sight. He was tall, thin, his face burned and as grossly distorted as a scarecrow's, his head almost bald except for a patch of hair on one side. He wore jeans and a sweater, and from the ends of the sleeves, both hands were burned and scarred. The bent, charred fingers of his right hand held a stiletto knife.

Mark though that Jimmie Wanlyn looked worse than any image from a horror movie.

Mixtures of emotions flooded through Mark. The first was the incredible relief that Christiana was alive and seemingly whole, apart from the bruises. Tearing through that was the fear, rage and horror at what had been done to her, and what might yet happen. And over the top of all of it, was the hatred for the wreck of a man standing before him.

"Wanlyn, this has to stop," Mark croaked through a dry throat.

"When you're both dead," rasped Wanlyn. "But only after you watch what I'm going to do to this bitch."

"Jimmie, for God's sake, it's over," said Mark. He moved fully into the room, stopping just a few feet from Christiana. Wanlyn also moved, stepping next to the bound woman, and placing the stiletto against her neck. Christiana flinched as the blade touched her skin. Mark moved back a step.

"Not yet, it's not," Wanlyn retorted. "When the bitch has been cut up a bit, and your guts are on the carpet, *then* it's over."

"Dansbury and Jerome are dead, Jimmie, don't you know that?" said Mark. "Your New America Council is blown apart. They're all in prison. There's no point in this."

"Yes, there is." The ghastly face twisted in a dreadful smile. "I've driven here, and it's taken me three days. I'm *hurting*, Ashton, and it's your fault. And Jerome's not dead, don't give me that crap. When I've had my fun with you two, I'll call him. He'll get me out of it."

"He's dead. Believe it," said Mark. He moved slowly along the carpet till he was level with Christiana's left side, but a few feet away. Her head had slumped down on her chest again. She seemed unconscious, and Mark felt a freezing flood of panic about her. But he had to sort out the immediate problem first.

"And General Rollings told everything," Mark added. "So we know how you killed Crawford."

"You're a liar!" The hideous voice was like a metal file against iron. "Now shut up, or the bitch gets cut." The knife dug a little into Christiana's neck, and she moved slightly, as if waking up. She lifted her head and turned her face to Mark. Her bruised eye had closed now, and fear distorted her face.

Mark tried to smile at her then raised his eyes to Wanlyn again. He moved a little further round the chair till he was nearly behind Christiana. His heart was thumping and his blood felt cold. The hair on his neck had risen, and he could feel the air acutely against his skin. He was about four feet away from the fireplace, still keeping about seven feet away from Wanlyn.

"Jimmie, how the hell do you think I know about Rollings, Dansbury and Jerome? How do you think I heard about the New America Council? I know about Geoffrey Payne, Tony Redman, Vanderbilt, Armstrong and

Eckhard, too. Where could I have got those names from?" He moved another two feet nearer the fireplace.

Wanlyn seemed confused and increasingly weary. His mad eyes flashed round the room, then closed for a few seconds as if closing out the sight. They opened again and Wanlyn moved the knife away from Christiana's neck, waving it threateningly at Mark. "Listen, you bastard, don't give me that crap! Soon as I get out of here, I'm going back to Frederick. Jerome'll get me a doctor, and Randy Crawford and I, we'll be right back..."

"Randy's dead, Jimmie," snapped Mark. He moved another foot. "You killed him. Probably with that knife you've got right there."

"You're going to get sliced, Ashton!" Wanlyn shouted. He moved away from Christiana, the knife held in front of him, the blade pointing at Mark's eyes.

Mark snapped his hand down, seized the boomerang by the long arm and hurled it desperately in a flat plane straight at Wanlyn. The weapon spun round once as it flew, and the long, heavier arm struck Wanlyn on the neck. There was a dreadful crack, Wanlyn's torso snapped backward while his head was flung forward against his chest. A hideous grating rasp came from Wanlyn's throat, and the body fell to the floor, collapsing against the side of the black chair as it dropped. Christiana gave a strangled scream in her throat as Wanlyn fell against her, the knife falling into her lap, the blade coming to rest against her thigh.

Mark leaped at Wanlyn, pulled the body away from Christiana and dropped it with a shiver of disgust on the carpet. He looked down at the grotesque face. Wanlyn's eyes stared fixedly at the ceiling and his tongue stuck out between his teeth. Mark had no further doubt. Wanlyn was perfectly dead.

Rapidly, he moved to Christiana. She was weeping furiously. Carefully, Mark stripped away the tape from her mouth, then took hold of the knife and cut away at the bonds holding her to the chair. As the last strand fell away, she fell into his arms, clutching his neck tightly, her tears flowing down his skin.

Slowly, his heart slowed to normal and his breathing became controllable. He lightly touched her bruised cheek, and she raised her head and looked at him. The left eye was fully closed, the bruises were turning green and blue, and her face was a mess.

"I think we'll be okay, don't you?" he said, smiling into her battered face.

She nodded and put her head back on his chest. "We'll be okay," she said, but her violent trembles told him that recovery would not be quick.

Half an hour later, with Christiana lying in bed, still occasionally shaking with tremors, Mark felt able to leave her and pick up the phone.

"Feathers, we've had a problem," he said, when he got through TF5's protective telephone reception.

"What? Are you okay, buddy?" The alarm was high in the big man's voice.

"We are now. Christiana's a bit battered. Wanlyn was here."

"Was?"

"Still is, physically speaking. Spiritually absent."

"Jesus Christ, Mark! You obviously need cleaning help. How the hell did it happen?"

"He was a great break-and-enter specialist, was Jimmie. He got in while Christiana was alone."

"But you got him?"

"Remember that boomerang I bought when we were in Australia?"

"The kangaroo-killer? Jesus, Mark, that's a nasty... That's what you used?"

"It worked like it was supposed to."

"Stay there, Mark," said Feathers. "Somebody will be with you in less than an hour."

"Thanks, pal. I owe you one." Mark felt a huge load drop away from him.

"Several." Feathers' deep laugh helped Mark's mental recovery even further. "I think you promised one of my colleagues the same thing."

"We'll be over there to pay, I promise."

"Soon, buddy. The Chief's expecting you, Lieutenant-Commander Ashton."

"Who?"

"Promotion, little guy. You're joining us full time, correct?"

"So I am. See you in a few days. I've got a wedding to organize."

"I'll be there for it."

"Make damn sure. You're the Best Man."

Feathers' deep laugh and the click of the telephone being replaced terminated the conversation.

Mark settled down to wait with his lady until a clean-up crew arrived.

Epilogue

The CNN newsreader smiled into the camera.

"This has been a dramatic week in America," she said. "The funerals took place this morning of two of America's richest men and most successful entrepreneurs. Charles Dansbury and Vincent Jerome who died within hours of each other last week were laid to rest at cemeteries on the West Coast yesterday morning. Both had been major donators to political parties and to charitable causes all over America. The President said that the country has lost two of its finest, the sort of men who helped make America great, but both had long and successful lives."

Her smile didn't change as she looked down at a page on her desk and then back into the camera.

"In further political events, the death was announced this morning of Senator Morgan Eckhard, a stalwart of the Republican Party and long considered a potential presidential candidate. The family reports that the Senator had suffered a sudden, catastrophic heart attack while hunting on a friend's estates in Maryland. He leaves behind a grieving daughter and loving wife.

"And it was reported this afternoon that the televangelist, the Reverend Jackson Vanderbilt has been hospitalized with serious complications resulting from

AIDS which he is believed to have contracted as a result of blood transfusions some months ago."

She touched her earpiece, looking down at her desk and then looked up again.

"We're breaking away for a moment to cover this late-breaking item just in," she said. "Jack, you're in Washington, at the steps of the Capitol. Can you tell us what's happening there?"

The scene flicked to a large, burly man wearing a coat against the cold wind that was blowing.

"Yes, Marilyn, this is Jack McDonald in Washington, the nation's capital. Just a few minutes ago, Senator Bryce Lombard told us he would be making a statement of national importance right here. I think the senator is about to start, so let's listen."

The camera moved left to the podium which had been hastily placed on the steps of the Capitol. A bunch of microphones looking like bulky vegetables with labels on them were fixed to the podium and people lined several deep on the lower steps and to the sides. Standing beside the podium was Senator Bryce Lombard and his wife, Margaret. Despite the cold, both looked cheerful.

"Ladies and gentlemen," said Lombard. His words were slightly distorted by the wind that echoed in the speakers of radios and televisions around the country. "I have watched this administration over the last seven years, and not been impressed. Sadly, I also have to admit that I was no more impressed with the previous administrations, either."

He smiled into the cameras and took Margaret's hand.

"I don't believe either party can claim any glory for its behavior in recent years," Lombard continued. "The politics of hatred have no place in this magnificent nation...."

He broke off as a yell of approval roared all over the steps. Lombard smiled and waited for silence to return.

"Nor have the politics of divisiveness, religious intolerance and fascism, of either the left or the right..."

Another roar of approval broke the continuity. Lombard smiled at his wife and waited again.

"I see no relief from this so long as we continue our present approach of putting party politics ahead of the nation's benefit. And let me make myself perfectly clear, and perhaps highly unpopular with many elements of my own party, this *is* what we have been doing for too long. I don't believe I can stand any more of it, and far more importantly, neither can you. I therefore announce my intention..."

The bellow of delight that went up from the surrounding throngs completely out-did any similar previous interruptions. Several moments passed before Lombard could resume.

"I therefore announce my intention today to run for the office of President..."

This time, the noise went out of control. Lombard looked in astonished amusement at the sight of the unabashed joy being displayed in the crowd. The CNN camera panned through the hundreds of people, showing wide grins of pleasure on all faces, including the news-hardened veterans of the other broadcast crews lining the steps.

Lombard gave up. He put his arms round Margaret and hugged her ferociously. When he turned back to the cameras, tears were running unashamedly down his face.

www.ingramcontent.com/pod-product-compliance
Lightning Source LLC
Chambersburg PA
CBHW052347020726
47503CB00001B/140